*An Elusi*

Vampires drink blood, they're supe ... Dominants. Every vampire knows those truths. A vampire's human servant is property, plaything, pawn--and the only living being a vampire can trust. Though she may own him, body, heart and soul, a human servant keeps a vampire from feeling alone in her dangerous, political world. But Kaela has a secret. She's a vampire with a burning need to submit, to belong to a Master, and definitely not a vampire Master, who will use the advantage for political or emotional domination. But what kind of human male will consent to becoming a vampire's servant, a 300 year life of utter servitude, to be her Master behind closed doors? An invitation to Eden offers her the chance to discover her elusive hero…and indulge the bliss of surrender.

§

We are very pleased to issue your Invitation to Eden, an exciting series from 27 of the biggest names in romance. Join us as we take you on an exciting adventure to Eden, where anything--and everything--goes!

# Elusive Hero

By Joey W. Hill

*Copyright 2014*

A book of the Invitation to Eden series and

A Vampire Queen Series novel

**Storywitch Press**
Charlotte, NC

**Elusive Hero**
A Vampire Queen Novel
Part of the Invitation to Eden Series

eISBN: 978-1-942122-02-9
Print ISBN: 978-1-942122-03-6

Published by Storywitch Press
Charlotte, North Carolina, USA
http://www.storywitch.com

Cover Design by Frauke Spanuth

This is a work of fiction. Names, characters, places, and incidents either are the product of the author's imagination or are used fictitiously, and any resemblance to actual persons, living or dead, business establishments, events, or locales is entirely coincidental. The publisher does not have any control over and does not assume any responsibility for author or third-party websites or their content.

Copyright © 2014 by Joey W. Hill. All rights reserved.

No part of this book may be reproduced, scanned, or distributed in any printed or electronic form without permission. Please do not participate in or encourage piracy of copyrighted materials in violation of the author's rights. Purchase only authorized editions

## Acknowledgments

This book ended up being a much bigger project than originally intended, so I owe a very special thanks to Lauren and Lee, two wonderful readers who did a proofing run in the eleventh hour for me, as did my critique partners Ann Jacobs, Sheri Fogarty and Angela Knight. Thank you so much, ladies!

I also wanted to send tremendous thanks to author Lauren Hawkeye/Lauren Jameson for launching the Invitation to Eden series and organizing the efforts of the 27 authors involved. Herding cats is a piece of cake next to herding authors! Lauren, you have my gratitude and admiration. Thanks for including me.

And thank you to the many Invitation to Eden authors who have been working to cross promote all of us throughout the life of this project, with special thanks to R.G. Alexander, Eden Bradley and all the Smutketeers. As one of the authors coming in during the last couple months of the series, I'm particularly appreciative of all the cross promo, and hope I was able to return the favor with my limited marketing skills!

Last, but not at all least, to my husband. Since this was our first independent publishing effort, he had sole technical responsibility, donning a publishing hat to learn how to bring Elusive Hero to all of you. I was far too busy writing it (not to mention I'm a technology dunce), so without his help, it might still be living only on my computer (laughter). He's a treasure, as always.

I hope you all enjoy Kaela and Garron's story.

# Chapter One

"Your tithe is late. And you have no valid excuse for it."

"With respect, my lady, I told you why it was late. We've had trouble this quarter…"

"That is a lie." Kaela folded her hands on her desk and met the gaze of the male vampire. He'd sat down in her guest chair with a casual sprawl, stretching out his legs and hooking his ankles, as if the chance to study his powerful, handsome form was a special gift he'd brought only for her. It didn't impress her. She was all too aware this meeting could end with her tearing his heart out of his broad chest and spattering blood over every square inch of her home office. She should have held this meeting in the garage with its built-in drain, but that likely would have aroused his suspicions.

"You think I'm a fool, Greg. You want to test the female vampire overlord, see if she's really capable of controlling you, worthy of your obedience." She let the tips of her fangs show. "You will provide the funds you owe before you leave my property. You will also pay me the funds for next quarter, as a sign of respect. Once you make your payment, I want you out of my home and headed back to yours."

Her gaze flicked to the clock, mostly for effect, because every vampire over the age of fifty instinctively knew the time of day. She was tipping over a hundred and seventy-five years now. Young for an overlord, but female vampires tended to mature faster. A necessary survival trait.

"It's three hours to dawn, and you live two hours and forty-five minutes from here. Waste any of that time with argument and you'll be suffering a terrible sunburn."

She was gratified to see him straighten in the chair, his posture tensing. While she didn't shift by an inch, she was coiled to strike, ready for this to turn into a fight. She shut down any fear, any reaction other than what she'd been charged by Lady Lyssa to do.

*Serve me well, Lady Kaela. That is what I require.*

She'd done so, and would continue to do so. Until another vampire was able to kill her.

Everyone knew Lady Lyssa had appointed her. That would give any vampire pause, because the head of the Vampire Council was terrifying. Further, Lady Lyssa didn't make careless choices. So while the former might have them speculating that Kaela was Lady Lyssa's friend, under her particular protection, the latter would have them wondering if she was a far more lethal opponent than she might appear.

Neither of those statements had been true when she'd become overlord, but Kaela had learned how to do what needed to be done so now the latter *was* true. Lyssa had said the magical words, hadn't she? Words that, if she'd known the impact they had on Kaela, would have ironically kept her from being considered for the post, and she would be dead by now. Or worse.

Greg held her gaze. Kaela didn't twitch, holding that lock. If he attacked, he would come straight at her, using brute strength. A feint to the right should do it, an attack to the left, because he was right-handed. She would go for the throat, take out the meat of it. It didn't kill a vampire, but it was agonizing, crippling. As he writhed on the carpet, she could decide whether to stake him or let him live. He was thirty years older than her. Not a large margin, but male vampires tended to be stronger than females of similar age, no different from most species. It merely meant a female had to plan her attack more carefully.

Soon after Kaela had accepted Lady Lyssa's appointment, she'd killed five of the vampires in her territory, with the full support of the Council. The California territory had been rife with corruption and illegal behavior, thanks to the previous overlord thinking he was too far from the Council for his activities to be of concern. He'd gathered a group of stronger vampires around him, cronies he allowed to terrorize the weaker vampires, circumventing Council rules, risking exposure to the human world with their bloodlust. She knew about it firsthand, because she'd been part of that territory, doing whatever she could to protect the weaker vampires and playing a dangerous game of politics to hold onto what she had, a string of personal security companies that gave her eyes and ears in key places.

Not bad for a made vampire who'd once been a Confederate spy.

Greg shifted, and averted his eyes. It was a point for her, but she didn't relax her guard, because it could be a ploy before an attack.

"Will you take a check?" he asked.

"A wire transfer. Fran is outside and you can give her the information. You may do that now and leave as soon as she verifies it."

He rose with a stiff nod. "My lady." This time he meant it.

She waited until he'd reached the door. "Greg?"

He turned to face her again, not giving her his back. "Yes, my lady?"

"I will not forgive this type of behavior twice. This is your only warning. You can benefit from being in my territory, profit from my leadership. I am fair. I will support and protect you as long as you follow the rules. If you do not, this was your last chance at leniency."

He gave her a short bow of acquiescence, and she marked with further satisfaction the way he was taking her measure, with more uncertainty and nascent respect. At her dismissal, he slipped out of her office, closing the door behind him.

She took a breath, one that went all the way down to the soles of her feet, and let it out. A tremor swept her, fueled by the sudden sick flopping in her stomach. She let the reaction have her for about thirty seconds before reining it back in again. Everything had its proper time, and she kept it all on a strict schedule.

She'd accepted the need to embrace a persona that really wasn't her own, but despite her hope that assumption could become reality, a much stronger part of her embraced something different. Something she could only indulge in a rich, solitary fantasy life in the short period before dawn claimed her for sleep. Or that brief time each night when she first woke. It was like one of those fairy tale curses, where she could go where she wished only in her dreams.

But she wasn't complaining. She was here to serve. Whether she realized it or not, Lyssa had given Kaela the one outlet in her real life that helped her balance the denial of the rest. *Serve me well.*

Less than five minutes later, her servant knocked and was granted entrance. "That was the fastest wire transfer I've ever done," Fran said, a twinkle in her somber brown eyes. "He's paid in full, with one quarter in advance, my lady."

"Good. Do you have my travel arrangements in order?"

At that, the twinkle disappeared. "Everything's in your carry-on. Front pocket has all the paperwork." Fran took a breath and stared a hole into the surface of the desk. "I also packed in case you changed your mind about me accompanying you."

When Kaela said nothing, Fran's jaw set. "I really don't like this," she blurted out. She flushed. "I'm sorry. I'm not trying to be impertinent. It's just…how will you get blood, my lady?"

"The same way I did before I had a servant. Don't question me, Fran."

Fran was an Inherited Servant, trained from birth to serve vampires, so the faint reproof was enough to have her dropping her gaze. Kaela was surprised the woman had been that forward, but Fran was worried about her. It touched her. It also made her weary, eager to be away.

"I'll be gone ten days. Take the money I've given you, take a vacation."

"You're going to Miami. How can you protect yourself during daylight hours? Do they know…"

"Stop it, Fran," she said sharply. "I'm quite capable of caring for myself."

It wasn't her servant's fault that she couldn't fulfill Kaela's true needs. Because Kaela understood what that felt like, only too well, she softened her voice, just enough. Everything always had to be so calculated. There were times she thought the precision of her life would slice her into pieces.

"You are a credit above and beyond the ranks of Inherited Servants, Fran. I am rewarding you by giving you some time off. Enjoy it. Be whatever you desire to be for ten days and don't worry about me."

"I am a servant, my lady. My only desire is to serve you."

That Kaela would think anything different obviously puzzled Fran. Kaela cursed her mistake. Though the possibility of terminal violence with Greg hadn't unsettled her in a way that could affect her judgment, the implications of this trip were something different. But she kept her mask in place.

"I know that. Which is why I'm commanding you to go enjoy yourself. Find a handsome Master in one of the clubs and offer him the pleasures only an Inherited Servant can give. You'll ruin him for anyone else." Kaela let her lips curve, her eyes glitter. "Come back with all sorts of lovely bedroom stories for your Mistress. We'll experience the pleasure of them together."

Fran had been an active Inherited Servant for nearly thirty years. She'd served at the Council headquarters for twenty years, and been Kaela's second-mark for the remaining ten. Kaela understood Fran had been placed with her initially as eyes and ears for Lyssa. So when

Lady Lyssa granted her permission to claim Fran, give her the third mark that would make her Kaela's full servant, all hers, a permanent addition to her household, it had been another sign of Lyssa's approval and trust. Inherited Servants were highly valued, trained to serve high-ranking vampires.

Kaela had treasured the honor, but indicated she was satisfied having Fran in her household as a second mark. During the years since, Kaela had made it clear as often as appropriate that she was very satisfied with Fran's services, yet willing to let her go if Lyssa wished to assign her to another vampire who wanted to fully mark her.

Lyssa had not yet reassigned Fran, so that was where the situation stood. Kaela knew she was unusual, a hundred and seventy-five year old female vampire who hadn't taken her first full servant. The Council head had never questioned Kaela about that, so Kaela assumed Lady Lyssa understood the solitude and self-discipline a female vampire in a leadership position faced in their world. Perhaps Lyssa leaving the Inherited Servant with her this long, even as a second mark, was yet another statement of her support of Kaela in her overlord appointment. Kaela hoped so, even as she bore the guilt of denying Fran what every InhServ wanted most. A vampire who claimed her fully, all the way down to her soul.

Fran was a treasure and an asset, no question. An excellent assistant, intelligent and infallibly courteous, she was also passionate and well-trained in the sensual arts. She was beautiful as all InhServs were, with soft skin, a lush body, curling copper-colored hair and eyes brown like polished creek stone. She responded with enthusiasm to everything her Mistress offered her. The second mark allowed Kaela access to Fran's mind, and the few times she delved there, she saw the shadows, indications that Fran knew there was so much more her Mistress could give. According to Fran's training, it was just a matter of proving herself worthy, but Kaela knew the InhServ was more than worthy.

The problem was her Mistress wasn't the proper receptacle for such a generous gift.

Kaela often enjoyed Fran's body when she took blood from her, and she made sure to give the girl pleasure when she did. She was able to do that most successfully when Fran told her "bedtime stories" about her sexual service for past Council functions, describing in detail the creative performances that had been demanded of her and other servants, a part of almost every social vampire gathering.

Fran probably thought what aroused her Mistress so much during those recitations was Kaela imagining herself as one of those vampires, restraining Fran with use of rope, chain, cloth, doling out stinging or thudding punishments against lovely, supple flesh, forcing orgasms that would make her hoarse with her own screaming. But it wasn't the vampire's point of view that captivated Kaela.

Fortunately, Kaela's suggestion that Fran bring her back more "bedtime stories" from her vacation trip made the InhServ's gaze light at the implication. She nodded, though she couldn't conceal the wistful note in her voice. "Very well, my lady. You know where I am if you need anything. I am yours."

*No you're not, dear girl. But hopefully one day you will belong to someone the way I wish I could, but never will.*

§

Ten days. She was free for ten days. Or she was making the biggest mistake of her life.

At a little after one a.m., Kaela made the transition from the jet in Miami to the puddle jumper that would take her to the Eden resort, located on an island in the Bermuda Triangle. She'd boarded the plane without comment, though the female pilot had looked surprised by her nonchalance, as if used to passengers who were nervous about the dragonfly-sized plane with its bumpy ride and roaring engines.

For her, crashing in a plane meant a long walk through water to get home. A miserable prospect, but certainly nothing to fear.

Kaela embraced the cocoon the loud engine provided. She just wished it could drown out her thoughts. At least she didn't have to converse with the pilot. The absurdly young woman guiding the plane wasn't intrusive, however. She'd picked up on Kaela's unwillingness to chat and matched it with a comfortable silence. With Kaela's enhanced hearing, she could sometimes hear Joely--the pilot--humming to herself. She didn't know the tune, but it was pleasant, a good mesh with the growl of the engine. The girl smelled good as well. Engine oil, soap and cotton. A light perspiration odor, feminine and appealing. Her blood would probably taste like her personality.

Complex yet simple, possessed of a lovely humor and grace, with a trace of poignant anguish beneath the surface. A daisy.

Kaela needed to feed, but it wasn't critical yet. She'd been told that need would be amply met when she reached the island. The invitation she'd received weeks ago had promised her a lot of things.

*There's no such thing as vampires.* That was what most humans believed.

*There's no such thing as a vampire submissive.* That was what all vampires knew.

The human world thought vampires were a supernatural fantasy that happened in movies and books, because that was what vampires took great measures to ensure the most prolific species on the planet other than insects believed. But whatever species one happened to be, whether unicorn, fairy, vampire or cockroach, one tended to trust one's reality. A vampire could be just as skeptical about magic as a human. The reality was she really shouldn't be on this plane, believing in a fantasy that could get her killed. Or worse.

A vampire submissive. It didn't exist in nature or, if it did, it ranked just below the blinded, three-legged member of the wolf pack. A very brief anomaly, soon to be torn to pieces or turned out to starve to death. Starving would be preferable. Probably.

Kaela crossed her legs and folded her hands on her knees, refusing to allow either one to shake. Because she wanted to reach into her purse and finger the vellum paper of the invitation once more for empty reassurance, she deliberately didn't. She'd done that enough it should look as worn as the corners of a favorite book. Instead, the cream paper and raised lettering gleamed the way it had when she'd received it. The weight of the paper, its silken smoothness, the faint vanilla scent, made one think the color had come about from the invitation being dipped in actual cream, which enhanced the words written upon it.

*You are cordially invited to spend a week at the Eden resort, where reality is whatever you want it to be.*

Oddly enough, she'd found out about Eden from eavesdropping on a conversation. She'd stopped for an evening coffee at a diner, and had picked up on a discussion three booths over. The woman meeting with a friend was apparently bestselling romance author, Leila Connors. She'd been invited to the Eden resort some time ago for a writer's retreat and not only had tapped into her muse, but even deeper fantasies.

*"I know how insane it sounds, but that's how Sebastian came into my life. It started with the dreams I was having while I was there. It was like, as the book came to life in my head, he came to life...in my life."* The woman laughed shortly. *"No, I wasn't drinking that much. I'm telling you, there's something about that island. I think if you're invited there, anything you desire--if it's meant to be--could happen."*

Usually Fran did all of Kaela's administrative tasks, but she'd looked up the resort on her own, dumping the cache afterward just to be safe. Even so, a week later an envelope marked for her eyes only arrived via a private delivery service. Fran had passed it to her unopened because it looked official enough to have come from the Council or another overlord.

The envelope had included the invitation to Eden. While the arrival of the document was astonishing enough, the invitation had included an unsettling note in a bold male script.

> Lady Kaela, I understand your world comes with many demands. I believe Eden can provide you a respite from your current responsibilities and answer your deepest wish. The one you can't share with anyone else. This is my direct line. Please contact me for more information.

Her title, "Lady Kaela" was associated with the vampire world. She was a made vampire who had achieved overlord status, no small feat, so she was proud of the title. But a human outside the vampire world shouldn't know about it. Plus her street address wasn't common knowledge in the human world, everything coming to her through a post office box.

> I can assure you that you will have complete confidentiality and discretion to pursue whatever desires you have while on Eden. I'm sure you will appreciate the irony that Eden, like your world, does not make public all the ways we can meet our guests' needs. But you'll find my island allows those such as yourself the chance to be at ease...to be who you truly are.
>
> –Theodosius Vardalos

According to her Internet research, he was the owner of the island, the mysterious billionaire who granted no interviews and was the brains and money behind the exclusive, by-invitation-only Eden resort.

The invitation had been accompanied by a small box. Opening it in the privacy of her bedroom, she found it contained a bubble-wrapped crystal sphere. The sphere caught the light of her lamp as she held it up, sparkling rainbow beams across her desk and skin. But the note with it indicated it wasn't for decoration.

> Open the crystal over a bowl. Immerse your hand and then expose it to the sunlight. Only for a moment. The effect doesn't last longer than that away from Eden.

When she turned the sphere over and over, there was movement inside. Liquid. Opening the side latch to drain the contents into a bowl, she'd inhaled the scent of sandy beaches soaked by sun, something she hadn't experienced in many years. Some sand drifted to the bottom of the bowl.

Just past dawn she'd tried it, crazy as it sounded. Hidden behind the heavy drapes, she'd slowly extended her drenched hand through the small opening, ready to jerk back at the first touch of burning agony. Her heart had tripped a beat as she felt sunlight touch her flesh and warm it only. He was right; it only lasted a moment. When she started to feel that warning pain she brought it back, stared at her hand, the bowl of water. Then she re-read the whole note.

> I know your desire is not to embrace the sunlight, but far darker desires. However, I am hoping this small demonstration will help you gain confidence that you might find what you seek here.

Two weeks passed before she called Vardalos. She had plenty of enemies who resented her appointment to the overlord position and would love to trip her up with an elaborate plan like this. However, everything she researched meshed with what he'd sent her, as well as what she'd overheard in that diner.

On top of that, there was his voice. When he started speaking on the phone line, she was pulled into the sensual timbre. There was command there, power, as well as sorrow and wisdom. This was not a person you fucked with, or who fucked with others. She read people well, and he sounded like a person who knew what it was to fight through adversity simply to exist.

"Why?" she asked. "Other than the exorbitant price I can afford to pay to come to your island?"

"While I do appreciate those with the income to help maintain the island, money is not my main purpose for running Eden. You have your secret desires, Lady Kaela. I have mine, and fulfilling the fantasies of others is part of what brings me peace, the closest thing I've found to it. Much as your service to Lady Lyssa does for you. Fair enough?"

"You know that unmarked humans aren't permitted to know this much about my world. It carries a death sentence."

"There are exceptions to many things in Eden. You will be safe here, Lady Kaela. That is my solemn vow, and my life surrendered to you if I'm wrong."

With that voice, the commanding presence he had even over the phone, him surrendering anything to her wasn't the first thing that came to mind. She'd licked her lips, a nervous movement, and battled back the reactions surging inside her in an alarming manner.

The pilot's raised voice drew her from her thoughts, returning her to the present. "My lady, we're approaching the island. It's quite something at night. Well, anytime, but I especially like the night approach."

Kaela leaned forward to gaze out the window, her fingers tightening on her knees.

The castle was an uneven pyramid of glittering lights that expanded in reflection against the dark waters surrounding the island. It was the crown on a vast and hilly terrain that sloped down to the sea on all sides. With her vampire eyes, she could see even more detail as the plane started its descent. Tall spires, stone pathways. It had a few modifications, but overall it was the type of castle she'd seen in Ireland on her travels. The information about the island had confirmed that. Theodosius Vardalos had had the castle transported here, piece by piece.

It was the type of place a person with dark desires might never want to leave, because it might hold the answer to them. She suspected not everyone felt like that, trying to reconcile a place built for defense and long battles in tropical resort surroundings. But it underscored light against dark, the key difference between want and need. To get the most out of what you wanted, you had to have what you needed first.

As the plane landed on the water and taxied toward the land, she saw a wooden dock sculpted in a zigzag path up to the mainland, as well as a gold plated sign mounted on an outcropping of rock. *Welcome to Eden, where reality is what you want it to be.*

Want versus need. It was truly dangerous for her to be here. What she wanted was something she'd never even said aloud, but Theodosius Vardalos had.

During that phone call, she'd asked a second question, though she'd not intended for it to leave her lips. "You said you thought you might have what I seek there. What exactly do you think I'm seeking?"

"This is a secure line, so there's no need to be alarmed by me speaking the truth. You are something incredibly unique in your world, Lady Kaela. A vampire submissive who craves a human Master's hand. While you are at Eden, you can have that fantasy."

She'd hung up on him as if the phone had grown tentacles to reach out and strangle her. She'd even found herself all the way across the room, staring at it.

The one rule in the vampire world that never changed was "might made right". She had been satisfied being just one vampire in a territory, paying feudal tithes to its overlord as part of her business costs, but the overlord had overstepped his authority in a variety of brutal, unacceptable ways. It had been second nature to her, trying to protect other vampires as best she could, and then fortunately the Vampire Council had removed him. Kaela had waited like the others with the hope of a better overlord being appointed, then Lady Lyssa had summoned her to fly to Georgia and stand in her presence.

"Kaela, you took exceptional measures to protect others from Graham's misbehavior. Ten of the most influential vampires in your territory agree you would make a suitable temporary overlord. We agree. Should you be able to hold the position a year favorably, then it would become permanent." While Kaela was dealing with the shock of that, Lyssa had met her gaze. The last royal member of the Far East clan had jade eyes as piercing as the tip of a spear. "Settling things in your territory will not be easy. Should lethal measures be necessary, you have our permission to circumvent the usual approval process. You will contact my direct line, make your case, and I will endorse your decision during that call, if warranted. Should it have to be after the fact," those jade eyes glittered, "make sure your case is well supported."

Soon after, Kaela had held a gathering of her territory vampires at her home, a meet-and-greet-the-new-overlord sort of gesture. While the vampires she'd protected were clearly supportive, her purpose had been to determine who was going to be a problem. Peter Ailsworth, a vampire a hundred and fifty years old, had been the first to challenge her. When she'd taken him to the ground, she was willing to grant mercy, but he'd kept fighting. So she'd staked him and instructed two of the watching vampires to burn the body. She'd gone to her bedroom, thrown up and cried. Then returned to the dining room to share dinner with the remaining vampires and view sexual entertainment performed by their servants.

Just a normal day in the vampire world. Except for the throwing up and crying. She doubted Lady Lyssa had ever done either of those things. If a vampire showed weakness or surrender, she might as well just accept being the slave of other vampires for all her long, long life. Yes, there was a hierarchy among vampires, and there were plenty of vampires stronger than she was, but she'd learned how to play the game to demand the proper amount of respect and carve out her boundaries.

She hadn't called Vardalos back that night. Or for weeks afterward. She'd hung that crystal sphere in her window, thought about the way the sunlight would sparkle through it during the daylight hours when she couldn't see it. But at night she'd hold it up in front of a lamp and let it spin, watching it until it hypnotized her with all the possibilities it represented. At the end of week five, she'd sent back the RSVP in the envelope, indicating the dates she would be coming. Within three days, she received another "for your eyes only" missive that gave her the travel arrangements and the plane ticket from Miami to the island that Fran didn't know about. So here she was.

Worst case scenario, she'd have a vacation on an island paradise that offered every amenity. Spas, casino, five star restaurants, breathtaking views from many winding hiking paths… The booklet about the island's offerings was nearly fifty pages. On the last page it indicated what Vardalos had. *These are only some of the pleasures Eden can offer you. We invite you to come explore the ones that are right for you.*

Around the middle of the brochure, the sexual amenities were discussed. Club Sin was a fully equipped and staffed BDSM club inside the castle. There was also a section of the island for 24/7 Dom/sub play in an open air environment that included pools, gardens, wait staff to bring around drinks, hors d'oeuvres, toys…

She imagined herself there, the touch of the night air on her body, naked because that was the way her Master wanted to display her. His strong, capable hand would rest on the small of her back. The silver collar around her throat would pull against her jugular when he tugged at the attached leash. He'd bid her kneel at his feet as he ordered a drink and watched the others play around them. Sliding the toe of his shoe beneath her buttocks, he'd press the hard leather against her pussy, chide her for how wet she was, making the surface of the shoe shine with her shameless arousal.

The hunger that rose inside her at the image was the same hunger that populated her world. Not in vampires but in their servants, offering up their submissive desires to their fanged Masters and Mistresses. She saw it so often, those feelings should seem banal, stereotypical to her. Instead, every drop of their desire she witnessed was a hazardous addiction.

As if that wasn't insane enough, she was surrounded by male vampires who were all sexual Dominants. The trait was a given for all vampires, male or female, an unmistakable part of their genetic makeup. Because of that, male vampires had always provided a temptation she knew was a death trap with her name written on it. She'd shut herself down to it years ago, erecting a wall so thick and strong none of it reached her vulnerable core. That--in addition to the possible need to kill him--was part of what had made her immune to Greg's self-perceived charms.

Yet even when she fantasized in the early dawn hours before sleep claimed her, it wasn't a vampire master she desired.

It was a human one.

A human male for whom sexual Dominance was about mutual pleasure, not political gain or a chance to declare open season on her vulnerabilities. If any vampire knew she harbored an abiding desire to be restrained, forced to submit, all choices taken away so she could serve the pleasure of a Master, she'd stake herself rather than face the horror her life would become. The kind of mastery she hungered to have had nothing in common with the brutal domination vampires imposed in their political machinations upon one another.

Because of that, a vampire's closest relationship--though none would admit it--was with their third marked human servant, because in their world that was often the only person a vampire could fully trust. But Kaela expected vampires believed that was because they also fully controlled their servants.

Yet not all servants were natural submissives. Lyssa's own servant, Jacob, might well emerge as a Dominant if he wasn't bound to the vampire queen, for she'd sensed that vibe from him more than once. But his desire to serve his queen overrode everything, a delicious dichotomy.

Knowing her preferences, Kaela had deliberately requested a female InhServ, grateful Lyssa gave her that choice. How dangerous would it have been for her, if Lyssa had assigned her a male InhServ who had a personality like Jacob? He'd have certainly sensed her desire for a Master during those ten years, no matter how much she'd kept her desires locked away.

Yet Fran came with her own hazards. Giving a submissive servant to a submissive vampire? It would be amusing if it wasn't so fraught with peril. How often had she had to check her actions because she found herself trying to make sure Fran was happy in ways that would clearly indicate she was trying to serve her InhServ, as much as Fran was trying to do the same for her?

She was a freak of nature. This was madness. A mad desire she could no longer contain. For over a century and three-quarters, she'd been everything she needed to be, not only to survive but to thrive. She took nothing for herself, even though it appeared she'd acquired everything a vampire could want. Reputation, respect, even fear, God help her. But all she wanted was the bliss of…surrender.

Perhaps it would be easier if she hadn't once had the pleasure of surrender. A long, long time ago, when she was human. With Jared.

The plane bumped the dock, jolting that thought out of the forefront of her mind. Two men in khaki shorts and black polo shirts bearing the Eden logo were hooking lines to the plane. Joely twisted around. "Ma'am? You're free to disembark. The porters will get your luggage."

Kaela remained seated. She could tell Joely to turn around, take her back. They'd make it before sunrise. She knew places she could go to ground in Miami until sunset, when she could take a plane back to California.

Instead, she rose at last and made her way past the other sets of seats to that opening.

The two men offered their hands to help her safely to the dock. While she didn't need any assistance balancing, and they wouldn't know she was a vampire overlord, she knew what kind of behavior was expected from someone with her demeanor, her obvious aura of authority and importance. She always knew what was expected. Giving them a cursory nod after she was firmly on the dock, she left them to deal with her two suitcases. She held onto the carry-on which had a couple of blood packs on ice, just in case.

She was aware of their lingering gazes. She'd been a beautiful mortal, which had helped her be a successful spy. Becoming a vampire had only enhanced that beauty. Now when people saw her, they saw long red hair rippling like silk to her narrow waist, pale skin like cream and a body made for pleasure. If they looked into her oddly vibrant golden-brown eyes, which were rimmed with a dark ring around the iris and fringed with reddish-gold lashes, they lost their tongues entirely. But their lust, their mindless reaction that could drive them to their knees before her, wasn't what she wanted.

Then she saw what she did.

## Chapter Two

A half-moon scattered lightning bolt patterns along the water lapping against the dock. As her gaze followed the wooden boards with the same zigzagging path to the shore, she saw a man standing at the end. Even with her enhanced senses, she couldn't penetrate the darkness to see his face, as if the island intended to cloak him, intrigue her, make her want to draw closer. She moved silently by instinct, despite her usual caution about revealing her vampire nature among humans. But Vardalos knew what she was, didn't he? Everything about this place suggested it held so many secrets, one vampire was going to be a drop in the bucket.

He was tall, broad-shouldered. He had that way of standing that powerful, military-trained men or large animals did, aware of their strength and carrying the confidence that went with knowing how to deal with threat, crisis or…anything.

Was she going to unleash her fantasies here on the docks? Maybe. She had over a century's worth of self-discipline, yes, but she was here because that restraint had grown thin enough for her to take an incredible risk. So she kept moving toward him, even as she recovered herself enough to school her expression to impassivity, and her body language to that of someone who expected nothing for herself, but who was prepared to deal with…anything.

Her steps slowed at that. God, if this was going to be same-shit-different-day, she'd rather just turn around and get back on the plane. At least in her real life, she was in an environment that reinforced that discipline.

He had his head cocked and though his face was shadowed, she could feel his attention. Most humans in her own world didn't meet her eyes unless invited to do so. Even in the oblivious mundane world, most humans wouldn't hold her gaze for more than a second, but when she drew close enough to see his eyes, they were on hers. The angle of darkness kept her from knowing what color they were, but they were piercing. As startling as a gunshot in the darkness.

A flutter went through her breast. It had been decades since she'd had the luxury to consider whether or not the power of a man's gaze would compel her to lower her own. She knew just how important a message that was. Life changing.

But her life couldn't be changed. No matter what happened here, she had to get back on that plane in ten days. Because of that, she resisted the compulsion, unsettled enough by it to be defensive. She redirected her attention to absorb other things about him instead.

His head was shaved, the broad skull matching his strong, square cut features. Yet what caught her eye, as soon as she was close enough to see them, were the scars. One jagged line ran diagonally from his cheekbone to cross his nose, which would have been straight and fine as an aristocrat's if not for that bisecting groove. The scar ended at the hinge of his jaw. As if that hadn't come close enough, another scar started under the left ear, taking an equally harrowing route across his throat, making her question how he'd survived a wound so deep around the vital jugular and carotid pathways. The scar disappeared into the collar of his black polo shirt. Combined, the two marks made a crooked pattern not unlike the dock.

She thought his head was shaved because of the additional scars there. She couldn't imagine hair being able to grow in smoothly over the gouges and short slashes that reminded her of a map. Perhaps made by some form of shrapnel, an explosion of metal.

His brows were thick black silk matching the sprinkling of hair on his forearms and the signs of chest hair curling out of the throat of his shirt, suggesting he would have had black hair on his head.

She wondered why he hadn't had the damage minimized with cosmetic surgery, but maybe he couldn't afford it. Despite the mantle of authority he bore, she was sure this wasn't the Master of Eden. He wore a black T-shirt with the same embroidered logo as the porters' polo shirts, suggesting he was staff. Instead of shorts, he wore black jeans and athletic shoes.

She had no objection to the difference in wardrobe. The shirt stretched over his chest with admirable effort, and the jeans hugged strong thighs, accenting a noticeably well-packaged groin area. She expected he had a similarly excellent ass. But she dealt with male vampires all the time, so seeing a powerful, fit male wasn't what made him so appealing. Heat rolled off of him, as well as power…control. Her body tightened in so many ways, instinctively recognizing what he was, what she wanted.

Her blood hunger surged to the surface, because with vampires it was pretty much coupled with physical lust. Feeding was an erotic exercise unless one had to rush it for survival, and she could almost taste the virility that would infuse this man's red blood. He could nourish a girl for a good, long time.

This was a human, she reminded herself. She could break him, take his life with as much effort as breaking a nail. Yet somewhere low in her belly, she was trembling. She had a sudden vision of a lion tamer being circled by a lioness. Not one of those poor creatures who lived their lives in cages, transported from city to city, forced to entertain people rather than experience the open, free lives God had intended for them, but a truly wild, powerful creature, able to break the lion tamer with only a swat of a paw. But something about that lion tamer, the fix of his eyes, the stance of his body, said he was a predator worthy of respect, fascination…making the lioness want to come closer and perhaps allow herself to be leashed, as long as he understood and respected what she was, what she truly needed.

The man extended a hand to her, palm up.

No words. He just kept that dark gaze locked on hers. He didn't tell her to take his hand. He didn't need to do so.

*Eden can provide you a respite…* Vardalos's words. She wasn't sure if she'd really believed it, or had wanted it to be true so much she'd been pulled in by the right combination of words and a pretty brochure. It should take more than one magnetic male to do it. Or maybe not. Maybe she was so hungry for this, she'd let herself be beguiled by Vardalos's magic water and set aside logic, suspended disbelief and let it happen. Maybe the lioness was letting herself believe the impossible.

No. Even if that needy part of her wanted to be so gullible, she was incapable of handing over control to someone who didn't deserve it. There was a long way to go between fantasy and reality. Who she'd become made her too wary. Could a human male earn a true surrender from her, even for a ten day fantasy?

And what if he did? What if this male eliciting such a strong reaction from her was able to brush up against her fantasies? What if Vardalos was successful in giving her what she craved?

She needed to turn around and get back on the plane. This might be the greatest risk she'd ever faced as a vampire.

Yet she stayed motionless, even though her hand was twitching, telling her it wanted to place itself in that strong grasp.

"Going to make me come to you?" he said. His tone, low and even, warned her there would be consequences for that. The timbre reminded her of a dark cave near the earth's center, resonant with heat and solidity. Those tremors in her lower belly increased.

The discordant roll of a dock cart bumping across the boards disrupted her reverie. The porters transporting her luggage had caught up to her.

"Where we taking her, Rand?" one of them asked.

In her peripheral vision, Kaela noted the other porter scanning her high breasts and trim waist delineated by her silk-shot knit shirt, her hips etched by her snug above-the-knee skirt and legs accented by two-inch heels. She'd dressed formally for travel, because it projected the right image. Detached, in control. Untouchable. There was nothing as intimidating as a beautiful woman with a cool stare and an impenetrable force field of self-confidence.

As such, she ignored him, but Rand didn't feel the same way about it. His shadowed eyes glittered coolly at the ogling man as he answered the first porter.

"You're not taking her anywhere. Her luggage goes to Level B, the west wing. Suite A."

The other porter recognized the admonition in Rand's look, giving him a quick nod as he moved away with the other attendant, though she caught the muttered exchange between them.

"What's got Master Frankenstein's drawers in a twist? And Level B, west wing? Didn't even think we had rooms in the west wing…"

"Tell me what color your eyes are," she said.

She should be able to penetrate the darkness enough to tell, but she couldn't. The darkness must be making his pupils so large, they took over everything else. Rand brought his unsmiling attention back to her yet remained silent.

This was the mundane world, she reminded herself. Humans were used to polite questions, not statements sounding like demands. But she knew that wasn't why he remained silent, or why she restated it.

"Would you mind telling me the color of your eyes?"

"They were blue, once. Still are, in the right light." After that odd statement, he extended his hand. "Want to try this again?"

This time she went along with it, placing her hand in his grip. As soon as it closed over her fingers, that tremor she usually contained so well ran from the point of contact up her arm and down her side, making her left breast and hip bone tingle, the sensation curving under the crease of her buttock to arrow between her legs, as if the contact had set off a string of electric impulses.

His thumb ran over her knuckles, an intimate caress, a reassurance. She closed her eyes, absorbing that touch, even as she took another step closer into the shadow of his body. When was the last time a single touch had brought her a feeling of…sanctuary?

There were a few male vampires who had his size and breadth, but none of them felt as large as he did. She thought of what the porter had called him so unkindly, but she thought of it as a compliment. In the human world, her kind were mostly considered monsters, too.

She opened her eyes, looked up into his face. The moonlight was different at that angle, and for just a second she caught a glimmer of what he'd said. A faint hint of cerulean blue. If he had in fact had black hair before the extensive scarring, that--coupled to his strong features, "used to be blue" eyes, and impressive body--would have made any woman's head turn. Though in truth, he wasn't having any trouble holding her attention now.

"You know, people often mistakenly confuse Dr. Frankenstein's name with his creation," she said. "Mary Shelley never offered his name."

"No. People tend to fill a void. In the book, Frankenstein called him a variety of things. Devil, wretch. Ogre. Whereas the monster referred to himself as Adam."

There was a stilted note to his voice, the words formed like bold script, each one a stamp on the air between them, no room for misinterpretation. He was looking at her as if he intended to lean in even closer, take a detailed accounting of her every feature.

Her pulse beating high in her throat, she laid her free hand on his chest to ground herself. She was used to touching humans when she desired to do so, and Vardalos had said blood would be provided for her when she landed. So this must be dinner. Something held her back from the automatic assumption, though, despite the growing hunger. His heartbeat was steady and strong beneath her hand. He laid his over it, a quelling gesture.

"I'm Garron Rand," he said. "I'll take you to your room now. I'm in charge of your care while you're here."

Without further explanation, he tucked her hand into his elbow and led her off the docks. A cobbled main road lined with graceful trees and island foliage seemed to lead up to the castle, but he turned off onto a narrower, less manicured path carpeted only with pine needles and marked with round pavers. While she was as graceful as all vampires were, the thin heels of her shoes weren't made for the uneven terrain. He stopped, glanced down.

"Take them off, my lady."

He was soft-spoken about it, but the direct command stirred her. She could break his hand, all five fingers, with nothing but a squeeze of her own, yet the words that sprang to her lips, a demand that he at least say please, died before that look.

He'd addressed her as "my lady". There was an intriguing difference to the way he said it. She couldn't exactly place what that difference was, but it wasn't disrespectful.

Thinking about that, she took off her shoes. He held one of her hands, steadying her, not really necessary, but she accepted the pleasure of absorbing the strength in that grip.

"If you stay on the pavers, nothing should hurt your feet."

Removing her shoes from her grasp, he looped the straps over his wrist before taking her elbow and guiding her onward. The foliage here was close enough to caress her skin, the stiff tickle of ferns, light-as-feather fronds from tall decorative grasses. She could smell the sea air, but mixed with it were interior scents, dark jungles, lush green places, fresh water sources. Stone. Because of the castle, she scented a lot of stone. Castles had dungeons where all sorts of torments could happen. Delicious torments.

She could hear the blood beating in his throat and made herself think of other things. Time to cut through the air of mystery and put this on normal footing. "So you're my personal concierge. You don't look like that's your usual job here."

"You'd be surprised." The side of his mouth quirked, which pulled at the corner of his eye in an intriguing way against the resistance of the bisecting scar. She expected others found it macabre, but it increased the intensity of his focus, the flash in the affected eye. "I started as a bell guy and know most of the jobs here, so I still pitch in wherever needed when we're short-handed or busier than usual."

"This doesn't look like the type of place that Mr. Vardalos allows to be short-handed."

"No, that's true. But staff members occasionally take a vacation."

"What do you do when you're not 'pitching in'?"

"Security, part time bouncer at a couple of the clubs. With my looks and training, that's easy work." He said it matter-of-factly. "The rest of the time I'm one of the staff Masters at Club Sin."

"Oh. So I'm paying for your services as a Dom."

The thrill of confirming what was obvious about him came with an irrational feeling of disappointment. Theodosius ran a resort that excelled at giving people exceptional vacation experiences, commensurate with what she could pay. Rand was probably a fantastic Dom, so she should look forward to seeing how her money would be spent. How he could serve her needs.

"No, my lady." Garron stopped, retaining her hand as he turned toward her. "When Mr. Vardalos told me you were coming, I told him I wanted you, and cashed in ten vacation days. While you're here, I'm off the clock."

She stared up at him. "You--and he--assumed I would accept that?"

"No, my lady. You'll decide what control you relinquish. I'll decide how to handle that."

A cryptic statement, but the hard-to-read expression made her feel like most of the decisions rested in his hands.

"So what exactly have I paid for?"

His lips quirked again. "An expensive resort vacation on the exclusive, invitation-only Eden resort."

§

She was shockingly beautiful. Garron wasn't surprised Bill and Waylon, the porters, had practically drooled all over themselves. What surprised him was his possessive reaction, how instant it was. But he'd been thinking about her for over a month, hadn't he? Ever since Theodosius had conducted an extensive series of conferences calls with him to discuss the situation, the Master of the Island preferring voice communication to face-to-face meets.

He'd told her the truth, that he'd done pretty much everything from grunt work to upper management jobs here. Whatever Vardalos needed, because the man had saved his soul. For the past few years, Garron had preferred the hands-off anonymity of being a paid

Master at Club Sin, but doing extra hours as a bell guy or wherever they needed more hands kept his adaptation skills sharp. As such, filling in had become his primary means of occupying himself during leisure time. He liked getting people's belongings to their room or back to the plane, responding to their questions and needs. Yeah, some of the bigwigs that came here liked to order him around, but far more often, they relied on his guidance, his ability to negotiate things they didn't know how to do, letting him take the lead.

He liked seeing people come here with unfulfilled hopes and dreams, insecurities and personal shit to work out, and leaving with excitement about what lay ahead, a sense of peace because of what they'd finally figured out. He had a front row view of slice-of-life, happily-ever-afters without being in the middle of them himself.

It wasn't that he avoided life. He just hadn't found anything that made him want to be center stage about it again. Until Vardalos had told him about Lady Kaela, a vampire overlord. A female of extraordinary strength and will who hungered to be a submissive in a shadowy world that had zero tolerance for her desires.

During his ten years on Eden, he'd seen a lot of unexplainable things. Well, check that. It was possible to explain all of it, if you believed in magic, time travel and a plethora of WTF moments. So hearing that vampires were real hadn't been too much of a stretch. But until she got off the plane, he realized he'd still kind of expected her to be one of those Goth, blood-drinking wannabes.

While Waylon and Bill might only have seen a woman so off the charts hot she was almost unreal, he'd seen the waves of preternatural energy vibrating off her. Because of his injuries, he didn't see all that well with his eyes, but she had a sensory impact like a hammer to the chest. It was the one thing his not-for-shit vision gave him, and why he didn't take advantage of glasses or corrective surgeries for his eyes. Being able to detect the deepest needs of the submissives under his command through the vibes they put off more than made up for crappy vision. Yet in addition to those energy signatures--auras, as the crunchy-granola sandal wearers would call them--he also had a knack for intuiting body language, expression, intonation. The other Doms at the club said his gut was like The Force, but having a second sense for the details that were important, a byproduct of his military training, enhanced it.

He'd watched Waylon step forward to help her to the dock. She had the grace and speed to make it there herself, Garron was sure, but as an overlord, she was used to being treated with deference.

As she drew closer to him, she became even more potent. Long golden-red hair, honest-to-God like the thick waves of silk women only had in movies or hair commercials. Pale skin, yes, pale like a vampire, but so unblemished and tempting touch. Christ, the slightest mark he put on her would show like a brand, a thought that made his cock harden. He'd been told her vampire healing abilities would make most marks disappear quickly. That was all the encouragement he'd need to make them reappear, just as fast.

A small mouth, lips painted coral. Her willowy body was sculpted like blown glass, but she had generous breasts and a way of walking that drew the eye to the curve of hip and buttock, made a man want to plunder, use her hard. She exuded sexual promise like a siren, but the indifferent way she'd reacted to Waylon and Bill told him she put more stock in less obvious strengths. He saw it in her gaze, the set of her chin and the way she held herself. Her beauty was backed up by a maze of complicated contrasts. They told him he hadn't made a mistake, following his gut and telling Theodosius he wanted her.

Lady Kaela's submissive nature was as clear to Garron as he suspected it was hidden from others; a treasure buried so far down it would take both of them to bring it fully to life.

High-powered, on every level. If she was told to accomplish something, whether it was invading France or fixing him a beer, she'd do the first with extreme prejudice and the latter with enough sass to incur a promising punishment.

He also recognized a killer, because those in that exclusive club tended to know one another. That promise of savagery gave him relief, a kinship. He sensed the soul beneath, all the weight it carried. There was an irresistible explosive energy in a suppressed submissive, one that required the proper combination of gentle pushes and rough shoves to control, channel and ultimately set off the detonation.

Vardalos had given him a potion from one of his God-knew-how sources, and told him if he drank it daily, he would match her strength. He'd also equipped Garron's private room in Club Sin with restraints that would let him control a vampire, give her the helplessness she might crave.

Garron had dumped the potion, because that was the easy way, and he wasn't a Dom who took the easy way. As he absorbed everything about her now, he knew that had been the right play. Her surrender wasn't going to be based on his ability to physically subdue her. Her whole life was governed by those kind of rules.

She might not realize it yet, but this wasn't going to be about physical strength at all. It would involve something far more formidable. Will.

He'd keep the restraints in mind, though, because they both might find some pleasure in that.

Bill was correct. Level B was the same level as Club Sin, but up until recently the west wing of that level had been used for storage. Theodosius had ordered a major renovation three months ago. Now there was a suite down there, appointed to provide every luxury for a vampire overlord. And well-equipped for a Master to handle a challenging submissive.

Vampire or no, she'd looked tired from her trip, so he'd taken the shortcut. However, once he opened the access door to the maintenance elevator, he guided her in and pressed the button that would drop them off at the first floor level first, because everyone enjoyed the pleasures of the castle entrance and he wouldn't deprive her of that. With his wide shoulder span, he adjusted to stand behind her in the small elevator. She was probably used to having a human following her, but he was close enough his breath stirred her hair. When he slid his hand to the small of her back, he felt that little quiver and saw the slight tilt of her head, showing he had her full attention.

He shifted so his hip and upper thigh were against her buttock. His cock, nice and rigid in the jeans, was a couple inches from being against her ass, but he was more interested in watching her reactions than instant gratification. He kept his fingers along her lower back, making short, light strokes. Casual and easy. Not saying anything, just positioning himself in a way that assumed instant intimacy and ownership without pushing it too hard, too fast. She was getting more still, which in a human submissive he expected would have equaled more shallow breathing, tiny frantic pulses at her throat. The slightest touch, movement or word meant something when it came to Dominants and submissives interacting. It never failed to fascinate him, draw him in, make him want to demand even more. He could demand a lot from this female. She'd need it as much as he did.

It didn't matter how often she'd fantasized about it. From what

Vardalos had learned, Garron knew this would be her first time acting as a submissive since she'd become a vampire. He knew a great deal about what went through the head of someone handling that experience. He wasn't known as one of the best Masters at Club Sin for nothing. He was one of the highest paid pro Doms Vardalos had, not that it mattered much to Garron. He banked the money and forgot about it for the most part, except when he needed to buy necessities or something he particularly wanted to add to his dungeon equipment.

The elevator came to a halt, opened onto the lower lobby level, and now her breath drew in for a different reason. Yeah, the castle had that effect.

There were always guests awake on Eden, but this time of night in the lobby it was mostly a scattering of staff, so as he guided her up the wide marble staircase to the main lobby, she could look without being too guarded about her surroundings. He stayed half a pace behind her, so she was still aware of his presence at her back. It was interesting to note she seemed to accept that as a sufficient protection, her gaze sliding forward, up and to the sides only.

She tilted her head back to take in the vaulted ceilings, the array of stained glass. Whatever wonders she'd seen in two hundred years, she still seemed pleased by the castle, for her lips curved, her eyes lighting with an expression of conservative delight.

He knew about other things that could happen in the lobby upon a guest's first viewing, things most humans might discount or rationalize, even if they felt or saw them. He expected a different level of awareness from a supernatural creature, and he wasn't disappointed. Because he was watching her closely, he saw when she became aware of the flow of energy, her brow creasing. As her gaze drifted over to the nearest fountain, he shared the pleasure of seeing her react to what the magic wrought for her.

The sculpture there could be perceived as many things, but standing so close to her, cued into the energies around her with his hand resting on her hip, he was pretty sure they saw the same thing. An entwined couple, the male intimately close behind the female, one hand on her hip, the other curved over her throat as she tipped her head back on his shoulder in a gesture of surrender. As Lady Kaela's hand drifted up to her own throat, Garron's own desires rose another notch.

Slow and steady. He'd take it slow and steady, even though he expected his reaction to her smallest gesture was akin to the way blood hunger felt for her. He'd seen her gaze light on his throat, and remembered that Theodosius said she would need to feed soon after she arrived. It wouldn't be the first time he'd bled for a good cause, and the last time hadn't been near as pleasurable to contemplate.

Dark thoughts, but for once, he didn't have to banish them. She was a creature of darkness. Poignant, terrible memories could mesh with the possibility of dark pleasures, rousing his lust and sadism, his anticipation of the way pleasure and pain could come together with her. Want and need. Lust and…connection. That was what he'd been lacking with submissives lately. He let them in far enough to give them an unforgettable experience but no farther, and left himself mostly untouched. Theodosius had pointed out--with undisguised irony--that it was hard to connect when Garron was purposefully keeping himself at a distance, but a man had to be inspired to want to connect.

When Garron could tell she'd seen her fill, he moved across the expanse of marble toward the main elevators. She wasn't much of a talker, but neither was he. Not until he had something to say or ask. Stepping into the west wing elevator with her, he pressed Level B, entering the code needed to bypass the elevator's restriction from that floor. At her look, he nodded.

"There's only one suite on Level B at this time. Yours, my lady. Mr. Vardalos and I are the only ones with unconditional access to that floor. Housekeeping, maintenance and food service all have to be cleared through me, so you'll be undisturbed during your daylight rests."

Her brow arched. "I'll be given the code."

"No. Usually guests are given a patch that allows them access to their specific room and amenities. But for your specific needs, I'm your patch." The elevator doors opened into a carpeted hallway, lit by the sparkle of a crystal chandelier. A small table holding a vase overflowing with fresh roses was in the hallway. Her gaze slipped over them, noted the red color swirled with a trace of black. "If you desire anything, you call me," he continued. "The communicator I provide you will allow you to talk to me whenever you wish."

"So I'm paying for an expensive resort vacation, and I can only gain access to amenities through you?"

"You can indulge every amenity that I allow you to enjoy."

He knew that was a little strong, but he wanted to see her reaction. Her eyes narrowed, but he saw the curl of her fingers. She was balancing what she always had to be with what she wanted, and she wasn't yet sure if he could be trusted with that part of herself. The little nudges he was giving her, the touch in the elevator, the presumption of him holding her room access, were pushing her nerves toward testiness. Good. He wanted her to test him however she desired. Sometimes it was like the slow opening of the package, versus tearing off the wrapping, but sometimes it was a mix. If a few paper cuts were involved in the process, so much the better. It wasn't really worth it until blood had been shed.

He opened the double doors to her accommodations. Vardalos had designed the suite the same way he designed the luxurious rooms on the upper floors of the castle, only rather than windows with incomparable island views, he had curtains framed around screens that gave her that same views via full color video feed. Mazes of dimly lit flower gardens, spotlights outlining the elaborate animal topiaries. The skyline view of the clean Caribbean architecture of the clubs, restaurants and casinos, now lit up for the guests to indulge in the sparkling nightlife. The ocean behind it all, currently a dark but weighted presence. The curtains fluttered as if the "windows" were open.

"During the day, if you're awake, you'll get to see what it all looks like in the sunlight."

"That scent…and the wind. It's real. And the sound of water?" She turned on the ball of her foot. "It's in here as well."

"Yes, my lady. The wind comes from there." He pointed to the venting in the stone walls. "Mr. Vardalos doesn't believe any suite, even one for a vampire, should be shut away from the natural beauty of the island."

Moving to the one side of the room still covered by velvet drapes, he tied them back to reveal the miniature grotto. A waterfall poured down the stepped formations of the grotto with a pleasant rushing noise, into a ten-foot circumference wading pool. The surprise on her face turned to delight.

"It's lovely."

"Mr. Vardalos will be pleased that you think so. You're the first to use the suite." He offered his hand to her, was pleased himself when she didn't hesitate this time, placing her slim fingers in his grasp so he could draw her to the pool's edge. "When the sun rises, there's a system in place that will filter its light through the openings for the waterfall. It will put half the pool in sunlight, depending on the time of day, and the waterfall as well. If you're in the pool or have your hands under the falls, you won't be harmed by the rays. Mr. Vardalos wasn't sure if you'd be interested in that, but he wanted to give you the option."

She said something he missed because her head was down as she gazed at the flow of water in the pool. But knowing other guests' reactions to the wonders that Vardalos and his engineers, architects and designers pulled off, and seeing the spurt of light energy around her, he deduced it was a one-word accolade like *amazing*. Looking at her bowed head, he had the same word for the potential wonders she presented to him.

She lifted her head, gave him a piercing look. "You can't hear me, can you? That's why you talk the way you do."

He made a mental note not to assume this one was ever too lost in thought or sensation to miss important details. It had taken some of his co-workers months to notice the flesh-colored hearing aids in his ears, let alone what he suspected she'd picked up, the cadence of his voice, influenced by the muffled sense of it in his own head, as well as the echo sensation from the hearing aids. Truth, though he'd learned to work with them, he hated wearing the damn things.

"I can hear you, except when you look away from me and lower your voice. But I have a sense for knowing what people say, even if I don't pick it up exactly."

"So one of your submissives ducking her head to mutter 'overbearing bastard' doesn't go unnoticed?"

"Not a chance." He showed his teeth, appreciating her. Tilting his head, he showed her one of the small devices in his ears. "I'm mostly deaf without them."

"He can do this"--she looked toward the waterfall--"make the sun not burn a vampire's flesh, but he can't fix your ears."

"Perhaps he realized protecting your lovely skin is far more important than giving me back my hearing. I don't disagree with him."

Her brow creased at that, but she looked amused. "I thought Masters like to mark lovely skin."

"I do. But I want every mark on it to belong to me."

She went still again. He wanted to keep pushing on that sign of arousal, but it was also a sign of hypervigilance, because he was changing her paradigm so drastically. So he paced himself, waited on her next step.

She sank down on the cushioned bench next to the waterfall. When she put her fingers in the water, he watched it glisten over her knuckles, splash her wrist. Her red hair spilled over her shoulder as she leaned over, looked into the nest of black rocks at the base of the grotto. They formed a shallow basin that collected the water before it overflowed into the bigger pool. "There are fish in here."

"Yes, my lady. The water comes from the island's underground water sources and flows out to a much bigger waterfall at one of the island's larger grottos. So some of the fish find their way up here. Usually the smaller ones looking for a respite from being chased by the bigger ones."

"Hmm." She didn't smile at that, but she inserted her hand into the pool, standing up so she could reach farther into the water. He moved closer, watched. She seemed to barely move at all, but when she brought up her palm, a blue and gray spotted fish was cupped in it. She kept her hand just below the surface so the fish wasn't out of water, but her hand was so still, the creature didn't seem all that concerned with the confinement. She slid her hand from beneath him and he swam away.

"There's always a way for the bigger fish to get to the smaller fish," she said. "The only hope is that sometimes the bigger fish doesn't have dinner in mind. Or worse."

He drew a towel from a shelf built into the stone wall. With her gaze upon him he dried her arm, her fingers, rubbing them thoroughly. When he finished, he put the towel aside, clasped her wrist. Fine-boned as china, with an intense energy humming beneath the skin. She wasn't used to being touched without permission, and he could see the war in her about that, clear as the warning flicker in her gaze. He tightened his grip, gauging the pulse.

"I'm going to give you a massage now. Learn more about your body so I'll know how to properly care for you." He nodded toward the bathroom. "Take everything off and put on the robe hanging on the back of the door. There's a dumbwaiter in there for your clothes if you want to use it. You can put them in there, press the signal light, and they'll be returned cleaned and ironed within a few hours."

She lifted her head, met his gaze. Her brilliant eyes had one message. *Fuck you.*

And then she moved.

§

She needed to be left alone for a few hours. She needed time to think, regroup. His brief touches in the elevator, the way he brushed his body against her, had been startling but not even slightly unwelcome, which was all unsettling enough. He'd dried her arm as if he had every right to handle her more intimately. Now he wanted her--no, ordered her--to remove her clothes and submit to a massage?

Alarms went off in her, triggers that didn't care how intriguing he was. But she was hungry. She was going to take care of that and then tell him to give her some goddamned space.

No human could match or anticipate a vampire's speed, so slamming him against the wall and taking him down to the tile on his back, her heel on his throat, was easy. He promptly closed his hands around her ankle and twisted.

Strength or not, that kind of maneuver required her to spin, pull back, but he didn't let her go. He yanked, so she had to go down to roll free. When he seized her from behind, banding both arms around her, she broke the hold, sprang away, turned and hit him in the face.

She was teaching a lesson, not trying to kill him, so the spurt of blood from his lip could have been worse. She'd hit him hard enough to drop him, though, so she gave him points for still being on his feet. The man was built like a mountain. He touched his thumb to his mouth, tasted the blood in a thoughtful move that twisted the knife of hunger. His lips split in a feral grin, a dangerous spark to his eyes.

"Done proving the obvious, my lady?"

She narrowed her eyes. "What?"

"That you can kick my ass." He tilted his head, considering her from head to toe. "Want to go another round, just so you're absolutely sure? That first shot was barely a tickle. I didn't know vampires hit like girls."

This time she hit him mid-body, took them back to the wall

again. Fabric ripped, and she saw he'd caught her shirt so it was off her shoulder, the neckline of the thin knit torn. Her breasts, held in golden satin lace, were now visible and quivering. She wrenched free and hit him again, this time a solid connection with his jaw, and swept his legs, sending him crashing to the tile again. As he went down, he snagged the waistband of her skirt and yanked, hard. The skirt was a snug fit, but his strength split the side zipper and dropped the garment to her upper thighs, hampering her movement. In that key second, he was able to bring her down on top of him. She drove her elbow into his inner thigh, close enough to his testicles that she heard a grunt…and a chuckle.

She squirmed away, sprang back to her feet, and glared down at him. With a toss of her hair, she shed the ruined shirt and skirt. Flicking them away carelessly, she stood before him in the gold satin panty and bra set. Once one became practiced at excessive internal shielding, external shielding required no more than a passing thought. She could be naked as an infant and conduct herself as if she were wearing full body armor. Even if the way his unhurried gaze coursed over her braced legs, the nip of her waist, the rise and fall of her breasts, spread heat over every visible inch of her skin.

Her attack didn't seem to disrupt that placid energy that hummed off him when he got back to his feet and squared off with her once more. She should have torn his shirt off the way he'd tried to do with hers. She'd like to take her fill of that muscular expanse, taste his flesh, his blood.

"I'm hungry," she said. "You're in charge of my care. Give me blood."

"You're the badass in the room," he said, though the sharp laser of his eyes belied the mild tone. "Why don't you just take it, my lady?"

When she said nothing, he knuckled the blood away from his mouth. "Would it help if I could overpower you? Force you to my will with physical strength? I suspect there are plenty of male vampires in your world who could do that, and you wouldn't be losing money on a fancy vacation."

She pressed her lips together. "Do you think you can play games with me?"

"No. Which is why this isn't a game. You know exactly what I'm doing. You just want to control it, which defeats the purpose, don't you think?" He studied her. "All right, point made. We'll skip the massage, for now. Let's go visit the main grotto and waterfall. We need to talk awhile."

She wondered if he meant her point or his own and what his point had been. She closed her hands into fists, uncurled them. "It won't make a difference. I think this was a mistake."

"But you don't know for sure. Let's go find out. The plane won't be back until tomorrow night, so what else do you have to do?"

"I could explore the amenities of the island. You told me there were plenty."

He gave that lopsided smile again, but she was keenly aware the intent focus of his eyes never left her face, as if he was cataloging far more than her words. "I want to do something to help you get into a better frame of mind for this. An experiment. Are you brave enough for that?"

She stiffened. "I'm not afraid of you."

"I think you're terrified."

In her world, an opponent recognizing fear was like a wolf scenting blood. Yet his tone softened, just enough to lock things up inside her, keep her watching, waiting. "Why wouldn't you be?" he continued. "I can't even begin to guess at what it feels like, denying a vital part of yourself for years so you wouldn't end up someone's slave. You have walls that are miles thick. I'm not here to knock them down, Kaela. I know you need them to survive. You have to let down the drawbridge, let me in. I have to earn your trust for you to do that. I get it. So let's go talk and work on that."

He stepped closer. She eyed him warily. She could kill him. The fact that it seriously crossed her mind told her he was right. She was scared. By the situation, by being so far out of her element, but so close to something she'd denied herself for so long. All he'd done was tell her to don a robe and she'd attacked, seeking control because she'd realized somehow he'd already taken some of that from her. She suspected he'd pushed her that way as an icebreaker of sorts. What a strange man.

He didn't look down, but he found her clenched hand at her side. His large fingers covered her fist, caressed, teased, until her rigid fingers slowly opened up. Lifting her hand, he kissed her knuckles, keeping his eyes on hers as he turned her hand over, kissed her palm, her wrist. She drew in a breath as he held his mouth over her pulse, his thumb gliding up and down the delicate skin of her forearm. Her body swayed in toward him and suddenly she was even more aware that she stood so close to him in only a couple scraps of underwear, while he was fully dressed. It made her feel…that he was the one in control.

Only if she let him, and she wasn't there yet. Not even close. No matter what her body was saying. She'd learned to ignore its wants a long time ago. Mind over matter, always, because her life depended on her head, not her heart.

"What experiment?" she said, trying to pull back.

He touched her chin. For a man with such a startling appearance, he had tremendous sexual confidence in his touch, as if he knew his frightening visage was inconsequential to what he could make a submissive feel. "First the waterfall," he said. "But I still want you to go take everything off and change into the robe first. I'll feed you soon. Can you accept that much for now?"

She wasn't sure she could accept anything, but she nodded. She watched him, bemused, as he let her go to recover her skirt and blouse. Folding them into a neat pair of squares, he handed them to her. "If you'll put these in the dumbwaiter, they'll mend or replace them as well."

He didn't apologize for ripping them. No more than he'd apologize for ripping clothes that belonged to him. That was the point, wasn't it? She needed to stop assuming his thoughts, because it made her want to reach up, touch his split lip. When he'd kissed her hand, he'd left tiny smears of that blood on her skin, and the scent was heady. She wanted to put her mouth on his, bite that offended area, make it bleed anew so she could taste him. It was as if she were a fledgling again, trying to control bloodlust.

As if he anticipated her alarm at that thought, her need to do something immediate and drastic to put things back in perspective, he put a calming hand on her shoulder. Under her curious gaze, he pressed his thumb against his bottom lip, putting pressure next to the split. When he felt the blood well anew--or perhaps he saw the avid sparks in her gaze, the signal of her parted lips, the gleam of her fangs--he swiped his thumb over the spot, collecting several drops.

"Stay still, my lady. Still as a statue."

Nothing could be as still as a vampire. It was one of many things that made them deadly. But she couldn't still the thundering of her heart as he reached out that short distance between them and painted his blood on her lips with sensual care, like an artist at a canvas. The tip of her tongue came out, an involuntary motion, and teased the taste off her bottom lip, touching his thumb. He let it rest there while she sampled his flesh, his blood.

A human's myriad scents were as detailed as a book page. She'd registered his interested arousal as soon as they met on the dock, but now there was a more focused attention to it, his cock likely finding even less room in his well-fitted jeans. She detected a faint tightening of his muscles, but other than that, he was almost as still as she, watching what she was doing.

What would she do if he pushed his thumb into her mouth, an unspoken command to close her lips on it, suck it like he'd want her to suck his cock? On her knees. She'd seen that reaction in the eyes of any male vampire who wanted to prove he could overpower her. She would have expected it here, but what she saw was a reflection, as if Garron's sexual energy merely opened her to a mirror of her own desires and needs. She wanted to be on her knees, sucking a Master's cock. Maybe sucking this Master's cock.

She stepped back, a little too abruptly, but he let his hand fall to his side, his expression as steady as before.

"A meal soon. First the robe and the waterfall."

His tone made it a simple command, not a matter for debate. With a lack of other immediate options, Kaela circled around him, moved toward the bathroom.

"My lady?"

She paused at the door, glanced back, but he wasn't looking at her. He was studying the small waterfall, his hands now slipped into the back pockets of his jeans, his weight rocking lightly on the balls of his feet, a position that inadvertently drew attention to the breadth of his shoulders, the fine ass and columns of his thighs. He was built like a brick house and looked like he could dismantle one, brick by brick.

"Jewelry too," he said. "Take it all off."

She didn't say anything, but disappeared into the bathroom, closing the door. Like the rest of the suite, it anticipated every comfort she might need. Ironic, given she felt miles from her comfort zone. The large tub had silver fixtures that gleamed, thanks to their cleanliness and the row of bell-shaped lights that cast muted white light over the room. Another spray of colorful tropical flowers was on the vanity, so vibrant that all the gleaming white and silver surfaces reflected hints of their color. If she had a reflection, she wondered what it might look like tonight. It was probably best that she didn't know.

She removed her underwear and found the robe. The silken fabric caressed her skin like a spa treatment and clung to her curves, showing the jut of her nipples and molding the flare of her hips, the cleft of her buttocks. When tied, the robe was at mid-thigh, short enough to display her legs and make her think twice about what might be revealed if she bent over, but it wasn't so short she'd feel unclothed. Yet it was definitely a garment intended to display her assets for a waiting Master.

That thought gave her pause. He'd been strong, quick, not easily intimidated. He hadn't seemed afraid that she could seriously injure him, which was either foolish or something else, something she appreciated. Sometimes the most important advantage you had was making your opponent believe that, no matter what he did, your will wasn't going to break.

Unless you wanted it to do so.

She frowned at the thought. Maybe their talk would help her figure all this out. Maybe not. But if not, he'd said it himself. A plane would be available tomorrow night.

She belted the robe, emerged. He'd taken a seat in an easy chair that faced the bathroom, so when she stepped out, his full attention was on her. While the chair would have been roomy enough for her to curl up with a book, take a nap, it fit his size. He had his hands resting on the arms, his knees spread in a casual pose. He wasn't waiting on her as much as he was expecting her, a subtle difference she picked up from his body language.

It probably wasn't even calculated. In the human world, men who enjoyed sexual Dominance might get involved in the BDSM scene to embrace it fully. Yet there were some who, with or without the environment to define it, were Masters. It was clear which one Garron was, because he wouldn't have gotten this far with her yet otherwise. Though the steps might seem small to him, they were vast leaps for her. Which was why all of this was so damned disquieting.

His gaze coursed over her, noting the male-pleasing features of the robe. "Do you use that to get what you want?" he asked, his voice neutral.

"My body? At times. I use whatever tool is necessary to do what has to be done."

"An honest answer. Those are the only kind I'm interested in hearing." He stood. "Come with me, my lady. Trust me, the waterfall is worth the trip."

He took her back to the hallway outside her suite, only this time he led her to a smaller elevator at the end of the hall. He keyed in a code and it opened immediately. Once in, he pressed the button to take them down another level. Seeing there were two levels below this one, she wondered how it was possible to go that far into the ground of an island without hitting water. Another of Eden's mysteries.

As the doors closed, her sharp senses detected a faint cry. A repetitive thudding, not exactly like music. The combination made her cock her head, but the sound was gone as the elevator engaged, moved down. Garron didn't react to it, but she didn't think he'd missed it. So far, he hadn't seemed to have any trouble hearing her, or registering her reactions, but he clearly paid very close attention. She wondered if that was because of the hearing handicap, or part of being a Dom at his level of expertise, or some other aspect of his background. She didn't yet know where the scars had come from, but his demeanor and her suspicion it was from a spray of shrapnel suggested a military background.

"You said there weren't any other suites on this floor, but I can hear…something."

"It's in a separate wing, but the BDSM club is on the same level as your suite," he said. "You're probably catching echoes in the elevator shaft from sessions happening there."

"Oh."

The doors opened, bringing her a stronger smell of earth and rock, the more distant scent of salt water. This exit put them in an unfinished tunnel, so she felt like she was exploring a cave. The stone beneath her feet was smooth and damp, small pools of water gathered in places that had her shying at first at the contact, but it was warm, pleasant. She could hear a muted roar, further evidence that they were headed toward the larger waterfall and grotto Garron had described.

They went up an incline, down, around a curve, Garron's body brushing hers as they navigated the turns. Out of all the scents she was absorbing, his was the most pervasive, and she found herself welcoming and anticipating every time he touched her.

"It's easy for someone with strong submissive cravings to think they're ready for something before they really are," he said conversationally. "It's why a lot of subs plunge into a relationship with a Dom too fast when they first hit the scene. You won't have that issue. But beyond that, you have to have a Master that gets it, who knows when to take it slow or speed up the pace."

"Hard to slow down when you only have ten days to do the job."

"I told you. I don't have a job these next ten days." There was humor in his voice, but a wealth of other lustful promises. "You're my vacation."

"If that's the case, you're misclassified, Rand. You're more masochist than sadist."

He chuckled at that, his grip on her arm sliding down to enclose and caress her hand. "I'm not going to rush this, Kaela. We move at the pace I set. The right connections, the moments of trust, can happen in a blink. But only if you don't rush it, no matter how fast the sand runs through the hourglass."

"Cryptic wisdom is barely a breath from empty bullshit."

"That's entirely true. It takes an intelligent woman to know the difference."

She wasn't sure if she shouldn't break his fingers after all, but she settled for letting him guide her on yet another upward incline. This one brought the scent of fresh air and hints of greenery, flowers. The thunder of water grew louder, sending a hum through the rocks.

"Here we are."

They emerged from the tunnel, Garron ducking to clear the overhang. They were outside the castle in an area of dense foliage and discreet pathways. A scattering of stone benches carved with Celtic designs circled a beautiful lagoon that had a rock wall built around it. The waterfall, tall as several levels of the castle, poured along an array of sleek rock in a jagged pattern that reminded her of the dock. A mist hovered over the water, containing a haze of colors from the moonlight. It appeared they had the place to themselves at this late hour.

He drew her toward a stone bench. When she expected to sit on it, he shook his head, directed her to sit on the low-lying ledge around the pool, put her feet in the water. He took a seat on the bench behind her, sitting to her left she could see him in her peripheral vision. He braced his foot next to her hip, his arm stretched out on the back of the bench, all his attention on her where she sat on the ground below him.

Fran often sat at Kaela's feet during vampire events. If it was after the sexual entertainments, she was usually naked, her skin still dewed by orgasm, her head bowed. Kaela would idly stroke her, keeping tabs on her physical and mental state, because the haze that happened after a particularly demanding performance could be extreme. Subspace, they'd call it in the human world. Servants had it as well, that hypnotic trance state that was part euphoria, part numbing peace. She knew because she had seen dozens of servants experience it. She'd even experienced it a couple times as a human, though she hadn't known to call it that. Jared had instinctively known to care for her with extra attention, realizing she needed help grounding again.

*Stop it. Stop thinking of him.* She was already off balance emotionally. Thinking of the man who'd been part of her life as a human would not help.

Garron leaned forward, resting his forearms on his spread knees. He slid a fingertip along her shoulder, drawing her out of her thoughts. "You know," he said quietly, "one of the best Doms I ever met is in a wheelchair. There's something in each of us that says who we are in the pecking order of things, who we can trust. Those are the ones to whom we'll surrender. Sometimes things have built up in our lives, debris, trash in the moat. Until we get rid of that, wade through it, it's hard to figure out who we can trust to guard that fortress."

She looked down at the water, the way it swirled around her calves. There were little fish here as well as some larger ones. Trying to figure out what her legs were, they nibbled at her skin, a teasing contact. "Is this where you convince me physical power isn't relevant to submission? To a vampire? Physical power is everything in my world."

"I'm not sure that's true. I expect you're not the most physically powerful in your territory. But you do a hell of a job either convincing them you are, or that they're all better off with you in charge. You just have to have enough physical power to make them put aside pride in favor of the overall benefit."

She really did wonder how Theodosius Vardalos knew all this about her. And about vampires. She should also find out why Garron accepted she was a vampire so matter-of-factly. These were all things a responsible overlord should do, to protect the vampire world as a whole. Do a threat assessment. But that wasn't why she was here. She didn't want that to intrude upon this.

"There's a reason it's called a power exchange, my lady," Garron said gently when she remained silent. "There's a reason a submissive can abhor the reality of rape, but long for the edge play of a forced seduction. In the room, you overpowered me physically. But what does your heart want, your mind want? Even if you're Hercules, there's always someone stronger physically out there. Correct?"

"Right." But she didn't lift her gaze to him.

He sighed. "Choice is the only true power that exists in a Dom/sub relationship, the guiding credo in everything we do. You suspend disbelief to enjoy a movie, cry over a book. We can get lost in our imaginings and empathy and find a power and magic in them that can strengthen us in our real lives in ways we can't envision. Even more than if we strangle back those imaginings."

"I don't have that choice. Haven't had that choice."

"You do here. Kaela." He reached out, brushed a fingertip along her jaw. "The trick is finding the mind or personality strong enough to hold us up when we need to let go."

"That doesn't exist in my world."

"But maybe it can exist here."

She stared back down at the water. Silence ensued, and she wondered just how he was interpreting her lack of response.

Putting one hand under her elbow and another at her waist, he pressured her to rise to her feet. While she let herself be guided to sit down on the bench next to him, she kept looking at the water, not questioning why she couldn't look at him. Wouldn't. The silence became laden with something else, a feeling that became even more weighted as she felt his hands at her waist again, this time slipping the tie of the robe.

Suspend disbelief, she told herself. Just let it happen.

He spread open the cloth, the humid mist touching her bare flesh. Now she did turn her attention to him, met his eyes. He didn't lower his gaze, and it made the moment more potent, that he'd exposed her naked body, but hadn't chosen to look at it yet.

"Stay still for me. Time for that experiment."

When he removed a coiled object from his jeans pocket, a dozen thoughts and feelings swirled through her like a capricious breeze coming through an open window, scattering papers on a desk, sending them into disarray, a lack of order.

It was a collar. Nothing elaborate, just a silver band no wider than one of her fingers.

"For a lot of submissives, there's a shift of consciousness when you put a collar on them. They let go of some of their worries, get more inside their heads, more in tune with what they're wanting. I'm going to put this on you, let you wear it for a little while, see how it feels."

"Like letting a horse feel a halter for the first time to prepare her to be ridden."

His lip quirked. "If you want to go down that road, sure, but you're getting a little ahead of me."

She pursed her lips. "I doubt that."

"Lift your chin, my lady."

She tried to see self-serving lascivious intent in his expression. Turn him into a man who had the arrogance to think he could top a vampire. She was a challenge to his testosterone, his ultimate goal being to fuck her, conquer her. Nothing more.

There were times she wished she weren't smart enough to see through her own defense mechanisms. Desire for her came off him in waves, yes. She expected that from a human male, no different than what she'd expected from the porters. It was Garron's control of it, the way he refused to let it distract him from what he was doing, and how he channeled it to feed an even more intense action-reaction between them, that made it different. His control was capable of scrambling hers, and his confidence in that wasn't arrogant. It was as if he had a window into her soul and was following her own cues, her needs and desires.

Trying to suppress that internal quiver, she lifted her chin. She could do this. It was a gesture, was all. It didn't matter that, when his eyes warmed with approval, her toes curled against the rock as if she'd been given a gift.

Garron guided the collar around her throat, his fingers stroking her as he buckled it. The strap didn't rest on her collar bone. It fit just below her jaw, snug, compressing the arteries and her windpipe enough to feel restrictive, the buckle below the hinge of her jaw.

He caressed her jaw above the collar's hold, her throat below it, soothing her. Even so, her pulse fluttered like a line of butterflies, her body going even more still. So did her mind, all those dozen thoughts dying down to puzzled whispers. A quietness took over, while other parts of her became far less calm. The tissues between her legs had contracted hard when the strap constricted.

A different level of consciousness, he'd said. All from placing a collar on her throat.

He drew her to her feet, and she stood mutely as he slid the robe off her shoulders, let it fall and pool around her feet. She was standing naked in front of a fully clothed human male, wearing nothing but the collar he'd placed on her neck.

She didn't need to breathe, yet she was making shallow, desperate little breaths.

"Ssshhh…" He ran his fingertips down her jugular, all around the collar, and slid them into her hair, massaging her nape, his thumb tracing the silver band. "Easy, my lady. Just breathe. I know you don't need to do that, but I expect the act calms you as much as anything. It's just a collar. Christ, you're beautiful."

Her attention snapped back up to his face. He said it fervently, reverently. It wasn't practiced, part of some elaborate strategy. Even as he was staying conscious of her every reaction, he was genuinely savoring, absorbing every inch of her, from the way her hair fell down her back and over her shoulders, to how her painted toenails gleamed as her toes dug harder into the stone.

"Is it always the same charge for you…no matter what she looks like?"

Not sure what emotions she was feeling, she couldn't inject any into her voice, not consciously. Her beauty had always been just there. Another shield over whatever she really was. Sometimes a vulnerable woman, sometimes a monster, sometimes a vengeful warrior. Sometimes an ugly wreck of grief and rage, despair and yearning.

"Yes," he said, meeting her eyes. "I've had the pleasure of mastering submissives who fit someone's ideal of beauty, and those who are so far from it they've forgotten beauty is in the eye of the creator, not the beholder." He stroked a hand down her hair, caressed her elbow. "All this beautiful hair alone would make a man kill to fuck you, to wrap his hands in it." When he reached her wrist, her fingers started to curl, anticipating him tangling his own with them, he shook his head.

"Stay still, my lady. I'm touching you now. I'll determine how you touch me when the time is right. Just feel."

"So you see yourself as God? The creator?"

"Hell no. I try to reach a place with a submissive where we look inside one another and find what a creator sees. When I get there, the sub doesn't doubt her beauty or worth. She sees the absolute perfection she is."

His voice, that stilted rumble, could mesmerize. She had her gaze fixed on his mouth, and quelled an urge to lay a palm on his chest, feel his voice like the thunder of the waterfall, a sound heard below the surface of the earth. Below her surface, for certain.

"Time to go back to your room," he said, and withdrew another item from his pocket. A blindfold.

"I want you to trust me to get you back to your room. You've seen the tunnel, know where we're going. This way you can absorb the way it feels, walking with me like this."

Naked. In his collar. If he hadn't just made it clear they'd take the same path back, she might have refused, but still caught up in the spell of his words, she gave a bare nod of acquiescence. As the darkness descended, she managed to suppress a flicker of panic with a couple rational reassurances. He wasn't tying her hands. She could get out of the blindfold whenever she wished.

He touched her throat again, clipped something to the collar. A tug told her he'd fixed some type of tether to it. He'd collared, blindfolded and leashed her, and she'd barely been off the plane two hours.

It was too much. But as she went rigid, began to pull back, he made a little hum in his throat, a soothing note. He moved next to her, putting his hand against the small of her back, thumb stroking the upper curve of her buttock. He had hands large as bear paws, it seemed, and they compelled a mesmerizing calm.

"Just stand here, my lady. Feel it, get used to it. Nothing is going to happen to you."

She knew how empty reassurances of safety were, but she found she could be just as susceptible to their comfort when accompanied by his touch, the press of his body. A second mark servant could speak inside his Mistress's head, and she wondered how that would add to the tempting sense of sanctuary between Master and sub.

Once every five years, vampires assembled at the Council Gathering. Usually held in a sprawling estate or castle, the event required extra staff, so servants of lower echelon vampires were often drafted to serve as extra help. During that time, they were naked except for head masks to conceal their identity. It underscored that those servants were there to serve the pleasures of the visiting vampires indiscriminately and with enthusiasm, to honor their Master or Mistress. The idea had spawned quite a few more fantasies for her, the first year she'd attended.

There was a wide gap between fantasy and reality. When she imagined another vampire seeing her like this, or Garron offering her up to serve others, her fingers itched to do violence to stave off the panic. She forced herself to calm, but it wasn't only her own efforts that helped. The way his hand rested on her waist, the wrap of the tether around his hand that allowed her to feel its slight tug, made her think he really wasn't the sharing kind.

By all the saints, she was getting ahead of things, her mind running amok. They were just standing by a grotto, him giving her the opportunity to trust him during a walk back to her room, in a familiar tunnel where they'd be seen by no one.

"Ready?" he said, his voice a pacifying interjection into her tumultuous thoughts.

Apparently so, because she was in motion, walking with him. The tether was a gentle pull at her throat, and his hand never left her waist. His body brushed hers once again as he guided her back into the tunnel, placing a brief hand on the crown of her head. While he'd had to bend significantly to get through the tunnel opening, she'd only had to duck her head, but he still protected her from scraping the rough archway. Once in the tunnel, he eased her back into a straightened position, kept her moving forward.

The sensory deprivation heightened the scents of earth and wet rock. Which increased other senses as well. She felt every brush of his hip against her buttock, and each finger resting on her lower back sent individual tendrils of heat into her lower belly. The tug of the tether had her nipples stiffening, and the constriction of the collar around her throat made her imagine his grip there instead, holding her down, collaring her with flesh and bone as he spread her legs and plunged into her, commanding her to wrap her legs around his hips, take him deeper. His skin would heat, the blood rushing to his cock, making him thicker and harder, and she'd hear his heart thundering, his life essence calling to her.

Her fangs were lengthening, and she realized she'd rested her hand on his side, was screwing her fingers into the fabric of his T-shirt. As she thought of him teasing that blood over her lips, her nails dug into the flesh beneath. She wanted to taste him. Needed to taste him.

As they made another turn, he gave her a gift, proving how insightful he was. Sliding an arm around her waist, he crowded her against the stone wall, himself against her body. Surrounding her with all that strength and weight, he cupped the back of her head, brought her mouth to his throat.

"Ask my permission to feed, my lady. You need your Master's permission to eat, to drink, to sleep."

He was so close she could practically taste his skin. He had his hand wrapped in her hair, but that wouldn't stop her from taking what she wanted. She could strike like a snake, as lethal as one if she desired.

He'd said as much earlier. *"Why don't you just take it?"* But that was his point, wasn't it? Any male vampire could force her to his will, just as she could force Garron to hers. Her body quivered in his hold, shrieking at her to ignore all that, to just take. It should be enough. It was enough for other made vampires.

Even if they didn't have overt dominant tendencies before being turned, it was as if the chemical change ferreted out and magnified every subtle hint of them so the vampire could survive in a world where it was all about a hierarchy of dominance. That was what her sire had assumed would happen to her. He'd been wrong.

She was the anomaly. The human woman she'd been, the Confederate spy, had possessed the strength to manipulate and deceive, to become whatever was necessary to serve, to try and make her world a better place. Her turning had latched upon those qualities, magnifying *them*, while leaving those deeper yearnings untouched. Her submissive desires had been stronger than any single or combined dominant tendency within her. Provoked by Garron's command, they surged up like a tidal wave.

He smelled like all the things around her--salt water, stone and tropical jungle--as well as the cotton of his shirt, a faint aftershave. Beneath that was his essence, the unique scent she would inhale if she visited his quarters, wore one of his shirts, or woke in the middle of the night in his arms. She wanted to do all of those things, fiercely and immediately. She wanted to wake up in such a life, all the rest a bad dream.

Her reaction had to be caused by the sorcery of the blindfold and collar. She'd seen servants go into a euphoria from such basic tools of mastery. Why should she be surprised that they had a similar effect on her, when she'd fantasized about wearing them so often? She didn't care about the whys. Yet, despite that, she found she couldn't make that last step and ask for permission.

"I want…" Her fingers closed into balls again. "I want to feed."

"Yeah, you do. You look hungry. So be polite and ask." The edge in his voice increased the quiver through her limbs. What kind of punishments did Garron deal out to disobedient subs?

"I can't. I've never… It's like I'm opening myself up far too much."

"It's just us. I can see—hell, I can *feel* your reaction to wearing my collar, being naked like this. It's humming off every inch of you. The blindfold helps you get lost in your own responses and emotions. It creates a cave like this inside you, where those things echo and bounce back, intensifying everything. I love the tight way you're holding those gorgeous lips, holding it all in, because that means what you really want to do is part them, let me in. My mouth, my cock. Cry out your pleasure, ask for permission to exist, let alone take a pint from my throat."

He leaned in so close his breath was caressing her lips. "You've imagined this countless times, my lady. Haven't you?"

She made an incoherent sound as he wrapped the tether tighter around his large hand, rested it on her sternum so she felt the weight of his touch, the deliberate pull against the collar. "You want a Master who will keep you naked but for his collar all the time, so you know you're his. Totally his. He'd take you to his bedroom, hook the tether to the headboard, put you on your hands and knees and fuck you like that. Put his hands on your hips so every time he pulled you back to take his cock harder, you'd feel the yank on the leash, the collar. His ownership of you."

Her fangs lengthened to their full size, something that she didn't usually do until they were embedded in flesh. They were nearly a half inch, curving over her bottom lip. His hand was close enough that when she dipped her head restlessly, she grazed the sharp tips over his knuckles. His other hand dropped, his palm so broad it cradled her buttock. His fingers insinuated themselves into the cleft, an intimate invasion, causing her to lift on her toes against him. Her mound brushed his erection, an impressive steel bar under his jeans, sending a jolt of pleasure through her body.

"Ask," he demanded.

"Please let me drink," she said, the words wrenched out of a place of fear and need. If he waited another second, she would simply take, no matter the consequences to her sanity, to her belief about her control. It would be over before it ever started. The thought plunged her spirits into a different kind of darkness.

His grip on the tether eased, but only to move his hand to her nape and bring her forward so her mouth was fully against his throat. She sank her fangs into him, and that was a jolt of pleasure as well, the first flood of metallic, rich taste. When she all but purred from it, she heard his answering growl of satisfaction. He increased his grip on her ass, not holding back on his strength. Pulling her thigh up along his hip, he shoved her back against the tunnel wall, dropping his hand lower to seek a different pleasure for himself. As she had his first taste of his blood, he had his first exploration of her pussy, the slick lips that she was sure coated his knuckles with her arousal as he pressed them into her. God, he had fabulous thick, long fingers. She worked her hips on him as she was drinking, her hand drifting up to his jaw.

Catching her with the hand holding the tether, he wrapped a loop around her wrist, holding it against her throat, making her keep it to herself as he explored her cunt, teased her clit and made her writhe between hard stone and his muscled body. Her bound fingers convulsed under her jaw as her other hand clutched his T-shirt, fingers clinging to the waistband of his jeans beneath.

He broke her hold on his throat after she'd had no more than a few swallows. "Enough for now," he said roughly.

It was and it wasn't. It was enough for her immediate needs, an adequate snack, but it didn't balance anything else. She gasped as he continued to work her on the hand dipped below her thigh. She was up on one set of toes, the other leg clinging to his hip. He was pushing against her as if they were fucking, and she was rubbing her mound in a crazy pattern over his erection as his fingers kept up their diabolical dance inside her.

"I'm still hungry."

"Yeah, you are. But you'll wait a bit."

He pulled his fingers out and she smelled her musky scent. While he let her slide back down to her feet, he kept her pinned against the wall. Tying her wrist to her throat had freed both his hands. He spread his palm out beneath her bound wrist, which put the heat of his hand over the cleft between her breasts, a sensation that spread over a much wider area. As her scent grew stronger and tangled with the faint mint of his breath, she heard the provocative sound of gentle sucking, and realized he'd placed his other fingers in his mouth to taste her. Hearing and smelling that without sight, his aroused body hard against her, had her ravenous for things so much more fathomless than blood. Yet the need paralyzed her as well.

"I'll feed you soon. Then you'll feed me," he said.

She wanted to do it now. Everything in her raged for it, couldn't believe she was allowing herself to be restrained by little more than his words and the pressure of his body. Her nipples were tight and hard, her pussy wet and willing. But as he freed her wrist and tugged her onward, his hand again on her lower back to guide her, she followed his lead. In the darkness, with the collar on her throat, she had no care for who and what she was supposed to be.

"It's getting close to dawn. Time to put you to bed.

## Chapter Three

*Time to put you to bed.* Like a child? Was he insane? Or was she?

The walk helped her settle, regain some perspective, wonder what he intended to do next. Back in her rooms, he kept the blindfold on and brought her into the bedroom, put her down on the bed in a sitting position.

He left her, moved to a closet. She heard racks sliding along a metal bar, clothes in the closet.

"Did Bill and Waylon unpack my clothes?"

"Hardly. These are a couple things I had put in here prior to your arrival, things I wanted to see you wear."

The rack made a little ping as an item was removed from it. He was standing before her, dropping a garment of fragrant silk over her head. He guided her hands through spaghetti straps, settling in place what felt like a lacy nightgown that pooled at her hips, leaving her bare-assed on the bed but the fabric folded in her lap.

As he removed the blindfold, he stroked her hair from her face, combing his fingers through it before he set the blindfold aside. She blinked, and though she'd not yet seen the bedroom, the first thing she wanted to see was him.

Because she'd been denied sight for that short journey between the grotto and her suite, the structure of his face and dark brows, the jagged path of the scars over his face and throat, the scattering of them over his broad skull, seemed sharper, more vivid to her.

"If you wore leathers and a patch, everyone would think you were an outlaw biker."

"Maybe we'll get a chance to role play this week. I'll put that on the list."

Even though she saw a flash of amusement in his gaze, that intensity she'd felt through his touch and the press of his body against hers was still there. He was just as aroused as she was. She was used to touching Fran whenever she wished, so she reached out to run her fingers along the ridge of his erection before she even thought about it. He caught her wrist, squeezed it in reproof. Folding her arms against her upper body, he used the tether to wrap both her wrists against her neck this time, securing the end of the leash to the collar. The position put the sides of her hands against the pulse points on either side of her throat.

"Hands to yourself, my lady."

The leash and collar were fragile things, so easily breakable. She fingered the links of the leash caught in the collar. The metal loops dug into her wrists, against her sternum, a titillating pain. When he disappeared into the living area without explanation, she let her gaze drift over the room, a weak effort to recall herself from the bright edge of lust, reclaim some of the self-control that being restrained made her want to abandon.

A gold and green area rug with a Celtic style border lay on the floor, a thick cushion beneath her feet. There were more live screens showing island scenes, framed by curtains so they looked like windows. There was a wet bar, entertainment center, a desk and a couch, making this room as comfortable and versatile as the main sitting area.

The bed was a replica antique, the mahogany headboard carved with an ornate scene of Victorian women playing with dogs and flowers. Something that would grace a titled lady's room in a different time. Jared had given her a little music box like that once. Not that exact scene, but that kind of thing. The bed was covered with a thick comforter, cupping her backside like a nest. The pillows looked equally inviting, for sleep as well as for other things. She imagined Garron piling up several up those pillows, putting her over them so he could do all manner of things. He'd hike up the pretty nightgown she was wearing, pull all that ivory lace and figure-molding fabric out of his way so he could do the type of things she usually fantasized about just before dawn.

So her attempt to distract herself from the heat of her desires was failing. Obviously. Or maybe her mind had turned in that direction out of habit, because she could feel the dawn's approach, even down below the earth like this. Jet lag didn't apply to vampires. No matter where she was, she responded to the cycles of sun and moon. Particularly the sun. She was old enough to resist it, such that she could stay up almost close to midday before the sunlight lethargy that affected all vampires to some extent would impair her, but perhaps here, with Theodosius's magic water, it would be different. While a part of her was ready to recharge out of habit, another part was so overcharged she might explode if the right wire was touched.

Garron returned with an electronic device that looked like a remote control for a television, only broader and heavier, the base shaped like an oblong egg. He set it on the nightstand and unwrapped the tether from her hands, unhooked it from the collar, but he kept his hand on her shoulder, his thumb sliding along that snug strap as his attention slid over her. This time she had the feeling he was evaluating her physical state as much as taking pleasure in her partial nudity. Her breasts were almost spilling out of the low cut lace bodice of the gown, the translucent fabric showing the smudge and shape of her nipples.

"Do you need the bathroom, my lady?"

"I know where to find it if I do." She arched a brow, nakedness notwithstanding. Some part of her did it just to see that crooked smile, the glint in his eyes. His pupils seemed to merge into the irises in a way that made them almost indistinguishable, except for occasional hints of a swirl of colors, like two paints when they were first mixed.

"Your choice." He cocked his head. "In the tunnel, before you bit me, you said 'it will be over before it starts'. What did you mean by that?"

She hadn't realized she'd said her thought out loud. She lifted a shoulder. "It's difficult to explain."

"Difficult or uncomfortable?"

She didn't have to answer him. But she met his eyes. "I had the feeling, if I went ahead and took your blood before you agreed…"

"That this is like Jeopardy? One wrong answer and you're out? You only get to take home what you've already won?" His brow creased. "Actually, I'm not sure if that's Jeopardy. Some of my co-workers watch game shows in the break room."

"There's a break room on Eden?"

"Wherever there are employees, there's a break room." He took a seat next to her on the bed, propping his arm behind her. Because the back of the gown scooped down just above the dimples of her ass, his biceps pressed into her bare back. He smoothed his other hand down her thigh. First using the palm, then one finger, taking a pass over her knee. Sliding back up her thigh, he sent a frisson of sensation up both legs, between them. Then he retraced his path along that seam toward her knees once more. Still only using one finger.

"Open your legs, Kaela."

She did, albeit slowly. Yet he didn't dip lower or take advantage of the position, which just made the throbbing want between her legs resume its insistent beat.

"When you're sitting with a Master, you stay open to him. So he can play with your cunt if he wants. You sit up straight…" He adjusted that muscled arm behind her so she did straighten, lifting her chest as part of the movement. His gaze slid over her approvingly. "So he can see your breasts, high and proud, the nipples stiff, begging for his attention."

This was the type of thing she'd seen new servants have to learn, though in more extreme conditions. Submissive 101 for servants was throwing them into an orgy populated by sadists and seeing how they did. She thought she preferred Garron's way, even if there was an element of sensual torment that might make her as insane as the other method.

"If you had taken my blood before I agreed, it would only mean you'd earned a punishment. And that I need to figure out a different way to help you understand what it is you're really seeking." He brushed his thumb over her lips, her cheek bone. The constant touching was a marking, a way of getting her used to the fact that he would touch her how he wanted, when he wanted. She understood that, even as she wondered at the way the knowledge made her want to tremble as much as the contact itself.

"It's not pass-fail, Kaela. It's a journey, and Masters like bumps in the road. If you didn't give me reasons to punish you, it wouldn't be half as much fun."

Now he was teasing her, but not in a soothe-the-little-girl's fears way. The set to his mouth, the lock of his gaze, showed her the sadist within, the one who would take pleasure in doling out a punishment, at kissing away the tears he'd caused. Garron wasn't a gentle Master, and he obviously looked forward to showing her that side of himself. The way her body became taut in response and that hunger rose anew said she could complement that craving with her own desires.

Before she could take that thought any farther, he rose. Sliding an arm around her waist, he brought her to her feet, letting the gown fall into place. He pulled down the covers and scooped her up as if she weighed nothing, placing her in the bed and tucking the covers around her.

"You'll sleep awhile now. When you wake, I'll feed you again. There'll be some breakfast things. Theodosius said vampires can't eat much real food, but you enjoy sampling. We have several chefs here that could make dishes for angels." He picked up the tether again, snapping it on her collar and looping it over the post of the headboard. As she watched, bemused, he took a spool of thread from the nightstand, broke off a piece and ran it through two of the links before looping it to the post, tying it into a firm knot. "Lift your chin."

She did, eying him, and he did something similar to the collar buckle, his fingertips brushing her sensitive throat before he tucked the small spool in his pocket. "You don't get up for anything without contacting me."

So that was the reason for the bathroom question. If he thought she was going to call him if she needed to do that… "Why?"

"Because while you're here, unless you decide you want something different from your Eden experience, you belong to me." He said the remarkable statement simply, putting a hip on the bed and bracing one hand on the other side of her. He twined his fingers in her hair. "Now's the time to get advance permission for reasons to leave the bed. If you want to lay them out for me, I'll consider them."

He'd *consider* them? She was changing her mind about his lack of arrogance. The man had plenty, with extra to spare. "Even if I agreed to something like that," she said tightly, "how am I supposed to contact you for things not on the list? Telepathy?" Which brought second marking him back to mind, something she pushed away. The situation was outrageous enough.

He picked up the item that looked like a remote. "This is the communicator. This button calls me. It won't go to a voice mail or any bullshit like that. I'll have it with me at all times."

"What if you're taking a nap?"

The lines around his eyes crinkled. "I'm a very light sleeper, my lady." He nodded to the headboard. "If you leave the bed, you'll break the thread on the tether, or the collar, depending on which you remove. I'll know you disobeyed me."

"And this should bother me, why? I'm not asking permission to go to the bathroom. I'm an adult."

"Yeah, you are. Capable of making your own choices." Leaning over her, he brushed a chaste kiss on her forehead. She thought about biting off a piece of his ear and spitting it at him. Instead she absorbed the heat of his body arched over her, the strength in the hand that touched her cheek. Rising, he strode to the doorway, but he paused there, looked back. "Kaela, I expect you to fight me, to fight yourself. Usually there's plenty of time to do that. But if you want to make the most of this, see where it can go in the time we have, you're going to have to give yourself permission to have this experience sooner than later. I think you've wanted something like this long enough to make that possible. Think about that as well."

She had her hand coiled in the tether. With one pull, she could not only pop those threads, but the links themselves, probably gouging the finish of the post and taking out a piece of sheetrock with the recoil of the chain. She thought of doing it now, in front of him, and seeing what he'd do. He really couldn't do anything, could he?

But he knew that. So did she. Who was she fighting? Him or herself?

His eyes rested on her clenched hand, visible over the covers. "There's another option as well, my lady. If you prefer, I could turn you over to a professional Dom. It would be included in your resort price, and he could help you pursue your submissive fantasies in a more structured way, where you hold onto more control. You wouldn't be the first submissive who came here who changed your mind about what you really want."

He was as calm as a professional Dom would be, no hint of his own feelings on the matter, which rankled her further. She met his dark eyes. "So it's your way or no way?"

"As I said, my lady, you're not part of my job. I'm a Master personally interested in you as a submissive. So yeah, if you want my company, it's my way. But if you don't, no harm, no foul. There are several excellent Doms on staff I could recommend to you."

"I don't want to know about any others. Not right now." The first statement was kneejerk, the second an amendment, leaving her options. Maybe this wasn't the best set up for her. That was the voice of controlled reason, the one that guided her life every damn day, down to the second.

"Understood, my lady." No emotion betrayed itself in that resolute face, the relaxed stance of his powerful body. A body her own still hungered for. "Just keep in mind, imagined fantasy and desired reality often aren't an exact mirror. If you decide you want something different than this, just break those threads, contact me on the communicator and we'll see what else Eden can offer you. Otherwise, I'll see you in a few hours after you sleep."

He shut off the light, leaving her in a luxurious nest of bedding, the gurgle of the waterfall her only company.

§

Except for her own damn mind, which wasn't good company at all. Her irritation, her worries about his words, her damn spinning mind, kept her from sleeping. But at length, she was just lonely. Sad. Unsure of what to do. She kept twisting her fingers in the links of the tether, but then she turned on her side, slipped both her hands in a folded position on the pillow, put her cheek on them and drew her knees up, a position of self-comfort.

The threads weren't about a grown woman having to ask to go to the bathroom. It had been a straightforward, powerful reminder that she was under his care. Alone, she could admit it had scared her, because she wanted that feeling to be real, so very much. It had been so long since she'd been under a Master's care, yet it was still the most vivid memory of her life.

*Jared.* She remembered kneeling over his grave in the rain behind the ruins of their small farm, not caring that her dress was soaked, that she was cold. She was alone. What did any discomfort matter?

A Confederate soldier, determined to fight for the South's autonomy from the Northern states, he'd been cut down in the first year of the War for Southern Independence. The history books called it the Civil War now and made it sound like the whole thing had been driven by the evils of slavery, because history books were always written by the victors. An important lesson for her, then and now.

While he was off fighting, she'd run the farm. When a pack of Union deserters had come through, looting the area, she'd driven them off with the help of the neighbors. She'd forever won their admiration by taking down the mounted leader with Jared's axe, though she knew the wild swing that embedded the blade in his thigh had been desperate luck. She'd had no fighting skills to speak of then, just the fury of a woman defending her home.

She and the others had dragged him from his horse and he'd bled to death. Despite his transgressions, she'd unsuccessfully tried to staunch the wound. Ten days later, Jared's body had come home in a pine box, on a wagon drawn by a mule and guided by a man who looked as old as she felt when she understood that box held her husband.

At the time, she'd been too numb to realize it, but in the later weeks, months and years of the war, she realized what a mysterious miracle it had been to be able to put her husband to rest. Neither side was prepared for how to handle literally thousands of dead during wartime. A shallow or mass grave was the best fate for most, with far worse for others. The old man would not tell her who had paid him to bring Jared home. She learned that much, much later.

Jared had been her first and only Master. Of course, they didn't use all the terms they used now. Yet when they made love, when he held her wrists to the bed, her desire would rise like the tides, and he'd noticed it. He was as much of a natural Master as she was a submissive, and they explored so many things together. Playful children, madly in love, so young. Even though he'd been twenty-eight, ten years older than her eighteen years when they married, she knew now how young they both had been. She'd been twenty-two when he died, and she'd thought she'd break apart when she lost her Master, her lover, her husband, her heart.

The grief had given her the strength of hate. She'd walked away from her past and put on the mask of a Union sympathizer. That, and her looks, had allowed her to feed information to the Confederacy, sway some battles. She'd taken greater risks as the war became more desperate, as she began to fear it would all be for naught. Maybe she'd wanted to be killed. Even so, she'd often wondered how it would have changed the war if she'd gotten that last missive through. But she'd been captured, and that failure had weighed on her heavily for a long time.

Because she was a woman and beautiful, she had it better than most, turned into an unpaid camp whore, eventually serving the needs of the captain in charge of the prison camp, as well as his higher ups when they came for official visits.

In the end, the resources of the industrial North triumphed. Decades later she would get past the hate, realizing that humans would forever kill one another on battlefields, the same way vampires would always fight for supremacy within their much smaller world.

But there had to be something left over to make it meaningful.

Something real. Her hand settled over the collar on her throat, stroking it.

She realized she was staring at the communicator, sitting on the nightstand. Reaching out, Kaela closed her hand on it, brought it back into the covers with her. She lay there another half hour, wondering.

Turning onto her other side, she fingered the communicator. She knew she was being fanciful, but it seemed to hold the warmth of his fingers. She held it to her cheek, moved it to the pulse in her throat, felt the beat against the metal, the faint hum of the device.

Whatever his motives, Vardalos had gone to great lengths to craft an environment that assured her she could exercise her cravings, but Garron had picked up on her recurring despair that it just wasn't that easy. What if she couldn't surmount her defenses to take a single step closer to her desires?

Garron had gotten past the first line. Maybe even the second. But there was still a long way to go. Merely saying--"Look, the stage is set. All you have to do is step onto it and start…acting."--wasn't enough. That was the problem, wasn't it? She could act all day long. She didn't know how to be her real self.

This was hopeless. She shouldn't have done this. Because he'd been holding it, she tucked the communicator under her cheek. She liked the way his hand had felt on her face. That at least didn't get a rise out of her insecurities. Vampires were sensual creatures and indulged that sensuality almost as carelessly as humans breathed.

"Garron Rand," she murmured. The name rolled off her tongue. Garron meant guardian. It suited him well. He looked like a man who'd been crafted of the clay of warriors, a man who bore the marks of his battles. It was in his eyes as well. He held control because it gave him pleasure, release, and fed a dark need.

*We don't have to rush…* He'd said that, yet he'd also said she could change her mind, go with a pro Dom. But she suspected there'd been a lot simmering beneath that controlled courtesy.

She always took time to figure out her opponents; their strengths, weaknesses and what motivated them. Over the years she'd improved at it, such that she could often size someone up within a matter of minutes. He was a Dom, through and through, and he'd likely be a demanding one. Sometimes cruel. The thought didn't dismay her, because she suspected he could find the part of a woman's soul that desired that cruelty. He'd never strike without pleasurable cause.

But beyond that, he remained an intriguing mystery. She believed him when he said this was voluntary, that he wasn't being paid to top her. Despite her earlier defensiveness, she knew it wasn't because she was some kind of testosterone challenge for him, a Dom mastering the big, bad vampire.

"Garron," she breathed again. She wanted to put her fingers between her legs, but that was what she did in the hours before dawn alone. It seemed too sad to do it here.

"Kaela."

He spoke in her ear, and she jumped, not expecting it. Had she somehow activated the communicator by speaking his name? Or maybe she'd accidentally hit that direct call button, though she hadn't heard it ring.

"Yes."

"What do you need?"

She stayed silent. In her world, there was no nervous chatter, no "I'm sorry, I didn't mean to dial you", especially when she wasn't sure that was truly the case. "I don't know. Something."

She might be seeking something impossible to achieve in a limited time period. A pro Dom might be the best experience she could get. But she wanted something real, and Garron with his ten vacation days was offering her something real. Which made her wonder why it was so important to him. Did Theodosius offer his employees the same chance he offered his guests, to turn a lifelong fantasy into a reality, no matter how temporary? She'd had Jared for barely a blink of her current lifespan, yet it was the greatest treasure her mind held.

"I don't want a professional Dom." *I want you.*

"I'm glad to hear that, my lady." Despite the staid response, she picked up the potent undercurrent of a male staking out his territory. It confirmed her earlier suspicions of what she'd detected behind his courteous offer to give her care over to a pro Dom. It made her smile, even as her hand tightened on the communicator, her body curling around it, an unconscious desire to bring herself as close as possible to that stimulating tone.

He'd changed position, his voice more pronounced. "Did you break the threads?"

"No, I didn't."

A pause stretched out between them. "So did you call me because you want permission to go to the bathroom?"

"I may not break the threads, but I will hang up on you."

His chuckle sent intriguing little surges through her body. "So I've found a hard limit. You won't bat an eyelash at fire play, suspension, being caned until you're bloody or fucked up the ass with a tree branch, but nix on the asking me to go potty."

"The tree branch might need to be negotiated. And if you ever say 'go potty' again, I will not only ask for a pro Dom, I will turn in a scathing evaluation to Mr. Vardalos that says you are an unmannerly jackass with an exceptionally tiny penis."

His deep-throated laugh made those surges transform into something that swirled and hitched in her chest. "I like that frosty edge to your voice," he said. "You just barely avoided adding 'peasant' to the end."

"I thought it was implied well enough not to be overstated." She smiled.

"Makes me want to tie you up and stripe your ass."

"You have those kinds of fantasies? Lady of the manor and big, brutish stable hand who's going to take her down a peg or two?"

"Sounds like you have," he responded. "Which isn't surprising, since you have to be overlord all the time. Why don't you tell me about one of those fantasies?"

"Are you my confessor now?"

"I can be anything and everything, Kaela. You already know that. You just don't know if you can trust me."

"You haven't earned it."

"No. But there has to be a first step."

He'd gotten serious again. She couldn't remember the last time she'd had an equal give and take conversation like this. She didn't encourage familiarity with Fran, for obvious reasons, and with vampires…same problem. Because she couldn't afford to slip up.

"All right," she said at last. And took that first step. "I think I had that particular fantasy for the first time around 1910. I was visiting a business associate in London, and he had a stable full of beautiful carriage horses. He was resisting the introduction of the automobile."

"Who could blame him? Ford hadn't come out with the Mustang."

She smiled again. "There was a man who worked in the stables, a big man who was gentle with the horses but who watched me in a very non-gentle way whenever I came to visit them. I don't ride but I enjoy watching horses, from a distance. They don't really take to most vampires."

"They sense a tiger's been put on their back."

"Yes. But I could watch them in the paddock. I remember one day that stable hand was leaning on the fence, just far enough away from me to seem respectful, but close enough to be…a presence. When I looked his way, there was this expression on his face… The way he wiped his knuckles over his mouth, the dirt of a hard day's work on him…"

"Tell me what you imagined, Kaela." His voice dropped lower, a part of the darkness swirling around her. She closed her eyes and let it take her.

"I imagined him following me back to the stables. I'd be irritated by the way he was looking at me, and would order him to saddle my horse. I'd be sharp with him, impatient. Instead of obeying as he always did, he'd sneer at me, take liberties. He'd come up behind me, press himself against me, all sweat, the smell of horses and man, put his filthy hands on my breasts, pull open the habit I was wearing. I would turn around, intending to slap his face, use my crop…"

"But he takes it away from you. Tells you that he's not going to saddle a horse for you until you learn how to ask nicely, the way a lady should. He decides putting you over a saddle for a nice hard ride might work better for him."

Heat rippled over her skin. She wanted him to keep going, and he did, taking her fantasy away from her and expanding it.

"He'd put his hands in your hair, tug it out of that smooth, perfect twist. He'd yank you over to the saddle he was cleaning before you arrived and started ordering him around. He'd push you down over it, pull up your skirts. You'd be struggling, even as you're getting more excited, fighting the shameful pleasure of being overwhelmed. What would happen?"

"He'd use the crop on me." She noticed she sounded a little breathless. "I'd feel the first strike over my underwear, but that's not enough for him."

"No. It wouldn't be. He'd want to see the marks he's leaving on your pale skin. See how your pussy is getting wet, because after that punishment, what you really want is him to drive his cock into you, fuck you over that saddle, teach you a lesson once and for all. Teach you not to put on airs around him."

This was insane. Inappropriate.

"It's sheer fantasy, Kaela," he said softly at her pause. "Nothing wrong with it at all. Are you wet?"

She thought again about taking that first step. "Yes. And hungry. Really hungry."

"You have to earn your meal. Are you willing to earn it?"

"I…yes."

"Nothing as sexy as a woman who makes up her mind and doesn't back away from it. The communicator has a detachable earpiece. Remove it, put it inside that pretty, delicate ear. The one your stable hand would probably lick and nibble, stick his tongue into, even as you squirmed and tried to bite him. He'd grab your delicate jaw in his big hand, hold you still so he could do it some more."

A little shaky, she nevertheless lifted her head, looked at the device and figured it out. "Done."

"Good. Now, put that longer piece between your legs. Make sure the rounded part is against your clit."

She blinked, but complied. Just the contact of the smooth rounded base was enough to have her pussy flexing at the pressure.

"Cross your ankles, and hold your thighs together." His voice not only filled her head, but everything below it. "Keeping your legs tight together will keep it up against your clit. Imagine I've wrapped rope all the way from your ankles up to your thighs. You can't spread your legs, no matter how much you want to show your Master how eager you are to be fucked."

She jolted as it started to vibrate. "What…how?"

"I have the controls to the vibration feature. You won't come, Kaela. Not without my permission. Now keep telling me about your fantasy. What else does he do to you?"

"What…does he want to do to me?"

"Every inappropriate, dirty thing he's ever imagined doing to a highborn lady like yourself." Garron's voice had thickened with lust. "He wants to see you come from his touch, his mouth, his cock. Every time he watches you ride, every time he sees you from a distance, he's had fantasies of taking you over, teaching you to surrender to him. Doesn't matter that he's just a stable hand. He knows when he has you like this, you're all his. You belong to him. You give yourself to whatever you both desire. That's all that matters."

"Yes. The rest doesn't matter."

She pressed her hips into the mattress, lifted up, because the stimulation of the vibrator and his voice, the fantasy, was making it impossible for her to be still.

"Are you moving, Kaela?"

She must have jostled the phone piece. "Just my hips. Not my legs."

"Don't move at all. Nothing below the neck. Let it build, make you crazy." His rough whisper was like fingers skating down her navel and over her mound.

"When you're pushed over that saddle, he hits you with the crop until your ass is marked with a dozen welts. He doesn't hold back, even when you cry. The tears and your curses turn him on. He's tied up your legs, ankles to thighs just like I described. He likes the way you cry out in pain, even as your thighs try to spread, your pussy lips glistening. He takes the head of the crop, slides it into that slick honey pot, rotates it to gather some up and brings it to your mouth, makes you suck on it and taste yourself. He has you lift your chin, close your eyes, and flicks the end of the crop over your lips, your cheeks. Not hitting you, teasing you. He gives you another smart smack on the ass, because you started to lower it. He wants it up high, wants to see your cunt."

"Oh…" He'd changed the vibration, made it stronger. Her body pulsed with need. She was going to come in no time if he did this. "Garron…"

"Not until I say."

She opened her eyes, startled to see him standing at the end of her bed. The early morning sun was flickering on the waterfall, and that, plus a nightlight in the bathroom and her enhanced night vision, let her see him, though he was cast in the dreamlike gray of the mostly dark room. She couldn't remember the last time she'd been so absorbed that she'd allowed someone, vampire or human, come upon her unawares. Normally that would have brought her sharply back to earth to marshal her defenses, but as his gaze moved over every inch of her, she saw an unleashed possessiveness that distracted her. Captivated her.

Moving to the side of the bed, he carefully removed the earpiece, caressing the shell of her ear. Her lips parted beneath that stimulation, his intent focus. "Hands over your head," he said. "Hold onto the bed rails."

He wasn't asking any questions now, his mind entirely on domination, not negotiation.

When she complied, he locked his grip over her jaw. His hand was so big his thumb and forefinger slid under her ear lobes on either side, pressed into the base of her skull. He put enough pressure in the hold, she heard her pulse start to pound under the grip. His eyes glittered, mouth in a thin, hard line.

"If I was that lucky stable hand, I'd wrap a bit in a cloth, put it in your mouth. I'd tie the reins around your head, stretching that sinful mouth. I'd wrap the slack over your forehead, your eyes, the bridge of your nose, tie it all tight. I'd use baling twine for your wrists, rough stuff to abrade your pale skin, so soft and delicate because you lie on cotton sheets and your maids rub fancy creams into it. I'd tie your hands over your head."

Staying still from the waist down took an act of will so strong she was shaking from it. That, and the fierce look that captured his expression, only made the stimulation of the vibrator worse.

"I don't ever want to let you go back to your manor." He gathered up the cover, yanked it in one hard pull to the end of the bed, revealing her body in the slick satin of her nightgown. It had ridden up when she placed the vibrator between her legs, when she'd squirmed before he commanded her to be still. The froth of lace at the neckline exposed the areola of one breast. His gaze devoured that, moved down over her hips, her thighs that she was still holding so tightly closed, but oh, how she wanted to spread them. She'd taunted him with the comment about the size of his genitals, but she'd seen and felt enough of his cock to know he wouldn't be a comfortable fit. He'd fill and stretch her, demand that she take him to the hilt.

The vibration between her legs was driving her lust at every level. That, and his presence in front of her like this. Commanding her. Taking her over. She was under his control, swept along by the fantasy, so immersed she'd let him come into her room without her even knowing he was there.

She wasn't a vampire who let go of control like this. Had she lost her mind? She knew what she had to do to survive, what she couldn't allow herself. But Theodosius Vardalos, a man she knew nothing about, had said she could, had produced this male who seemed to know just how to reach inside of her…

Too many coincidences. While one part of her mind had accepted the possibilities enough to get her on the plane, rationality--along with all her caution and fears--surged to the forefront again, a cold shock to her system. How many close calls had she had, when she'd trusted the wrong vampire or person? She knew better than this. Though the rest of her was on this wild rapids ride, her survival instinct refused to believe this could be possible.

When Garron's grip increased, that instinct seized the reins.

She wasn't even aware she'd made a conscious decision, which she knew was why she took them both by surprise. Suddenly she wasn't in the bed. She slammed him to the floor, no matter that he was a foot taller and outweighed her by a hundred pounds. She was going to sink her fangs into him, taste his delicious blood, take over, make it clear she was in charge of the situation, that he couldn't take advantage of a moment's weakness, that she was prepared for any contingency…

"My lady."

Had he said it more than once? She tried to focus, realized the strap of the nightgown was off her shoulder, fully revealing one breast. Her hair had fallen over one eye, and her fangs were out again. She probably looked like a flesh-eating siren, capable of shriveling a man's testicles with fear.

Her chest was heaving with so many conflicting desires. She already had his wrist locked in her other hand, her fangs against his pulse. She could tear into it, make him bleed out even as she drank, like enjoying the heavy flow of a water fountain against her lips, heedless of the water wasted, splashing to the ground. She'd take what she needed, enjoy the sparkle of crimson, like the sparkle of sunlight on the waterfall twenty feet away.

"My lady."

It was the lack of urgency that penetrated the howling storm in her head. There was no desperation in his voice. Just firmness. An absolute, unshakable expectation that she'd heed him. The even tone was like a patient but stern father, except the sexual electricity that crackled through her at hearing it was a canyon length away from any reaction she'd ever had to her long dead father.

"You know…" Garron spoke in the same steady way, quieting the roar of bloodlust, though it, and physical lust, continued to pulse through her. "That stable hand knows the consequences of his actions. Once she's free of his mastery, once she's back in her big house with her comfortable bed and all her servants, his lady will likely come to her senses. She'll order her house servants to come and bind him, have him beaten within an inch of his life. Maybe even have him turned over to the local constable so he can be imprisoned for his presumption. He doesn't care. Primal instinct drives him, along with what he knows lies between the two of you, no matter what heaven and hell throw at them. He embraces it, doesn't cower from it. Or the consequences."

As she stared at him, Garron reached up. His knuckle brushed her cheek, then he curved his hand around her throat. A move as easy as when he'd wrapped the collar around it, but just like that, once his hand circled her throat, he constricted it in one decisive move.

"In your world you're taught that it's all force, that the power of the vampire can overcome anything." His gaze flicked over himself, flat on his back and held down with her one hand on his throat and her knee jammed against his upper abdomen, below his rib cage. "That's true, to a point. But you came here, even with all the forces in your world telling you not to do so. You took that risk because, in the end, the heart wants what it wants. It's stronger than any force on earth and will override any power to make its choice. So make your choice."

Releasing her neck, he closed his hands on her biceps. Drawing her down a few inches toward him, he lifted up, bringing his face close. Now his voice wasn't even. It was menacing, his eyes sharp as swords. "That's the last time you manhandle me. You'll be fed when you learn to ask nicely. And when I've had my pleasure. You're here to serve my needs. Not the other way around. You get only what I give you. I'm the only one in this room who will be taking. So let go of me. Now."

He'd understood her trust couldn't be easily won. He'd said he'd expected her to fight, and to keep fighting. He'd also told her she had to give herself permission to make the leap. He didn't seem to feel those three things were necessarily in conflict, though they left her feeling confused. He wasn't, however. She saw that in his eyes, along with something else that had her pulse fluttering a different way. But at his direct order, she found her fingers on his throat loosening.

The other strap of her nightgown had tumbled. He caught it on his thumb, tugging it down, her jutting nipple catching the fabric before it dropped, leaving her naked from the waist up. Cinching his arm around her waist, he lifted and pulled her over to straddle his lap. His cock pressed between her legs. Then he did the unthinkable, something so ill-advised yet so ballsy she knew it had to be deliberate. Digging his fingers into her hair, he jerked her head back, and set his teeth to her throat.

All vampires had a visceral level, one that was so far beyond civility a rabid wolf would seem tame in comparison. Every one of them had to learn how to stay above that level, because to fall into that pit meant full blown bloodlust. Combined with all the other drastic changes she'd experienced today, Garron sinking his teeth into her throat triggered it.

She shoved off the floor, taking him with her, and heaved him up against the dresser. The upward thrust bounced him down hard on the surface, knocked him back against the mirror. The glass shattered behind him. She followed him right behind her throw, was up on the dresser with him, her knee planted between his legs, against his testicles. Before he could react, her fangs were buried a half inch in his throat, her hand dug into the hard muscle over his heart like talons, as if she could plunge through his chest wall to take his heart.

She could.

She swallowed the first ecstatic mouthful of blood, such a generous draught it escaped her lips, trickling into the pocket of his collar bone. She had her other hand clamped on the back of his skull, his flesh firm and smooth beneath her palm, except where the scars were. Her nose was against the scar that started under his jaw, where someone had obviously tried to slice his throat and damn near succeeded.

The warrior in him had understood her reaction this time was different. He was fighting for his life, trying to break her hold. He'd realize he couldn't. The predator in her shrieked with cold pleasure. After years of control, of grief, hate and rage, she could do as she wished. She could kill and take, and feed, and…

She glimpsed his eyes, fierce and intent. Even during this, he was seeking her gaze, seeking to make a connection. His expression was unrelenting, unsubdued. Still wholly unafraid. At least for himself.

*Oh God. Oh…*

She let him go so suddenly he rocked forward, pieces of the mirror falling around him on the dresser surface, to the floor. She scrambled with no grace toward the corner, toward the best position to turn and put up a fight, but she couldn't control her own movements. She crashed into the wall, spun against the stone, hands up in defense, fangs bared. Her arousal ran down her legs, dampening the short skirt of the gown. Her nipples were hard and tight, her heart beating high in her throat. Her body throbbed.

She was hissing, a feral noise she also remembered from her first days being turned. Never had she lost control like that…not since she'd been a fledgling. Her sire, Seth, had been there then. Protecting her from herself, protecting others. She'd never thought she'd need that stabilizing influence again. But Garron had awakened something in her so overwhelming, and that, along with that savage bite, had unleashed a primal reaction, the way she'd respond to a threat from another vampire.

*Kill him. Destroy it before it destroys you.*

What had hold of her now was pure fight or flight, and she didn't do flight. She wasn't a big fan of live-to-fight-another-day. Everything was the sharp, bitter, here and now. She could take him down, keep him down. Kill him. She, who'd dealt with a roomful of fifty vampires, was perceiving this one human Master as a greater threat to her wellbeing.

She wanted what he'd been about to give her, but it was everything attached to it that wasn't simple, the significance of all of it. Damn Theodosius Vardalos. Had he thought about the risks to Garron? Though the Master of Eden seemed to know so much about vampires, he'd discounted how little human life meant to them.

"No. I can't do this. I'm sorry. You need to leave. Now. I'll hurt you if you stay."

He straightened, standing before the dresser. Glancing at the glass scattered over the floor and dresser, he tilted his head, considering the diamond shards littering the shoulders of the T-shirt. Reaching down, he grasped the hem, removed it in a sinuous movement that revealed his lower body to the waist. The man was layers of tough, lean muscle over the large frame. As he turned to drop the shirt on the dresser, she looked at his broad back. There was more scarring there, as well as a stark black and red tattoo between his shoulder blades.

It was a coiled single tail whip, the end split into three barbed tips that spread out in a fan just beneath his left shoulder blade. Inside the coil, between his shoulder blades, was script.

*Serve and protect. Master and cherish.*

The words were done in red, several of the letters elongated so they looked as if they were dissolving into drops of blood.

He turned to face her again. He had scars on his chest, too. Small, shiny round scars from bullets, more shrapnel scars. Whatever had blown up near him, whoever had shot him, tried to cut his throat--any or all of that should have killed him. She could have killed him minutes ago, because she hadn't been mindful of her strength at all, hanging onto any level of control by a thread. Yet here he stood, as substantial as Atlas or Hercules, as if he would be standing as long as a mountain stood.

Which was foolish thinking, because she knew how fragile human life was. But this man pulsed with life. Life and lust.

Her gaze coursed down from his chest to the ripples of muscle over his abdomen, to the hint of hip bones and lower abdominal muscles that disappeared into his jeans, so her track led her over his groin, and the impressive evidence of virility there. Nothing indicated she'd cowed him in the least. From his reaction, she thought he might have some Viking in him, threats only rousing the warrior in him. Rousing him, period.

She despaired at the wave of red desire that rose in her to match it, fighting with an emotional reaction that was going to drown her. Serve, protect. Master, cherish. He could offer her all those things.

"You need to leave," she said again, moving her gaze to the opposite wall, looking anywhere but at what she hungered to have, the need so overwhelming she didn't think she could move without causing herself greater agony. "I'm not in control."

"No, you're not." He was moving stiffly toward her. She'd put him down hard. She'd be surprised if she hadn't cracked something.

"This isn't going to work. I don't want to hurt you, Garron. Please." She threw up a hand as he drew closer. "Stop. I mean it." She moved to another corner. He couldn't stop her. She was too fast. How could she have ever lost her mind enough to believe she could be successfully dominated by a mere human? She couldn't do this with vampire or human. It was a fantasy that was meant to remain an actual, only-in-her-head fantasy. "I have a blood pack in my things. I'll drink that. Tell Mr. Vardalos I want to go out on the next nighttime plane. I'm sorry. There's nothing wrong with you. This just won't work."

She tensed as he approached again. "Stop. I can hurt you. I can't control that."

"Yeah, you can. Because I say you can."

This time when she lifted her lashes, he was meeting her gaze, and what she saw there didn't let her look away. Ruthless determination, and a passion that couldn't be matched by a roaring fire. He wasn't going to stay away. He was going to dare her to kill him. To defy him. To refuse him.

"You did all that on purpose," she accused. "Have you lost your mind? I could have killed you."

"But you didn't. And you won't. I had to prove that to you. Saves time, don't you think?" He took another step closer. Though she told herself to move again, she didn't. She sank down against the wall, put her backside on the floor in the hope the physical grounding would help with the mental one. Dropping to his heels, he braced his hand above her shoulder as he reached down, traced her lips, a fang, with the pad of a callused finger.

She closed her eyes, shuddered.

"Theodosius gave me a potion that would make me stronger than you. Faster."

She snorted out a hysterical half laugh. "Tell him to get back whatever price he paid for it. It's not working."

"I didn't take it. I won't be taking it."

She opened her eyes. His touch on her lips was distracting, almost as distracting as his eyes, locked on hers. He leaned in, all heat, pressing against her even though he wasn't physically against her. Yet.

"Why?" She let out a little hiss as he tapped on a fang, caressed the corner of her mouth.

"Same thing I told you earlier. I assume there are plenty of male vampires in your world who could bring you to your knees, master you."

"Control me. Torture me. It's not the same."

"No, it's not." He looked grimly satisfied with her response. "I expect that was part of what just happened, why you reacted to what I did that way. You're a tough bitch. No one's going to make you do what you don't want to do. But what really sets it all off is you're afraid I can master you without ever lifting a hand against you. As afraid as you are of that possibility, you want it more than you want anything. You want to call me Master and mean it."

He paused, gave her a penetrating look. "Yet that's a point of no return, isn't it? When you were fantasizing about it, you never thought it could become reality. If there's a chance it can actually happen, it changes the whole playing field, doesn't it? Affecting things way beyond ten days."

An ache was taking over her throat, spreading out in her chest. "I've had to be on my guard too long, Garron. This is just…I can't believe I came here, let alone let myself believe that something like this could happen. I just don't think I have it in me to trust you enough. As much as we both need me to trust to make this happen."

"Once again, you're taking too much on yourself, my lady." He sat down next to her, drawing up his knees, linking his hands loosely over them, sitting shoulder to shoulder with her. Or, given his height, shoulder to cheek. After the intensity of the past few moments, it was a casual move, almost friendly. She gave him a wary look.

"I know all about Eden seeming too good to be true," he said. "Before I came here, I was having nightmares pretty much every night. Refused to take any drugs, because that just made me feel trapped in the dreams, which was worse. First night I was here, I slept like a baby. That freaked me out more than having the nightmares. It took me awhile to get used to what this place can do, what it all means. Telling you that isn't going to make it any more possible to accept in the ten days you'll be here. Or maybe it will. You seem pretty extraordinary to me. A lot smarter than a big dumbass war veteran with bad PTSD."

He flicked a piece of glass off his knee, laid his head back against the wall and closed his eyes, as if he had all the time in the world to wait her out. Maybe he did. She studied him for a long pause, then settled back against the wall, putting her shoulder against his biceps.

The quiet companionship helped. She made herself calm down, using the techniques she'd used at the beginning, the things Seth had taught her. She wasn't too proud to treat herself like a fledgling, if the result was not putting the man next to her at greater risk. But after she'd found that center again, the hollowness was there as well. She put her head back against the wall, stared at the broken mirror.

"Have you ever had something you wanted so much that, if you ever did get it and then lost it, you'd want to die? Not the way people say 'I want to die'," she added. "Even when they're down and depressed, there's this line past which the instinct to survive will trump those feelings. Like the person attempting suicide who gets on the ledge, almost falls off by accident and starts screaming for help."

He stayed silent, waiting for her to finish the thought. Waiting for her to answer the question he'd posed, that hung in the air between them. "Yes," she said slowly. "If you're able to give me what I hoped to find here, I think I might meet the sun, rather than do without it again."

He put an arm around her. Said nothing, just held her to his side. Which made it impossible to resist putting her cheek on his shoulder. The broad, rounded expanse was solid and welcoming.

"You know," he said, "when they were putting me back together, and I was going through endless rehab, and surgeries, and more rehab, and more surgeries, I had a lot of days I thought, this just isn't worth it." Garron paused. "I mean, maybe I was meant to die, and these doctors, my buddies and especially me, just needed to accept it. Three of my closest friends were blown up with me. There weren't any pieces of them to put back together. They had to clean some of those pieces off me to make sure they weren't my parts. Some of the guys in my unit made the joke that it was good I didn't have anything amputated, else they might have stuck the wrong pieces on me. Then I really would have been like Frankenstein's monster, right?"

"There's nothing monstrous about you," she said softly. When she lifted her head and met his gaze, a tide of feeling for him swept her. What had just happened, the violence of it, compared to the quiet now, underscored how he was managing the situation. Honestly. He'd shown her anger and humor when he'd felt them, and now insight, giving her a window into a terrible time of his life she could understand. He was treating her as an equal, a confidante, not holding himself away from her, emphasizing that the two of them were bound together in this remarkable situation.

That tide of emotion she was experiencing was gratitude. Even if this didn't work out, she was grateful for the chance to finally connect with someone, talk honestly about herself. And, riding that surge of feeling, she wanted to give him something for that. Immediately.

She'd noted how his brow furrowed as he talked, as she talked, as if he was fighting a faint headache. She could give him something no one else could. It would be temporary, just like his gift to her, but an offering just the same.

Lifting her hand, she touched his ear. He tilted his head, a curious expression on his face as she felt the shape of the hearing aid, figured out how to remove it from his ear. She shifted onto her knees to remove the other one, stretching her body out against his chest. He let her do it, his hands briefly resting on her waist, her side. When she had the small objects cradled in her hand, she braced her forearm on his knee, looked down at them, back up into his face. "It's easier to talk without them, isn't it?"

She knew he could read lips, had seen the way he watched her mouth. He also seemed to pick up just as much of what she was saying from her body language. "My hearing is exceptional," she added. "So when it's just us, you don't have to wear them. You don't have to worry you're not speaking clearly enough, too loud or too soft. You can whisper or mumble, and I'll know what you're saying. It's easier that way, right?"

His gaze softened and he touched her face. "Vampires are supposed to be mean. You're not. Violent, sure. Possibly cruel at times. But mean, no. Not being mean counts for a lot in the world."

"Not in my world."

"Maybe you're worrying about the wrong world."

She shrugged, settled back at his side. Guiding his arm back around her, she put her head against his shoulder once more. She turned her face up to him so he could read her next question, though. She liked the careful way he watched her mouth, her facial expressions. "So what happened to get you out of that dark place, during all the surgeries?"

"One day, I'm in the hospital, feeling a million miles from anyone, and this nurse who mothers everyone on the ward shows up with a picnic basket. Through pieces of our conversations and talks with my buddies, she's figured out what my favorite foods are, and has cooked up the best fried chicken, mashed potatoes, gravy and apple pie you've ever tasted. So she perches on the edge of my bed, feeds me, listens to me, reaches out and touches my face, strokes my cracked and scarred head. When she gets ready to leave, she just puts her arms around me, hugs me against her big Mother Earth breasts, where you feel like everything will be right with the world. Even when your world is a cracked egg with the yolk running all over a dirty floor."

He cleared his throat. "She says 'Son, it's pretty simple. I don't care who you are, there's nothing in the whole world that doesn't feel better after you've had a good meal and the right kind of contact with another human being. You don't have to have the answers. You just have to have the feeling that you can handle them.'"

Garron touched her chin, made her look up at him. As he leaned in, she thought he was offering a kiss, but as her lips parted for that, he bypassed the opportunity, instead sliding closer to hold her, his bare chest and throat against her face, his arms circling her. The nightgown was still tangled at her waist. She hadn't bothered to change its position, even when removing his hearing aids. As a result, she could feel him against her breasts.

He brought them both to their feet, her against the wall. A different level of intrigue took over as he pushed the nightgown all the way off of her before hiking her up and guiding her legs into a locked position around his body.

Once he had her there, he went still, letting her feel his bare shoulders under her hands, his chest against her, his hips spreading her thighs wide for him, his groin pressed firmly to hers, reminding her of the throbbing need between her legs.

He didn't move, didn't stroke her further, just held her like that, looking at her, seeing her, saying nothing. The position emphasized his strength, let her absorb the muscled power of him pressed against her body so fully, pinning her to the wall. His silence, the full contact that suggested so many possible actions, none of which he was immediately executing, making her guess what he'd do next, were incredibly stimulating, resurrecting the weighted, delicious tension between them.

The nameless feeling that bound them, that connection, also resurrected, making her protests and fears die with their two bodies melded together like that.

"See there?" he said, low. "As I said, I can overpower you, my lady, and I don't need greater physical strength to do it. I see your need for surrender, and I can bring you to that. It boils down to a willing choice."

The will. It was all about the will. He'd said that too, hadn't he? She had a formidable will, the will to live when she'd wanted to die, to rule when she'd only wanted to serve. Face to face with him, she felt the strength of a will as great as her own. Perhaps greater, because there was an incredible message pounding through those words. If she surrendered her will to his, his will would care for her. All she had to do was make the choice. Could she do it?

When she'd first become a spy, then later a vampire, then an overlord--hell, every challenge of her life--she'd learned to deal with those things by taking it minute by minute. Then hour by hour. Day by day. So maybe she needed to do the same here, starting from scratch.

Moment by moment.

His eyes were still locked on her face. Under that gaze, she shuddered once. Blinked. Her pulse hammering between arousal and terror, she did the unthinkable.

She lowered her eyes.

His fingers flexed on her in reaction. He stayed motionless for at least another dozen heartbeats, letting her feel the gravity of that decision, making sure of it. She wasn't sure of anything.

"There it is," he murmured. "That click. That first tiny sign that you think you can give me your trust. People think it's deference or subservience, and that's part of it, but as every creature in the wild knows, you don't take your eyes off of what you can't trust."

Her pulse elevated even more, and he must have detected it. "Easy, my lady. First the right kind of contact."

Wrapping his hand in her hair, he dropped his other one in between them, trailing his fingers down her upper abdomen, over the indentation of her navel. She licked her lips at the whisper of a touch over her mound and then a tiny sound of need came from her as he found her damp core. He stroked, teasing circles over her clit and the petals of her sex that had her hips lifting to his touch, her nerve endings catching fire.

He lifted his gaze to hers again, locked. "Come for me, Kaela," he said quietly, "and then you can take however much blood you need."

His hand on her hair tightened, pulling at the scalp, immobilizing her head, and his clever fingers began to knead and flick. That was all it took. The orgasm surged up against his touch, straining for release. She fought that wealth of feelings, even as he spoke against her ear.

"Come for me, Kaela. Trust me to take you where you need to go."

A climax. So straightforward, so easy, but it meant so much. She struggled against the flood of fear, the instinct to fight, but this time as that feeling rose, he anticipated her. He plunged his fingers into her fully, holding her up against the wall with his body weight while working her ruthlessly. He tilted his head once more, taking the artery farther from her greedy lips. As a moan broke from her lips, he chuckled, a faintly malicious sound that sent chills over her spine and made her whole body constrict. His hard eyes pinned her.

"Don't fuck with me, my lady. This blood comes with a price. Your obedience."

The words were like bullets, and they struck the target. Her body convulsed, arched, struggled, and the climax strangled its way past her reservations. She cried out, throwing her head back so it hit the stone wall. As she continued to writhe, he closed the distance between them again, cupping her skull to protect it and bringing his throat within reach again.

"Feed, Kaela. Take what you need."

"Give…I need to give what I need…"

He nodded against her temple, understanding her meaning in a way she wasn't sure she did herself. Even so, she bit into him with the manners of a starving wolf. His strong arm banded around her, holding her as she took the first sweet gulp.

A first step, he'd said. It was a hell of a first step, as precarious as stepping out on a ledge that might give way. For the first time in a long time, she had to remember when to stop, so she didn't drain him. She wanted to drain him. His biggest danger to her and to himself was that he made her forget he was mortal.

But he was right. Sometime during the past few pivotal moments she'd decided, whatever the consequences, she wanted those ten days. No price was too high. God help him, he'd made it clear he was willing to pay that same price, and she wanted what he could give her too much to deny herself.

## Chapter Four

At length, his hold on her hair became a stroke. As she let her fangs retract, she licked him, swirls over heated male flesh. She nipped and suckled, her hands gliding over his chest, his biceps. She pushed back abruptly, overwhelmed by all of it.

"Easy, my lady."

As he let her down, she pushed away, needing the space. But she was swaying, turning. The world seemed topsy-turvy. When he tried to get close, she evaded him. Stumbled. A vampire never stumbled.

He stayed at a distance, probably to keep her from staggering in a different direction. She sank down to the floor, trying to get a grip on herself, but it felt like waves were crashing down on her. Each attempt to raise her head, gain control, was knocked asunder by the next wave of disbelief, of feelings that had been held back so long. He must think her a fool, a decades-old vampire cut adrift by simple submission. Yet it was a priceless gift she'd never thought she'd be given again, one that could tear her to pieces with its reality in a way that being deprived of it never had.

He came to her, stood beside her where she sat on the floor. As he touched her head, her eyes closed. He began to stroke again, exerting a gentle pressure so she gradually leaned in, until her head was against his knee. He was threading his fingers through her loose hair, combing it, tugging on it, outlining the curve of her ear, moving around to her jawline, making her lift her chin. Hooking his thumb in the collar, he traced her soft skin beneath it.

"That's it. Just give yourself to me, my lady."

"I'm afraid." Words she never, ever said, now spoken in dawn's semi-darkness to a fantasy, a mysterious stranger who would be her undoing. "I'm always afraid. And alone."

"You're not alone right now. Are you?"

"I don't know."

He knelt behind her, a man like the shelter of a tree. His arm slid around her waist, and his other hand moved from her jaw under her hair, to her nape. With more inexorable pressure, he began to bend her forward, moving with her.

She was disoriented enough to give him the control, to let him fold her the way he wished. He bent her over her knees, a fetal position that brought her forehead to the floor, his hips cupped over hers, his chest against her back. His arms slid free to circle her shoulders and head, his lips to her crown as he sheltered her like a cave over a hibernating animal, dark and hushed. The heat of him surrounded her, his breath on her hair, his heartbeat against her back.

With his blood inside her, his scent upon her, she let it happen. Her arms were folded at her sides, and she slid them forward so her fingertips touched his forearms, crossed over her head. She curled her hands over them, brought them in beneath her chin, pulling him in a tighter arc over her. He complied, adjusting so his arms were wrapped over her chest just below her throat. His head was tucked against hers, his mouth cruising along her throat.

"Do you want me inside you, Kaela?"

"Yes."

"Stay still then. Just like this."

Her fingers tightened on him. Yes, she wanted him inside her, but only if he didn't have to move from this position. His heated chuckle against her ear warmed the cold fear in her. "Figures a vampire would be a pushy sub." But he held onto her with one arm and somehow managed to free himself from his jeans with the other hand, opening them enough that he could guide himself to the slick heat between her folded legs. The press of his body brought her up a few inches off her heels, just enough that he could achieve the desired angle. He fitted the head of his cock there, broad and thick. She quivered, her labia spasming over him.

"Hot, wet and tight. Just the way I like a sweet, submissive pussy."

Even Jared hadn't spoken to her like that, because they'd been too young, too unsophisticated. Yet Garron's words were raw, primal, anything but polished. "Don't move, my lady. I'm fucking you for my own pleasure. You're serving me. Aren't you?"

"Yes," she whispered, then closed her eyes tight.

His lips touched her cheek bone, her jaw. "You're too tense, too afraid of this." He adjusted his hips, slid in another inch. She made a noise of deep need. "Yet your body's screaming for it."

Her nails bit into his flesh, found blood. He let out a quiet growl, not an admonition, but a reinforcement of the savage act. When he pushed in several more inches, she tried to raise her hips, but he kept her pinned down. "This is all about my pace. My control. Let me take you where you need to go, Kaela."

She was at least satisfied to hear the strain in his voice, and a breath escaped her at his thickness, his length, as substantial as she'd expected. He was as aroused as she was, and that knowledge shattered her even more. She put her forehead down between her arms as he slid all the way home, stretching and filling her. In this position she had no control over her own pleasure, so as he withdrew halfway, slid back in, the seesawing motion sent crazy whorls of sensation through her clit and pussy, into her lower belly and shooting up into her chest, causing wild flutters to her heart. She began to make helpless, aroused noises.

"That's it. Let me hear you, my lady. Serve me well. Give me pleasure."

She couldn't think past her own overwhelming response, but she expected that was what he meant. This spiraling ecstasy seemed to be feeding his own actions, for his thrusts grew stronger. And still he kept her from moving.

"Please…"

"Beg all you like, my lady. You're mine to enjoy as I wish. You'll come when I'm ready."

The angle he was employing kept him out of range of any clitoral massage, yet sent mini-climaxes ricocheting through her cunt, skittering over her like electric current. Her mobility was restricted, her body a tight ball beneath him, yet she was vibrating like a tuning fork.

"Please…"

"That's it. All you have to do is beg."

Her reality was being destroyed, and she was letting it happen. Welcoming it. She fell over that edge, her pussy clenching him hard, sensation spiraling through her, a compressed cyclone in her current position that had her screaming out without any ability to restrain herself. He only encouraged it by rising on his knees, pulling her hips up and increasing the power of his thrusts, rocking her forward like a doll.

"No…no…" She didn't know what no meant, except she was still afraid and she didn't want him to stop. He didn't, working her through the full orgasm until she was shuddering at his barest move. Even then, he wasn't done. He pushed her back down into that coiled position, his cock still hard and thick inside her. He wouldn't let her hold onto her fear. As she came down from the violent climax, he curved tightly over her again, his voice against her ear.

"What does your mind want? What does your soul say when it reaches out to me?"

She couldn't answer that, but he left it there. One more deep thrust that wrested a guttural groan from her and then he was withdrawing from her body and lifting her. He put her back in the bed, himself around her.

"If you don't let yourself have these ten days," he said at long last, "if you get dressed and leave on the next nighttime plane, do you think that changes anything? You'd regret denying yourself the chance of seeing where this could go. That regret could grow so large it would eat you alive from the inside."

"You think I'm already past the point of return."

"Yeah. I think you were there when you decided to make this trip, before you ever stepped foot on the island."

She knew he spoke the truth, but the pull of the sun, combined with the confused state of her body, half lethargy, half please-fuck-me-into-oblivion, pushed her away from any decisions. His fingers, stroking her hair, her face, her shoulder, made the only decision she was capable of making. She gave herself to sleep.

§

Garron sat in his private room in Club Sin, studying the monitor which showed him the feed from Kaela's room. He'd dealt with some paperwork, checked the readiness of certain toys and pieces of equipment he had in mind to use upon her, but mostly he'd watched her sleep during the afternoon hours. Sitting in his chair, turning it slowly left and right, he kept his eyes trained on the monitor, but his thoughts were covering far greater ground. Toys and equipment were the least of what a good Dom employed to take a sub on the journey. So much of it was a trip of the mind, and to do that right, it was critical to stay several steps ahead of his submissive. Though he found his reaction to her was putting them more neck and neck than he'd experienced in quite a while. Not an unpleasant feeling, just different. Intriguing as hell.

Once he'd left the bed, she'd gradually migrated back to the center, sleeping on her stomach, her arms spread, one leg bent, the silky limb outside the comforter an unconscious tease. It hadn't taken her any time to take over the bed in his absence. Though he didn't like to think of her facing so many things on her own all these years, he was caveman enough to be pleased with the evidence that there hadn't been anyone sharing her bed, at least not long enough to change her preferred sleeping arrangements.

They'd made some small progress. Despite his admonition that there was no need to rush anything between them--primarily because it couldn't be rushed--he was far too aware of how short ten days were to cover the emotional transition that needed to happen. The only balls he had in his court were how Vardalos had set the scene, helping her believe she could open up in a way she'd craved for so long, and how much she actually did want to embrace her submission.

Then there were his actual balls. Which had turned out to be pretty necessary, dealing with a sub who could kill him with less thought than it took him to snap a pencil.

Fucking her, pleasurable as it was, didn't mean much. A less experienced Dom would have thought that was the major breakthrough. But from his understanding, the vampire world was all about kinky sex that didn't necessarily touch the power dynamics locked in place like armor. The most important event in those hours together had been when she let him curl over her, give her sanctuary, intimacy. A sense of safety that had nothing to do with the differences in their strengths, but the emotional haven she needed. She needed so much more, though, and she hadn't opened that door more than a crack. But it was an important crack. In that same short time, he'd become determined to handle everything that came out of it.

Vardalos had known that. He knew Garron had been in Eden long enough. His growing restlessness signified that things had healed, that it was time for a purpose. When he was in the military, he'd stayed behind as a contractor when others pulled out because he'd known what needed to be done. Even if it was a lost cause with dwindling numbers, it didn't mean it wasn't the right thing to do. He remembered the eyes of the children, watching the soldiers leave. At that young age, they'd cared nothing for adult politics or zealotry or big talk about self-determination without shit for fire power to back it up. They wanted to be able to play ball in the street, go to school.

Not worry if their friends, parents, their dog or themselves would be dead by the end of the day, if another part of their unpredictable life would crumble and be remade in another power-hungry idiot's image of the perfect world.

He remembered the kids playing near the base, asking the soldiers for candy. Little opportunists. His lips twisted at how innocently and transparently they used their charms. Their simple trust and hope had lodged in his heart. As a Master, he placed a high value on such trust, used that as motivation to earn and deserve it.

Despite the fact the vampire he was watching had a long history that made her the exact opposite of innocent and transparent, he felt that simple trust and hope reaching out to him from within her. The kind of Master he was had responded to her as if she was the answer to a question he'd been waiting to hear for a really fucking long time.

He liked Lady Kaela. Liked the way she fought, how unapologetic and yet complex she was, keeping him on his toes. Yeah, he enjoyed the hell out of his job, but this was more than that. He wasn't one of those guys who denied his feelings. He evaluated them in a pretty matter-of-fact way. Which was why he'd always been bemused by those who thought falling for someone was a long process, one that couldn't happen in a heartbeat. He'd known in a heartbeat he would stay in the Middle East, do what needed to be done, and that decision had nearly cost him his life. It didn't change the fact he would have done it again, because he knew that was where he needed to be.

He'd never met a damsel in distress who could put him through a wall. Yet he looked at her and saw a connection, a signpost that said this was the way he needed to go, whatever the cost. Consequences didn't bother him. Missing a sign post was the real bitch.

He shook his head and rose. Time for a breather from all the emotional shit. He hadn't let himself go over when she had, and his cock was bitching about that like a shrewish fish wife. Watching her had stirred him up, so what was unfolding inside him was good, straightforward lust. He thought she might be ready to enjoy that as well. Kind of a cleansing, the good dirty kind, before they got back into the real muck again.

Hell, his vampire might still kill him before the week was over. He grinned at the thought. So no sense in holding back. Before it was over, he'd make damn sure she knew just how demanding a Master he was.

§

Fran always waited to be called before she entered Kaela's room. But she knew Garron was there, sitting in the occasional chair a few feet from the bed, watching her. Without opening her eyes, Kaela imagined sliding out of the bed, going to him on her knees, kneeling between his feet, head bowed, waiting for whatever he desired. Maybe he'd stroke her hair with those strong, capable fingers that calmed things inside her. Maybe he'd open his jeans, force her lips down on his erection and make her service him. Maybe he'd do nothing but make her sit there while she trembled and wondered. Waited on him.

She'd fought and killed vampires who'd had a better than equal chance of killing her or worse, and yet, as she considered actually doing what she imagined, sliding from the bed to kneel between his feet, her courage failed her. But what if he ordered her? She wondered what it would be like to have him in her mind, issuing commands in that sensual rumble like a muscle car, hinting at all the power he could unleash. Would it sound like that, or be more fluid, like the command of a warrior angel? Without the hearing aids, his voice was low and steady, the syllables unbroken, a smooth and sure connection like the strength of his hands holding her.

For her to find out what he'd sound like in her mind, she would have to second mark him. Which technically would make him a second mark servant. He was no servant, but the thought of him being bound to her that intimately was too tempting.

All her worries of the previous day were hovering, and she didn't want to get lost in them. So she raised her lashes, and got lost in something else.

He was sitting in the chair, yes, watching her, fingers steepled, eyes thoughtful. And he wore nothing, every length of limb and layer of muscle visible. His erection, thick and stiff, brushed his hard belly. He didn't look concerned about his nakedness at all. He was just studying her, as he would a wild animal he was trying to tame to take food from his hand. Not so far from the truth, really. It was a titillating thought, another fantasy.

Desire shot through her, strumming through her thighs and punting all those worries over the dark edge of her mind. Especially when his gaze sharpened and he spoke in that muscle car purr.

"Sit up and let the sheet drop. I want to see you."

He'd put her to bed naked except for the collar. She could smell his scent on her skin, between her legs, and she didn't want to shower. Or wear any clothes at all that would detract from that marking. From his heated look, she wondered if he was going to let her wear any more clothes these next ten days anyway. Swirling became tight coils at the thought, centered between her legs. This was just a fantasy, one she could enjoy without repercussions or worry. Yet it felt so real to her. Too real. Regardless, she pushed herself up, her long hair falling over her right shoulder as she let the sheet crumple to her waist. His attention went to her breasts, the slope of her abdomen, her shoulders.

"Play with your nipples. I want to see them get tight and hard."

She cupped her breasts, her lips parting at the flicker in his gaze as she manipulated her nipples between her knuckles. She didn't think anything other than his intent regard was needed to get them to stiffen, but how he focused on her hands, her breasts, so exclusively, as if watching her do that was the most important thing in the universe, intensified her reaction. This was how she'd imagined it. Serving a Master, yet somehow feeling like the center of his world because her service was so essential to him.

He clasped his cock at the base, began to idly pump it, thumb rubbing the glans as he watched her. Her gaze went to it, and she licked her lips.

"Hungry this evening, are you?" His hand slid down, back up, squeezed himself, and she felt a similar sensation between her legs. He didn't seem in any hurry to order her to do anything else. He was just looking at her, using her as his personal pinup while her pussy got more slippery and the cool flesh of her breasts yearned for the heat of his hands.

"Come to me." Those dark eyes locked with hers. "The way you imagine your Master would want you to come to him."

The man apparently didn't need a second mark to hear her thoughts. Perhaps his skill as a Master had been augmented by having to watch body language so closely, read lips, do all the things someone mostly deaf had to do to comprehend the world around him. She'd always prided herself on her poker expression, knew she was good at it. He was just better. It was rare she'd met a man who could get the upper hand with her when she didn't want him to have it. It was even more rare--try never--that she'd met a man to whom she wanted to give that upper hand. With Jared it had been a natural evolution, never a conscious choice like this, a mature woman putting her soul into a man's hands.

When she hesitated, his lips firmed. "Don't refuse me, my lady. I have an alligator paddle you won't like at all."

Actually the idea of it struck her mind like a glowing brand, and she pressed her lips together. His brow raised.

"Christ, you're a temptation. Obey me and I'll reward you by blistering your ass. You won't be able to sit down until your vampire healing fixes you." His eyes glittered. "You're getting wetter. Your chin just lifted a little, jaw tightening a fraction. Shortened breath."

"It's not supposed to be this simple."

"It's not simple. It's just swift. There's a difference." He studied her. "Vardalos told me about the way vampires mark their servants. First mark, a geographical locater, so you know where I am. Second mark, you can speak in my head and I can speak in yours. Do you want me in your mind, Kaela? Unable to hide any thought from me, no need to speak aloud because I already know what you want and need, even when you can't quite tell yourself?"

*Yes.* But marking wasn't about that. It was what a vampire did to bind the servant to her, to make it impossible for the human to hide his or her thoughts. Fran only had access to the thoughts Kaela sent her, allowed her to hear. Yes, she could open her mind to Fran if she desired, but that wasn't the way the vampire-servant relationship worked. But Garron having full access to her mind, her body… Her pulse jumped unexpectedly, and she realized the hands he'd commanded to fondle herself were moving more sensually over her breasts, cupping, kneading, now pinching her nipples in a way that had her head dropping back on her shoulders.

"Kaela." His voice was a growl. "Get over here."

"It's not as easy as you just ordering me about." Yet her voice was thready as she brought her feverish gaze back to him, to the cock still jutting between his legs. It had grown thicker. She could almost feel the way it would stretch her, invade, pin her to the bed like a helpless butterfly.

"Nothing's easy about you, my lady. Crapping broken glass would be easier."

She blinked at the crudity, not sure if she'd just been insulted or complimented. She also wondered at the part of her that appreciated the moments when he let his own rough edges show. "So you are a masochist."

"There's not a big difference between the two sides of that coin. Otherwise they wouldn't fit together so smooth. You know…you can second mark me if you wish."

She started at the unexpected segue. He said it casually, but his direct glance said he was serious.

"We can't do that." She shook her head. "It's forbidden by the Council to second mark a human if there's no intent to bring them into our world permanently, since the mark is permanent. It's a death sentence for the human."

"It's different here." Garron gestured to the waterfall in the wall, where she could feel the remnants of the day's sunlight still fading from the rock. She'd fallen asleep looking at it, the miracle of seeing that slash of sunlight in her bedchamber. "The same magic which makes that possible allows you to second mark me, let me into your head, without it being permanent. Once you leave the island, the mark ceases to exist and the connection will disappear."

That wasn't possible. But sunlight on her skin hadn't been possible, either. "You're not a servant."

"Servant can have a lot of meanings. Or mean nothing. It's just a word."

"I won't risk your life based on the word of Theodosius Vardalos."

"You risked yours based on his. The waterfall, the things he knows… Do you think he'd tell you the mark would be eradicated when you leave if he didn't already know it would?"

"I don't want you to be a servant."

His gaze flashed like a blade unsheathed. "I'm not, Kaela. Mark me or not, it doesn't change that."

Her earlier concerns, that somehow this was all an elaborate trap, returned, but were gone just as quickly. It wouldn't make sense. If she second marked a human, the control was all hers, and she would have detected if another vampire's mark was upon him, trying to seek a way into her mind in an unguarded moment. But it didn't make the idea, already too tempting, any more feasible. She wouldn't let her own desires endanger him any more than they already had.

"I can't do it. It's bad enough that I've pursued this as far as I have. I should have left on the next plane."

"Not allowed. You're my vacation, remember? If you leave, I have to go back to work."

She made a face at him and he gave her a tight smile. His hand stilled, though it stayed wrapped around his distracting cock. "All right, we'll leave that alone for now. I'm going to tell you how this day is going to go. Would you like that?"

After a long, heart thumping silence, she nodded.

"You're going to come over here, kneel between my feet and suck me off. Then I'm going to decide what I want you to wear tonight. I like the look of that dainty little collar and tether on you, so that may be it." He paused, arching a brow. "Want to hear more?"

"Yes." Her hands had dropped to the bed, were fisting the sheets.

"Then come here." He pointed between his feet. "The way you imagined it, Kaela. Impress your Master. Make me even harder, so I can't think of anything but fucking your mouth, shoving you down on me until you make those little helpless, hot noises because I'm being too rough. But you don't want me to stop until I make you choke on my come."

He considered her, lips twisting. "I'll bet it's been a hell of a long time since you went down on anyone. You couldn't do it to a servant unless he was trussed up, to make it clear you're doing it to torment him with your mouth, rather than serving his pleasure. But you couldn't risk even that, because if you're like most subs, it's hard not to lose yourself in that feeling that takes over when you're sucking your Master's cock. I don't have to tell you what that feeling is, do I?"

She shook her head. Her eyes felt too wide in her face. She was holding onto his every word with ten times more fascinated attention than she'd given to Fran's most involved bedtime stories. Probably for the reasons he'd just stated. She couldn't afford to get too lost when the words were coming from Fran's lips. She could with Garron.

"Kaela." He fisted his cock, rubbed his thumb over the slick slit. "Over here. Now."

A vampire had incredible speed, but they were also as lithe and flexible as cats. She slithered to the floor in a sinuous stretch of upper torso and thigh, and closed the ten feet between them on hands and knees. No thought to it, just putting everything into the sway of her hips, the toss of her head to get her hair to fall back against her shoulder blades and spill forward again. It tangled with her fingers as she moved toward his feet, his knees, the tempting organ that rose between his thighs. She could almost already taste him. Her breasts swayed with her movements, brushing the insides of her arms.

She'd unconsciously bared her fangs. From the spark in his gaze, the slight tension in his body, a soldier's reaction to potential threat, she knew she looked dangerous. She liked that, liked challenging him that way. Yet when she reached him, something else took over. She laid her head on his inner thigh, watched his hand move up and down his length. Inching forward, she laid her lips on his knuckles.

Releasing his cock, he laid his hand on her hair, stroking as she imagined wrapping her lips around him and sliding slowly, slowly down his turgid length. But not until he told her she could.

Just when she thought he would, he nudged her up so she sat back on her heels. When she smoothed back her hair from her face with both hands, he had another command for her.

"Stay like that. Hands laced behind your head."

Another standard submissive pose. She automatically spread her knees, arching her back. A little moan broke from her lips when he gripped her breasts, giving her the heat she craved. He flicked the tips and shifted forward in the chair. As she kept her chin up, her eyes resting on the wall of his chest, he pressed his cock between her breasts, closing her curves tight around it. She wanted to put her mouth between his well-developed pecs, work her way down that defined abdomen to the organ that had her salivating.

"You promised…" She had to clear her throat, stifle another moan as he pinched her nipples again, pushed his cock more insistently into that cleft. "To tell me more about…the day you had planned."

He grunted, but pumped himself a few more times between her generous curves, making it clear his pleasure came first. She realized she'd arched her back further, pushing her breasts into his palms.

He gave them another squeeze, a rough caress before he slid back. Not too far, though, because he tangled his hand in her hair. Instead of answering her, he pushed her face down toward his lap.

"Lick me first. Balls to head. Convince me you deserve the whole thing in your mouth."

She couldn't think about this, didn't want to do so. She didn't want thought to interfere with the incredible flood of sensation between her legs, the flutter his every word was causing in her chest, increasing the tingle in her nipples, the ache from every orifice wanting to be filled by him. She complied… Obeyed. She traced the ridge of the glans, followed the throbbing veins down to the base, nuzzled his balls, inhaling his musky scent. Creating a swirling pattern all the way up and around, she took tiny nips and suckles as she went, small infractions but ones he allowed. If the clench of his fingers in her hair were any indication, he approved, and that made her more enthusiastic.

Garron muttered an oath. Holding her head fast, he angled and thrust his cock all the way to the back of her throat, a clear message that play time was over. He expected her to get down to business and service her Master.

Oh God. It had been so very long since she'd done this, at least for reasons she wanted to remember. At the first taste of him, the way he stretched her mouth, she closed her eyes, savored the taste of the man. He'd been hard pretty much throughout, and she wanted to feel him release, jet in the back of her throat. She wanted to have to work to avoid spilling a single drop of his seed.

He gave that appealing growl, and she inched closer. Closing his hands over hers, he unlaced them, guided them down to his bare thighs. She made a sound that could only be described as grateful, gripping muscle and firm flesh. The man was as resilient as stone and wood, things of the earth. She sucked harder and he flinched.

"Fangs, baby," he reminded her. "Easy."

Baby. How long had it been since she'd been called that? It made her feel warm, fluid everywhere, and even more determined to give him pleasure…to please him. She adjusted her grip, used her tongue and lips to better effect, and managed only to score him a couple more times. She wanted him to come, not because she could *make* him come, like making a servant do her bidding, but because it would tell her she'd served him well.

She remembered the first time she'd done that for Jared, a shock to both of them in their naïve world where sex was genital penetration and some kissing and touching. Oral had been…taboo…forbidden…delicious. Yet being on her knees before him had made something click inside her so strongly, she'd fantasized about doing it all sorts of times and places, just to prove how much she wanted to serve him, give him pleasure.

She put all that suppressed yearning into her efforts now. And Garron repaid her with frustration, slowing their pace with a tightening of his hand in her hair, drawing it out, making it clear he'd build to orgasm only after he made her work her ass off for it.

She wondered if he'd jacked off when she'd slept. Otherwise, he had amazing stamina. Amazing control.

Releasing her hair, he slid forward so that he pushed deeper into her throat, bracketing her with his thighs as he curved over her, gave her ass a heavy smack. She whimpered against him, especially when he used the reach of his long arms to put a hand between her legs. His fingers pushed into her, his thumb teasing her rim.

"So you want to hear more about the day I have planned for you." He made an impressive effort to keep his voice even, though she detected the strained nuances that said he was as turned on as she was. "I have my own play room at Club Sin. That's Eden's BDSM club. It's outfitted with my equipment, adjusted the way I want it done. There's a new set of restraints that Vardalos had brought in special. A vampire can't break them. Once you're in them, you'll be entirely at my mercy. Yeah, you like that idea. You're wet as a fucking hot tub."

He took her hands from his thighs, pulled them behind her back. Crossing her wrists, pressing her knuckles in the shallow valley above her hips, he manacled her there with one large hand, squeezing her delicate bones as he renewed his rhythm of pushing her mouth down on his cock with his other hand on her head. His ass flexed against the seat as he shoved himself against her gag reflex. She controlled that enough to take all of him, suck and lick harder. He was getting closer, breath rasping, grip getting tighter, restricting her movements even more.

"I'm going to mark you, again and again," he said hoarsely. "Paddle your ass, flog all that beautiful, pale skin. I like giving pain to a submissive who craves it, Kaela, whose pussy gets all flushed and slick from it. You'll come over and over tonight until you're not thinking, not asking yourself any questions. Nothing exists except what I demand of you. I'm going to work you hard, until you want to call me Master so much you'll beg for the privilege."

She'd do anything he wanted. She just wanted to feel him let go, wanted to know he'd come in her mouth and she had that part of him inside her, however he wanted to do it. Fucking her mouth, her ass, her cunt. She was just a creature of unfulfilled wants that wanted all of them fulfilled now, and the way to it was in serving him. She'd beg him to let her serve, to just do this for ten days…

His fingers constricted, a little less controlled. He was thrusting into her mouth, his breath clogging in his throat. She pleaded with every lick, every nip, every long, sucking stroke. And then at last he rewarded her.

He bucked up, started to come. As the first salty spurt hit her tongue, she made an encouraging noise, doing her best to keep up as he kept coming, filling her mouth, her swallowing throat, spilling out over her lips though she used her tongue to gather it, slide it over him as she kept sucking, drawing out his climax to give him the ultimate amount of pleasure from it.

"There we go. That's my girl." His grip was easing, his fingers sliding along her hair rather than pulling it hard, and she went from sucking to greedy little licks, nips at his testicles, kisses on his inner thighs. "Sweet girl. Beautiful vampire…my sub."

When he finally stopped her, he made her keep holding him in her mouth, a flesh and blood gag as his fingers slid along her jaw, along her frantic pulse. She'd given him release, and she was so close to it herself, she could barely think straight. When he finally lifted her face, letting himself slide free, his gaze slid over her features in that slow, measuring way, seeing the flush of her pale cheeks she could feel. As he wiped her mouth with a thumb, she smelled his seed there.

She turned her face into his palm without thought, and he made a pleased noise. He lifted her to her feet so she was standing before him, so he could put his arms around her and kiss the tip of one breast, tease it with his mouth as she stood still, torn between a million emotions and the storm of her own arousal, still unsated. He followed the tracks of her arousal on her inner thigh with his fingers, and she made that needy noise again. Her hair when unbound fell almost to her hips, and he tugged on a lock of it.

"Go to the dresser and bring me everything that's in the top drawer."

There was no balking about it this time. As she obeyed, she was bemused to discover two things. One, she wasn't entirely steady on her feet. Two, while she slept the mirror had been replaced, along with the rug. The floor around it was entirely clean, not a sliver of glass.

"Does Mr. Vardalos have an army of field mice on his payroll?" Her voice sounded hoarse, another intriguing thing.

"I let the Club Sin cleaning staff come in while you were sleeping. Under my supervision of course. You were out, my lady."

She wasn't going to think about the significance of that, that she was allowing this male she barely knew watch over her while she slept. She'd kept her door bolted and locked the first five years Fran was in the house.

"Dresser, my lady. I'm getting impatient."

She realized she was standing in front of it, head down in thought. Now she jerked into motion, sliding open the drawer. When she saw the contents, her heart started to thump erratically again. An alligator paddle, just like he said. The name was a misnomer. It wasn't made out of alligator skin, but the paddle's impact surface was designed like it, like rows of pyramids with the tops cut off, leaving square blocks and spaces between that would leave a memorable impression on the flesh. Next to the paddle was a pair of clover nipple clamps and a butterfly-shaped clitoral stimulator.

Turning, she saw he was standing. He'd picked up a pair of folded jeans from the floor and was sliding them on. The things she held in her hands were forgotten as she watched the play of his upper body muscles, the ripple across his shoulders as he pulled the jeans up to his hips, over his taut ass. No underwear. Tucking his cock back in, he zipped the jeans, but carelessly left the top button undone when he sat back down, beckoned to her.

She was used to seeing gorgeous male servants in all manner of dress and undress, yet this powerful scarred man had her arrested, to the point he had to speak to break her out of her ogling. "Kaela, bring them here."

Guiding her between his knees again, he took the toys from her, leaving her standing. He didn't say she couldn't use her hands, so she laid her hands on his shoulders, enjoying the width, the firm skin. The man had a neck like a tree trunk, which fit the proportions of the rest of his body. She was so aroused, yet there was another part of her, restless and needy, that had words spilling from her mouth.

"Does he have someone?"

He didn't answer her right away. Unclasping the straps on the clitoral stimulator, he hooked them over her thighs, running another ribbon strap down through her outer labia, her buttocks, clicking it into a three-way hasp between the dimples over her ass. As he did that, he brought her closer. She caressed the wide expanse between his shoulder blades, ran her fingers over the tattoo. When she looked at it, it felt as if the message on it was intended just for her.

"Who?" he asked.

"Sorry. It feels like…never mind. The Dom in the wheelchair. Does he have a permanent sub?"

"Yeah, he does. She loves him, would do anything for him. He's the same way about her."

He caught her hand, bent his head over her palm to kiss it. Hesitantly, she raised her other hand, touched his bare skull. Tilting his head up, he laid his big hand on her shoulder, giving her a light squeeze against her throat before he turned his attention back to what he was doing.

Her mind fragmented as he pulled the straps taut so she felt the pressure against her clit, labia and rim, all the erogenous points. Though her mind went quiet, that ache in her throat didn't. "That's nice. About the two of them."

"It is. What was the 'never mind', Kaela?"

She shook her head. She couldn't tell him that sometimes it felt like he was in her mind like a second mark. Maybe even a third, because supposedly their range could be even more expansive…if the vampire allowed it. *Stop doing that. Just because he or Vardalos says it's okay to second mark him doesn't mean it is. It's one thing to risk your life. That would be risking his, if they're wrong. Or lying.* She didn't want to contemplate any deception here, but that sly voice wouldn't let up.

If he was second marked, he *couldn't* lie to her.

He straightened, making her hands slide from his back to his shoulders. She wished he never wore a shirt. She loved feeling her palms against his skin, and the man had an amazing upper body.

"We'll come back to it." His tone changed. "First I want to talk about you taking blood without my permission yesterday."

He gripped her forearms, taking her hands away from him. Putting them at her sides, he tapped them, a signal to keep them there as he picked up the clover clips from the side table where he'd placed them. He rolled the metal in his palm, over his fingers, idly playing as her gaze latched onto them.

"When a submissive misbehaves like that, she's testing her

Master." Closing his free hand over her right breast, he started squeezing and tweaking her right nipple, an obvious functional intent, preparing it for the bite of the metal. "Afterwards, she'll feel regret, uncertainty. She doesn't know how to fix it. That was the way you felt yesterday, wasn't it? Say it. I want to hear it."

"Yes." She had to admit it was. She swallowed back a tiny yelp as he pinched her harder, rolling the nipple between fingers acting like pincers. But for all that it was uncomfortable, she just kept swaying toward him.

"If I'd acted angry, how would you have felt?"

"Maybe angrier," she said. "Defensive."

"Good. Honest answers. How else?" In one smooth movement, he attached the clover clip to that throbbing nipple. The biting pain was immediate, but he caught her hands. She could have thrown him off, but his sharp voice stopped her.

"Breathe through it. Answer my question. Breathe."

"I don't know…I wondered…I wasn't sure…how to say I was sorry. How to…earn forgiveness."

Could she believe she wanted that, needed that? That she'd even said it aloud?

"It causes a sub a lot of stress, those kinds of questions. But it's not your job. If you've misbehaved, it's up to me to decide how to absolve you."

He started to work on the other nipple and she had all she could do to stay still. The bound nipple was throbbing. His free hand closed over her thigh and he ran his thumb up the sensitive inner side, letting her feel the fluid marking her there. "You're in pain, and yet your clit is as full and flushed as the head of my cock when you had it in your mouth. You have no control here, Kaela. You can act up, beat me black and blue, but all that does is show you're feeling out of control, uncertain about the scenario. You can't take command of this like you can as a vampire overlord. You came here for a very different experience, but that's the experience you know, so you retreat to it when you're feeling unbalanced. When I earn enough of your trust you rely on me for your balance, you'll figure it out. Another deep breath."

She had to stop herself from backing away before he clamped the clover clip in place. It hurt. God, it hurt. Once again he caught her hand. "Breathe. Breathe through it. This will help." Reaching between her legs, he pressed the back of the stimulator, a weight that spiraled through her cunt. The rubber butterfly started to vibrate in a pattern that tingled along her labia and stroked her clit like a heated tongue.

Her moan was less inhibited this time, and she couldn't stop the twitch of her hips. Rising, he moved the chair, guided her hand to clasp the top of it, leaving her in a supported position as he went to the bed, returned with the tether. She'd woken without it attached and had frankly missed it, enough that she lifted her chin to make it easier for him to hook it to the collar she still wore. His gaze on her was proprietary, pleased with her, and that was all her mind could handle now. With those vibrations between her legs and the clover clamps squeezing her nipples so painfully, there wasn't room for anything else. Which she was sure was his intent.

He shoved the alligator paddle into his back waistband. "Blindfold goes back on now. We're going to my private room at Club Sin and I want you focused on all the things I'm going to do to you there."

Darkness descended. Everything was the throbbing in her nipples, the stroke of electricity across her pussy. The sadistic man made her walk, and it was difficult, all those sensations making her unbalanced. But he had his hand at the small of her back, the tether wrapped over his knuckles so it was a consistent, distracting pull against her throat.

Back to the hallway. Through her arousal and confusion she heard a door open and he ushered her over the threshold. She thought they passed through some sort of connecting room, perhaps a storage area, because she scented cleaners, old wood. Then they were back in another hall with plush carpet, and tropical scents that suggested the same kind of venting system as in her room, allowing the aromas of the island's nature preserve down into these lower levels. But her sharp ears caught something else, reminding her what she'd heard in the elevator.

The thrum of music and the sound of a whip striking. A cry of pleasure, of pain. The scent of sweat, of sex, of need and want. Her senses were acute, so she knew they weren't in the club yet, but quickly approaching it.

She was blindfolded, going into an area she didn't know. Her nostrils were flared, taking in every scent, her hearing on full alert for noises. How did she know she wouldn't be set upon by enemies, no matter that she was the only vampire here? She couldn't trust anyone but herself. His world was not her world. Her world was little different from that of a rabbit in a thick wood, the creature never able to relax her guard against lurking predators.

"Easy." Garron had his hand on her again, was stroking. "I know it's tough for a fighter to be blindfolded when you aren't familiar with your surroundings. Just a little while longer, my lady. Just a short exercise in trust. I won't let anything happen to you. Or creep up on you." His hand dropped, cupped her buttock to give her a pinch. "Except me."

She couldn't retort to that because her senses were focused on another human, close by. As if he could read her thoughts, he filled in the blanks. "It's Bridget. This is the staff entrance into the club, but we keep a manned desk here in case someone wanders down the wrong hallway. Mr. Vardalos values the privacy and safety of his guests above everything else."

"Good evening, Master Garron. Your room is ready." The woman had a purring voice, one that made it clear she appreciated everything about Master Garron. Kaela barely resisted the urge to show her fangs.

"Thank you, Bridget."

Moving forward again, she followed Garron's lead through a door and into another hallway where those thrumming drumbeats and the scents of pleasure and need grew even stronger.

"Club Sin has several large main rooms with a lot of beautiful equipment, and private curtained alcoves around them, but it also has two wings of private rooms. We're about to cross a section of the main club to get into my wing, but we'll be sticking to the fringes."

"Your admin sounds like someone you've sampled before."

"Bridget is a submissive, yes. I've had sessions with her before. The staff practices together, enjoying one another so we remember why what we do is never just about playing a role and getting a paycheck." His grip dropped, caressed her upper buttocks. "She and I don't have a relationship, my lady. I'm unattached."

It didn't mollify her, and it should have. Actually, she knew it shouldn't have bothered her in the least. He was dedicated to her for ten days and that was enough. That was all she could ask.

"We're about to enter that main area. There won't be anyone

close enough to us to engage us in conversation. Nor will they. No one will be touching you but me. All right?"

She nodded, then remembered he wanted to hear words. "Yes."

He opened a door, brought her through. It felt like they stepped from the doorway through a wider opening, perhaps an archway into a bigger room.

The door had significantly muffled the noise. Here the music vibrated through the chest, the soles of the feet, and those sharp cries, the snap of a whip, were far more vivid. She found herself focusing on Garron's hand on her hip, her back, his body brushing hers, like a focal point to walk a tightrope. She didn't realize she was leaning into him like a storm shelter until she inadvertently stepped in front of him. If his arm hadn't been around her waist, she would have tangled up and tripped. Before she could get flustered by that, tear off the blindfold, he came to a halt. She was surrounded by the hum of conversations, of commands given and received, of whimpers and sobs, gasping breaths. But no casual conversation. Despite the distant thrum of dance music, this area was intended to give Doms and subs the ability to connect.

She should be freaking out, and she was, somewhat, but all those sounds inundated her with images as well. Images of herself doing whatever the subs she couldn't see were doing. Garron holding the whip, the key to the cuffs, his hand to the back of her neck, his gruff orders to spread her legs.

When he'd caught her, she'd turned toward his front, her arm folding against his chest. Now her fingers curled in his collar, discovering he'd donned a shirt before he left her suite. Once again he was fully dressed while she was naked, except for his collar, the stimulator and the nipple clamps. To anyone watching, she'd look like a sex slave. His. He stroked her back, her ass. He used his other hand to tweak the chain connecting the clips, gave it a little tug that sent searing pain through her nipples. But the reactive jerk of her hips increased the more immediate threat of the clitoral stimulator. "Oh…"

She sucked in a breath at the flood of feeling, of panic. She was going to come. "Garron."

He slid his fingers between the stimulator and her pussy, pinching the wet lips in a way that cut that intense sensation, yet the direct contact of his hand upon her became the catalyst. She had a short, intense mini-climax against his fingers, pressing her mouth against his collar bone to muffle her groans. He cupped the back of her head, holding her as she shivered and jerked against him.

"Fucking gorgeous," he said against her temple. "That's just the way I want to keep you tonight. I want you so mindless and needy you'll come from the touch of a feather. But only if I'm the one holding it."

She braced her forehead against his chest, fighting to pull herself together. Everything she'd imagined and more, Garron was doing to her. How was it that Theodosius Vardalos hadn't asked her about her fantasies, hadn't had her fill out a questionnaire of limits and preferences, yet this male seemed to pick up on so much, keeping her spinning? He said he used his instincts, and she believed it, because she felt like she had his total attention in a way no man had ever paid attention to her before. Uncanny.

She was still throbbing, feeling like she could come again in no time. She was sure he knew that, but he was leading her onward, making her do her best to walk upright with all those pleasant and less than pleasant stimulations keeping her to a hobble. Then they were out of the public room and back in another quiet hallway. A code was punched in, and he'd eased her into a room, closed the door. This was his room. It had that same sandalwood aroma that Garron carried on his flesh, as well as a light rosewater scent, clean linen…lavender. Was it from the efforts of a cleaning staff, or from the mix of whatever oils and lubricants were probably available in the room?

"So this is where you do sessions with other guests, other staff members."

"Yeah. Mostly. Though a lot of them prefer public floor play." He touched her face, turned her toward him. "But for these ten days, my submissive has me all to herself."

He'd picked up on the edge to her tone. If he'd been smug, she could have shot back a barbed response, but he sounded satisfied by her need for possession. That only twisted her irritation into a more compelling, more confusing need.

He used the tether to lead her across the room. Gripping her wrist, he guided her palm until it met the stone wall, telling her he'd taken her to the back. A chain rattled and he fitted a cuff to her wrist, some kind of steel that fit snugly. Not tightly enough to press against her wrist bone, but too small for her to slip the cuff easily over her hand. He threaded the chain into a frame above her, lifting her arm out to her side and just above, securing her bent arm at a 45 degree angle. After he did the same to the other, he knelt and spread her legs past shoulder width, cuffing them to the floor.

Rising to his feet, he inserted his thumb into the hinge of her mouth. "Let's take care of these fangs."

Though she tried to jerk her head back, startled, he slid a metal bit between her lips, strapped it around her head. "You may be stronger than hell, but my guess is your enamel breaks like anyone else's. You won't be trying to bite your way out of that unless you don't care about that pretty smile."

He balanced the abruptness of that by stroking her back, her hair. This time it was to do more than enjoy the lustrous strands, though. Separating them out into three thick ropes, he began to braid them. She was impressed by how efficiently and swiftly he managed it, even as little shivers of sensation chased one another up and down her spine as his fingers brushed her.

He'd left the blindfold, nipple clamps and vibrator in place. The vibrator was still humming against her clit. With all these different forms of stimulations, he was trying to get her worked up higher than even last time, she was sure. Her legs and arms were spread, cuffed in place, and her trembling was back. It was ridiculous, because nothing could truly hold her. Or could it?

"These are the cuffs and frame that Vardalos had brought in special," he said, as if reading her mind. "You can't get out of them, not without substantial effort and concentration. I plan to destroy your concentration, take it away from you entirely until you know you have to ask my permission to have it back."

He thought he had her captured. Reflex had her giving the cuffs a yank, not really believing him, and then her heart hitched in her chest as she found yes, they were stronger than she'd expected. Far stronger. The frame didn't budge, either. She was used to everything she touched being something that would give under the pressure a vampire could bring to bear. It was why one of the earliest things a made vampire learned, after controlling blood lust, was physical self-restraint so they could hold things designed for a human grip without destruction. Like wineglasses, eggs.

She yanked harder. She was caught. Truly caught. Unable to get free. She'd fantasized about it, but reality meant she was vulnerable to attack. Yet the more she pulled, the more her nipples throbbed and the more her hips jerked against the vibration. She was gasping, aroused, panicked…

"Easy," Garron murmured. He'd finished with her hair, had wrapped her braid around his hand, his fingers massaging her nape.

"Take off the blindfold. Take it off." Her voice was muffled, so maybe he didn't understand her. If she could have that much control…

Instead he removed the gag to bend and press his mouth against hers. Gentle, using the tip of his tongue to part her lips, tease them and her fangs, coax her tongue to play with his. He was making a quiet hum in the back of his throat as he did it. Cupping her skull, he stroked her face even more gently, with sensual, drugging intent, making her focus on the strength in his hands, cradling her like an egg. Caring for her.

She kissed him back with desperation and far less control, tried to nip at him. He merely held her face still, kept playing with her mouth, making love to it in a way that had her swaying forward in the chains again, her body against his. He bent his knees and held her waist so he could press his cock against her core, letting her feel that demand even with the denim separating them. He was seducing her into giving up control. Making her okay with something she could never be okay with. Or could she? She'd fantasized about it. She had.

He was giving her what she wanted. But that panic had resurrected a fear she hadn't experienced in so long, the years having pushed it below better memories.

She wasn't a woman who allowed the horrors of the past to control her present or future, but some memories took over if the circumstances were right. She was caught in unbreakable chains, more vulnerable than she'd been in decades.

*No. I won't let that ruin this. I won't.*

But she had a feeling she was going to need help with that. The question was, was Garron as good a Master as he seemed? Could he drive the fear away?

She had a feeling if anyone could, it would be him. At least she hoped that was the case. She wanted him to be that good. That was probably just as worrisome a compulsion as that darkness of her past, rising to sweep her away in its grasp.

## Chapter Five

As she pulled against the right chain, testing it, Garron stroked her hair, tugged it. "That's it, my lady. Make sure of it. You're caught, and all mine."

Back when he'd been studying her in the monitor, he'd contemplated whether the worst of the physical struggle between them was over, and concluded "not yet." She had too many reasons to stay hypervigilant, and too many triggers for them. She was right, what she'd said earlier. It was a miracle that she'd suspended disbelief to come this far. Vardalos was good, but not that good. She must have been near a breaking point to come here and risk so much. He'd seen her express a fuck-the-consequences reaction a couple times now, reinforcing that theory.

A vampire having a midlife crisis. He could handle all that. It was just a matter of managing those triggers with her, staying ahead of them.

He circled behind her, left a kiss on her temple. She was doing that body quiver thing again, and he banded an arm around her waist. She preferred full body contact, did that little melting thing against him every time, yet when he cupped her breast, tested the hold of the clover clamps, she flinched. Time to get rid of those. They were moving into the wrong kind of pain.

Moving around to her front, he unclamped the clovers, and her face tensed in response, her body bowing against the pain. He put his hand against her back and knelt to take her right nipple into his mouth, spreading his lips wide so he could suckle not only on the tender bud, but mouth the flesh around it. He covered the other nipple with his hand, pressed on it, a gentle palm massage as she made tiny noises of distress, caught up in the discomfort of the blood returning.

He soothed only as long as was needed to get her past the initial agony and straightened. Capturing her mouth with his, he put his hand between the clitoral stimulator and her body. As he rubbed a slow rotation over her clit and mound, she made uncertain complaints in his mouth, disjointed things that turned into a sexy little sigh of frustration as he removed his hand. Since he was all about feeding a sub's frustration, seeing how hot he could make her, he raised the setting on the clitoral stimulator before he stepped back. As she started to yank against the chains again, work herself against the ankle cuffs, he circled her, watching, measuring.

"Yeah, you'll be doing a lot of that. We're going to test those bonds, my lady. See just how strong they are."

Thinking about what Vardalos had told him a second mark was, he was intrigued by the idea of being in her mind, of how much more information that would give him as a Master. He could watch the flow of reactions in her head, see them matched in her body, her facial reactions. He'd relied on the other signs too long to become too dependent on what was going on in her head, but it would be a gift, getting both. A woman's reactions could be a tangled mess when she was aroused, the emotional and physical a complex tapestry that required his full concentration. He suspected being in a female vampire's mind might be just as much information overload. It would take some skill to manage all of it, but his instinct for a submissive's needs were finely honed. He was up to it.

He frowned now, because those instincts told him something was off. She was aroused, yes, the stimulator and the situation working together, but her jerking against the bonds was becoming a real fight, fueled by a touch of panic he'd sensed minutes ago, a short wave that was now back in greater strength in the vibrating energy around her.

He wasn't touching her or talking. She'd been using that to stay in the here and now. Realizing it, he quickly moved back in, touched her face, cradled it, let her feel the press of his body against hers. She liked his size, had fitted herself to him like she was under the shelter of a tree several times. It was an early sign of trust. He removed the blindfold, a tactical decision. The flood of relief in her gaze told him it was the correct one. He'd trapped her in darkness with something that had frightened her, something not in this room.

Stroking her jaw, her temples, he spread out his fingers so they were fanned over her cheeks, eyes and forehead. He held them there, over her closed eyes. Through that contact, he felt her trying to steady herself.

"Where did you go, my lady? What memory took you from me? From this room?"

She shook her head. He could push, but she wasn't ready to talk about it. He'd made himself a firm promise he would keep this session in the more physical realm, that a period of pure pleasure was needed before he threw them both into the emotional end again. That plan might have to change, but for now he made the judgment call to keep with his original strategy. It might just break the other loose.

"All right. But keep your head in the game, else we're going to chat and share our feelings."

That won a small smile out of her, and he brushed his hand along her shoulder, the silken skin of her hip. Yeah, she'd made herself tense.

Some Masters were service tops. He had a fair bit of that in him, but he liked to mix it up. The only problem with staying a hundred percent in that service top zone was it didn't allow for the mutual benefit that could come from a Dom making it all about what pleased *him*. Done correctly, it could pull a power service submissive out of the wrong headspace as she tried to keep up with his demands, as he made her take whatever he wanted to do, which could make her arousal intense to the point of losing her mind, a high he'd gladly ride all day long.

Roan Abrams was the Master who'd designed Club Sin. During the times he returned to oversee further renovations or special Sin events, he and Garron had shared a few beers and debated the pros and cons of that, because Roan was a dedicated service top. But in this case, there was no room for debate. Garron was going to drive her fucking crazy, drive her to do things she'd never do in her ultra-controlled world. And enjoy the hell out of it himself.

Pushing the stimulator up onto her mound kept her feeling the vibration in an indirect way but removed it from his path so he could play with her pussy as he wished. He kept his hand down there for quite a while, kneading, flicking, thrusting, pleasing himself until she was making those little noises in her throat, bucking against his hand. He wanted whatever had panicked her long gone. While he wanted to pull deeper things out of her, take it beyond play between them, he didn't want those images to be what she carried out of the starting gate. He waited until he was sure her mind was a swirl of red lust. She was jerking against her bonds, but now she embraced the helplessness. Feared it in all the right ways. Her cunt was so wet he followed the tracks down her inner thighs, swirled patterns in the honey. Her thighs strained.

"That's it, my lady. Keep fighting those manacles. Remind yourself you're spread for my pleasure." Adjusting the stimulator back over her clit and putting it on a lower setting, he stepped back and stripped off his T-shirt. Moving back in, he brought himself full against her again. Yanking her head back, he spread slow, lingering kisses up and down her throat, her sternum, rubbed his chest against her breasts, liking the way her nipples stabbed him, how she tried to rub her mound against his cock, even with the interference of the stimulator and his jeans. The vibration tingled through his rigid shaft but he moved out of range, watching her lips twist in frustration, her head tilt as she tried to follow him with hearing and smell.

Going to the cabinet that held his supplies, he withdrew a dildo the average thickness and length of a man's cock and lubed it up from one of the pump bottles on the counter. There were three kinds. One standard lube, one with a warming oil, and one flavored with some spices that could make a woman writhe and scream from the fiery touch on her nipples or clit. Definitely not one he used in the anus, unless he was in the mood to cross the line of criminal sadism.

The only way he'd be doing that was if one of the bastards who'd mistreated her was in those chains instead.

He knew that was what had happened. He'd seen the signs before. In her world, there had to be some bad times when another vampire had taken what he wanted from her. Up until now, he hadn't seen those indications of sexual abuse, but she was a warrior, a leader who couldn't afford getting caught up in brutalities of the past. He understood that, as much as he understood that putting her in situations where she was helpless might bring them back to life. He was going to make her craving for more of what he was doing far greater than any memory.

Parting her buttocks, he probed her ass with the slick tip of the dildo. Eased it in past tense outer and inner muscles. "Push out against it, let it all the way in. You resist it, it burns. There you go, my lady."

His own arousal cranked up several notches as he got it seated, imagined his own aching hard dick in there. "Hold it with your muscles. Keep clenching down on it. Your cunt muscles will work at the same time and everything will start to feel like one long climax. But you don't come until I say, do you?"

She shook her head. "No, Mas--"

She cut herself off like she'd bitten herself. He steeled himself not to pounce like a tiger on a morsel of steak. "What was that, my lady?"

As he passed a light hand along her back, he found she'd gone rigid as a board, so he let it go for now. Before it was done, he'd kill to hear those words come from her lips. Now, though, he put himself against her back, his mouth to her jaw. "Can you give me everything I demand, my lady? Can you serve your Master better than any sub ever has?"

Nothing like rousing a competitive streak in a power sob. A long pause, then she nodded, a hitch like a sob coming from her. He nuzzled her jaw, inhaled her scent, a flavor of powder and lavender, a metallic undercurrent of blood. He could almost feel her rolling the phrasing around in her head. *Your Master...*

"Then I think it's time for a punishment," he said.

Pulling the alligator paddle from his back waistband, he trailed it down her back, let her feel the edge, the broad slapping part. When he got to her buttocks, he rotated the handle against the flared dildo in her ass. "I'll bet you haven't been stretched here in awhile. Do you push your fingers in there sometimes when you're alone, think about being taken, your face pushed in the mattress, my hands yanking your hips up so I can plow your ass?"

She nodded again. Because she was so graceful, he was beginning to love that unsteady jerk of motion. While farther down the line he might demand a *yes, Master* or *no, Master*, since he didn't rely on his hearing for stimulation, body language was often far more arousing to him. Every twitch she made went straight to his cock and the fire burning inside him to take, possess. It was a state he often experienced during a session, but there was an extra intensity to it with her, knowing how far they had to go--and how hot that flame would be by the time they got there. He might incinerate them both.

"I'd drop down over you, cover you, grip your wrists for leverage, but also to stroke them as I fucked you. A reminder that I never forget you when I fuck you. You're never just an object. You're *the* object."

His object. His property. His lady.

It might be a little harder to keep this out of the emotional arena than he'd expected. She trembled under his touch. When her lips parted, he spoke harshly. "No talking unless you want that gag back in."

He forced himself to step back. "A little warm up, mainly because I love the way my hand feels, connecting to your pretty ass."

He spanked her once, twice, the slap a blunt, solid sound in the quiet room. She sighed, a sound of relief and need at once. He did it a few more times, drawing the blood up to the surface of the skin, giving her a nice rosy blush. She rocked at the force he put into it, and he ran his hands up along her arms. The muscles were tight. By the time he was done she'd need a nice full body massage, one of his favorite parts of aftercare. Usually it got him worked up enough he'd fuck his sub again while she lay there exhausted, staring up at him with shining eyes and slack mouth. He'd like to see that in his lady's face. While every sub who'd gifted him with her willing submission was special, they all felt like warm ups toward this. This was a female who needed every skill he had and would be as demanding a sub as he was a Master. They'd test each another's limits with every interaction. Right now she still wasn't sure of herself, but he could tell the signs of it, in those little fights they'd had.

Yeah, the little fights that had left his ribs bruised and his skull almost split like a pumpkin. A grin split his lips. "Time for payback, my lady."

She jerked at the first slap of the alligator paddle. It was a vicious brute, tough and unforgiving, and it left a nice pattern on female flesh. It was nice, working with such a physically powerful woman who nevertheless had curves. One of his subs had been a competitive weight lifter, all hard muscles and very little body fat. She'd been beautiful, yes, like having an exotic creature in his care, but if he had his preference, he wanted a woman who had generous breasts and a heart-shaped ass. Lady Kaela reflected the best parts of Aprodite and Artemis. Goddess of beauty and huntress both.

He ran his hand over her ass after he hit her three times in the same place. She exhaled that shuddering sigh again at his contact. Reaching in front of her, he brought the stimulator up another notch. She whimpered, her legs fighting the bonds, trying to rub herself against it. He cinched his arm around her, held her fast and started applying the paddle to both ass cheeks, her upper thighs, back to the butt again. As she got close to a cusp, he pulled the stimulator away from her, made her pussy clench on empty air, and spanked her some more, until the pain took her away from the edge. She was making all sorts of noises, soft cries, words it seemed like she was trying to strangle back. Not because he'd bid her be silent, but as if she was used to having to be quiet about her pleasure. He was having none of that.

"I want to hear you, my lady. Else I'm going to make this hurt a lot more."

He pinched a nipple, gave her cunt a few smacks with his hand over the stimulator before he stripped that from her. She let out a little protest, and he gave a nasty chuckle. "Yep, not going to let you get off with that, my lady. You have to ask me. Beg me. I can keep your climax out of reach for hours, break your mind in half."

She was going to more cavernous levels inside, pulling him down with her. He could follow because he saw the path in front of him, in the way her head tipped back, her mouth worked, her body flushed as she shook, jerked, fought her bonds. Forget the second mark. What would it be like to have that third mark, be able to follow her down to her soul, see what happened when subspace took over, wrapped itself around every part of her, inside and out?

"No…I can't take anymore…please…"

"Yeah, you can. You're just scared to let go."

He seized her around the waist from behind, set his teeth to her throat, shoved his rigid cock against her ass, against the dildo. When he forced his knee up between her legs, a decided impact that made her strain against the chain, she groaned with pleasure. She wasn't holding back any more.

He reached up, clasped her hand above the manacle and shifted his body to give her bottom another whack, earning another short shriek from those lush lips. Her fingers clamped over his hand, hard enough that the bones creaked alarmingly. Oh, yeah, she still had some fight in her. The blow he gave her this time was a definite reprimand, and triumph surged through him as she not only understood loud and clear, but responded appropriately. She convulsed, let him go, but he saw the flash of her fangs, heard that little defiant hiss.

He flexed his aching hand and used the other one, spanking her marked buttocks, stopping to work the dildo in and out of her until she was making those whimpers again. 'Going to be my dick in there before this is all over. I'm going to fuck your mouth, your cunt and your ass, my lady. Then you're going to wash my cock with your manicured hands so I can do it all over again."

"Please…"

"That's it. Ask me for what you need. I'm in charge of all of it, aren't I?"

"Yes…" It was a desperate whisper, charged with painful arousal. It made his heart hurt to hear it. But he had to keep pushing. That hiss and the attempt to lock up his hand had told him that, as well as his gut. Time for a different tactic. Pleasure could overcome her where pain couldn't.

Setting the paddle aside, he went back to work on her with his mouth. Kisses down the sensitive nape, the shoulders, moving the braid aside to work his way down her spine. He started humming in the back of his throat, giving her further sensation, letting the thick rope of hair tumble back in place as he straightened to ease the dildo from her ass. Using a flavored wipe to clean away the chemical lube, he massaged her blissfully tight opening before kneeling behind her and replacing the wipe with his mouth, teasing those sensitive rim nerves. He held her buttocks with hard hands while she bucked and cried out.

At length, he left that to kiss his way down each leg, to her feet, her toes. She went really still then, her lips pressed together. She became less still as he worked his way up her front. He bypassed her cunt, went around it, teased her navel. Nuzzling the crease beneath her breasts, he made moist circles around the still swollen nipples before descending again. When he put his mouth over her clit, warming her there with swirling flicks of his tongue, short nips, she shuddered like an earth tremor.

"Please…" she whispered again.

"Please what?" He kept his mouth on her, let his tongue ease into her pussy, play. She tasted sweet as divinely ordained sin, the best of both worlds. An animal cry came from her. His rigid cock had gone numb, the circulation cut off under the hold of the jeans. He was going to have to fuck her or jack off soon, or he wouldn't be able to concentrate beyond his own lust.

"Please…"

"Say it, my lady. There's only you and me."

A tear slid down her cheek, and he lasered in on it. She swallowed noisily and he rose, went to the wall behind her. He retrieved a belt, made sure she heard the clink of the buckle. Wrapping the strap under her arms, he cinched it over her sternum so her breasts tilted up higher, the nipples getting stiffer. He bent, licked one then the other, keeping his knuckles wrapped in the short fall of the belt, pulling her roughly toward him, as much as her bonds would allow. She was his. His.

He loosened it, moved behind her, doubled it over and gave it a sharp snap. Didn't touch her with it at all, but the noise made her jump. Her breath hitched, that near sob again. He opened his jeans, got them out of the way and applied more of that lube to his cock, pressing himself up behind her so she'd feel what he was doing.

"I can't…"

"Tough. I say you can." He parted her buttocks, guided himself to that tight hole. "Push against me again, only this time you're taking me, not some fake dick. You're taking me." As he began to ease slowly into her, he felt her breaking apart. He put his mouth to her ear. "Your Master, my lady."

He'd given her a push, and she was so close to the edge of the cliff he could almost see her start to flounder. Perversely he wanted to grab her, hold on, keep her from the fear of that flight, even as he knew he was the one who had to ruthlessly shove her over. He didn't usually have trouble detaching, staying cruel enough to deliver what the sub needed. But that was because he always let them go when it was all over. They went back to their lives, leaving him with pleasant memories. He didn't want pleasant memories of her. He wanted her.

"You know why I'm fucking your ass first? Because in your world, this only happens when someone's topping you. Proving they're the biggest, baddest thing in the room. In charge. In control. What do you want, Kaela? Tell me."

Her head fell back on his shoulder, and he felt the war inside her as if he could see her being torn in two. "What do *you* want?" she gasped.

It was what she'd asked when they were walking through the stable hand fantasy, and he cupped her face, stroked the pounding pulse in her throat. "Is that more important to you than your own desires?"

A pause, and then she gave him the one word he wanted to hear. "Yes."

He gave her the time to understand the significance, hear it as clearly as he did. "So what is it you want, Kaela?"

"To give you pleasure."

"How do you do that?"

"Any way you demand."

"But how do you do that, my lady?" He let his lips cruise along her jaw, whispered the next words. "Look inside. What do you want? What words are there, just waiting to be spoken? You've thought them when you've touched yourself, imagined your Master."

She was strangling on emotions, her body like a taut rope. He ran his hand up and down her throat, as if stroking a cat. Her head tipped back on his shoulder again.

"Say it," he murmured, and he felt the ache move into her throat, the way she swallowed under his hand. "How do you give me pleasure, Kaela?"

"By serving you."

"Bingo."

He tamped down the surge of satisfaction. It wasn't the time. She needed his full focus, because those three words snapped the rope, bringing back the panic. He'd closed her into a narrow space surrounded by his demands, his words, challenging her reality in every way, and facing that was more unsettling than mere manacles.

Settling into her, he put his hand fully around her throat, squeezed it tight enough she felt the constriction. Fingered that collar he knew did all sorts of delicious things to her mind. "You're mine, my lady. In these bonds, I could pick up a stake, end your life. But you aren't afraid of that, are you?"

When she shook her head, he tightened his grip more. "Why?"

"Because…you won't hurt me. Not that way. You make me feel…cared for." She started to shudder. "Like Jared did."

Because she was so lost in her head, he wasn't going to pull her out of it by asking who Jared was. Plus, whoever Jared was, he was past tense.

"All right. Hold on, because I'm taking you on a ride, and I'm not letting you off until I'm good and ready. Give me pleasure, my lady. Serve me with your body, your heart and soul. Don't you hold a damn thing back. When it's just you and me, you don't have to hold anything back."

She caught that sob in her throat again, the one that made him want to take off her bonds, cradle her in his arms and hold her until the last sunset for all eternity. But that wasn't what she needed. He began to work his hips against her, stroking in and out, making all those sensitive nerve endings in her ass thrum down to her pussy. He didn't touch her clit at all, just let her build to that crescendo. She struggled, her ass working against him in a way that had him gritting his teeth for control. Cupping her breasts, he teased and pinched the nipples, rubbed and pulled on them, using those generous curves for leverage as he started to thrust even harder. Smacking his pelvis against her ass with each thrust, his testicles hitting her cunt, had her squirming even more. He knew her ass was sore from his punishment, and he wanted to keep it that way as long as he could. Though her vampire healing would give him an excuse to start all over, wouldn't it?

He pulled out when she was shuddering erratically, her body jerking.

"No..." The word slipped from her, a single protest, and he bared his teeth in a grin, stepping in front of her to tip her chin up, stare into her eyes with his best I-will-so-kick-your-ass look. "What did you say to me?"

The woman who could break him into little pieces and tear out the throats of other vampires did a double take before that look. Then those beautiful eyes swept down before his hard stare. An unthinking act of submission, no hesitation at all this time, just pure sub instinct. It told him just how deep inside herself she was. He'd successfully pushed her beyond the reality of who she was, even past the fantasy of who she wanted to be, into the real Kaela, at her core. Her whisper proved it. "I wanted you to stay inside me."

"I am inside you, Kaela." He gave her temple a light tap. "But you meant my dick in your ass, didn't you?"

"Yes. No. Just...inside me. All the way inside me." She was fighting for her words, having trouble organizing her thoughts, but he knew what she meant as naturally as he knew what it was to breathe. For women, the physical connected to the emotional, down to the spiritual, to the lowest levels. But there was more he wanted, and he was willing to deprive himself to get to it. He wanted to knock her so far into subspace, he'd be the only one who could reel her back in.

Going to the sink in the corner, he filled a bowl with water and picked up soap, a wet cloth. Rolling a small table in front of her, he set the bowl on it and began to wash his cock thoroughly, rubbing it, stroking himself, thinking about whether or not he'd give himself a climax this way first, with her golden eyes trained on the movement of his hands, her lips parted, her expression obviously one of hunger.

"You said…I could do it." She almost whimpered it.

"You will. When I'm done fucking you all the ways I want."

Pushing the basin and table aside, he brought two waist-high T-frames from the corner. Using the track system on the floor, he locked them down a few feet in front of her, spacing them out where he wanted them. He didn't need to measure. Experience and a glance at those long, slender legs told him approximately where they needed to be placed. With the same efficiency, he moved in front of the T-frames, bent and unsnapped the chains holding her ankle cuffs. Sliding an arm under her thighs, he lifted her, reattached each ankle to a frame so she was suspended by arms and legs in a hammock pose. He added the necessary straps to support her head, neck and shoulders. And her hips, so her knees were higher than her head, her ass canted up. She might be vampire, such that she could hang from her wrists and ankles without permanent damage, but he didn't want her distracted by that kind of discomfort.

As he stood between her raised, spread legs, her pussy and ass were gorgeously vulnerable, all his for the taking. They were glistening with her juices, her clit flushed and full, the lube giving the rosebud opening to her ass a slick little sheen. He indulged a nice visual of pumping his cock over her, painting her flesh with his seed as she hung there, helpless. The image was more than enough to send him over the edge, but he clamped down on it.

Retrieving the butterfly stimulator, he put it back on her. As he took his cock in hand to stroke, he reached out and turned it onto its highest setting. "Changed my mind, baby. Want to watch my sub come hard, with not a damn thing you can do to stop it."

Her eyes widened, lips parting. Her gaze flicked to him, a delicious panic, and she started to buck at the sensation, pulling at the bonds.

Her mouth worked in breathless protest, but there was no room for anything but reaction now. He seized the thick rope of her braid, kept his fist tight on it so she had to stare into his impassive face as the climax took her, as her body shook, as a scream broke from her lips. Removing his hand from his cock, he put it on the butterfly, working it against her swollen lips as she writhed and screamed some more. It wasn't enough for him, so he slid two fingers below it, into her spasming tissues, letting her tight pussy clench him.

"Nooo…no…" The words were torn from that coil of need inside her. She wanted this, she didn't want this. She was afraid, she would tear his heart from his chest, she couldn't…she didn't…

"Doesn't matter if you're afraid, and yes, you can. You will, my lady. Do it."

He saw it break free. That coil of emotions exploded over her, overwhelming her, scaring her to the bone even as the climax was taking her over.

She yanked against the bonds, snarled, her fangs elongating, her eyes showing crimson lights. He hung onto her hair grimly, moving with her so he didn't tear out a handful, but he stayed mindful of the teeth because she was thrashing, and clearly looked as if she'd bite a good chunk out of him if she could.

"Easy, my lady…easy."

There was no reasoning with her. The energies around her were a wash of red and gold, colors too bright to do anything other than obliterate quieter emotions in the wave of passion and violence, need and loss of control, and all the emotions that came with that.

*Crack!*

He jerked his head back, just as the link in the broken chain missed his face by the width of a hair.

§

She caught his hand, slammed it against the frame, held onto it. Vaguely she was aware of his grunt of pain, but she realized he once again hadn't tried to retreat. He'd increased his banded grip around her waist, which meant he'd bent forward. Letting go of his hand, she snaked her arm around his shoulders, yanking him down to her. As she sank her fangs into his throat, he let her go. But not to fight her. As she swallowed his blood, he reached between them to rip away the stimulator. Then he angled himself and thrust into her, hard enough to make her shudder with a mix of pleasure and discomfort. He wrapped that iron hold around her waist again and pushed deeper, taking from her as she took from him.

His blood was salt and earth, metal and fire. Thinking of everything he'd said about the second mark, every denial she'd made to prevent her from even thinking about it, she embraced the former and ignored the latter. She made another leap of faith.

Against the roar of decades of discipline and good sense, she released the serum of the first mark. The geographical locator. If he was within a couple thousand miles of her, she would know exactly where he was.

And then, since he had roused her ire, she released the second mark behind it.

His body stiffened, because releasing them together was a burn like actual fire, coursing through the veins, licking at the internal organs. It was a warning of what a vampire could truly do to a human if she put her mind to it. If she third marked him, she'd own his soul, could crush it with her mind. It was the ultimate gift a human could give to a vampire, the ultimate surrender of will and choice.

She'd never wanted that from a human. But she'd envied Fran not only the willingness to offer that, but the ability. Garron was fighting through the pain, a light sheen of sweat on his skin, and she wanted to touch those straining muscles, all of them. She stroked and gripped the hard biceps, pectorals, his broad shoulders, all while keeping her mouth locked on his throat. She wanted to drink forever, take his essence into her as if she could hold that part of him that had been able, miraculously, to dominate her for a few precious moments. She'd use it as an elixir to get her through the interminable days and nights that would stretch before her when she left Eden.

His free hand flexed on her buttock, a twitching spasm that helped her recall herself. She retracted her fangs, jerked her head back, knowing her eyes were wild, blood on her lips. She thought *Oh, God, what did I do*, then she saw his face.

*Want to play rough, do you?* His eyes were as filled with violent passion as hers were, but the thin look of his mouth, the obsidian glitter of his eyes, the way his silky brows drew down, told her she'd crossed a delicious line, opening up a side of him that might terrify a lesser woman. It only made her crave his aggression. Then she realized she was hearing his voice in her head, at the same second he registered she had.

He reached up, jerked on the clip that had shortened the intact chain holding her other wrist. The increased length gave him enough slack to put her on the floor, him holding her with one arm. Her legs, still cuffed and chained to the T-frames, were now straightened such that her ass was a few inches off the ground. Altering his grip so he cupped it in both hands, he plunged back into her with ruthless intent, the position allowing an even more demanding penetration.

*Look at me, Kaela. You look into my fucking eyes.*

She saw plenty of things there. Anger, but it was controlled, passionate. He knew she needed his fury. She felt it in his mind. He went up onto his knees, hiking her legs up around him, her hips even farther up in the air, and started hammering into her, fucking her, taking everything he wanted. It broke open a powerful need inside her, but when she reared up, he planted a hand in the middle of her chest and shoved her back to the floor.

"You stay where I put you, my lady. You're in enough trouble."

Her cunt clamped down on him in reaction to that, but she obeyed. Even though the vicious need and violence were rolling through her, she craved his dominance, no matter that she could turn the tables in a heartbeat. She kept making this a struggle of might over right, which told her just how much she'd embraced the truth of the vampire world over seventeen decades, but it had been necessary, ensuring no one would make her do anything she didn't want to do.

But that wasn't what she wanted here…was it? He'd said it wasn't about physical strength. It was about will, and his will to control and hers to surrender were running neck and neck.

She was mixed up, volatile, not in control again. Fear stabbed her like a needle. She could hurt him badly, because he would no more consider retreat in a fight than she would. She'd seize control only if she took it from his cold, dead fingers.

*You closed your mind, my lady. Open it up. You won't hide from me.*

It was like opening a gate on an impulse, a frightening whim that could have terrible repercussions. She hadn't trusted anyone like that, not since Jared.

But she did it for Garron.

She opened up, trembling at his anger, at his force, at what he was making her do, at what she was allowing herself to do.

Trust. She couldn't trust. Not because she was a vampire, though there was that. But because she knew what it was to lose trust, to not be able to trust anyone in the whole wide world. She'd seen the ugly side of the soul and couldn't ever forget it, because once seeing that side, she'd known it was possible to find it inside any one, given the proper trigger.

He knew how to make it hurt, he'd been correct about that. He was slamming into her so forcefully, the impact held pleasure out of reach, but it was clear from his thickness stretching her that he was aroused to an animal level. That just goaded her own desires, despite her tumultuous thoughts. Yet abruptly he stopped, still holding her so close, inside her as deep as it was possible to go. With his grip on her ass he lifted her and began to knead, to slowly rotate her on his cock, sending spears of sensation through her.

*It hurts, does it?*

Her gaze flitted up to him, and now she saw a different look in his eyes.

"Say 'yes'," he prodded.

"Yes." Her throat had that odd ache again. Something…she needed something, the emotions unfolding in her exponentially. "I shouldn't have done that. Mark you like that. Without your permission."

*No, you shouldn't have.*

His gaze held her and she swallowed over that unfamiliar feeling. Or rather, one that used to be familiar, something she'd had to leave behind long ago. Regret.

*I'm sorry.*

§

When she'd broken the chain in her agitation, everything sensible had told Garron he needed to jump back out of range, but he'd never been known for being sensible. Loyal, determined, and sure where the line passed from black to white, no matter how much grey fog lay over it. That was what he was known for.

He caught her hand, put it on his side. Her fingers pressed into his muscled bare flesh, nails digging into him, puncturing. He kept his hand over hers, let her feel him there.

"Mine, my lady," he said softly, holding her eyes. "You don't say no to me, do you?"

She was panting, her fangs curving over her bottom lip. The right one had cut a groove in her flesh and he leaned forward, brushing his mouth over it, tasting her blood. As he did, he gave her a firmer thrust. "Answer me."

"No. I don't…I can't…"

"You can do anything I give you permission to do."

"Garron…I want…I need…I…" Words failed her and her head

dropped back, eyes squeezing shut. He cupped her head, brought it back up to look at him as he continued to move inside her. In and out, stroking those tissues, bringing her back toward the climax he wanted to inflict upon her, if he could hold out long enough himself. He'd never let go of control like that before, but he'd done it deliberately, showing her that he had as much of an animal nature as she did. Now he could take it down a notch, give her pleasure again, even as the energy vibrating between them remained volatile, unresolved.

He wouldn't let it deprive either of them. They were still on the roller coaster, and whether uphill or down, he wasn't letting up a bit. He inhaled her scent, a woman's musk, blood, fragrance. Her hair had a special aroma of its own, and he wanted to take it out of the braid, wrap it around himself. He wanted to put his face between her legs, bring her to climax that way, immerse himself in that scent as well.

"You'll do what I tell you to do. When it's like this, I'm in charge. Aren't I?"

Her eyes had that desperate light. She was so afraid. He could feel it inside her. It was as if she thought her life was literally in his hands, and she hadn't trusted anyone like that in so long…

He kept stroking until her muscles were clenching him on every stroke, her hand clawing into his side as the rest of her stayed in their bonds. He pushed her over the next climax, wondering if he was going to have blue balls before this was over, because he was determined not to come until he'd gotten them where he intended them both to go.

She arched and bounced, sinuous as a snake, and he gritted his teeth as she squeezed down on him in a way that showed she was mindful enough to be determined to make him come. He rewarded that bit of impertinence by pulling out when her pussy was still clutching down on him in aftershocks.

Kneeling, he went after her with his mouth, suckling away all the juices from her orgasm, wetting his finger with them and playing around her rim. He took advantage of her helpless state to tighten the chains, lift her legs higher in the air, readjusting the band beneath her head and shoulders so he didn't put her into a near head stand. It gave her physical comfort and him the position he wanted to continue to explore her as he wished. He wasn't giving her mind time to reset. Whenever it seemed her mind needed further focusing, he cracked the flat of his hand against her ass.

This was his element, and he was fully in the groove. He could make a woman beyond helpless in this room. He could take her to the point she'd lose control of her bodily functions, underscoring that he was in charge of everything, including her dignity, but the point wasn't humiliation, not for him. It was to prove she could trust him with all of that. He could break her down to the most primal, base form, and he would still cherish her, see all the treasure she had to offer him. He would kiss away a sub's tears, clean her up, hold her coiled and exhausted in his arms after multiple climaxes, multiple emotional breakthroughs where he took her through every childhood fear and insecurity and brought her out to the other side. He made her see her value and worth in his stern, approving gaze. When he held her after all that, knowing he genuinely held not only her life and body but her soul and heart in his grasp, he knew his purpose in life. To give her that gift.

All of that had been preparing him for this. He was sure of it.

She worked him hard, whether she knew it or not. He took her up to that peak again with his mouth, with the torment of his fingers. He pinched her ass several times, holding the clamp so she felt the pain, reacted to it in confused response as he kept licking her cunt, thrusting his tongue inside, mixing the pain and pleasure in ways that kept her from wrapping her mind around all of it.

*Please…I can't take anymore.* She may have said it aloud. In his position he couldn't have heard it, but in her mind he heard it loud and clear. He loved that, the ease of hearing her voice, but it didn't alter his attention on the most important thing. Her. Things were cracking inside. She was back at that precipice. He sensed…something, and he wanted to see how it played out, despite the shaking, broken note to her voice that twisted his heartstrings.

Pulling back from her, he gazed down at her body. At some point she'd caught hold of the loose broken chain with her free hand and had hung on to it as a way of restraining herself again. He wondered if she'd even realized she was using it that way, but he did for sure.

"Yeah, you can take more. Else you wouldn't still be able to talk or think that clearly. I've got plenty I plan to do to you, my lady. You think about that while I get the next phase ready."

Moving over to the counter and cabinets that held his supplies, he surveyed what was in front of him, cocking his head as if thinking about what he wanted to do next. He could feel her eyes on him, wondering. It only took a matter of seconds. Without his touch, without his voice, she began to shake, much as she'd done earlier. This time he was in her mind, so he saw the emotions go from simmer to boil in the face of his casual indifference, his deliberate decision to force her to confront her feelings and thoughts without distractions.

*Garron.* It was a thought, then a whisper, a child lost in the woods. "Garron."

He could hear her, inside and out, but he kept his head down. She craved that ultimate surrender, yes. But sometimes, before he could get a sub to what she really craved, he'd have to clear some debris off the field. Sometimes that debris was thick and high enough to make a landfill look small in comparison, but that was part of what had to be hurdled. What he saw in her head made it more than worth it, an obstacle past which a sweeping quest awaited, full of revelations, challenges and glory for the Master who embraced all that she was.

Not only could he hear her without strain, he could *see* inside her. Since that kind of sight didn't involve his eyes, he was seeing everything crystal clear. It was heaven. He could hear the emotions that wrapped themselves around the words like an illuminated script, full of color, emotion and artistry.

But as those colors turned to darker shades, he realized she was drawing too close to hell. He abandoned his wonder at the new sensations and went after her. He wasn't going to leave her there alone.

Disembodied voices, distorted shapes, then voices, memories, rising in a jumble. A grave, cold rain. Bloody battlefields. Soldiers wearing Union uniforms. Then in various stages of undress, lounging around a room, drinking, smoking cigars. One of them jamming a cigar on the inside of her thigh, since she was tied spread eagle to a bed. She'd already been well used by most of them, but they were nowhere near done…

"No." He was back to her, up against her as she thrashed. He pushed aside the kneejerk reaction to protect, to get her out of the bonds, to soothe, and looked for an anchor point beyond that, a key to get through to her mind. "Kaela. Kaela, ssshh." He held her twisting body. "Jared. Who is Jared? Stop. Tell me who Jared is."

He barked the order, brought her to a quivering halt. Repeated it in a more gentle voice. "Tell me who Jared is, my lady."

She'd gone so still, her fingers curled into claws.

*I've killed other vampires. I've killed humans. It was necessary.*

He kept stroking her hair. "I've killed, too, my lady. It was necessary, just. Even if it wasn't righteous. That's not what I asked. Tell me who Jared is."

As that quiver went through her again, her lovely eyes stared into his. She could ask to be released, but she hadn't. He was mindful of that, so again fought down his own desire to let her go. That horrible image had captured her mind, but Jared's name had broken its hold, so he said it again, like a safe word for both of them. "Jared. It's okay. Who is Jared?"

*He was my husband. At the beginning, before I was turned. He died during the War of…during the Civil War.*

"The War of Southern Independence." He picked it up from her mind and managed to win a painful twitch from her tempting lips. "I am southern, my lady. Alabama born and bred. My grandparents preferred calling it the War of Northern Aggression." He beefed up the drawl to make her smile a little more, but the infusion of warmth was such a contrast to the other emotions she was fighting, it undermined her further. A sob caught her so he slid an arm around her waist, bent and nuzzled her throat, nudging her chin out of his way so she had to drop her head back. He suckled the major artery pumping beneath the skin, teased her with the tip of his tongue, his other hand cupping her elbow, sliding along the tender skin of her stretched and bound arm.

"Those bastards who had you tied down? What happened to them?"

He raised his head to meet her gaze, soldier-to-soldier. It beat acting on what he actually felt, a testosterone-driven rage to hunt every one of them down as if that could eradicate what had happened to her.

*Long dead, not by my hand. I was a Confederate spy. They captured me.* Her chin set, even though her lips were trembling.

"They held you helpless, took what they wanted." He let his hand slide all the way up to her fingertips, then he moved there, kissed her knuckles, her wrist above and below the cuff, started working his way down. He spread out his palm on her abdomen, a solid touch there, moved the other behind her, cupped her bottom, slowly kneaded as he nuzzled and nipped at her arm, making her jerk and tremble.

"I don't know what you're doing," her voice quavered.

"Reminding you of the difference. Yes, you're caught, my lady. You're at my mercy. That's where the comparison ends."

*You make me feel…helpless.*

He lifted his head, stared at her. "Like they did?"

She shook her head. "No."

"Good." The anger in his gut eased. "Then don't let me see you get that shit confused again." He bared his teeth in a wicked smile. "Or I'll let you go. Take you out for dinner, and have some nice, safe vanilla sex with lots of cuddling afterward."

Her gaze warmed with a variety of responses. Gratitude, intrigue, relief. As well as other things that turned his world on his axis as much as he was doing to hers.

"You're mean."

"You have no idea," he managed. "Trip my sadist trigger, baby, and I'll make you regret it. There will be flowers. Candy. Kenny G."

Her eyes glowed even brighter. He slid his hand down over her mound and cupped her, rubbing his thumb over her clit and making her squirm in the bonds. Her lips parted as she absorbed the arousal, letting it mix with the sorrow, fear and memory, balance it once again. She might be a tossing ship, but she refused to be sunk.

With relief, he saw that, despite the horror of such memories, she didn't view herself as a victim, had never viewed herself that way. Normally that was the most crippling obstacle to getting over such a thing. She'd acted against men like her captors in wartime, used information to turn the tide of battles that might have killed their friends, other family members. Their punishment beyond capture had been motivated by rage. The dark sadism all men carried in them had been goaded, demons brought to life by hate. She understood that, had realized it wasn't personal. Vampires might have an immortal lifespan to analyze personal trauma, get past it, but they had no time to wallow in it or milk it. Life was brutal, tough. If you didn't want all of it to be that way, you had to figure out how to move forward.

He saw all those thought processes in her mind, wondered how conscious she was of all those layers, or if it was just who she was. Regardless, he admired her stoicism. Her strength.

Beyond that, her human past had obviously been the key to opening her up, helping her claim the submissive needs she'd always yearned to embrace. Jared had been her Master, the only Master, and his time with her had been too short. If the male had loved her as much as she'd loved him--and Garron had no doubt he had, because this woman inspired a man's devotion as much as his territorial instincts--he was giving Garron a blatant fish-eye message.

*Make it happen, you fucking bastard, since I can't.*

## Chapter Six

After a little breather of just stroking her, touching her, getting her focused on arousal again, he released her legs and brought her back to the original standing spread-eagle. He fixed the broken link and felt her attention build as he did it. She'd gone quiet, her mind a slow spinning top. No longer agitated, her body on a low hum, waiting for more of what he had planned. That was where he wanted her mind.

Retrieving a different ointment from his personal stores, he stood before her as he spread it on his fingers. He coated her clit and labia with it, reaching further between her legs to apply it to the tiny creases of her rectum. It had a soothing blend as well as a lubricant. For his own pleasure, he put some on her nipples, making them glisten. The ointment sparkled, metallic pieces part of the mix.

Returning to the counter, he put away the ointment, retrieved a violet wand and opened his tool box, choosing a mushroom-shaped electrode to fit into the neck. The violet wand made a humming noise as he turned it on, the mushroom casting a lavender light. Behind him, he heard her draw in a breath as the oil started to do what it did. It would warm at first, start to tingle, then stimulate. Then he would add to it with the wand.

He came to her, began to pass the mushroom-shaped glass attachment over her nipples. The metallic pieces sparkled as she arched in surprised reaction at the electricity passing through them. She rocked up to her toes, fingers closing on the chains holding her manacles. "Garron." It was surprise, trepidation, pleasure.

He leaned forward, kissing her lips, her cheek, her forehead, her eye brow, touching her face all over with his lips. She whimpered. Out of all the sounds she made, that pleading note was his favorite. Especially since he expected nothing like it had crossed her lips in some time.

Straightening, he went back to creating more magic for her. An even flow of movement over the nipples, down the stomach, to the cunt, tipping his elbow up or down as needed for stronger sensation. He stayed away from direct contact with the manacles, since that would result in too intense a charge for what he was wanting to accomplish. She started to dance under his touch, and this time he stayed mindful of how hard she was jerking against her bonds.

*Please*… Subs always used that word. It was like an aphrodisiac to a Master. Please stop. Please more. Please…just please. It was his favorite word in the whole world for all the things it meant, especially coming from her lips and mind now.

Words were keys, clues to the inner psyche. When he demanded them from a sub, it wasn't to stroke his ego, but to get farther inside them. He knew which ones were key transition moments. He always treasured the first time they were spoken, and this time even more so.

"Please, what, Kaela? Say my name. Tell me who I am." He slid the wand over her clit, heard the static crackle as he passed it up and over, down and around in a swirling pattern. The slick tissues convulsed again.

"No…I can't…no…"

"You'll come as often as I want you to come. You make me so fucking hard when you come, my lady, I may not ever let you stop. I may keep you chained here all ten days, screaming my name and your cunt gushing, over and over. Give you water to keep you hydrated, let you feed from my throat, and beg me for release… When you say no, when you try to fight it, it makes me more determined to keep you chained up."

He moved the wand over her breasts again, down over her pussy, over all her flesh, watching the streaks of electrified color move between the device and her body. Her glazed eyes were on them as well, her mouth working but no words coming out. Except one.

"Master." *Master.*

His fingers tightened on the wand, and he forced himself to keep his head down an extra second, savoring the sound of it.

She broke again, her body straining. He saw the first flickers of mental and physical exhaustion, the climax carrying her away with no resistance, telling her just how helpless she truly was. That panicked her, such that she started to fight again. He knew how to work with that, so as she rolled off the climax, he was using the wand to take her up once again. Even as the tears started to roll, he catapulted her back to that peak once more.

She sobbed, broken words coming out of her mouth. "Master….no more, please. Master…"

He set the wand aside, but only to strip off his jeans. He'd tucked himself back in when he needed the restraint, so it was a relief to finally make himself as naked as she was. He released her lovely legs, coiling them around his hips. He put his arm around her waist, holding her to him as he released her wrists. Carrying her to the mattress in the corner, he laid her down on it, himself on his knees over her.

He felt how fragile she was now, her eyes clinging to him, her lips parting again as he gripped her thighs and pushed his cock into her. Her hands fell above her in an unconscious posture of surrender.

Slow this time, inch by inch. He held her hips, worked her on him. She understood without words, even without thought, that he wanted her to lie still, let him move her upon him the way he desired. She was deeply, fully submissive, the way she'd obviously yearned to be for so long. Her fingers curled over her head, her throat working, and still she cried, silently, the tears slipping down her cheeks.

He adjusted, stretching out upon her, bracing his elbows on either side of her head. She hid her face into his throat as he worked his hips, driving in and out, slow and easy, a reminder as well as a provocation. He wanted to take her to climax again, but this part wasn't so much about that. This was all about connection.

"Say it again, my lady," he rumbled against her head. "Put your arms around me."

They coiled over his shoulders, his back, as her face pressed more tightly in his neck. *Master.* "Master," she whispered.

"My lady," he responded. "Mine." He kept moving as her heart and soul emptied into him. He was surrounding her, holding her like he had the other night, giving her shelter. In that darkness, her face against his throat, she could let go.

It took some time, but he made sure he pushed her up to one more climax. She came through it even more exhausted. Numb, out of her head, disoriented…floating. He'd put his lady into subspace, and he'd never worked so hard for something he wanted so much.

He was bleeding, bruised and still nursing a hell of an erection, but he'd gotten where he'd intended to go. He stayed on top of her, holding her, soothing her. He'd worked subs through subspace and subdrop before, and this was quite a bit of both. He used his arms and body to warm her chilled flesh, rocked her, kissed her temple, the bridge of her nose. She was truly hell and gone, so far inside herself, as if she'd like to lose herself there and never come back. It was desire and grief, loneliness, loss and longing, ecstasy and pleasure wrapped in such a confusing mass he knew he would have to do some long and hard thinking on it, on how best to handle it to be the type of Master she needed.

The one thing he knew for sure was he damn well wanted that challenge.

He'd never had the honor of seeing it happen so deep, so strong, but he wasn't arrogant enough to think that was all his doing. He might have known how to turn the key in the lock, but what lay behind that door…it was all her. He *was* arrogant and possessive enough to want to keep that magic for himself forever. He'd never seen such treasure in a submissive's response.

He'd exhausted a vampire. He'd have no small satisfaction about that, except he knew a great deal of the exhaustion had come from the fluctuations of her mood, her inner war between want and need, duty and survival. What she could live with. Fuck, he knew all about that kind of struggle.

As if his intimidating appearance didn't make it plain, he was a very physical man. He knew how to use violence to achieve objectives and protect the defenseless. He knew how to use intense sexual encounters to take a submissive to a whole different level. But the way to that, particularly with this female, was through the brain, the heart. The soul. He had to convince her she could trust him with that part of herself and to do that, he might have to do something he hadn't done before, at least not to the extent that would be necessary. Let her get as into his head as he needed to get into hers. In the case of a vampire, that was kind of a literal thing.

But first things first. It took quite a while, but at length he had her calmed down enough to move to a grounding phase. Rising to his feet, he lifted her, took her to his massage table and laid her down on it on her stomach. She watched him with vacant eyes as he used the Velcro straps to hold her hands and feet to it. A reminder of her submission, something to help steady her in her current state.

"Master?"

He lifted his head, met her gaze. Her eyes were glistening, as if she wasn't aware she couldn't stop crying. But that was to be expected. It was clear her tears had come at a hard cost, as if it had been a long time since she'd cried. He expected she'd taught herself not to do it, not to indulge the weakness when there was no shoulder to spill them upon.

"Yes, my lady?"

She moistened her lips. "May I ask something?"

"You can ask. I'll decide whether or not to answer."

It wasn't something she was used to in her world, he knew, and it was fascinating to see her fluctuate between two identities, the one that would deal out punishment for impertinence, and the one that craved him to be a hard-ass with her.

"Will you…touch my face?"

Such a simple request. But to a sub in this mode, it was like requesting the moon, a child hoping their dream would come true. Knowing his set expression would tell her he was thinking about her request, he finished restraining her. He picked up the massage lotion, spread it on his hands. When he started to work on her shoulder, she let out a purr, melted beneath his touch. He smiled, bent and kissed her ear, nuzzled her cheek. Pressing his own against her, he gave her that requested contact.

"You did very well, my lady. Your Master is very pleased with you."

She hiccupped over another tiny sob. She still hadn't recovered enough self-awareness to calculate her responses. Straightening, he continued his way down her back.

Her gaze flitted to his arm, saw streaks of dried blood. "I hurt you."

"You tore me up like a tiger, my lady. But I don't worry about scars."

Another tear slid out of her eye and he tsked, catching it. "You're free to use your claws on me. If I can't hold my own with you, I'm not the Master you're seeking."

She wanted him to talk, he saw it in her mind, anything so she could hear the rumble of his voice, hold onto it like an anchor.

It was a fucking charge, to be in her head like this. He thought about his earlier musings on having the third mark. Vardalos had said the second mark was a mind to mind thing, but the third mark went all the way to the soul. Whatever that meant. Though as a Master, he expected he understood even better than most what it could mean. The pot of gold at the end of the rainbow.

As he massaged her, he probed gently through her hazy mind, seeing how far he could go with the second mark. He knew when he reached that point, because it was like another door presented itself, a fortress within a fortress. Her consciousness slipped away beneath it like smoke.

The door the third mark would open, he suspected. The threshold to her soul. Feeling like he'd already had the privilege of briefly crossing that line during this session, he knew he wanted to go there again. And again.

He withdrew to see her fingers kneading the table padding as if she needed to be touching something. She needed some more grounding. So did he, else he might lose control and start all over again with her.

On that wry self-admonishment, he began to talk about the island, all the things that were here. The forests, the hidden streams, the exotic flowers that appeared in unexpected places, like fragile treasure. Thunderstorms where blue forked lightning shot over the ocean waters and one could smell the ozone, feel the electric current in the air heating the skin. He massaged her with both hands, but when one of them came close to her bound hand, she grasped it and wouldn't let go, her eyes closing.

§

Despite how good the two-handed massage was, Kaela didn't want him to pull away and was relieved when he didn't. He started to stroke her back, her flanks, the nape of her neck with his one free hand, letting her hold the other.

At length, he moved her to a mat on the floor, placing a blanket over her to keep her warm. Sliding a chair up next to her, he took a seat there. He was watching over her, a quiet reassurance like a tree canopy. She probably needed to stop thinking of him in tree analogies, but there was something so reassuring about a large, sturdy tree…

She adjusted so her cheek was on his shoe, her temple lying against his jeans cuff, since he'd pulled his pants back on. He braced his other foot behind her, so his ankle and calf were against her back. She couldn't stop shaking, inside and out, but that wasn't the worst of it. She wanted to say things she couldn't say.

*This is a safe place, a safe zone, Kaela. You can say anything you want here.*

*Because it's just a fantasy. A temporary respite.*

He grunted and stood, pushing the chair out of the way. Lying down in front of her in one lithe movement, he stretched out on his hip--facing away from her.

She immediately pressed herself up against him, her face between his shoulder blades, her cheek against the coiled whip tattoo and the red letters enclosed in its circle. Reaching back, he threaded her hand under his arm, over his bare chest, and held her firmly there. He could have faced her, but he seemed to know this worked better for her, where he couldn't see her face, where she could just anchor herself against him.

She would never have a third marked servant. It was so obvious, wasn't it? She'd had so many fantasies involving this vacation, but the reality facing her now was painful, impossible.

The only one she wanted as a third marked servant was someone capable of dominating her. The deepest wish she had, the one that would bring balance to her life, could not come true.

Maybe she never should have come here to learn the truth. Ignorance might not be bliss, but it made life far more bearable. Now that she'd had this with him, she couldn't imagine ever depriving herself of it.

He turned, propping himself on an elbow. Sliding a fingertip down her sternum and over her breast, he returned to her face to touch her cheek, her chin. "So what would that look like, Kaela? Your Master being your third mark servant?"

§

Her gaze snapped up to him. He'd shown he was capable of absorbing so much from her--body language, unvoiced yearnings, and some of the most subtle thoughts in her head--even before she'd second marked him. Of all the magics she'd found on the island, that one amazed her the most, since it wasn't magic at all. It was the man.

"It's ludicrous. It's--

"Yet you've imagined it. In detail." He gave her a thoughtful look. "I want to know what it looks like in your mind."

She shook her head, but he caught her chin, lifted it and gave her that stare which made things go all fuzzy inside her in a way that shouldn't affect her how it did. He was a human.

"Is your mind open to me, Kaela?"

She'd shut it back down out of habit, the way she did with Fran. She opened it up again, though it took some effort. Decades of caution weren't so easily reversed. If it wasn't for the set-up, the fantasy elements the Master of Eden had provided, it would have been entirely impossible. Was Garron in her mind, examining everything he found there? How did she feel about that?

*It doesn't matter how you feel about it, Kaela. If you submit to me, you open up all of yourself to me.*

She felt that trickle of resentful reaction she'd felt before she'd second marked him, then she remembered how she'd felt after she'd taken that choice out of his hands. As if she'd betrayed herself, as much as him. She'd let fear take over, though she'd fought much worse things in her life.

"He would be in my mind, because he could be. But I wouldn't block him." She paused, realizing that was exactly what he had just demanded. "So even when he's having to behave as my servant, meeting the demands of my world, I could hear his voice in my head, know he was still in control. But it's impossible, because he would have to act as my servant, truly be that way, in front of other vampires. How could someone who is truly a Master…like you… bear that?" She touched his face. "I couldn't bear it," she whispered.

His eyes stayed cool, the lips firm. "You're taking too much on yourself. A Master makes his own decisions, doesn't he?"

"It doesn't matter. This is a vacation. This is what I can have. I won't talk about it anymore."

"Take that high and mighty tone with me, my lady, and you'll find yourself back in those restraints."

This was a ten-day fantasy. What gave him the right to talk about it as more than that? She didn't want him to do that, make it harder than it was.

He gave her another thoughtful look at that, but didn't say anything else. Just rose and pulled a robe out of a closet. He put it on her, letting her do very little to help him with that before he picked her up and put her back on the mattress. She watched him pack away his equipment, leave instructions for their care to the submissive attendants who ensured that all of it stayed clean and ready for his next session. She was quiet, inside and out, watching as he typed out a text on his phone. He paused, swept an appraising look over her, went back to the text. A few minutes later, a knock came at the door. She heard a female voice, saw a slender arm pass a glossy Eden gift shop bag through the opening. The voice belonged to Bridget, the woman at the desk.

She remembered then she could now see through his eyes, so she caught a quick, blurry glimpse of a lush brunette in a velvet red corset before the door closed. She blinked. Blinked again. Now she understood why he looked at her in such a careful, measured way. The man had terrible vision. How on earth did he read lips so well? Why didn't he wear glasses?

When he turned to look at her, she realized something else was going on. He could see auras. Not just a vague halo of light, either. It was as if a different part of his mind other than his sense of sight detected the energy signatures, and they were complex, detailed, beautiful…

"Yours in particular," he said. "Yeah, it helps with reading lips, though I can't really explain how. The auras give me another sense of what's being said, along with body language and the rest."

"You think glasses or surgery would mess with it."

"Maybe. I don't really want to take the risk. It gives me something, when I'm working with a submissive. Something I'm not willing to give up."

Any more than most vampires would be willing to give up the soul connection with their servant. Yes, for some of them the servant was merely a valued tool, but for those like Jacob and Lyssa, it went far beyond that.

She thought about the second mark connection she already had to Garron and understood that far more than she was comfortable saying. Why was she thinking about this? It didn't matter. He wasn't leaving with her.

Her gaze flickered up to his again and they held that contact. Her attempt to push away the thoughts and his awareness of them formed a humming energy between them. At last, he spoke.

"My lady, you looked through my eyes because you were curious about Bridget, weren't you?"

Her relief that he wasn't going to push her on the issue was supplanted by an inexplicable defensiveness. She bit back on a dozen things she could have said, settling for, "Yes. She's very lovely."

His eyes glinted with humor. "I didn't give you permission to be in my mind. You just want more punishment, don't you?"

She was pretty sure the answer to that question was a resounding *yes*, but she simply offered a noncommittal shrug and pushed up from the mat, combing her fingers through the wisps of hair that had come loose from her braid to frame her face. His look said he'd heard that *yes* loud and clear, and that it would be his pleasure to accommodate. Her skin heated under that regard, but he merely tossed the bag to the floor in front of her. Opening it, she saw two scraps of cloth, a bikini. "Put that on. We're going to take a dip in one of the pools. It's shallow," he added. "Only five feet so you can stand."

At her little sigh of relief, he gave her a wink. "Vardalos mentioned vampires are uncomfortable in water over their heads."

"That man knows far too much about us, and it's not a fear. It's just a preference. We're not buoyant. We sink." She considered the swimsuit. "There's not a lot of this. Why even bother?"

"Because I want to see you barely wearing it." He gave her an appraising look. "Put it on."

She felt spots of color in her cheeks as she responded to the order. During the heights of her arousal, it had been a little easier to accept her instinctive compulsion to obey his commands. Even so, she shed the robe and donned the bikini. Though there wasn't much to it, his gaze was hot and appreciative. The bra cups were low enough she nearly spilled out of them, while the press of the sides and straps kept her breasts pushed up high with a tempting valley of cleavage. The bottoms were Brazilian cut with little beaded ties that could be pulled free easily.

She was used to being seen as beautiful. Being seen as her Master's possession, inciting his desire with her every move made her slow down, take more time with it. She was still enjoying a dreamlike state of post-arousal, but the more he stared at her like a wolf wanting to devour, the more that was turning in a present tense direction. Vampires were known to be insatiable. She'd never been happier about that trait.

§

He was going to die of a hard on. Garron imagined Theodosius writing that one up for the mainland authorities. He'd probably give up on it and just pay them off, saying that Garron had died at the hand of a homicidal maniac yet to be apprehended. Easier that way.

He leaned against his work table, fueling his frustration with the view as she stepped into the bottoms, re-tied those little strings and fitted the top around her luscious tits, making his mouth dry at how she reached in and adjusted them, sexy as hell. She started to twist her braid into a knot, but he shook his head.

"Take out the braid and leave it down. I want to see it look like mermaid hair, all silky while you're swimming."

She slid the band off the end that he'd twisted there, and began to unravel the thick strands. He stayed where he was, watching, letting her see his pleasure at merely watching her perform the task. The way she combed her fingers through it, freeing it to rest on her shoulders, was almost as enjoyable as doing it himself, savoring the feel of it, the way her eyes darkened when he pulled on her scalp.

"Vampires don't swim you know," she said. "We're too dense."

"Wading is fine. I'm not going to ask you to compete in freestyle. Though seeing you do the backstroke would be every man's wet dream."

The teasing was putting her feet back under her, restoring her fire. She tossed her hair back. "I'm not here to be on display to others."

"No? So you had no interest in checking out the 24/7 area?"

Her bitten lip, the spark in her eye, told him she did. Leaving that for now, he moved around her, considering her from head to toe. "Stunning. But you're used to hearing that, aren't you?"

"No. It's a given in our world." She lifted a shoulder. "Vampires are sexy, sensual, erotic, beautiful, handsome. It is what it is. It doesn't mean anything."

"It means something to me." He stepped close to her, touched her mouth. "I'm not talking about your measurements, how pretty your hair is or the silk of your skin. I look at you and I see you in those restraints over there, begging. I hear you saying 'Master' for the first time in that desperate whisper, your voice trembling on the cusp of climax. When I take you out around other people, that's a window into who and what you are that they don't have, you spread and begging for me. It makes you more than beautiful. It makes you a goddess to me."

She lifted a hand, traced the scar over his face. "It works that way for me, too," she said, wondering. "I see far more than the way you look."

"A good thing," he said wryly.

"No." She shook her head. "I like the way you look, Garron. But it's a matter of opening your eyes to really see what's in front of you.

I look at you and I feel the gentleness of your hands, hear that tone in your voice that makes me tremble for reasons I don't understand. I can break you, and yet I feel this delicious edge of fear when you threaten to punish me, tell me to obey you. You were frightening, right after I marked you. I was afraid of you and…it aroused me."

She had no idea how her words could take him to his knees, make him want to worship her, even as he visualized all the ways he could make her surrender to him. He settled for taking a tight grip on her hand, and clearing his throat. "Good."

He linked fingers with her, changed topics. "For the next little bit, you can ask me anything, talk about anything. I know part of you wants to stay in character full time, because it's easier for you to treat this as a pure fantasy, something that won't chase you once you leave here, but I think that would be the wrong tactic to get the most out of this. My goal is to give you what you need, not necessarily what you want."

She didn't yet realize how far he was willing to go with that, maybe because he was just starting to figure it out himself.

She frowned, obviously not liking him disrupting her effort to keep her expectations down to a ten day fantasy, but that was just tough. When he slipped the collar from her throat and pocketed the slim strap, he saw the flicker in her gaze, a protest she bit back.

"And another thing," he said casually. "From here forward, you don't get to call me Master unless you ask and I say yes. I don't let a sub do that automatically until I'm sure she understands exactly what it means to call me Master."

Oh yeah, he was pissing her off a bit. He saw the flash through her mind. She wasn't "a sub", any faceless submissive, one of his harem or another guest who came through the Eden club, paying for his services. He shifted a little closer to her, using the intimidating body language to tell her he was aware of the attitude. She stiffened but her gaze lowered. Progress.

"That goes for getting in my head," he continued. "You keep your mind open to me, but you need my permission to be in my head. I'm sure you can do it without me knowing, but I'll pick it up in how you anticipate me, and that will disappoint me, Kaela. It will tell me you don't respect the boundaries your Master sets."

"You said I couldn't call you that."

"It doesn't mean that's not what I am."

It gratified him to see her resentment about not being allowed in his head had nothing to do with the edge the information would give her. She wanted the connection and, after having it such a short time, he had to agree, it was fucking fantastic. He wouldn't mind it being two-way himself. He didn't care if she saw where he was going with things, but at the moment it was better if she just focused on one thing, and that was what he was telling her, not what he was thinking. What lay behind the orders would be way more complicated for her to handle at this juncture.

He touched her cheek. He didn't need a window to her mind to read it through her golden-brown eyes. Resentful, troubled, aroused, confused, pissed. She was never just one thing. He liked that about her. "I want you in my head, too. But for the immediate future, I want your focus on you and what I tell you to do."

She nodded.

"Okay. Let's go to the pool. I'll drop a rock in it and we'll see which one of you sinks faster."

*I can rip your heart out of your chest, human.*

She might not be listening to his thoughts, but she realized he was reading hers. He bit back a smile, though he wondered if hearing his response would unsettle her the way it did him.

*You already have, my lady.*

§

Eden had no less than a dozen different types of pools. The lagoon pool, his intended destination, would be one of the quietest ones this time of night, but since it wasn't technically in an area where being buck-ass naked was okay, they needed to stop at his place so he could grab one of his own swimsuits. Passing through the trio of pools and adult water slide that were the main social hub for the party set was a necessary evil for that. Even at this late hour, it would be hopping.

Because of that, Garron snagged a sheer body scarf with beaded fringe from one of Eden's many discreet boutique shops. As well as a pair of matching rhinestone sandals to protect her feet. Having Kaela knot the scarf at her hip added a translucent veil over her backside that only enhanced the temptation of what was there, and of course didn't conceal the feast of her breasts at all. In the end, he gave her one of his extra staff T-shirts he kept in his room at Club Sin and had her put it on. Even though he was aware of her speculative look, he didn't respond to it. Yeah, it was kind of a surprise to him as well. He had every intention of indulging her interest in Eden's 24/7 BDSM area eventually. Hell, if he took her there, she might be stripped down to nothing but his collar.

Yet that didn't change his feelings a bit about exposing her to the mainstream jet set crowd. For whatever reason, he felt she was more vulnerable there, where less rules were in place. In a formal BDSM setting, behavior toward subs, no matter how beautiful, was structured and controlled by the respective Masters and Mistresses.

As such, he kept a light hand on her lower back as they moved into the area that was always too lively for his taste.

*I get the feeling you prefer quiet places,* she thought. *Walks along the beach, a book, a cup of coffee in the morning. And no, I didn't read that from your mind. I've seen policemen going into a crack house who look more comfortable than you do.*

She reached out, touched his side. "I'm fine, Garron," she said. "I have to be around humans quite often. I was one, remember?"

He gave her a rueful smile. "Sorry."

They'd just come out of an intense one-on-one that had been ongoing, in point of fact, since she'd arrived. This was like emerging from a cave. Even in a normal sub session, he usually did something to transition himself from one environment to the other. His time with her had been ten times more intense than that, putting him as much into his head space as she'd been in subspace. He realized now he should have circled around the cocktail set. He'd been through enough PTSD therapy to know what triggers to avoid, and he was feeling too vigilant. Adjusting his body closer to her, his eyes noting every sound and movement, were indications of it. His instincts for danger were turned up to high volume in a way that didn't fit here and he knew it. Self-awareness didn't change his nerves being on edge, however.

Kaela's hand slid behind her, tangled with his on the small of her back, as if she was letting him hold her arm behind her back. But she exerted gentle pressure on his hand and shifted her body so that he was cupping her ass, his thumb sliding along the cleft in blatant ownership. The satisfying flare of arousal in her mind was matched by his.

He lifted a brow, glanced down at her. "Topping me, my lady?"

"No sir." Her full lips pursed as she lowered her lashes in a way that said she was doing something different. A combination of flirting and reassurance at once. She might not be in his mind, but she understood body language almost as well as he did. He'd never in a million years have expected her to call him *sir* like that, but it successfully snapped him out of the fugue and brought him into the present.

He gave her a squeeze and slid his hand back to her waist. Putting his hand on his submissive's ass in a club environment was an appropriate message. Doing it here would be disrespecting his lady, and he'd no more tolerate that than he'd tolerate anyone else doing it.

When he saw her cheeks tinge with color, the pleased surprise in her gaze, he tugged her long hair. "You are listening. Didn't we talk about that?"

"We did." She closed her hand over his on her hip again, caressing his knuckles. "I was worried about you," she said. "I wanted to make sure you were okay."

He wasn't sure how to feel about that. Without access to her mind, his defenses might have gone up, making him think he had to prove he was in charge, but he saw it wasn't that. She didn't see any conflict between him being her Master and both of them wanting to watch one another's backs. Him by covering her with a T-shirt, her by checking into his state of mind.

He'd had relationships with a small handful of women, where some of that reciprocity existed, but this was the first time he'd looked into a submissive's eyes and seen a hint of a true equal, someone who had no expectation or desire that him being her Master would absolve her of her own desire to watch out for herself…or for others.

Something to think about. She touched his mouth, the scar on his throat. "No," she said. "It wouldn't. I don't think it's supposed to work that way. Do you?"

He hadn't ever given it much thought, since his relationships here were professional and temporary, all about caring for the guest who turned everything over to him. Not so much about trusting himself in her hands.

"Hmm," she said.

"Stop reading my mind," he told her sternly, but a smile struggled on his face. "Else I will totally kick your ass when we get to my place."

"You say that like it's a threat."

He sighed, put his hand to her back and gave her a playful push before they were walking again. Mission accomplished, though. Things were easier now, the noise and splashing not bothering him as much. They followed the perimeter of one pool through a crowd of guests standing in clusters, drinking and laughing. Others were in the pool, swimming and flirting. More held drinks and conversations while sitting on the lip or on lounge chairs, all ways to see and be seen. The five waitstaff and two bartenders manning the tiki hut were hustling. It was one of those evenings where, if he wasn't engaged at the Club, Garron would have been pitching in. Evidence that he had no real social life, according to Vardalos. There was the pot calling the kettle black.

"Look, there's one. Hey, *you*."

Another thing that hadn't helped his management of the noise was that he'd put in his hearing aids, knowing he was going to be around people other than Kaela. The cacophony of white noise was overpowering, even when he turned down the volume. Now what had sounded like a distant snippet of conversation was actually close, a guest calling out to him. He saw it in Kaela's mind when she touched his arm.

A man he'd seen at check-in earlier in the week, who'd obviously remembered Garron worked here despite the lack of official uniform, was headed his way.

"Apologies, my lady," he muttered, and turned to acknowledge the guest.

While all those Vardalos invited to the island received exclusive invitations and were vetted, there were some Garron knew served a "conflict purpose", challenging the true visitors about the nature of their fantasies, helping them find their way to them. This impatient male, reeking of entitlement and alcoholism, with bloated blood vessels on his nose and cheeks, had to be one of those, because otherwise Garron couldn't see Vardalos letting him set foot here.

"I asked for a drink five damn minutes ago."

*Should have brought your stash from your room to tide you over*, Garron thought. His attitude toward the man didn't improve as he saw his bloodshot gaze go to Kaela and cling. Ignoring male attention as usual, she was watching the play of light over the pool and studying her surroundings, but Garron gave serious thought to scooping the guy's eyes away from her breasts with a jagged-edged grapefruit spoon.

"What are you, deaf?"

Garron cursed himself for looking away. Usually he paid close attention to what a customer was saying. "I'm sorry, sir. What was that?"

Most the time, the hearing aids went unnoticed, but he realized the torchlight around the pool must have caught the glint on the tubing, for the man's gaze zoned in on the side of Garron's head.

"Well damn, I guess you are." The man made some elaborate hand gestures, a mockery of sign language, and mouthed his words in an exaggerated fashion. "Think you can send someone this way who knows English? And how to bring me my fucking drink?"

Garron wondered if it occurred to the asshole that being obnoxious on a remote island in the Bermuda Triangle--where there was no lack of ways to dispose of a body--put him square on the top of the clueless heap. Then he saw Eaton returning with the man's drink. From the young man's harassed look, Garron suspected the guy's drink request had involved a trip into the vaults. Eaton gave him a long suffering look before schooling his face back to professional courtesy.

"Here comes your drink, sir," Garron said, turning back to the guest.

But the man was no longer paying attention to him, and Kaela was no longer to Garron's left. She was standing in between him and the offensive man, her back to Garron, but because of their mind connection, he heard what the man said to her…as well as her response.

The man gave her an amused look. "Decided you liked the look of a whole man instead of that scarred freak show, didn't you, sweetheart? Why don't you come have a drink--"

He punctuated the question with a yelp that could have come from a poked Chihuahua. Thanks to the man's brief-style swim trunks, a poor choice for so many reasons, Kaela had reached down and clamped a hand over his balls. Her grip was hard enough to elicit that high pitched squeak and turn the man to quivering Jell-O as he realized movement would be inadvisable.

"You know those little stress balls people use to keep their hands strong?" she inquired pleasantly. "Thanks to those, I can tear your tiny little testicles off with no more than a twist."

She must have given him a sample demonstration, because he let out another pained grunt, his desperate gaze seeking rescue. Ironically his eyes found Garron, probably in the name of male solidarity. Garron had to admit his balls twinged sympathetically. However, the waves of violence rolling off Kaela suggested it wasn't yet the right time to intervene. Timing was everything when defusing a bomb.

"Those who don't respect others get taught respect," she said shortly. "You need a rather extreme lesson. Unless you start saying the right things."

"I'm sorry," the man stammered.

She cocked her head, spoke in a menacing tone. "To him, you worthless piece of shit. Not me."

Lady Kaela understood the line between brutality and civility. Garron expected she usually made rational decisions about stepping over it, especially in a human environment. Yet in her head all he saw was her replaying this man's treatment of her Master. On every replay, she was becoming all the more certain that what was needed was a poolside castration.

With alarm, he realized she would do it. She was an overlord confident of her ability to take and give life, who was used to making those decisions, enough not to doubt herself when that judgment had to be made. She was scary as a hanging judge. But doing things that drew unwelcome attention to a vampire was not a good thing for her, or the vampire world as a whole. From what Vardalos had told him as part of a whole list of cautions, she could be in deep shit with her Vampire Council if that happened.

It told him he wasn't the only one who'd been unbalanced by the intensity of their Dom/sub play. Though he couldn't have anticipated this scenario, Garron should have been more on top of that. If he didn't do something to distract her from her current course, Vardalos would owe a rather substantial apology to a guest publicly neutered during late evening cocktails.

Eaton had stopped a few feet away, his gaze darting between Kaela and the man before going to Garron. Garron raised a finger, a quiet command to hold his position. Closing the gap between himself and Kaela, he pressed against her back. He slid his hand over her shoulder, caressed her throat as his other hand rested on her waist.

She was rigid as a board, but her acceptance of his touch made him feel like he was calming a dragon who allowed only him within the range of her fiery snarl. He embraced the feeling, even as he realized the hefty responsibility that came with the honor. She would mutilate this male without remorse.

"We're done here, my lady," he said quietly. "Point made. Stand down." *Sticks and stones, my lady. He's just a pathetic asshole.*

After a bated moment, she nodded. "This matter is done. Neither I nor this man"--she jerked her head at Garron--"will hear anything more about this, or I'll find you again, won't I? It's a small island with a tremendous amount of water around it."

Garron had to suppress another smile as she pointed out the same thing that had crossed his own mind. The asshole bobbed his head like it was on a string. She tilted her head toward Eaton. "Look. Here's your drink. All that bad behavior for nothing."

She backed another step into Garron. It made it easier for him to turn them together, her close against his side as he maneuvered them into a walk. As they cleared the pool area, moved onto another path screened by vegetation, he slid his arm fully around her, but she shrugged away, moved ahead of him. He gave her the space, watching her thoughtfully as she pulled it together. She'd closed her mind to him, so he stopped, patiently waited until she noticed he wasn't following. It took about twenty paces. When she turned, he saw the crimson light in her eyes, the tightness of her face that said the anger was still with her.

He raised a brow. "Problem, my lady?"

She shook her head, which of course meant nothing. "Why are there *always* people like that?" she demanded. "Those who take advantage of someone weaker, in a position of less power? You use your sadism as a gift, a way of cherishing and giving pleasure. You understand what power is. It's a gift or a curse, a tool or a poison, but in its purest form, the way it's meant to be wielded, it's…"

"Creation," he said. "You can create good things from it. Relationships that last, a stable foundation, a kingdom, a household, or build a rocket and fly to the moon."

With a sigh, she shifted her gaze to a clump of crimson exotic flowers beside the path. As she did that, he closed the distance between them. He didn't touch her, which got her attention, especially when he crossed his arms, gave her a neutral look. "It's also a way to help a submissive know when she can let go. When it's not her job to take care of things."

"I know you could have broken him in half. But you would have lost your job. He knows that, too. That's what I hate. It turned him on, being able to order you around like you were nothing. Nothing." When she closed her eyes, he put his hands on her shoulders.

"You've been there."

"Every made vampire has been. Probably most of the born ones. It makes you determined never to be one of those treated like nothing, ever again. An incentive program for upward mobility, if you will. I get that. It's how we survive. But pointless cruelty like that, just to make him feel better about himself… I try not to let hate consume me, but I could cheerfully tear his limbs from his body and watch him bleed to death."

"Probably best not to go that way," Garron advised. "Theodosius has a limit on the number of guests we can kill each month. I think we've reached our quota."

"Oh?" Her lips curved, despite the shadows in her eyes. "What does he do with them?"

"Feeds them to his Kraken, of course. And the Kraken can only have so many a month. Don't want him to get fat."

Her shoulders eased down and he massaged them, tilted her chin up with a thumb. "It's okay, my lady. You're a woman used to being in charge, no matter how much you crave submission. Correct?"

Her brow creased. She wasn't sure where he was going. That was okay, because he was going to be crystal clear on this one.

"During that first fight we had, I made it pretty obvious that I won't let you walk over me. You received that message, else we wouldn't have been able to go any farther. Understand?"

She frowned. "I don't know."

"I'm saying that if I choose to embrace a subservient façade, I have a reason for it. It doesn't touch who or what I am." He wondered if she understood the underlying significance of that. From the sharpening of her gaze, and her shoulders tensing under his hands again, he thought she did. He'd leave it there, but he wanted her to keep chewing on it. Despite the displeasure of dealing with him, the obnoxious guest had provided a good opening for that, at least.

He looped her hand into his elbow. "Come on. I need a

swimsuit."

## Chapter Seven

The apartments on the fringes of this end of the resort weren't as posh as guest suites, but Theodosius treated his employees well. The rooms were comfortable and had lots of windows to provide good views of the ocean or forest. Their spacious, open air layouts were reminiscent of homes Garron had seen in Hawaii.

He'd never played with a sub here, even a staff member. He'd never had that kind of connection with one, where she was given permission to see what kind of Dom he was in his personal space. He kept it in the confines of Club Sin or the areas designated for BDSM play because he understood when he let a sub cross this threshold, he was considering a relationship, something that would include yet expand the Dom/sub dynamic significantly.

He hadn't reinforced to Kaela that she had to stay out of his mind, but she didn't seem to be listening now, because she had no reaction to those thoughts. Which was probably good. After he turned on the entry way and kitchen lights, he turned to watch the beautiful vampire drift through his main living area, taking in everything, what his décor said about the man he was.

He winced at the thought. He was a minimalist when it came to decorating. The living room had a futon with a quality cherry wood frame and a bamboo coffee table. He had a bookshelf with a few titles on it, a compact, hi-powered stereo system for music. The kitchen was stocked with what he needed.

As she stepped out onto the deck, fingering the potted plants there, most of them arranged by the Eden landscapers who put their touch on everything, he went to his bedroom to find his swimsuit. He didn't really go for the Speedo look because it always felt like he was wearing bikini bottoms, but one of the staff subs had talked him into a pair of shorts that hit high on the thigh and were snug enough to make the girth and length of his cock measurable to the eye if he was hard.

*"Master Garron, if your sub gets a good look at you in those, she'll do anything for you."*

He'd snorted at that, but had agreed to them, as well as a pair of normal swimsuit shorts for leisure swims. He'd actually found the tight style worked well to do his laps in the ocean in the morning, but women had other reasons for appreciating the aerodynamic fit.

He didn't angst over the drawbacks to his scarred appearance, so emphasizing the attributes he knew would please women was a matter of practicality in his profession. But Kaela wasn't about his job. As he decided to wear the shorts for her, he realized his motives were somewhat different than usual. It was the first time in a while he'd thought about whether a woman liked his appearance overall... Or chosen what to wear because she made him feel good about himself and he wanted to honor that feeling with extra effort on her behalf. Kaela made him feel as if she liked...well, all of him.

He shook his head, found himself smiling. He was an idiot.

Turning his thoughts back to her, he expected she was enjoying the view of the water from the deck. A light screen of plants for privacy and barrier was followed by the beach sloping down to the water, about a hundred yards off. He'd stood on that porch during storms, watched the surf get closer. One time it had reached the deck, sloshed over the edge, wet his feet and ankles. He'd turned his face up to the howling wind and driving rain and thought how that fury had felt almost soothing on his scars. Funny, because he typically didn't enjoy wind in his face because of how it made them feel. But a storm was different.

He slept on the futon, so his bedroom was just to hold clothes, his workout equipment and a desk to handle his paperwork and bills, not that there were many of those. Lodging, healthcare and utilities were part of the job perks, so that just left groceries and the infrequent impulse buy. Didn't need anything like life insurance, because he didn't have any beneficiaries for it, so no point. He didn't really care about how they disposed of his body.

"You should," she said. "It has served you well, suffered for your choices."

He turned. It had been years since he'd turned his back on a door when someone else was in his house, yet he had with her present, without thinking about it at all. When she spoke from behind him, having moved with that unconscious vampire stealth, he hadn't started. Perhaps because they were sharing minds, she felt as present as his own self.

More than that, he felt safe with her. It was more than the thought he'd had at the pool. He genuinely felt as if he could trust her to watch his back, the way he watched hers. There weren't many in the world he'd say that about. Definitely none who'd accomplished that in less than two days.

Her gaze flickered. "Here I was thinking you only had crude reasons for watching my back."

"Well, there are a lot of good reasons to watch your back. No reason to limit myself to just one." He took her hand, tangled their fingers. "I can't seem to keep you out of my head, my lady."

"I was trying to stay clear, until you left the room. I missed you."

She said it simply, yet it wasn't simple at all, the way the words made him feel. She stepped closer, into the shadow of his body. She gazed up at him, lifted her hand, traced the scars on his face again, followed them down to his neck. She liked touching them more than any woman he'd ever met. It was as if she knew they were the vital key to who he was at the bottom of his soul. Her stroke soothed the raw edges that came along with them.

She'd been honest, and he gave her back the same. "I like hearing you in my head. When you talk, I don't have to strain to listen. I can almost tune out the verbal, focus only on the mental, even though I have to sort it out with your thoughts, what's speech and what's thought." He smiled faintly. "Could cause some embarrassment if I mix those up."

She continued to study him, her hand drifting down his chest, nestling into the T-shirt he'd donned at the club. He put his hand over hers. "What are you doing?"

*Listening. Just…listening.* Her lips curved, her eyes thoughtful. *Being in your mind is like listening to the ocean. It whispers and roars, murmurs and laughs…it doesn't mind others listening to it, because it's self-contained. It knows who and what it is. It's both a place full of mystery and shadows, yet sparkling light in so many colors and brutal honesty…*

He thought he could feel her there in his mind, like the touch of her hand in places that so often remained untouched. His heart, his soul. Had he opened his soul to a woman, ever? He gave a vital part of himself to subs. That was important, for it to be as powerful as it should be, but did he open up this layer? Though he'd thought about finding that door inside her, the one that, if the third mark was shared, could be opened to him if she so chose, he hadn't thought about that same door in himself, or the sudden desire to give her that access. That reciprocal access was a way to an even more powerful connection with a submissive he wanted to keep for his own? Keep forever?

Her gaze flickered up to his, held. "If I gave it to you here…would the third mark be the same as the second? Temporary? Gone once I leave?"

"Vardalos and I didn't talk about it," he admitted. "But it stands to reason, doesn't it? If the second mark goes away, and that's a prerequisite for the third…"

The idea hung between them, ripe fruit, heavy with temptation. All it lacked was a snake peddling it, but they didn't really need that, did they? All they had to have was the desire in one another's eyes.

"I'd like to be able to stand inside your soul, Garron Rand," she said. "I expect it's very much like the man containing it. A stronghold. A safe haven. A place I can say I've had the privilege to be, at least once in my life."

He cupped her face, sliding his fingers along the fair brow, the sculpted cheekbone, the delicate chin. "Beauty and the beast."

"I expect either one of us could be the beast, couldn't we?" She tilted her head into his touch, a response and a caress at once. "I didn't want Beast to turn back into a pretty prince. I liked how he could be vicious and gentle both. You have to understand both sides of the coin to understand the value and purpose of each."

Her gaze slid over his scars. "There are male vampires so beautiful it's arousing just to look at them. Some can also be as cruel as spoiled children, just because no one can tell them no. You understand the word no, Garron. You understand the force of that word, the consequences, the anguish of it. The lessons that can be learned from it. You understand denial and pain, and you know how to turn those things into pleasure for a woman."

"I want you to stand inside my soul," he said abruptly, eyes boring into hers. "I want that. Let me give you that."

Her eyes misted a little. "I'm not sure. I know you say it's temporary but…I'm just not sure. I've barely been here two days, Garron."

He was reluctant to postpone it when it seemed they were both willing to do it, but as usual his gut gave him guidance, seeing her conflict. "Then we wait a bit."

But he wanted to keep her mind on it. His gaze strayed back to the dresser. She'd said giving him a third mark, even temporary, might be too soon, and what he was thinking now could fall into the same category. Even so, he slid the top drawer open and reached into the back, closing his fingers over the box tucked behind neat rolls of underwear and folded socks.

Feeling her eyes on him, he gave himself another moment, thinking it through, but he already knew it was the right choice. What was in the black velvet box had been purchased from a silver shop years ago, after his rehab, when his buddies took him to Hawaii. He knew it had been goaded by sentiment, thinking about a permanent submissive he knew he'd probably never have. But he'd never given it away, letting it travel with him from place to place.

Since he'd come to Eden, he'd realized there were very few strong impulses in life which were random. It was as if there was a thread taking a man toward something inevitable, and he set down his intentions along the way, marking that trail.

He opened the box, lifted out the contents. He heard her draw in a breath, felt that stillness sweep over her body, through her mind. The choker had been crafted with heavy silver links, each one twisted into the figure eight infinity symbol and connected to the next. No other adornment, the weight of it a statement of its own.

As he turned to face her, he wasn't sure what he was going to say, but it turned out words weren't necessary. Both her slender hands cupped his large fist, her head bowing so she could kiss the silver links wrapped over his knuckles. The tremor in her hands matched something in himself.

"I know you're worried about how you'll deal with things when you leave, my lady," he said, as steadily as he could. He touched her chin, met her eyes. "But no matter what happens, I want you to take this with you. It will remind you…you can always come back to me. I'll always consider you mine, Kaela. Maybe that will help."

§

Help and tear her to pieces at once, to know her dream existed in reality. But she'd take it. Kaela would prefer that to the alternative. She lifted her head, her chin. "May I wear it now?"

He moved behind her to thread the necklace around her throat. She put her hand up to touch it, hold it in place. "You have the strength to break it if you need to do so," he said.

"I won't."

As he adjusted it, he removed three of the links. In his mind, she saw he hadn't known what size neck the woman would have. He'd just known he'd put it on the neck of the woman who would be the one he'd want to always wear it.

Her fingers flexed on the choker. When he fastened it in place, her hand remained there, her breath shallow again. "Master?"

"Yeah." He had his hand on her nape, curved over it as she bowed her head and he leaned in, nuzzled her hair, pressed his body up against her.

"I want to…" She turned, stepped back. As his gaze rested on her, she removed the T-shirt he'd loaned her, revealing her body in the scant swimsuit. Her attention went down, and then the rest of her did, her breasts so ripe and full in the swimsuit top they had a little quiver as she knelt before him. Resting her hands on his thighs, she fixed her gaze on the strained state of those wonderful swim shorts. When she'd first come into the room, she'd zeroed in on them, the way the fabric molded and creased over his muscular buttocks, emphasizing the strength of his thighs, the power of his upper torso. She was pretty certain he'd never have chosen such a style himself, so she blessed the woman who'd talked him into it, even as she had a perverse desire to do her harm. "I don't want to go to the pool yet. I want you to be with me…here."

"You were listening to my thoughts."

"Yes, Master. I'm sorry."

"No, you're not." But his voice had that stern sound that said, rather than being displeased, he was considering exactly what they might both want. He wanted to take her here. Take her in ways neither of them would ever forget, and the sexual heat that surged from him over that idea made her tremble. It was as if the session in his room at Club Sin had been days ago, and she wanted him just as much, all over again.

"Stay on your knees."

Moving to his desk, he opened the top drawer, withdrew a quill. It wasn't a quill with a built-in pen, like most of them were. It was an actual quill, and he took a small pen knife from the same drawer, sharpened it even further. There was a pad of paper next to him, but she didn't think he was preparing to write.

"Eyes down, my lady." He didn't look up, which made the flutter in her throat and chest more frenetic as the seconds drew out. He hadn't said she couldn't talk, had he?

"What do you really want, Master?" she asked softly. "What can I give you that no other sub can?"

She jumped as he closed the drawer with a decisive slam. He wasn't angry, just catching her attention, but his tone told her he was ready to draw the reins tight. Excruciatingly tight.

"I didn't give you permission to call me Master, did I?"

"No." She shook her head. "I apologize."

"You don't ever apologize to me, Kaela. If you do something wrong, I'll punish you, in my own time and way. Now look at me."

When she did, he was putting the pen knife aside, testing the point of the quill. He stared at it before he lifted his gaze.

"I want the chance to fulfill the dreams of a submissive who's like no other. Who needs it not just as a release at the end of the day, or to have fun, but because it's as vital as breathing or blood to her, and she's done the miraculous--gone without breathing for almost two hundred years."

"Rather easy for vampires, really." The wry humor didn't ease how tight the words made her feel, like she was wrapped up in rope from neck to ankles the way he'd described, completely helpless to him. His crooked smile didn't dilute the intensity of his dark eyes, either.

"Hard to do metaphors with you supernatural folk. Come here, my lady."

At last it occurred to her, why the address sounded different when Garron said "my lady." It wasn't obsequious in the least. It was possessive. *My* lady.

She went to him. She wanted to kneel at his feet again, so close to his erection he couldn't resist her. Her gaze slid over the terrain above and below, the ropes of muscles on his thighs, the layers sculpted over stomach and chest.

He caught her arm before she let her knees buckle. "Trying to top from the bottom is never a good idea, my lady," he said with deceptive mildness. "Nothing will make me meaner, faster. Open up."

When she parted her lips, he put the quill in between them. "Hold onto that. Gently. Don't drop it."

Her world tilted as he bent, banded his arm around her thighs and--no other word for it--tossed her onto his shoulder. The capable movement, indicating the sprawling strength and grace of his body, his palm gripping her ass, the choker pulling against her throat, exacerbated her desire for him, her need to feel him inside her once more. It seemed the wanting him never ended.

"Glad to hear it. But that pussy of yours is going to do without for awhile. Everything my way, my lady. That's just one lesson you'll learn about wearing my collar."

He employed the fireman's carry, her head hanging down, hands trying to find purchase on the rise of his ass, the rugged landscape of his muscular back, as he took her out of his office and workout room to the futon. Settling down in the center, he turned her so she was draped over his legs, hips arched over them and knees sunk into the couch cushion. He gripped her face, turning it toward him. Taking the quill from between her lips, he set it beside him.

"You need a good spanking, Lady Kaela," he said shortly. "Being in my mind when I told you no. Calling me Master before I gave you permission. You may heal fast, but pain is pain, and I could leave you black and blue with my hand alone. I think I should wear your ass out good. Shouldn't I?" His tone sharpened, making her start.

"Yes." She was whispering.

"I didn't hear that."

"Yes sir."

"Better." He wrapped his hand in her hair again. "Breath control's off the table with a vampire, more's the pity. I think you'd like that, my lady, me controlling whether or not you get to breathe. But you'll get some of the effects of it like this." He pushed her face down into the seat cushion and jerked the ties to the swimsuit bottoms, pulling them off before he began rubbing firm circles over her buttocks, a sensation that had the nerve endings begging, all her erogenous zones tingling.

"You disobeyed me partly because you're still floating in that post-subspace, where there's more intimacy. I don't mind that. Even like it. But you recouped your energy more quickly than a human sub, so now you're disobeying me because I'm giving you too much room to think. So get ready to lose control of your mind. And anything else I want to take from you."

Jared had spanked her a couple times. The first time had been an accident. She'd dropped hay in his hair and he'd threatened to spank her. She'd teased him by flipping her skirt at him as if she'd lift it.

He'd driven the breath out of her, catching her up against the loft ladder and yanking the skirt up himself. She thought he was going to take her there, tear through her thin drawers. As a result she'd been instantly, gushingly wet. Eventually he'd done just that, but first, he'd drawn back his hand and…

*Thwap!*

She shuddered. She didn't want to think about all the things that could go wrong about this once she left the island, things that felt like subdrop multiplied by a hundred suicidal thoughts. She wanted Garron to help her stop thinking.

She got her wish.

He leaned over her, hooking the coffee table drawer with a foot, and withdrew something. When she started to turn her head in that direction, he pushed her face back down into the cushion. "Not your job to see what I'm doing, my lady." He tapped one thigh. "Spread these for me. Shoulder length apart. Put your arms behind your back, wrists side by side."

The position increased the pressure of her face in the cushion, made her wetter, and she moaned as he indulged himself, sliding two fingers inside to scissor and play. He unhooked the back of the swimsuit top, untied the neck, pulled it from beneath her so she was naked except for his choker.

"You make a man want to fuck you to death, my lady." Withdrawing his hand, he clasped both of her wrists and picked up what he'd taken out of the coffee table drawer.

She realized what it was as soon as he began threading her arms into it. A corset sleeve, meant to lace a sub's arms together behind her back, going from wrists to upper arms, as tight as could be tolerated. She'd seen modifications to them used at vampire events and vividly imagined one on herself. The strain on the shoulders, the way her breasts would thrust out, the tightness of the hold.

As the sleek, tough fabric molded to her limbs, her breath caught. She didn't breathe at all as he drew the lacings taut, increasing that sensation.

"Yeah, there you are. You like being restrained, my lady. It turns you on ten different ways and puts your mind back where I want it. Keep floating."

Which was exactly how it felt. The ties holding her to rational thought were cut like balloons, letting her drift and spin, even as her body throbbed, begged for even more. Anything he wanted to do to her.

He was pulling her shoulders back in increments until he had her upper body off the couch. He moved a cushion under it to hold her, indulging his desire to fondle the breasts that were now thrust out. She gasped at the tweak on her nipples before he placed another bigger cushion under her chin and pressed her face back into it, putting less strain on her neck.

Her shoulders ached from how far he pulled them back, locking her in the arched position. But he knew she craved greater levels of discomfort than a human sub. It pushed her deeper into that place in her mind. The iron bar of his cock against her belly said he fucking loved being able to push past those boundaries, indulge desires he'd never been able to pursue this far before.

With every restraint he added, her mind…went away. She had little licks of panic over it, but they were distant, intriguing reactions, not able to organize themselves into a full revolt as before. Her legs were spread, her pussy so wet she was sure it was dripping against his bare thigh. She loved that idea.

Now he cupped her jaw, lifting her face out of the cushion to tease the broad ivory feather of the quill over her lips. It made her want to lift her chin even higher, especially as he stroked it down her throat, over a breast. He was mastering her in his home. Like she was one of his possessions in truth.

"Damn straight about that. You're don't talk unless I command you to. Tell me you understand."

"I do." God, she wanted to call him Master now, but he hadn't offered it again, the chance lost, and she was afraid to ask. Afraid of what it meant. Afraid she'd beg. He'd said she couldn't talk anyway, a convenient excuse.

He moved her off his lap, laid her down on her side on the coffee table. Kaela licked suddenly dry lips as he lifted the quill. Opening his hand, he punctured the heel with the sharp end, efficient and deep, the welling of blood immediate. He waited as the blood formed a small pool in the cup of his hand. While he did that, he watched her, how riveted she became by that ruby bright flow.

He dipped the tip of the quill in it and leaned forward. "Eyes on the wall behind me, baby. You don't get to see what I'm writing until I say so."

Reluctantly, she obeyed. Her skin shuddered as she felt the press of the sharp tip and he began to write. It was scratchy, sharp, ticklish by turns, depending on where he was writing. Over the curve of a breast, around her navel, on her hip. When the blood clotted on his hand, he stripped off his T-shirt and punctured himself again. In the corner of her eye, she could see where. His pectoral, his biceps, his other palm…his throat. Except for his palms, he dipped the quill directly into the wound to ink the tip. Her nostrils flared, saliva gathering in her mouth as thin crimson rivulets of blood slid down his neck, over the curve of his biceps, down his pectoral, along the ridges of his abdomen.

And yet he kept writing. On her thighs next, then he turned her onto her stomach to make swirling, sharp scrapes down her back, over her ass. He cupped her chin, giving her support since the corset sleeve kept her arched up. She dipped her head enough to taste the blood on his palm and he gave her a sharp poke with the quill, an unspoken reprimand that had her pressing her lips tight together. She savored the small taste she'd stolen.

The lower curve of her breasts pressed into the ridges of the bamboo coffee table, a provocative friction. He leaned over her, his knees pressed against her shoulder and hip. He shifted his hold to her sternum, spreading out his hand there to give her additional support.

"Spread your legs."

When he wrote on her inner thigh, the feather curling over to tickle the seam of her ass, the back of the opposite thigh, she was whimpering, pleading without words, since he'd told her she couldn't speak.

At last he put her back on her hip and shoulder, facing him. He touched the bloody quill tip to her lips, her tongue, letting her have another taste of him.

"You can look now. See how beautiful you are to your Master, inside and out. I'm writing the words I think of when I look at you, my lady." The quill dropped, began to trace the word he'd written on one breast. "Strength." Down to her hip bone, her lower back. "Laughter. Tears."

His dark eyes were fire, capable of making her shake inside, everything susceptible to him. Even without giving him the third mark, she didn't think she had any shields that could resist his invasion as deep inside her as he wanted to go.

His gaze flickered, but he went back to tracing the words. "Rage. Grace. Breasts. Cunt. Ass. Legs." A smile touched his lips. "Because I can't help but think about those things, too. Being a man and all."

She realized she'd obeyed him so literally she hadn't even allowed herself to think in full thoughts, because that was a kind of talking. But she really wanted to know what the looping scrawl on her back had been. He'd written along either side of her bound arms.

Scooping her off the table, he settled back onto the futon with her on his lap, on her stomach. "Surrender, on this side. On this other, my name. In between…" Putting his fingertips on the narrow opening between her shoulder blades, he bent and put his mouth on it. "Mine."

Tears stung her eyes, unexpected, and she was suddenly short of breath, seeking air, forgetting she didn't really need it. That happened sometime when a made vampire panicked, as if muscle memory kicked in from their human days. She'd overcome it decades ago, because thinking she was hyperventilating during a fight could be fatal. But she was safe with him, and he'd overwhelmed her.

She'd told him she couldn't be marked, that she healed too quickly, and he'd adapted, marked her in a way that had to be washed off.

"Dangerous. Vulnerable. Just. Uncertain. Need. Incomparable. Irresistible." He etched those words as well. Then he removed the corset sleeve, taking his time so she felt the gradual easing of her shoulders, the caress of his hands as he stripped the tube off to free her arms. He traced the impressions the lacings had left, passed his strong hands over her shoulders kneading the strained muscles as he bid her to lay limp over his lap, her face down in the cushion again. It was ecstasy, the way she could be simultaneously so aroused and so tranquil under his command when her mind was captured by everything he was doing.

At last he turned her over, cradling her in his arms. His rigid cock pressed against her hip through his swimsuit.

She was covered in tiny crimson marks, his blood. The rivulets of it marked his chest, his arm, his abdomen. She wanted to taste him everywhere.

"Everything." That was what he'd written on the inside of her thigh. As his fingers settled there, he looked up at her, met her eyes. "You're the universe on the head of a pin, my lady, and it's in every line of your body, every look you give me. You're shaking so hard, so pale…"

Easing her to the ground between his knees, he stood over her to remove his swimsuit before he sat down, picked up the quill again. He punctured his inner thigh, a small notch where the blood welled quickly. Gathering it up on his fingers, he smeared it over his cock, began to stroke. She pressed toward his jutting member, but he closed a hand on her shoulder.

"Not yet. I'll tell you what you get to suck and when. Got it?"

"Yes…"

"Yes, what?"

A little breathy sigh of relief escaped her, and she saw his eyes get even more intent. "Yes, Master."

"Close your eyes."

She obeyed, lips parting. He must have levered his cock downward, because he rubbed it over the tops of her breasts as her chin quivered with the effort to keep it lifted despite the aroma of blood, of the pre-come gathered on the slit.

"I liked holding your breasts together and fucking them. Sometime, I'll do that until I spew. But for now, you drink."

He directed her to that puncture in his thigh, put her mouth over it. "That one puncture won't be enough. Use your fangs, my lady."

She really was more depleted than she'd realized by the session in his dungeon room and this. Stress could deplete calories for humans; she hadn't realized the same was true for vampires. In her odd floating state she found herself licking and savoring the taste of him, moving her mouth slowly on him as he stroked her head with that one hand. But her ears and the movements of his body told her he was stroking himself as well, his knuckles brushing her ear and cheekbone every once in a while as he masturbated while watching her feed.

She never wanted these ten days to end. Maybe she could pretend they never would, that she could just stay here in his apartment, be his always…

"Put your mouth on me now," he said roughly. "Take me as far back as you can."

§

Maybe vampires had better control of their gag reflexes. He

wasn't sure, but after she clotted the wound made in his thigh with only a couple quick kitten licks, apparently a perk of vampire saliva glands, she turned her head to the task he'd ordered and damn well pretty much took all of him. The little scrape of her fangs as his broad head broached that hot mouth sent a ripple of visceral pleasure through him.

She sucked him in, her tongue an agile gift, stroking and teasing, flicking and swirling. All while those succulent lips slid up and down his shaft, her hand circling his base to grip, the other cupping his balls, stroking. He kept her hair in his fist, loving the thick, shining weight of it, the way she gasped when he yanked her down on him harder, making her lose her balance so she had to grab hold of his thighs again.

*I'm the one in control here, my lady. You're servicing me, and I want you to push yourself. Take me deeper, suck harder. This isn't a beauty contest. It's about sucking off your Master, because he wants to come in your mouth, watch you struggle to swallow him down.*

She gave a half hiss against him, redoubled her efforts, and he felt the shift in energy to where he'd wanted her. She needed to be pushed and tested. Not too soft and easy. He'd given them both that a moment ago, but his instincts told him not to draw that out too long.

"Hands behind your back," he ordered. "You do this only with your mouth."

She didn't like that, wanting to touch him, but she complied. His balls were drawing up, his body rocking into her, cock thrusting into her mouth. He used the hold on her hair to give him leverage. Stress tears rolled down her cheeks and now she was fighting her gag reflex. When her fangs scraped him a little more enthusiastically, he rolled with it, pushing farther into her mouth but moving his thumbs down to hold her mouth open wider, straining her jaw.

"You bite me, I'll extract those fucking fangs with pliers."

He'd already learned that savage side of her responded to the threats, probably because he could call forth his own savage side that would genuinely mean it…in words. In truth, he'd murder anyone who caused her true fear or pain.

Her tongue kept working over him, and his cock convulsed. He pushed her down on him and held her tight there, her nose and chin buried in his pubis and testicles, his cock at the back of her throat. As he jetted, she tried to submit to that iron hold, not fight it. As for him, he had all he could do not to black out, the climax was so violent. He spewed come into her mouth three, four, five long streams, hips working, rocking against her face as she gasped, tried to keep up.

When he finally let her come up for air, he tipped up her face. Thanks to how insistent he'd been, there was no way she could have stayed pretty by girl standards. She tried to hide it from him, but he made a warning noise. "I'm the one who messed you up, my lady. It's my pleasure to look at you with tears staining your cheeks, your mouth smeared with my come and your saliva, your cheeks flushed and lips swollen, eyes bright. You look fucking beautiful to me."

His voice softened as she swayed. "Hold onto my knees." He molded her hands over them, made sure she'd stay upright as he stretched out over her to retrieve his T-shirt from the edge of the futon. He used it to wipe her mouth, nose and eyes, then covered her lips with his, scenting his climax on her sweet mouth. She kissed him back with fervor, conveying her own arousal. She was revved up, spinning, so worked up that when he put his hand down between her legs, her clit was as swollen and wet as he could want it. He thought about suckling that ripe fruit into a full explosion of juices into his mouth, but he had other ideas. Hell, he couldn't choose between all the things he wanted to do to her.

Catching the choker, he tugged on it, toppling her to her hip so she'd lean against the futon for support. He rose to don his swimsuit again, then pushed the coffee table out of the way. "Forehead down." She looked puzzled for one second too long, and so he pushed her there with his hand on the back of her neck, bringing her ass up in the air with a hand underneath her abdomen. He shifted her so she was centered in front of the futon, facing away from it, and gave her buttocks about ten swats, finishing up with a bruising knead of her backside, pinching her with hard fingers until she was quivering and trying her best not to flinch. Sitting back down on the futon, he bent forward and laid his lips on one shuddering cheek.

"Hold your weight on your hands, my lady." It was the only warning he gave her before he pulled her legs up, bracing her knees on his shoulders and leaving her face down over the edge of the futon between his knees, her head hanging down to the floor. As she scrambled to use that vampire flexibility to balance herself, he did what he could to destroy that balance. He lifted her lower body to his mouth and drank his fill of that full, juicy clit.

She came, instantly, violently, beautifully. He had to band his arms around her waist, as she clung to his legs, her upper torso twisting as she shrieked her pleasure. Her clit spasmed under his lips, her climax short, sweet spurts on his lashing tongue. He shifted his grip, grasped her bottom in both hands, kneading those sensitive globes as they writhed under his touch. He held her fast, made her feel every overwhelming sensation.

*Oh…too much. Too much…* "Stop…no…don't stop…oh God."

At a certain point, it was no longer a flood through her mind but was starting to reach her lips. She'd had to keep all those words locked in her mind during her masturbation fantasies, afraid her servant would overhear and guess what she truly was, what she truly needed.

*You don't need to do that here, my lady. I want to hear you. I know what you are and what you need.*

Amid the cries of pleasure, he heard the broken words behind them, spinning around in her mind like constellations around the sun.

*Want to give him everything…feeling…never thought…have again…*

The flash of her heart, wide open, so vulnerable, almost stopped his own heart. The climax blew through her like a tornado, leaving sensual devastation in its wake. She collapsed to the floor. Or she would have, except he held her, eased her down, put himself around her. She was in a fetal curl on her side, as small as she could make herself inside the span of his body arched over her. He pressed his lips to her temple, her mouth and cheek bone, her throat, then buried his face there as he coiled his arms around her head, held her tight, rocked her.

*It's okay, my lady. I'm here. I'm here.*

The way she kept catapulting into subspace so hard and deep, as if he were her oasis after decades in a desert, was the most amazing gift a sub had ever given him. He'd always known a sub's trust to do that was a gift, but this was beyond that. It felt the way a miracle should.

She'd zoned down deep, so deep he kept rocking her for quite a while, until hard trembling turned to little jerks, twitches, the occasional vibration. Lifting her from the floor, he kept her cradled in his arms, and carried her to the workout room. He had a massage table here as well, since twice a month the island masseuse came and did therapy on him, ongoing maintenance for those old injuries. He preferred to do that in the privacy of his home, rather than the more public area of the island's employee health clinic.

Hooking the table with a foot, he brought it out from the wall enough that he could move around it, lay her down. He eased her to a position on her stomach, put her hands down by her sides, spread out her ankles and used the slits in the frame of the table to bind both wrists and ankles, hold her there, just as he'd done at the club.

She could easily break the Velcro, but she needed the reassurance of restraint after that wild flight. Her fangs weren't even fully retracted. As he bent to kiss her mouth, he teased them with his tongue. She made another of those incoherent sounds, and the points receded. He didn't want her inadvertently puncturing those pretty, full lips.

She'd earned every bit of aftercare he could give her. He started to ground her once again with a full body massage, because it was clear she enjoyed aftercare. She needed to feel her Master's hands on her, owning her.

It was one of the reasons he looked forward to doing it. A reminder that the session might be over, but her ass still belonged to him. As well as everything attached to it. He thought of what he'd written on her, still saw the evidence in partial scrawls and loops, though some of it had rubbed off as a result of their movements. Though he regretted having to wash it all off, he couldn't take her to the lagoon pool that way. Moving to the open doorway of the bathroom, he kept a close eye on her as he ran a basin of warm water.

Coming back to her side, he wiped her down all over, every nook and crevice. When he put heated compresses on her anus and cunt, she made a noise of pleasure and languorous arousal both.

*I don't really need aftercare, you know. Vampires heal from everything, even strained muscles.*

Even the words in her mind were slurred, but that she'd attempted communication said her disoriented mind was trying to grasp some sort of control. He wasn't going to put up with that.

"Every sub needs aftercare, my lady. Now shut up, or I'll gag you."

He said it in a mild, gentle tone. She subsided with only a token sound of complaint, but enough to deserve a short pinch. After that, though, he massaged her neck, worked his way over her shoulders, her back, loosening the tense muscles. He'd coated his hands with a lotion that smelled like sandalwood spice, and she responded to that as well, inhaling it on a sigh. Every so often, she'd quiver under his touch, another reaction he savored. Hell, he savored everything she did, including the flow of her thoughts, so easy and uninhibited.

He was caring for her efficiently, confidently. Like he'd touch something, someone who belonged to him. She hadn't felt like she belonged to anyone since Jared, but she remembered the way that felt.

*It's a fantasy. A fantasy that will have to last a lifetime.*

The first part made him frown, then she spoke. Her words were still slow, dreamy, making him smile.

"Why did you say your eyes used to be blue?"

"The explosion affected the pigment in my eyes."

"I saw the blue for a moment, at the docks. Like cobalt. Beautiful. You're not very…tan." Her eyes were half shut. "Not quite as pale…as a vampire, though."

"Yeah, not quite that pale. Sunburn on the scars makes my doctor bitch. She and her latex glove scare me. So I stay out of the direct sun."

Her lips curved. "Every man's fear."

"Not fear," he said stoutly. "I'm just averse to having a doctor's hand up my ass."

"You don't seem to worry about how I feel about it."

"Master's prerogative." He leaned over her, taking a firm grip of one buttock. "I put my hands wherever I want and make my sub love it."

She closed her eyes all the way, but that smile stayed. "Too full of yourself as is. Won't…confirm that."

"Ah, my lady. Your mind already did."

"Cheater."

"Again, Master's prerogative. Any means, fair or foul, to make you surrender your soul."

"You and Lucifer."

"We text regularly."

The banter said she was returning to earth, but he liked how she stayed relaxed, inside and out. He retrieved the bikini from the living room, satisfied to find the bottoms had been sufficiently soaked by her arousal before he'd removed it. That was the way he wanted them to stay. He lifted her up like a rag doll, all that lovely hair streaming over his arm, and made her hold onto him as he fixed the swimsuit back in place.

"Fran dresses me sometimes. For formal events."

"It's been so long since I've been to a formal event, my lady, you might be called upon to dress your Master if we go somewhere like that."

The slip had cost him some ground. Her expression transformed to that wary, puzzled look. "I don't think we'll have to worry about that here."

"No. Probably not." That much was true. While the 24/7 area had a dress code, it certainly wasn't black tie. He tied the gauzy wrap around her hips again, made her slide her feet back into the pretty rhinestone sandals. "If you want to take advantage of the bathroom, go ahead. I'm going to call Vardalos, check in with him about a couple things. Then let's go for a swim."

"Yes, Master." She said it without thinking, caught herself, looked at him sidelong to make sure it was okay. Not because she regretted saying it.

Christ, if he was going to get an erection every time the word left her mouth, he'd need medical help before long. When he gave her a pinch, he caught the tiny smug smile on her lips. She'd probably dipped into his mind to be sure she hadn't screwed up. Only the spontaneous response that crossed her mind saved her from punishment.

*It makes me just as aroused to say it. Master.*

## Chapter Eight

Kaela sat on the lagoon's edge, her pale body bathed in moonlight as she gazed around her. There were other swimmers, but unlike the busy pool where they'd met the obnoxious male, there was enough room to have privacy. Particularly since the design of the pool incorporated voluptuous curves, overhanging vegetation and Grecian pillars placed within its depths. The result was a variety of shadowed alcoves, and the few other bathers were like ghosts whose sensual utterances drifted down on the wind. Sometimes there were hushed gasps, and those silhouettes she detected seemed like one shape, undulating as they came together in the water, letting their desires and the surroundings take them over.

Her vampire senses let her hear, see and scent clearly what they were doing. Since her mind was open to him, Garron could enjoy the same. She liked giving him that. In her brief glimpses into his mind, she'd seen just how hard he had to work to see and hear, even with the help of the auras. He leaned against the pool wall next to her, his hand gliding up and down her calf, playing with her foot beneath the water. Her hand rested on his shoulder, flexing as she responded to the stimulation. After the earlier intensity between them, everything was like a lovely, slow moving dream. She never wanted the sun to rise again.

"Take off your top," he ordered, low.

She didn't even hesitate, and she felt his approval, the only light and warmth she needed. As she untied the top, pulled it free, he turned, putting his hands on either knee to spread her wider, move himself between her legs. His palms slid up her thighs, thumbs pressing into the crease between thigh and sex before curving behind her, down into the swimsuit bottoms.

She wished he hadn't had to wash the words off her body. If a vampire's flesh was painted with her blood, and then a severe enough wound was made through the thin coating of that blood, the wound could become a permanent scar, overriding a vampire's fast healing ability. She wanted him to mark her like that somehow before she left. She thought of him carving *Mine* into her back with her blood, making it permanent. The necklace wasn't enough. Nothing would be enough. She didn't care about the risk to herself.

"Ssshh, my lady." He nuzzled her breasts. "No thinking. Just focus on your Master and what he'll demand of you."

She wasn't thinking clearly, but she didn't have to do so. Her fingers flexed on his powerful shoulders, slid over them to the back of his thick neck as he captured one nipple in his mouth, started a leisurely suckle. He caressed the seam of her ass, tightened his hold. He took her into the water with him, folding her legs high on his waist so he could keep her where he could tease, lick and suck on her breasts according to his own pace.

She made a warm hum in her throat, folded her arms over his head, held him to her as he moved. At length, he drew back and merely held her, waltzing through the water, making circles and glides while she arched back to wet her hair. As he adjusted his hands higher to give her support, she felt his gaze all over her.

*May I see what you're thinking and seeing, Master?*

*Progress. You finally asked permission. Yes.*

He was watching her hair wave beneath the water like a mermaid's, just like he'd said he wanted to see it. When he brought her back up, she folded her arms around him again, her breasts brought to his hungry mouth once more. She shuddered, held him tighter while he pleasured them both. As he did, he kept slowly turning them in the water.

*The only kind of dancing I do, my lady.*

*It makes it worth it to be in the water.* But she was okay with this, especially since it wasn't over her head. As she'd told him, most vampires didn't enjoy the weighted-down feeling.

He moved from her breasts to her throat, nuzzling, catching the choker briefly in his teeth before letting it go. "You had to take quite a few links out of this," she observed, lifting her hand to toy with it. It amazed her, how much she loved wearing it. "Were you expecting a big woman to be your permanent sub?"

*I love seeing it on you, my lady.* He lifted a shoulder. "When I'm choosing for myself instead of for the job, that's usually my preference. I'm a bigger than average guy. Sometimes the slim little things make me feel the way I do around Chihuahuas. I'm certain I'm going to break a limb like a toothpick. A girl with meat on sturdy bones is a pleasure to top. I like smacking a wide, round ass. The breasts are total bounty."

"So if it wasn't for my strength, you might have passed me over as too skinny."

"Well, you've got nice-sized breasts for your frame. I'd still have given you a second look. Maybe." He grinned when she pinched his shoulder. Catching her wrist, he linked their fingers. "My lady, the only man who'd look at you and see something breakable would have to be blind. I'm mostly blind and I still saw all it, humming below the skin. The asshole at the pool sure saw it. I'm surprised he didn't piss himself. Nice to know I can tell anyone who threatens me that my sub can totally kick their ass."

She sniffed. "You look more than capable of fighting your own battles."

"More progress. I think I explained that to you, didn't I?"

She rolled her eyes. "I think there's another reason you like a strong woman. You like pushing a woman physically."

"I do. Maybe it comes from sparring in the military. There's a rush to it, taking down an opponent but knowing it's not real, though it's done for real reasons. Touch of danger, competitive spirit, and a test of your reflexes and strength, all in one."

"You knew what I was from the first, but when we fought, I didn't sense any fear in you."

He kissed the juncture of her shoulder and slim throat. "A soldier gets past that. It's just a matter of getting the upper hand, and hoping like hell you'll figure it out before the other guy does."

She sobered, touching his face. "I could have killed you."

"After almost two hundred years, I figured you had some self-restraint. You know how to get pissed without taking a life. Maiming, crippling, those are your middle grounds."

As they drifted through the water, he kept them away from the other couples, eventually bringing them to a fixed point beneath the overhanging limbs of some kind of willowy fern with fragrant white flowers on it. Though they were shut tight for the night, the fragrance still permeated the air around them.

"You haven't seemed surprised that I'm an overlord." She curved her leg more securely over his hip, liking the way their bodies were locked together, so comfortably, yet with that low hum of sexual promise.

"There's no surprise in finding a sub like you in a leadership position. You're an aggressive overachiever. Service submissive so strong it's like a super power. I know you have a cape and tights somewhere."

He tugged her hair back, made her look up and notice the ceiling of flowers over her head. She reached up, enchanted with the burst of additional fragrance that a mere touch unleashed around them.

"Then there's the vampire thing," he continued. "You're a predator, my lady. You don't stop being a vampire just because you also are a submissive. It's probably why you've made it work as long as you have, but it's the root of the conflict, too. Trying to reconcile being a strong predator with your submission. You're a hell of an overlord because the submissive side of you works with people. You know how to figure out what people want, how to help them figure it out for themselves. But when push comes to shove, if you have to unsheathe your claws, throw down with another vampire to make things work out, you'll do that too. But that part's tough for you. I expect you get some type of physical reaction to those situations afterward. Panic attacks?"

At her bemused assent, he made a noncommittal grunt. "So you're kind of like David Banner and The Hulk."

"Or Jekyll and Hyde."

"A much prettier version."

That coaxed a smile from her. "It surprised me, that I could do it," she admitted. "But I truly think Lady Lyssa is responsible. Her words--serve me--let me serve as a Dominant, rather than pretending to be one, which is what I've done most my life. Long ago I started telling myself bedtime stories, fantasies to help me cope, knowing when I woke I'd have to be what a vampire is expected to be again. It's why I never let my servant sleep with me in that hour before dawn, though I know that hurts Fran, the lack of intimacy."

He cupped her face. "That's the hardest thing about all of it, isn't it? Fran."

She put her hand over his large one, her fingertips sliding into the spaces between his. "Yes."

As hard as it was to maintain appearances, even knowing her life depended on it, her treatment of Fran distressed and drained her more than anything else. It was right in her face, underscoring her situation. Having someone in her household so obviously devoted to her needs, wanting exactly what Kaela herself wanted, and having to hold it out of Fran's reach, knowing how it felt to have that part of herself denied, thwarted, put cracks in Kaela's heart. So many times when she'd seen that combination of hurt and puzzlement on Fran's face, she'd wanted to explain, but until a vampire third marked her, Fran's first responsibility was to the Council. Kaela would never put the woman in the position of dangerous divided loyalties.

It was why she'd kept hoping all along that Lyssa would retrieve Fran from her service for another worthy vampire. But aside from those occasional formal reminders of her willingness to let Fran go, Kaela's guilt had kept her from pushing hard for that, not wanting to let Fran think in any way she'd failed her Mistress.

Garron was in her head, so she didn't have to fill in the blanks that words couldn't cover. He kept holding her, touching her, forming a cocoon around her. She liked how strong and big he was, straightforward as that sounded.

"I guess I'm here because I couldn't handle them being bedtime stories anymore," she said softly.

She felt a little self-conscious about it, something that seemed silly in the face of everything she'd revealed to him thus far. "Lately it seems that one hour is the best part of my day, and my craving had become so strong…"

"You started to worry about how much longer you were going to be able to maintain."

Over the years, the need to release, to surrender, had become so overwhelming, she'd gone through periods where she'd tried not to give herself to those pre-dawn fantasies so often. Yet at dusk, she couldn't control her mind when she first surfaced from sleep. At dusk, all she wanted was to wake curled in a Master's arms, hear his sleepy command to spread her legs so he could put his mouth or cock there as he desired, as he locked her wrists in cuffs and made her his slave in all ways…

"Sounds like that could become my favorite bedtime story, too." Garron slid his hand up to cradle her skull. Tilting her head back, she trusted his hold as she reached up to brush her fingers over the ferns. He kissed the top of her breasts, let his tongue play between them.

"I haven't done this. Not in so long."

"What's that?" He could follow the words in her mind, like subtitles on the screen, and he thought her voice sounded like velvet. His pleasure about that hummed through her blood. God, she loved them being in one another's minds. She hadn't realized how alone she'd been all these years. Yet she knew what a miracle this was. This place, this male. It wouldn't have worked if Garron had been a different kind of Master or man.

"Simply enjoyed a lover. Being with him. Talking as if there was all the time in the world, as if time has stopped, just so we could spin this out and enjoy it forever. There's a magic feeling to it, like floating in clouds. I had it for such a short time, and it was so long ago, I shouldn't remember it, but being with you, it seems so vivid."

"I'm sorry you lost him, Kaela. And the life you planned together."

Her chin dipped, her eyes coming back to him. Her hands moved from his shoulders to his face, the scars. "I'm sorry for the losses you have suffered in your life, Garron Rand. And the pain that made you take refuge here so you could heal. Have you healed?" she asked softly.

She could tell it surprised him that she'd figured Eden was a haven for him. But it shouldn't. Intuition, being two steps ahead of everyone around her, was part of what had kept her alive. Him as well, she expected.

"Yeah," he said briefly. "You can slide into hell so fast. The trip back is a long road on foot. That's the only way out of it, though."

She nodded. "And every footprint can be marked with blood and tears, such that you feel like there's a trail following you wherever you go from there, ready to pull you back. I'm glad we both found our way."

§

That was all that needed to be said. It was more than the mind-to-mind connection that made that possible, but God above, it sure helped. Garron had never felt such a comfortable silence with a woman. It was like sitting by a river of their entangled thoughts and memories, watching them flow by as they sat on the bank, hand in hand. Or as they stood among them, as they stood together in the water now.

"So going back to that third mark thing," he said casually, "you just release some chemical inside me, like the first and second one, only I have to take some of your blood as well. Isn't that the way it works?"

Her gaze came back to him, and he saw her weighing it in her mind. Could she do something as forbidden as fully mark a servant who wouldn't be part of her life after these ten days? The thunder of need rising in her mind like primal drums, just from him bringing up the topic, told her yes. Yes, she could. Her fingers curved into claws on his chest, into the muscle.

"It's temporary, my lady. You can trust that. I asked Vardalos when I called him. He said it works on the same premise as the second mark."

He saw her flash of regret over the word "temporary", quickly quelled by her rational nature. He schooled his expression to neutrality, hoping she didn't catch any nuances from his mind that told her just how much he wanted it to be permanent, too.

"How does Theodosius know all this?"

"I've learned not to question his sources. He only lets you know what he wants you to know anyway. But he's never told me anything that's not true. He doesn't bullshit. If he's not sure of something, he'll tell you that. He was sure of this."

"Yes, you also take some of my blood," she said at last. "Before or after, it doesn't matter. Some feel taking it before helps guide the serum, like a marker."

"How would you prefer it done, my lady?"

Her eyes grew more luminous, her mouth fuller as her lips parted. He felt her thighs press harder into his hips, her fingers grip his shoulders. "Are you sure that…"

"I'm sure."

She might have been asking once more if he was sure the third mark would only be temporary, part of the island's magic. Or she might have been asking if he was sure he was okay with the binding of that third mark. Either way, the answer was the same. *Yes.*

"I would prefer my Master choose how he wants it done."

"I've been wanting to take a healthy bite out of you since you got off the plane," he said with a feral grin, and got an answering spark out of her gaze.

"That would have made the porters' mouths drop open for sure."

"They can mind their own damn business."

A good Master did his homework, prepared as much as he could for what his sub would need, and this was no exception. When Vardalos had told him how the final mark was done, Garron knew if the issue came up, he wanted to do it without stumbling, without gnawing on her like a dog on a rawhide. So though he was sure she'd laugh if she saw it in his mind, he'd used an orange, the theory of it the same as for medics who practiced injections, because it replicated human skin the best. While biting through the rind was a bitter experience, doing so now with his lady was going to be anything but.

He wrapped his hand around her hair in that way that engaged her attention instantly, his other arm banding around her waist to hold her fast. His cock was already hardening against the soft give of her pussy beneath the thin suit. "Last time I did this, I got thrown into a mirror. Good thing I'm in the water this time."

She gave him a haughty look. "The circumstances were different. For one thing you were trying to make me attack you. Plus you didn't break the skin."

He stroked his thumb along her pulsing artery. "So is my lady saying she'd welcome me being even rougher with her this time?"

Her pulse fluttered, all the answer to that he needed. He yanked her head back and struck.

He bit through her flesh to the artery, the taste of her blood telling him he'd done well. That and the extra bite of her nails, the gasp, her involuntary movement on him. While a mortal woman might have been alarmed to have someone take a healthy bite out of her carotid, a vampire took it as an erotic overture. One of those lovely moans slipped from her lips as her hips moved in invitation against his cock. Yeah. He wanted that, too. He wanted everything she had.

As he took her blood, surprised at how enticing the flavor was, he reached between them and slid two questing fingers beneath the crotch of the swimsuit. Though the water didn't provide a natural lubricant, once past the outer labia, he stroked and found her natural slickness waiting for him. She clutched down on him hard.

*That's it, my lady. Make me your Master in all ways.*

She gripped his head, telling him to pull back, that he'd taken enough. He began to lick the spot on her neck, providing the pressure needed to staunch the flow, if vampires clotted like humans did. Her hands cupped his bare skull, petted him as she rose and fell on his fingers, making him want to replace his fingers with his cock. If it had been a natural lagoon in the middle of a jungle, he would have rutted upon her on the banks until they were both covered with grass and mud, smelling of blood and earth. But he was just as good with manicured grass and a concrete lip. Whatever got him inside her sooner rather than later.

He brought his hand to her face, and she turned her mouth against the heel of his hand, then dipped lower. He saw the flash of her fangs, and she bit into his wrist, sending a swirl of fire through it, along with something else. Something that ratcheted up his desire tenfold, not that he needed any help with that when it came to her. Unlike those burning second and first marks, the pain this time was intense but irrelevant. He tore away the bottoms, pushed his own suit out of the way, and sheathed himself inside her in one brutal stroke that wrested a cry from her lips, even sealed over his flesh.

Cleansing fire, painful and yet fulfilling at once. He backed her up to the zero entry slope of the lagoon so he could lay her down, her head just above the water, and began to hammer his hips against her spread thighs. He kept her pinned there, his hands on her waist, making her take everything he was giving. She'd broken free of the hold on his wrist, the task done. He glimpsed a flash of ethereal blue on her fangs, a drop of it falling into the water and expanding like a tiny, fragile spider. That must be the third mark serum. In the real world, it would bind them together irrevocably. Here, it gave them enough of a taste of the possibilities he only wanted to demand more.

Putting a hand flat on her chest, he pushed her back as he straightened over her, keeping her in place as he worked her relentlessly. It was then that he felt it--the third mark taking hold.

That door inside her shuddered, the one under which she'd always disappeared like smoke.

*Open to me, my lady. You no longer get to be anywhere I'm not. Surrender to your Master, now and forever.*

She threw her head back, another cry breaking from her lips as a wave of near climactic pleasure seized them both. Not quite there, but so close it was too fucking good to leave the razor's edge. Framing her breasts, he leaned down, nipped and sucked, thrusting and thrusting. He wanted to fuck her to death. Wanted to fuck them both to death.

*Open to me, my lady. In all ways. Refuse me nothing.*

He dropped down over her, bracing one hand by her head, and grasped her throat. Her lashes flickered up, her lips parted, eyes wide and sparking with all the possibilities of the universe.

"Now," he growled. "Before I kick that fucking door down."

She trembled, and it opened, so suddenly it was as if he fell into her, even as he felt her step across the same threshold in himself.

To truly know one another, inside and out. Understand everything about how they had been born, how life had sculpted them, every thought and feeling that governed them. Because this woman was a mystery even to herself, for him it would be a delicious, chaotic tapestry that continually altered. He'd found his way inside a submissive's subconscious before, but it wasn't like this. He was standing fully inside Kaela's conscious and unconscious self, surrounded by the treasure that was there. Tears and anger, rage and joy, intellect and intuition, blind faith and measured calculation. Death and life, blood and healing.

There was so much detail, he closed his eyes to help him focus, even as his body continued on without any guidance, the rueful blessing and curse of being male. His cock didn't need any direction to do what was needed, what it wanted. God, yes… Balls deep inside her, fully locked together physically, was the best way to experience this complete meshing of hearts and souls.

Her own body rose and fell to his, small sounds of physical stress and pleasure coming from her lips at the force of his taking. She was so wet, he was sure he would have heard her cunt sucking on his cock with every stroke if they were on dry land. As it was, the lagoon waters lapped over his thighs and ass, along her shoulders, across her breasts, like an additional stroke by sensual hands, urging them onward.

"Christ…you feel…" There were no words. He brought her up to him in one forceful yank, wrapped his arms around her, felt hers wrap around him and they became another of the lagoon's melded silhouettes, meant to always be merged like this. Her life was cruel and unpredictable. He knew how to deal with that. What's more, so did she. He'd never experienced such strength from one person, man or woman. Yet he felt her longing to have a port where she could set down the sword and shield, not have to wield that strength every moment of every day.

He knew how to deal with that, too. That cagey bastard Vardalos. God bless his dark, mysterious soul. He'd known Garron needed a purpose as demanding and meaningful as the battlefield he'd left behind. She was it.

Ever since he'd nearly lost his life, hearing and sight, he'd had to fight his way back. During the endless torturous rehab sessions he thought might be the way to go for CIA interrogations instead of waterboarding or fingernail pulling, during the adapting to different ways of seeing and hearing, he'd tried to find himself again. Standing inside her soul, her standing inside his, was the reward. There was no need to strain to hear, to see, to feel. It was all here, within her. There was more waiting for him in the silence and the darkness of her soul than in every voice and sight in the whole wide, blessed world.

*Thank you, my lady.*

Did any vampire allow his or her servant at least one delicious breath like this, this deep inside their Master or Mistress? He doubted it. From what she'd implied, it was a one-way thing, the door to the vampire's mind forever locked, while the servant's mind could be plumbed to the soul if the vampire so desired.

Based on what he knew she needed from him, it made the thought he sent to her all the more critical.

*This is our contract, my lady, the only non-negotiable condition for me being your Master. That you never close me out of your heart, soul and mind. Not now, not ever. Everything else we figure out. Day by day, moment by moment.*

§

It was entirely possible for a woman's heart to be sliced in half. Kaela felt all he was feeling, even as she experienced her own reaction to seeing who Garron Rand was to the depths of his soul. She'd never had that pleasure with a servant, but she'd certainly been told about it. No words could describe it. He was entirely hers. She could crush that soul in an instant, destroy his mind and heart with the power she had in the third mark binding. Yet her mind kept returning to his words. *Make me your Master in all ways… It's not about physical strength…*

In the end, it would be about physical strength, though. It would be about what happened after she left this island. No matter what he thought, she couldn't take him with her. She certainly couldn't stay, no matter how addicted she was to what he could offer her. There were those who depended on her protection. The Vampire Council would come after her. Fran would be destroyed. Feeling like she'd betrayed the Council and her Mistress, the InhServ would commit suicide in her monastic cell back at Council headquarters, her shame and failure leaving her no other conceivable option. Vardalos and

Garron would die as well, for knowing too much about vampires. *Garron would die.*

Her Master made a surprised noise as she pulled him even closer, not measuring her strength, only knowing she needed to hold him as tight to her as possible with arms and legs, him buried inside her, so she could dispel the image of him dead at the hands of the Council.

No. This was what she could have. If she could have Jared back for only ten days, knowing she would lose him again after that, she'd still do it. As horrifying as that pain would be--and it would probably be ten times as much, because she'd know what it felt like ahead of time--she wouldn't even hesitate.

So she would accept this binding for the next few days, and afterward she would leave. There were things that had nothing to do with fear of the aftermath.

Did he hear all of that? He could have, and was choosing not to spoil this moment with disagreement. Or he could still be getting accustomed to the many intersecting lines of communication a mind-to-mind connection included, overt as well as passing thoughts, some directed, some random. Either way, she was glad for the focus to remain elsewhere. Suddenly, ten days felt like the shortest time ever.

Garron lifted and took them out of the lagoon, past the cobbled path around it to a patch of grass screened by ferns and more of those exotic red flowers. His eyes on hers, his mind inside hers, he removed the remainder of their clothes and put himself upon her again, slid back into her. Her legs twined over his hips, his muscular buttocks, and she reveled in his strength, his fierceness. When his lips met hers, she opened her mouth to him, making a soft plea as he explored her mouth with his tongue, with teeth. He stretched her arms out to her sides, made her leave them there, expecting her to obey his will. Every part of her, inside and out, inside him--because that was also where she was--capitulated.

He stroked inside her, watching her face, and then he pulled out, working his way down her body. His mouth teased her clit, played at her pussy until she was gasping and squirming, grabbing handfuls of grass to anchor herself. Turning her over, he pulled her up onto all fours and covered her. He slid back into her pussy, taking her over again as he pushed her to her elbows, dominating her physically, mentally. She had no need for thought or will beyond what he desired of her, and that thought alone was enough to bring her to climax, especially when she heard his voice, the thought echoed inside his mind.

"You'll come now, my lady."

She cried out despite the nearby bathers, because he just felt so damn good, stretching her, his thick cock filling her so deep. His hands closed over her breasts, cradling and gripping them hard as he reached his own climax with her, hips slamming against hers so she was driven against the ground, the heels of her hands creating furrows in the earth. He loved looking down at the slim line of her back, her buttocks quivering, her head down as she took all of him, as she gave all of herself to him, her cunt squeezing down on him as if it knew her Master's cock was the only one that was supposed to be there, now or forever.

*Best keep that in mind, my lady.*

When he finished, he was breathing hard, running on the emotions as well as the physical exertions. Which took another spike when he coiled his fingers in the heavy links of the choker around her throat and twisted a loop in it. Her whole body rippled at the constriction, her pussy giving him such a strong contraction his balls spasmed with the pleasure of it, especially as a short scream wrenched from her throat, an aftershock as strong as a mini-climax.

He rocked her through it, pushing in short strokes as she made tiny sounds of delight. Not until he'd wrung every last sensation out of both of them did he finally ease that hold and drop down over her. Bracing his palm beside hers, he coiled his arm around her waist. "Good," he murmured. "Good, my lady. You've served me well."

She shuddered, her forehead to the ground, and her hand moved over, hooked his fingers, gripped hard. He put his lips on the back of her neck, over the heavy chain, and stayed there. He breathed against her, his chest rising against her back, keeping that connection as she pulled herself back together. But she couldn't. She just kept shaking.

It seemed like every time he took her, she ended up back in this place. She didn't know what was wrong.

*Not a thing, my lady. You've just hungered for this so long, whenever the gateway opens, you go into the deep end. It's a beautiful thing to see. A total gift for your Master.*

Making another soothing noise, he pulled out of her, put on his swimsuit so quickly there was barely a breath before he was touching her again. Garron turned her over, scooped her up, and her arms went around his neck as if he was her last hope before falling off a cliff. "I've got you, my lady," he whispered, staying there on the ground, holding and rocking her.

*Please, I want to go back to the room. I want to be just with you. No one else watching.*

§

The way she held onto him when she was like this made his heart tilt. While it was pretty private here, he understood her request, even if he hadn't been so far into her head it was like having two different minds in his own, side by side. She always had to stay aware of her environment, of who might be in her space. She didn't want to hold onto any of that.

He lifted her in his arms. Vampires *were* extremely dense, her weight more than he'd expected, but he could carry her as far as she needed. He'd do it or die trying.

He'd collected the pieces of her swimsuit, putting them in the cradle of her body. This lagoon was on the fringes of the adults-only part of the island, so close to the BDSM public play area that nudity and sex play were tolerated. A guy carrying a naked female through it wouldn't cause any problems. Nevertheless, he was glad not to meet anyone along his way and he stuck to the darker, unlit paths, well familiar with them. He took the tunnel back to her suite and, once safely inside, he didn't turn on any lights. With bad vision, he was used to navigating more by shape and shadow, so that wasn't unusual, but it wasn't until he was halfway across the room that he realized he hadn't used the lights for a wholly different reason.

He could see in the dark. Not fully, but like the grey light of dawn. Yet the room was fully dark. Was it his imagination, or did his vision seem sharper?

He pushed that away. It didn't matter now. She was his full focus. This time he'd use a shower to ground and relax her. Going into the bathroom, he put her down on the commode and turned on the shower jets. Making sure of the temperature was a matter of lifting her hand, holding it cradled in his, and putting it under the spray. He felt it register, felt her desire that it be warmer, and accommodated. She was floating again, but basics like physical comforts seemed to be handled by a different department of the mind. He was bemused that he received that information not exactly in words, but in a shared satisfaction with the temperature. Fucking amazing. He could anticipate her every need not only by the instincts that had always served him well, but through the mind-to-mind connection.

Dropping his swim trunks, he got her to her feet. "Here you go, baby. I've got you."

Again her arms slid around him, held, while he moved them under the spray and closed them in. He combed his fingers through her hair, getting the chlorine off her. Despite all the excellent efforts to make the lagoon look like a real live lagoon, even down to the emerald green coloring, they still had to maintain it like a public pool to keep it clean. Particularly given what things humans did in it. Erotic, unforgettable things.

He smiled at that. She stood quietly in his arms, let herself be turned and rinsed. Every once in a while her eyes opened and she focused on him. He stayed hand in hand with her mind to be sure she wasn't thinking, wasn't chewing on any worries. That was where he wanted her, though he saw shadows he wished he could dispel. They were waiting just beyond the fringes to cover her, to turn this into something she needed to worry about. He'd hold that off as long as he could, be her umbrella against the rain. No one had ever taken care of her. Not like this.

Next on the list was drying all that long, silky red hair. He sat her down at the vanity, worked the towel over it, massaged her scalp. Picking up a brush, he began to comb it out. It was startling to see only himself in the mirror. He hadn't been sure what about vampires was fact or fiction, but the lack of reflection part was true.

Even so, he could feel her gaze as he braided her hair, finding a hair band in the well-stocked cabinet which had everything from mousse to ribbons and curling irons. He suspected a vampire's hair dried like silk, but since sleeping on wet hair didn't feel good to anyone, he did the braid.

As he fixed the band to the tail, he realized he'd been doing everything in the dark. He snapped on the shower light. Though it only cast a dim light over the bathroom, it still made him stop, momentarily frozen. He wasn't imagining it. He could see better. Not a hundred percent, but far better than before. Christ. And his hearing…he'd been listening to her inside her mind as well as to her voice, but now he realized he could hear the water dripping down the drain. He'd taken the hearing aids off for the visit to the pool and hadn't put them back in, yet he could hear the plop, plop of those drops, something he might have had trouble detecting even with the hearing aids.

Her hand covered his and he looked down at her face. The shadows were there, but a poignant smile was in her luminous eyes as well. "I'm glad I could give you that, if only for a little while."

She was worried it would affect him the way embracing her submission was affecting her. That it might be worse to do without it after having it again for such a short time.

"Who says it has to be a short time?"

Her gaze dropped and that tension returned to her shoulders. "Because that's the way it has to be, Garron."

Once again, they were back to her not wanting to talk about it, the walls of her mind closing. He tightened his hand on her shoulder, drew her attention back up to him. He shook his head. "You don't hide from me, my lady. We talked about this."

"Do you know with the third mark, a real one, I can destroy your soul, Garron?"

"No one can destroy someone's soul, my lady. You can mangle it, shred it, but in time it knits itself back together. It may not be the same, but it survives everything, just like a cockroach."

"You're so sure. But that was based on what you knew about life before. Now that you've felt me in your soul, you know what I'm telling you is true." Her gaze slid back down. "I've seen a vampire do it. Shred his servant's soul until she was writhing on the ground as if she were trapped in Hell with no way out."

"Why did he do that?"

"Because he could," she said quietly. "Someone at the dinner table, another vampire, doubted it was possible. He was proving it could be done, for their amusement and to satisfy their curiosity. It was early on, before I was an overlord. I had no power, no way to intervene."

He saw how that had damaged her, how a hundred different things over the years had chipped away at her humanity, her belief that anything was possible, that dreams were anything more than wistful fantasies that had to be put aside in favor of survival.

"There are many beautiful things about the vampire world," she said, softening that. "Amazing things. It's not all terrible. But the things that are terrible, are beyond nightmares."

"Yeah." He leaned against the vanity, his stretched leg brushing her knee. "The bomb that blew up my team, blew up part of an apartment building. Families. I remember lying there, the medic working over me, and I was so out of it, but not out of it enough. Some things are so clear, I'll never get them out of my head. My hand passed over something in the wreckage, and I picked it up. At first I thought it was a doll's arm, but a doll's arm isn't soft like that, wet. It doesn't have tiny fingernails like an infant does. It's funny...that's the last thing I saw clearly with these eyes of mine until you gave me that third mark."

As many years as she'd lived, he expected his lady had seen the carnage of war up close and personal. What he was telling her wasn't a new horror, but he saw it still had the ability to touch her. To ease it for both of them, he leaned forward, traced her cheek. "Gotta say, I prefer this view."

She linked hands with him. "Garron."

He shook his head. "It's a shitty world at times. It's also not so shitty other times. What's between you and me, that's a reciprocal arrangement, Master and sub. You have as much capacity to harm me as I do you."

She didn't say anything to that, but he was done talking about it, too. For now. He slid a hand under her hair, massaged, while she continued to play with his fingers. The links of the choker clinked as he stroked, and she tilted her head toward him, responding to the stimulation. She was staring at the waterfall, caught in the reflection of the bathroom mirror. Dawn had come while they were taking care of her shower, and the rays were sparkles across the water. Since he could see she wanted to go to it, he rose and lifted her again.

"I've never been carried so much in my life."

"Is that bad?"

She shook her head, increased her hold around his neck. When he lowered her to the seat next to the miniature grotto, she hung on so he went to one knee by her, keeping his arm around her waist, the other over her thighs, hand curved over one. She remembered, loosening her legs so if he wanted to go farther between them he had access, but he held off on that now.

Lifting his other hand, he closed it over hers to take it under the water, like he had in the shower, only this time they watched the sun warm her skin and he felt her wistfulness over that. "Magic doesn't exist everywhere," she said.

"Depends on what you call magic. I see it pretty much everywhere."

She closed her eyes. "But there are places where it can't exist."

"Only if you refuse to believe in it." He turned her hand over, watched the water glittering off her wet skin. "Most of us wear different faces to cope with our daily lives, my lady. If we can wear the honest one behind closed doors, with at least one person we can trust, it makes the other faces bearable. Even helps us enjoy them more, see the good things about those different aspects of who we are."

"Have you had someone you can trust?" She sought his gaze. "I never asked if you'd been married, or had someone before."

"A couple relationships, but I was too caught up in my military career to give them the time they deserved. It's only since I've been here that I've realized it's time…to go a different way."

She didn't want to think of other women. He detected an intriguing spurt of bloodlust at the thought, his fiery submissive. But other thoughts poured into her mind. She needed him to need her now, use her now. Make her feel like his submissive. Their conversation unfortunately had reminded her she would have to do without soon enough, making her even hungrier for everything he could demand of her now. She didn't want to sleep, even if the night's exertions and the encroaching sun were trying to pull her into sleep.

He could oblige her, since apparently even a temporary third mark made his cock spring to attention at the mere thought of sex, but he was pretty sure that wasn't what she truly needed. He wasn't going to rush a damn thing, because for him, this wasn't a ten day proposition. He took her back to the bed, though, reattaching the tether to the choker. Feeling her yearning stare, he hooked the chain to the bed post.

"Eyes down, my lady. No looking through my mind. One way only for now."

He felt a spurt of resentment at that, but he knew how to counter it. "Show me attitude and you'll sleep alone."

He rummaged through the plentiful supplies in the drawer and chose a fleece-lined cuff, another length of chain. He attached the cuff to her ankle and tethered it to the bedrail, slid himself up behind her.

"What are you doing?"

"Sleeping here, as I said." He cupped her breast, squeezed. "Making sure you stay where I put you so if I wake up in the middle of the day with a hard dick, my sub can take care of that. But go to sleep for now. I'll wake you if I need anything."

"We don't wake up at the height of sunlight," she said testily. "Not without great persuasion."

"I'll have to be persuasive. Or let you wonder what wicked things I did to you while you were out."

She let out a sigh petulant enough to make him smile. Usually he'd punish that kind of behavior, but he could feel enough things roiling inside her to know it ran deeper than bratting.

The way her eyes had glazed when he chained her had been distracting, to say the least, so he compromised. He slid his fingers between her legs, made sure she was ready for him. She was. He fitted his cock to her cunt, pressed inward until he was seated. He grunted a reproof as she squeezed down, rubbed her gorgeous ass against him.

"Cut it out," he admonished with a slap of her thigh. "We're going to lie here for a bit, just like this. I decide when it's time for us to fuck. Understand?"

She let out an erratic breath as he pinched a nipple, found it pebble hard. Shit, this was going to be as much of a punishment for him as it was a lesson for her. But he wouldn't be led around by his dick.

"Tonight we're going to go the 24/7 area. I want to show you off as mine, around other subs and Doms. Would you like that?"

"Yes. I think so." She hoped so. It was something she'd imagined, but he also caught a niggling reluctance her mind couldn't define. He felt some of the same himself, wanting to keep her all to himself. But he'd give her the full Eden experience. A throaty sound broke from her as he increased the pressure on the nipple.

"You'll see all sorts of things there, everything from public sex to Doms playing chess with the board balanced on the bare back of a sub."

"Have you seen that?"

"Yeah. They hooked him up to a fucking machine, spread his arms out wide enough they could put a sub beneath him to suck his dick while they played. It was to see how long he could manage before toppling the board. After which they both fucked and caned him as punishment."

Feeling her shiver, he dropped a kiss on her throat. "You like that, do you? Imagining yourself in his place?"

"That's what I do with Fran. When she tells me stories about her experiences as a servant, I imagine myself as her. But she doesn't have access to my mind, not the way you do. It's the first time I've been able to let myself show…why I like the stories. Will you tell me more…"

She paused. "May I call you Master?"

"Yeah. From here forward, whenever you want. And whenever I demand it." At the wave of pleasure from her mind, he increased his hold on her. "Though I'll live to regret it, I'm sure. Whenever you call me Master, I'm tempted to give you any damn thing you want. For a price."

She let out a half chuckle, groaned as he moved inside her. "I want to do everything to you I've ever done or thought about doing to a sub, you know that?" He felt her shiver again.

"I'd stay so distracted I couldn't think."

"That would be the point. I'd do a hundred things every day, big and small, physical and mental, to remind you that, no matter what you're facing, you belong to me. You have a Master who cares for you, who knows you, who needs you."

She stilled at that, swallowed under his hand when it closed over her throat, caught the chain. "Do you like wearing this?"

"Yes. So much."

"We'll figure out something like it you can wear all the time."

"Tell me other stories of what you've seen. Please?" He was scaring her, he knew. Taking her down that path she couldn't go, intruding on her fantasy of what was possible.

"We have a water tank with a platform over it. A frame is welded to the platform so you can suspend or restrain your sub multiple ways. You lower the platform into the water until it laps at her chin. Just like water guns at a carnival shooting gallery, the tank has jet hoses you can aim at the sensitive points, to stimulate or make her come that way. They work with the tank dry or filled, so if a Master wants to do it with the tank empty, make the roar of the hoses against the glass part of the experience, he can. That assault on the senses can make the sub feel even more out of control."

He saw her absorb that image, felt her muscles clench him even tighter. He took a steadying breath. He reminded himself he was trying to teach her about deprivation, the pleasures of waiting on his command, yet all he wanted to do was fuck her like he was a damn rabbit. He cleared his throat. "You can also fit her with an oxygen mask and take her beneath the water, deprive her of her hearing and sight. For extreme edge play, you take her under water without the mask, so she has to trust you to reverse the platform, bring her back up in time to breathe. Not all subs can handle that," he added.

Vardalos didn't trust guest Dominants with it either, mandating that a Club Sin staff member handle the water controls at all time. Even if the visiting Dom was calling the shots, the staff member had override power. Garron had done water platform duty plenty of nights. Protecting the guests from themselves as well as from each other was as much the job as anything else.

"There's other edge play stuff as well," he concluded. "Plenty of methods to see how much of your sub's trust you've earned.

She was feeding on his description, still milking his cock with those little involuntary contractions. He was just as bad, realizing he was pushing against her in a slow, short rhythm, keeping his cock moving forward and back in small increments inside her. She made a soft sound as he toyed with her nipple, keeping his grip over the choker on her throat to add to her passion.

As hot as they made each other, trust was the crux of it all, wasn't it? She might be an amazing supernatural creature, but trust worked the same across species. He knew what level of it he wanted from her, but he had no way of earning it unless she let him leave the island with her. A chicken and egg dilemma.

"Will you tell me more?"

"No. I want your fantasies. Tell me every wicked thing you've imagined or feared a Master doing to you. I want to know what limits I can push, break and destroy."

She quivered, but he saw it unfold in her mind and gave her throat a little squeeze. "Say it aloud, my lady."

"It's one that can never happen, but I imagine…you commanding me to my knees in front of the entire Vampire Council. Just to touch my face, but it says…I belong to you, not the other way around. When it happens, everything in me…sighs with relief." She paused. "There were lots of times over the past century I thought it would be better to come out with it like that, and die honest. True to myself. Since I became overlord, I buried that feeling. At least until I decided to come here."

The resigned way she said it gave him a spurt of fear, and he slid both arms around her, thrusting even deeper, earning a surprised gasp from her.

"If I thought for an instant you would ever try to hurt yourself, Kaela, I'd never allow you to leave."

"How would you stop me?" she said dully. "When it comes down to it, Garron, all of this is because I allow it, isn't it?"

He thought carefully about that. He'd told her to stay out of his head, but when he did allow it--or she forgot, as he expected she'd do for a while out of long habit or to protect herself--she could see how he picked up and discarded thoughts like clothes until he found the one to wear. In the meantime, she'd know everything in his wardrobe about the topic. But maybe that was okay. If she was following his mind, just like he was following hers, it was like learning a new language, where you had to weed through the different statements, questions and random interjections to find out what was truly being communicated. To learn the nuances, what was true and what was chaff.

"You're a vampire. Your life has been about what you can fight to achieve, how not to let another force you to their bidding. Dominant and submissive interactions aren't about choice and free will, are they?"

She shook her head. "It always depends on the motive of the vampire, what they want from you, what you'll let them believe they can have. It never ends."

"So your time with your human servant is your only real down time. Except you haven't even had that, because you've had to be something else. Until now." He coiled his arms tighter around her, withdrew and thrust back in, closing his eyes at how good she felt, clutching him with those slick inner muscles. "Kaela, would you say the time you spent with Jared was the best time of your life?"

*Yes.* It was there before she could stop the thought, and he made a quiet, admonishing noise.

"There's no need to censor yourself. You loved him, he loved you, and you were able to be honest and open with one another about your needs, your desires. You're in a position to know just what a fucking gift that was. He was your Master, and you would have served him however he demanded. Yet because there was love, he would never have demanded more than you were able to give. Than you were willing to give. It was a choice. Yes, you allow me to be your Master. I accept you as my submissive. There's nothing more powerful and frightening than choice. It's the field on which courage and love are tested."

"You do know I'm almost two hundred years old. Far wiser than you."

"Supposedly." He chuckled as she kicked at him with her free leg, and dropped his hand to grip her thigh, stilling her with the firm pressure there. "You are stronger than I am, Kaela. Wiser in many ways. I'm honored to have such a talented, beautiful, strong woman at my command. Begging for my cock, squirming beneath my hand when I punish her. Making her cunt slippery, feeling how she needs everything I'm doing to her, so she can let go of all of it, just to be a creature of pure feeling and energy."

He moved his fingers up to her mouth, teasing her lips, stroking the tips of her fangs, scraping the pad of one finger beneath one to test its sharpness. "I'm not going to ask how you learned to go down on a man without driving these into his tender parts."

"You didn't seem afraid of that."

"I don't fear you in any way, my lady. You're mine. Your heart is inside me."

He started to move again, slow strokes that built her up to a shimmering peak. Reaching in front of her, he found her clit, kneading it until she came once more, bringing him over that same pinnacle. They shared a quiet, intense climax, one that left them both resting on the same hazy cloud of awareness.

He stroked her hair, kissed her shoulder, her temple, her throat, adjusting his head on the pillow so his breath bathed her pulse there. He stayed inside her, his arms around her. When he could tell she'd closed her eyes, those lovely long lashes likely fanning her cheeks, he spoke again.

"Sleep. Dream good dreams of all the things your Master will demand when you wake."

It was like a vacation, the kind humans took. For a week they could be playful, whatever they wanted to be, in a new and exotic location. That was what she was telling herself as she drifted off. As well as reminding herself to live only in the moment, not think about what would come after, when she had to walk away from all of it. Yet no matter how far she went, she wanted to always feel that tether, Garron's collar on her throat. It might even make life after Eden bearable.

Garron grimaced. *Or far worse.* If she didn't agree that this could go beyond the island, he might have stripped her coping mechanisms, opened her up to self-destruction. That would be unbearable to them both.

# Chapter Nine

The 24/7 play area of the island was truly an adult playground. It had several pools, gardens, a five-star restaurant, movie theater, and endless indoor/outdoor stations like playgrounds, equipped to allow public scenes. There was even a paint ball arena. It was a resort within the Eden resort.

Garron had been with her when she woke at dusk and given her that fantasy she'd imagined for so long--what would happen if she woke in her Master's arms. He'd stretched her out, cuffed her to the bed, and taken her thoroughly, bringing her to climax. Straddling her head after, he'd put his turgid cock in her mouth, compelling her to suck him. But he wasn't done.

She was deeply thrilled and slightly terrified that the temporary third mark seemed to have an important trait that the "real" one did--endless sexual stamina for the marked servant, a necessity to keep up with the libido of a vampire Master or Mistress.

He'd unclipped the chains holding her cuffed ankles and fixed them to the headboard, her knees pushed up to her shoulders. He'd fucked her ass that way, kneeling on the bed, her hips cradled in his big hands. This time he reversed what he'd done the previous day. He gave himself no less than three orgasms before he was done, and only allowed her one at the beginning, leaving her aching, throbbing and crazy with lust. When she hissed at him in frustration, he'd flipped her on the bed and used a switch on her until pain balanced the pleasure and she'd minded her manners again.

God, the more he did to her, the more she wanted. Needless to say, he'd made sure he and his demands were her only focus. The only thing he'd allowed her to wear to the outdoor area was a thin short robe and his choker. At least until they reached the gate, where an attractive male sub with dark skin, pale blue eyes and rippling dark hair gave them admittance. He was wearing skin tight pants that left no doubt he was circumcised--and erect. Garron gave her a tap when she realized she was staring and she lowered her eyes, suppressing a smile at his grumble in her mind.

*Don't make me blindfold you, woman.*

The sub asked in a voice like honey if Garron wanted to check anything at the door. In answer, Garron removed her robe and handed it over, leaving her naked except for his choker and the leash he attached to it. As they stepped past the gate, there were enough people within range that she felt their eyes upon her. Being naked like this in front of them was more unsettling than she'd expected.

Garron put his hand on her, fingers caressing her upper buttock. "I'm the only one here that matters, my lady. Keep your focus on me."

He'd worn slacks, polished shoes and a gray silk shirt open at the throat. It made him look insanely attractive, which she hadn't expected, probably because his scarring and shaved head suggested he'd always look best in jeans, bad boy biker wear, or something in between. Yet the shirt and slacks were tailored to his powerful body, and his grace, the mantle of authority he carried, made him mesmerizing. Breathtaking, if she had breath to take.

She realized the reason for his outfit when she looked around. While all forms of fetish wear were permitted, including full nudity like hers, if a guest was dressed, it seemed they were expected to be dressed up. No jeans and T-shirts, no swimsuits outside the pool area unless it was necessary to display the submissive according to the Master or Mistress's desires. Male waiters moved around with trays of hors d'oeuvres, champagne and wine. Waitresses dressed like sexy cigarette girls carried containers of high quality sex toys, wipes and small samples of lubricants. A Dom could have everything he or she desired with a snap of the fingers. It explained why Garron wasn't carrying any supplies with him. Nothing to distract from the pleasure and fantasy of being here.

That was what she told herself, even as she found herself inexplicably moving closer to him as they passed by people who called out his name, gave him a nod and her penetrating, appraising looks. Her Master touched her often, but she let out a sigh of relief as he found a spot by the pool and sat down in a chair, putting a folded towel on the ground next to it and directing her to a kneeling position.

"Hands laced behind your head, knees apart. Eyes down."

While it sent a shot of heated arousal through her to have him order her into the posture, her lower belly was quaking about doing it in public. She complied, the air touching her bare pussy, the tips of her breasts.

"Nipple chains, Master Garron?" She saw the very shapely legs of one of those girls stop before him. "Perhaps a bullet vibrator or Ben-Wa balls?"

Garron made an approving noise. In her peripheral vision she saw him handle the balls, testing the weight and vibration. "Two sets of these. Put it on my staff account."

"Yes sir."

The woman moved on, her stilettos and seamed stockings a tempting view. Garron bent, sliding his hand between Kaela's open legs. "You hold these in, my lady. I want you to squeeze down on them like you do my cock. Every ten seconds."

He inserted them into her pussy, which of course was already wet. He pushed them up until she could hold them with her vaginal walls. Putting his hand on the back of her neck, he pushed her forward off her heels, bid her stay that way. Ripping open the lubricant the woman had given him, he worked it over the extra set of balls while she squeezed down on those other balls. She didn't have to worry about counting off ten seconds. She was aroused enough to be milking them involuntarily.

"Every ten seconds, Kaela. No cheating."

She had to really focus to do that, but that was the point. He pushed the other two balls into her rectum. This set had come with an attached string. Keeping it looped around his middle finger, he spread out the others over her buttocks, making slight movements so she felt the balls move inside her, the tug of the string, the press of his fingers on her ass. Then he took the loop end of the tether, threaded it through the string loop to the balls, secured the two together and sat her back on her heels. It made her keep her head up so the tether was a straight line down her spine, no excessive tension on the string that might pull the balls out.

A feeling of fullness, of…tingling. She knew some Ben-Wa balls were designed for more internal movement, causing vibration when the muscles contracted, and these were obviously them. She struggled not to squirm or wiggle, but she couldn't help the tiny flexes of her hips as the desire to move up and down, like she was riding her Master's cock, grew too strong to ignore. She bit back another gasp as each clench of her pussy did the same to her anal muscles, making her more aroused. Her response slid over her calf, dripping off her ankle.

"That's my lady." He stroked her spine, played with the tether, as her arms quivered in their bent position, fingers laced behind her head. "God, you make me want to fuck you all the time. You're so beautiful when you're like this. No coming until I say. You're getting close, aren't you?"

"Yes. Yes, Master."

"One of these days, I'm going to come just from you saying that one word."

She could do the same. She didn't even have to stroke herself. She simply thought "Master" and her whole body tightened with desire.

"Any Master?" He demanded

*No…I had a fantasy one for a long time. He had no face…he was a shadow.*

*How about now?*

She couldn't say it out loud, because it would shoot that not-so-delightful shard of poignant impending loss through her heart, but he wasn't in the mood to be kind. He caught the back of her neck again, squeezed. "Answer me, my lady."

"You. It's you."

"Good. Because if you know that, you know I want you to fail and come without my permission. Those switch marks healed way too quickly. I want to spank you here in front of everyone and make them wish they were me."

*Or me*, she thought, thinking of the submissives who might be watching.

He chuckled at that.

He could play her body so well, so quickly, and her desire for his domination, her eagerness to respond to it, only fueled it. But there were more people filtering into the pool area. More voices, more comments directed toward them. Garron was answering, casual conversation, and she tried not to flinch as chairs scraped, were brought closer. One of the people sitting close was a Mistress whose submissive was in the pool. At length he came to the edge, his wet arms propped on the concrete lip, only a few feet from Kaela. Even with her eyes lowered she could see he was watching Kaela, watching his Mistress, eyes flickering back and forth. He was a young Italian male, with expressive eyes and wet black hair sleek on his skull. She'd seen him get into the pool in an extremely brief white suit that would be transparent when he got out, all those olive-skinned ropy muscles a tempting contrast.

She didn't care about the beauty of the Italian male. She'd seen and known beauty plenty of times. She was more concerned about the people. When another chair scraped and she flinched again, she realized she was nervous and getting more so by the moment.

"May I touch her hair, Master Garron?" The Mistress was speaking. "It's so lovely."

She didn't know what he replied, if he said yes or no. All she knew was she'd turned her head and bared her fangs before she even thought about the wisdom of doing so. Despite the fact she was sure they'd think her red eyes were contacts, and the glimpse of fangs a surgical alteration for role playing, a sub acting as a vampire for Garron, the human woman's reaction was pure survival instinct. The hand was withdrawn quickly and the chair skipped back two paces with her still in it.

*Garron, I can't do this. I need out of here. Now.*

*Easy.* He touched the choker, slid his finger beneath it before gently removing the balls from both orifices and detaching the string from the tether. Despite her mental distress, his probing to extract the toys from her wet pussy and stimulated rim gave her an erotic shudder. Wrapping the items in a cocktail napkin, he gave them to a staff member to put in a used toy bin for cleaning and brought her to her feet with a firm hand under her elbow. "Excuse me," he said to the Mistress politely. "This is the first time my sub has been in a public environment, and we've reached our limit for today."

There were polite responses, things she didn't catch, but he was moving her away from the crowded area, onto one of those secluded paths Eden had in abundance even in the 24/7 area. Thanks to Garron's height, he was able to beckon over the foliage at one of the roving staff members. He had the man retrieve her robe. Keeping her head down as Garron put it on her, she tried not to be horrified by how she'd lost control. It had been nothing. Nothing but a woman reaching out to touch her.

*Sssh, my lady. Stop thinking so much.*

Garron tied the robe loosely at her waist, making her feel less exposed. He removed the tether as well. While a part of her protested, another part, the one that was scrambling to feel more in control, didn't stop him. He put his fingers under her chin.

"Look at me, Kaela."

His tone was neutral, and when she delved into his mind, seeking disappointment, shame, she found none. There was plenty enough of that in her own head.

He jerked her face up without warning, startling her into another hiss, a showing of teeth. She was never this out of control of her aggression. But before she could pull back, he'd slid a fingertip down her face, stilling her with the gentle gesture.

"It wasn't a request," he said mildly.

"I failed here. I can't do this part."

"You failed nothing." His eyes flashed. "Do you want to go back in there? Go back to what we were doing? You won't lie to me."

No, she wouldn't. She'd lied to everyone in the whole world for too long. If she lied to him, she'd be lost. She shook her head. "No. I don't want to go back to the pool with them."

"Why? Stop worrying about my reaction, and your unrealistic expectations, and think."

She narrowed her gaze at the reproof, but she considered the question, trying to get her feet back beneath her. Though there were still people passing, it was at a reasonable distance, leaving them in a quiet bubble. But when she looked back toward the pool area, where all those Doms and subs were grouped, the Doms socializing, the subs on display in a variety of ways, she recoiled.

Her uncomfortable vulnerability made her feel like she was at a vampire social gathering without any of her normal emotional shields in place.

Was it that simple? When she was with him, she could get lost in her head. For a while, when he'd first inserted the balls, she'd been able to hold onto that. But around others… It was too much like the public persona she'd had to put on for so long. She couldn't relax, as if the presence of others was a trigger to don her armor.

Plus she was a vampire. She didn't want to be vulnerable that way in front of…humans.

The shock of that stilled her. Garron was human, but he was different. He'd elicited a unique reaction from her from the beginning. Other humans she still saw as much weaker and even somewhat inferior, if she was being brutally honest. Her submission was a type of solitude, a gift to herself she hadn't had since she'd been a vampire, always on display or on her guard. When she was with just him, she could relax. Or rather, a vital part of her could, enough to surrender to him and be taken to sexual peaks she'd never experienced before him.

Whether it was Eden or Garron himself, it seemed the key that had unlocked this side of her was a key only he could hold. As if he was the only human she thought she could trust. She'd consider the idea absurd, except she'd reacted to him in a way she hadn't reacted to anyone in over a hundred seventy-five years.

An even less comfortable revelation was realizing that, sometime during those many years, she'd differentiated herself from humans, though she'd been one of them.

She lifted her gaze to him, found him waiting for her to get a handle on it. "Kaela, on one level, it's no different from any other submissive," he said. "You all have hard limits, even though it's difficult to accept that at first, because it's all about wanting to lose yourself in the Dom's desires. But you're different as well. You've had to keep your game face on, 24/7, for so long. Hell, even when you were a spy, you had to pretend to be something else."

She lifted a shoulder in uncertain agreement.

"Do you want me to help you approach this in a different way?"

She paused to consider that from all angles, but at last nodded. His eyes warmed upon her.

"Let's just walk around together, let you check all this out." He tugged her hair, won a half smile from her. "You're still here as my sub, I'm still your Master, but you're just watching, not participating. Nobody touches you but me. Got it?"

The biting coil of tension eased. His expression filled with amusement, not unkind. "You high-powered subs are all the same. You think if you can't leap tall buildings that you've somehow let your Master down. The truth is, when you let me know what you can't handle, you've given me exactly what I want. Your trust. Come on."

He pulled her in to kiss the top of her head. He kept holding her, rubbing his hands up and down her back, over her hips, back up to her shoulders and throat, tipping up her chin to press a lingering kiss on her lips. Warmth spread through her like the memory of sunshine, and when her lashes fluttered up at last, she saw him looking at her with a peculiar intensity.

"What was that for?" she said, low.

He touched her chin. "I don't like you being unhappy, my lady. Making you feel better makes me feel better."

"More manly?"

"Completely," he said, the crinkling around his eyes pulling at his face scar. "My testosterone just spiked, big time. Follow me."

She had a request first. He'd said to trust him, after all. "Would you…put the tether back on? I like the feeling that you're leading me."

He complied. Once the thin chain was back in place, the slack wrapped around his hand, he leaned in, kissed her cheekbone, spoke against it. "It's not a feeling, Kaela. I *am* leading you."

§

She had the opportunity to see the water tank he'd described, as well as a variety of other wonderful titillating things. She watched some more extensive violet wand displays with fascination, as well as the elaborate work suspension artists did, shaping their submissive's bodies with colorful ropes.

It helped that she saw other pairings of Doms and subs doing what they were doing, taking in the sights rather than actively playing, letting the visuals feed their own desires for private play later.

*Everyone is different, Kaela. There are Doms and subs who never take it past their own bedroom and are very happy with one another that way. Others that live in full 24/7 scenarios, complete with elaborate authority structures within their homes.* "Which is probably somewhat like the typical vampire-servant scenario."

He said that aloud, and she nodded again, her gaze fastened on a pair of men who had buried another man up to his neck in the garden and formed a frame of petals around him as if he were a plant. They were presently masturbating over his head, splashing their come on his face as if watering the "plant". It was whimsical, somewhat bizarre and ridiculous. Yet it managed to be arousing because of how involved they all were in it. She suspected the "flower' had some type of vibrator inserted in his ass or strapped to the head of his cock, because as they began to come, it was obvious from the contortions of his face that the same thing was happening to him. She wondered how reaching orgasm while fully immobilized, unable to move in any way, felt.

*I'll see if I can't figure out something that can hold my vampire completely still to test that. She responded quite passionately to being bound by rope yesterday.* Garron shot her a wicked look. "People liked the dungeon rooms of Club Sin so much, Vardalos had an underground area created out here as well. Would you like to see it?"

At her agreement, he took her into one of the gardens, to a stone structure that looked like a monolith at Stonehenge. Beneath the arch was a pair of ornate trapdoors, which were pulled back with golden ropes by two hooded, muscular males wearing the same kind of leather pants as the submissive at the entrance to the outdoor BDSM area. As the doors opened, she saw a winding stairwell descending into the ground. A whiff of exotic spices hit her nose. Garron folded her hand into his elbow and started downward, the doors closing over them once his head cleared the frame.

"Have they ever lowered it too soon and hit you?"

He squeezed her fingers. "Once. Clay did it on purpose. It was during one of our few maintenance days, when this area was closed to guests. I was going down for an equipment check. He wanted to be a smartass."

She chuckled at the image in his head of the young man who'd been on the left side, only in Garron's mind she saw him without the mask, all spiked blond hair and merry grey-blue eyes. He'd done his best to evade Garron's pursuit but had eventually been caught. Kaela got a vision of a head lock followed by a quite uneven wrestling match between Clay and Garron. All of it was tempered by her Master's deep affection for the slim young man.

"You're all family here."

"Some of us. It's like any working environment. You bond with some people faster than others. They're a part of my life now, and I'll carry good memories of them when the time comes for me to leave. I'll hope to have the chance to come back and visit them now and again."

*You bond with some people faster than others...* When he'd told her about being in the wreckage of the explosion, picking up the baby's arm, she remembered feeling a wave of relief, and one, all-encompassing point. *He understands. He knows.* He'd faced how horrible, fragile and wondrous the world could be. He knew how the threads of all those reactions often twisted together into a rope that could almost strangle the soul when overwhelmed by it all. He knew about that. She'd seen it in his mind, his eyes, his voice.

He knew everything she'd felt in the past hundred and seventy-five years, at an unconscious level that would never need to be explained. They'd simply feel it together.

He squeezed her fingers again, a meaningful gesture that she chose not to answer. She needed to stop following those thoughts in her mind to places she couldn't go. So instead she focused on the sounds drifting up the stairwell. Like Club Sin, she heard echoing moans and sharp cracks, the scent of blood, sweat, tears, heat, pain and pleasure.

Once they reached the bottom of the curving stairwell, she saw open areas marked off by dark stone pillars, the equipment positioned there indicating it was public play space. Garron directed her to a tunnel with an engraved sign over the mouth that read: "Viewing Chambers". The letters were done in a Goth-looking font with a tangle of purple and orange fairy lights around them, as well as coiled whips, an oversized Wartenburg wheel, manacles and chains. Once stepping into that tunnel, another branched off with a similar sign, only this one said "Private Rooms" and there were two staff members in front of a heavy purple and black velvet curtain screening the opening.

Garron continued along the Viewing Chamber corridor. She could see a scattering of people ahead of them, grouped in front of different spaces that looked like glass windows or cell doors, depending on the spot.

"The viewing chambers give you the chance to view sessions where the Dom is okay with it being somewhat public, but wants clear boundaries. You can choose a chamber with bars like a cell, or soundproof glass. Or normal glass, where you get some muffled noise from the rest of the club."

At the first window, she saw fire play in process. A naked man was lying on a massage table much like the one Garron had. Two women dressed in a scant amount of leather straps and chain ran lit torches over his skin in swift, smooth movements that appeared to heat the skin but didn't burn, if his ecstatic expression was any indication. The Dom, a tall, masked male in leather pants, thigh high boots and an open black shirt that revealed a smoothly muscled and tattooed chest stood to the side, watching. A clipped tag at his belt indicated he was a staff Master.

"That's Louis. He's a master at fire play. What he's doing there is pretty basic, so the session's probably just started or that's the guest's comfort level. I've seen him make a woman come just from doing fire play with her nipples."

Garron guided her onward. "Club Sin originally was just the one main area with a few private rooms, but Roan, the guy who helped with the design, learned fast that Eden needed far more options, and it just keeps expanding. This underground area was his latest design, with the help of other Sin staff and Vardalos's architects. I think they stole a few ideas from Disney and Universal for special effects and props."

"I've no doubt."

They passed a cell where the Mistress had a young woman chained fast against the bars. The girl was dressed like a nature fairy, with a crown of flowers and a gauzy dress that had been ripped to tatters, exposing her small breasts. They were pushed between the cell bars, held there by a rope harness that constricted them, made them look swollen. The Mistress was using a knotted rope to flog her ass and thighs. While she was doing that, a Master stood outside the cell, offering the watchers the chance to pinch or suckle a nipple, or slap the constricted breasts bare handed. As they passed by, the girl came, screaming out her climax. Without a change in expression, the Master stepped forward and shoved a ball gag in her mouth mid-orgasm, buckling it around her head as tears flowed. She continued to come as if his indifferent treatment increased the force of her reaction.

Kaela realized she was clutching Garron's hand at her waist. Everything said the girl was helpless to their sadism, yet she watched the way the Mistress stepped forward during the orgasm, put her body against the petite girl's back, ran her hand down her abdomen, closed a gloved hand over her pussy to gently massage as she bent, kissed her throat. Cherished, tormented, possessed.

*You're going to cut off circulation to my hand, baby.*

God, it made her knees weak when he called her that. When he touched her back, she drifted forward, past a couple more windows, an enema coupled with cock and ball torture, basic spanking, a flogging. She stopped in front of the next cell, finding the sight strangely hard to resist.

The Dom was dressed the way most people imagined vampire garb. White poet's shirt, tight black pants and Hessian boots. Bared fangs, long dark hair. He was sucking on his submissive's throat as she lay slack across his lap in a pale white nightgown showing the mauve color of her nipples. Her legs were spread and slack as he worked his hand beneath the wisp of skirt and exposed her, putting black gloved fingers inside her. Rose petals were scattered over her and on the floor. In addition to being an absorbing role play scene, it was involved performance art, the vampire and his victim probably into some type of theater as well as enjoying D/s together.

As she watched, she became aware of more people gathering at the scene. Garron moved them out of the group, putting some distance between her and them until they reached a window through which she saw a Mistress spanking her male sub with a wooden spoon while he clasped her ankles, his head to her boots.

"Does it seem laughable?" he asked, gesturing back toward the cell with the vampire.

She shook her head. "He looked dangerous, like he really would take her blood. Usually it's when they make vampires look tame, like they don't really want to hurt anyone, that they seem ridiculous to me. Because the reality is so different from that."

"I've noticed," he said gravely. His lip quirked. "I've seen flashes of it in your mind, usually when I mention my past submissives. You suppress the desire to do actual violence, but the impulse seems pretty real."

"It is. When humans say something like 'I'm going to kill my husband because he didn't take out the garbage', it's something they say, no thought or meaning to it. When a vampire thinks it…we want to do it. We crave doing it, can practically taste the blood as soon as we have the thought. It requires a great deal of effort to learn how to control the impulses, and you're never completely past it. No matter how old or experienced we get, bloodlust can be triggered. When it happens, suppressing makes it worse. We learn how to channel it."

"Hence the intense sex games with servants? Which I assume would make everything down here look tame."

A shadow crossed her face. "Yes. If you truly understood that, you wouldn't be pushing to be a part of that world."

It was the first time she'd acknowledged directly his push in that direction, but the set of her mouth said her bringing up the topic wasn't progress.

"The sex games and the politics are partial ways to deal with the bloodlust. The rest of it is just what we are. We can't afford to be killing humans without provocation or cause, or killing one another for the same reasons. There aren't enough of us to take those risks. We--"

Abruptly, Kaela broke off. Garron felt everything in her freeze and lock. Her head snapped up, gaze darting up and back down the corridor as she sharply pivoted, pulling against the tether as if it weren't there. He heard it in her head, the snarl, the shot of panic and rage together.

*No. It's not possible.*

"Kaela, what is it?" He couldn't make sense of it in her mind. When he touched her arm, she wheeled on him, her eyes shooting sparks. Showing him up close and personal that violence they'd just been discussing.

"He lied to me. Vardalos lied. There is another vampire here. Down here."

What the fuck? Garron caught from her mind that the threat was coming from the entrance to the tunnels, and it was too late to slip away unnoticed. If she'd detected the other vampire, the other vampire had detected her.

Amid the storm rising in her, he saw her spurt of relief as she recognized from his own reaction that he'd not been part of any deception against her. He wasn't as quick as she was to accuse Vardalos of malicious intent, but he admitted he was wondering what the hell his boss had been thinking. Not that Garron had intended to hit social media about his vacation with a vampire, but Theodosius had made it clear it was top secret, her life at risk if it leaked out.

One thing he knew how to do was prioritize in a crisis. At the moment, Vardalos's part in this, right or wrong, didn't top the list. His and Kaela's appearance--him an obvious Dom, her a collared vampire being led by a leash--was a much bigger issue.

Instinct had made him shy one step farther away from the bomb that had killed his team, an unconscious act that had taken him a long time to get over, a big part of him feeling like he should have died with them. Yet he'd seen enough of what her world was in her mind that he didn't question his instincts now. He had the choker and chain removed from her neck in a blink. Since there was no way that thing was going around his thick neck, he wrapped the choker around his wrist. Stripping off his shirt, he dumped it and the tether into a used toy bin. One of the girls was going by with a tray of toys, and he snagged the item he wanted off of it, sending her on with a curt snap of his hand.

With no hesitation, he strapped the spiked, two-inch wide leather band around his throat and shifted behind Kaela, despite every instinct that made him want to step in front of her.

Her eyes were darting about, her mind in turmoil, his presence forgotten as she tried to figure out how to make this work. He wasn't sure she'd even realized what he was doing. One of his other talents was getting a sub to slide into a different headspace, so using that skill now, he put firm hands on her hips.

"You're the California overlord, appointed by the Vampire Council. You're in charge and you'll kick the ass of anyone who thinks otherwise."

He said it as well as thought it, and the message penetrated. She started beneath his touch, turned. When she saw the collar, he felt her kneejerk reaction, a howl of protest, but he gave her a fierce look.

*Do you think trappings make me less of a Master, my lady? Or your absence of a collar less my sub?*

Her jaw set, and he gave her a brusque nod. "Your Master is giving you an order. Pull your ass together and show me that backbone of yours. I may give you orders, but no one else in this world does unless they want their throat ripped out." *That was what I saw written all over your face, the very first moment you put your hand in mine.*

Damn it, he wasn't getting through. Not enough. Over the past few days she'd given herself fully to her submissive core, guided by him ever farther into that well, and now she was floundering, suddenly drowning and out of her element, because her reality had intruded unexpectedly. She'd trusted in the fantasy and was feeling skewered by betrayal. Her mind was torn between panic and rage. He could feel that bloodlust reaction rising. Violence was not the proper response to this, but she'd said every vampire had a trigger.

So did every sub. Sliding his arm around her waist, he pressed his face into her throat, willing her to feel all his strength surrounding her. He exhorted her to remember that first night when he'd covered her with his body while she curled beneath him. *I know it takes years to establish the kind of trust between Master and sub that we're going to have to rely on in the next few minutes. But we're inside one another, aren't we? Hell, inside our souls. Trust me, Kaela. It's the hardest and easiest thing you'll ever have to do.*

His certainty about that wasn't just because of countless sessions with other subs, the experience that brought him. Or that the markings had taken them into one another's minds and hearts, bypassing years of communication games normal couples had to struggle with. It was because once they'd touched, connected, it was a fit that clicked, a perfect fit. It wasn't an assumption of perfection. More like finding the perfect place to build a forever home, brick by brick. Everything at first new, but the kind of place where, as the years together mounted, you knew you'd be willing to go through every remodeling, every repair, every unexpected busted pipe in the winter, because it was home. The place where you sat on the back porch to watch a garden grow or the moon rise.

*At least you didn't say watch the sunset, since I couldn't do that with you.*

Hearing her response was like seeing a boxer pull himself back to his feet after a near knockout. He wanted to cheer. He changed position enough to meet her eyes with fierce resolve, showing her how proud he was to be with her, to stand behind her. "I'll sit out there so you can watch it through my eyes, so we're doing it together. The same way we're going to do this together."

§

*"Every time I see a sunset, I think of how that was your favorite time of day. No matter where I am, I'm sharing that moment with you."*

It had been in one of Jared's letters. Not his last one, which hadn't been particularly significant. Unlike in the movies where that final goodbye often contained a significant, lingering pause, a final letter contained instructions on how to winterize the barn or asked after old Mrs. Willoughby on the other side of the hill. Or told Kaela what day-to-day things were happening in his camp. The type of beans they were eating, what they were mixing with their tobacco to make it last longer.

After his death, every word of every letter became significant. She'd re-read them often, until she was captured. When she returned home, everything had been burned to the ground and reduced to ash, including those. But the words had remained engraved in her mind, the phrases and thoughts rising to bring her comfort or inspiration when needed. Like now.

Kaela turned in Garron's grasp. As he eased his hold enough to permit it, she stared up at him. In mere seconds her world was going to be destroyed by the truth or she'd embrace the lie that kept it intact. Could she trust a human with everything she was? Trust him to understand, know what to do when she honestly didn't have a clue what she wanted to do? Could she truly follow his lead when her life hung in the balance? Or--more importantly to her--*his* life?

He was a man who'd faced death, horrendous injury, who'd led men in the field, men who'd had to trust him the same way. They had, because they knew he'd bring them home safe, if it was within his power. If he could have, he would have made a deal with the Devil for his perceived shortcomings in that area. As her gaze slid over his scars, she realized why he hadn't had them minimized. Everything worth doing and having had a commensurate price.

"Lady Kaela."

She'd been wrong. It wasn't one vampire, but two that she turned and faced.

Lord Richard was Region Master for many of the southern states, the post Lady Lyssa had held before she took over the Council. Before that, he and Lady Tara had shared overlord responsibility for the Alabama territory. Tara had remained in that overlord role, but the bond between them was apparently still strong, if they were at a resort island together. While she wondered what had brought them this far afield, she realized they were likely asking themselves the same question. Unlike her, their servants were with them.

*That's a matter of opinion, my lady.* Garron's thumb caressed the valley of her spine under the thin robe.

It should have been distracting, and it was, but it was a touch she embraced, that steadied her as well. She wasn't going to analyze the why of that. Instead, she gave Garron a brief flash of information about the two vampires and the servants standing just behind them.

Seanna was a black New Orleans native whom Richard had taken out of a brothel when she was barely in her teens, decades ago. Most servants aged until they looked late twenties, early thirties, but she still looked barely twenty-one. Despite that, she had a confidence, a sultry sensuality, that belied that. She was also almost as tall as Tara's servant Liam, a handsome blond male who looked like a young Brad Pitt. He wasn't as outgoing in personality as Seanna but served his Mistress with a quiet earnestness that made him acceptable and appealing at once. Since Seanna's arm was linked with Liam's as they strolled behind their Master and Mistress, it seemed they had a good rapport.

Kaela knew them as a twosome that had no difficulties staying within the lines of vampire society and protocols, and who were keenly aware of where those lines were. Even with Seanna's more flamboyant personality there was no overstepping the bounds for either of these servants. Both knew their place and served their vampires well.

"We just arrived this afternoon. We were unaware there were any other vampires here," Tara said, giving her a courteous and warm look out of her dark, expressive eyes. They'd met at several Gatherings, and were friendly acquaintances. Kaela knew that Tara had been born and made in the Middle East, her straight dark hair and olive coloring making her a head turner, though of course all vampires were. Richard, more reserved and austere, had the looks supporting that. He'd been turned in his forties and so his chestnut hair was threaded with handsome silver strands highlighted by his piercing gray eyes. As a Region Master, he outranked Kaela, and even when he and Tara were co-overlords, Richard had always been the more dominant of the two.

"It's an unexpected pleasure." Kaela said with equal politeness and warmth. "What brings you to Eden?"

"A vacation, if you can believe it. We were sent an exclusive getaway package. We thought it was a mistake, but well…it's hard to explain why we're here. All the reasons in the world not to go but the offerings were just too irresistible. And you?"

"Almost the same story." Her mind was turning, trying to figure out the angles and whys of it. As well as wondering if Theodosius Vardalos had a will made up in the event of his tragic, sudden and painful death.

*Easy, my lady.*

"How long are you here?" she said, hoping her smile didn't come off as a snarl. Since Tara and Richard continued to look genial, she must have accomplished it. A hundred and seventy-five years of practice really did come in handy.

"For the next week. And you?"

"I leave first thing tomorrow night."

She felt a flicker of startled reaction from Garron and closed herself down to it. "But you'll find so many wonderful things to do here."

"Like him." As Tara's gaze slid past her to Garron, Kaela suppressed the strong urge to stand in front of him. Not that she could have concealed his massive bulk with her far slighter form. However, if she bared fangs, she was sure it would tear Tara's gaze from its slithering over every inch of Garron's half-naked muscular form. "Isn't Fran here with you?" the Alabama overlord asked.

"No. I gave her a vacation as well." Something trembled hard and low in Kaela's belly as Richard's eyes flickered, considering. A vampire didn't travel without her blood source unless it was for significant reasons.

With a shot of utter panic, she remembered she had third marked Garron, something other vampires could detect. But maybe because it was temporary, that wouldn't be the case. Maybe.

"I've been thinking it's time to take…a more permanent companion, but my preference is a male." Kaela amended her language, knowing their assumption would be that their vampire identities must be concealed. "This seemed like a good place to sample the possibilities without any commitment."

After a weighted pause, Richard inclined his head. "I admit I was surprised when you accepted Fran as a second mark. You've always seemed to have far more attraction to males."

"Sometimes it's less distracting to have the gender that's not your primary preference." Kaela was satisfied to see them smile in response, even as it felt like a knife stabbed her in the vitals.

The way their gazes passed over Garron said neither of them detected the marks. Another boon to the temporary marking process, but the threat to Garron's life if that had not been the case wasn't going to be overlooked. Nothing about this situation was going to be overlooked. She didn't want to pretend here. She wasn't supposed to have to do so. Vardalos, that bastard, had promised his life to her if it proved any differently. He'd find she took promises very seriously.

Garron's hand was still on her waist. His fingers covered her hip bone, a small movement that gave him a more intimate hold on her. *You're not pretending at all, my lady. Your Master is standing at your back, watching your every move. Protecting you is my primary charge, even if that charge means ordering you to do everything necessary to protect yourself. Reach behind you and fondle my cock. Rub your hips against it. Make me harder in front of them. Now.*

As Tara continued to chat about the island's amenities, Kaela slid her hand behind her, finding the space between her buttocks and Garron's pelvis not that wide at all. She slid her fingers along the front of his slacks, finding him already semi-erect. Her fingers closed over the fabric, tightening and stroking as she rotated her hips against him as ordered, feeling a frisson of arousal as the organ immediately responded.

It was impossible that she could be this tense and be getting aroused at once, but vampires were like that. Or maybe it was the delicious danger of it and she was just hysterical enough to let it happen.

As he'd correctly surmised, vampires were used to such casual carnality, so neither vampire remarked on it, though she noted Tara watching with appreciation, as well as Seanna. She remembered Seanna was a pretty aggressive submissive, one who could be a service top with little effort. She was probably imagining in vivid detail the things she might be allowed to do to Garron if the vampires wanted to see some servant play.

No. Absolutely no.

"Join us so we can try some of the facilities together, my lady," Richard said. "We were headed for one of the communal rooms to play. We'd like you and your…" He gave a half shrug. "I'm used to referring to a submissive as a...servant."

"Masters and Mistresses call their subs many things here, sir. I'd be honored for you and my lady to call me that, if it's more comfortable for you all." Garron inclined his head courteously in their direction, but his gaze flickered over Kaela's face as she turned toward him.

Tara smiled, pleased. "He doesn't look like a sub, but he's very well-trained. Almost on the same level of the ones we brought, though of course there are some limitations. Things that can be overlooked because of the many pleasures of this environment."

Kaela was all too aware of what limitations Tara was referencing. Like the ability of a third mark to endure levels of pain and deprivation that made the edge play here look like beginner's BDSM, using toy handcuffs from a party store.

They were waiting for her response. One of the things she'd learned as a spy as well as a vampire was that sticking as close to the truth as possible was the best cover. "Garron is one of the dungeon

Masters, but as a paid employee, he is available as a switch if the guest wants a stronger personality to order around."

Tara chuckled. "Being who you are, you wanted the strongest one available. Lady Kaela, you are always wonderfully unexpected. But it makes sense. If you're going to be auditioning servants, you need to go for a powerful personality. Fran has always seemed so docile for you…more your secretary and personal assistant than someone who can satisfy our more demanding needs."

She wouldn't give away how close to the truth that arrow struck. She had too much else to focus upon, like what excuse would allow them to part company. Richard was the ranking vampire. Short of a demand on her time from another even higher ranking vampire, she was stuck. No. She could say she was engaged with another matter. Even if she seemed rude, she was going to do it.

*No, my lady. We see this through.*

Richard was assuming her assent, already pointing her toward their destination, Tara moving to link arms with her. In another second she was going to dig in her heels, appearances be damned. *You have no idea what they will demand.*

*I've seen almost every demand you can imagine in these rooms, Kaela. While I'm sure their tastes are even more extreme, beyond what Eden allows, I think I can handle whatever happens. I want to see how my sub handles it. It will tell me even more about what kind of Master you need.*

This wasn't a debate of hypotheticals. He had no clue what they could demand within those boundaries. Yet his knee pressed into the back of hers, and suddenly she was walking with Tara, Garron falling in behind her.

She was not a donkey, to be led around by the nose, forced to…

*To do what, my lady? What's the real issue here? What I can handle, or what you can bear to watch me handle?*

*It's not that. Damn it…*

*Will it make you think less of me, to allow myself to be treated as a sub? It ruins your fantasy, your desires?*

She wanted to grind her teeth, but she almost flinched at the sharpness of his tone.

*Yes or no. Simple question, Kaela.*

*No. Nothing could make me think less of you.* Her hands curled into fists. Fortunately Tara didn't seem to notice.

His voice in her mind went dead calm. *Then let me handle this, my lady. If you honor me as your Master, you have only one job. To trust me.*

# Chapter Ten

"Everything any Master or Mistress could ever want," Tara observed. Their destination looked like a giant crystal cave, the pillars and walls glittering with clear jagged rocks that reflected the fire flickering in the wall sconces. Once again, Kaela wondered how Vardalos managed this underground network on an island where the water table had to be close to the surface, but she was starting not to question any remarkable thing the island produced. At this point, she feared the real world would be a greater challenge for her to accept. How could Garron ever contemplate leaving such a place? Why the hell was she having that thought?

*Because you already know my intentions, my lady, no matter how you refuse to talk about them. We have a testing ground here, don't we?*

Tara had released Kaela to lean against Richard, comment to him as they surveyed the activity in the communal area. Scenes from playful to intense were being conducted in the informal spaces created by the pillars and array of equipment. Whippings, spankings, fire play, electric play. Even some role play like in the enclosed rooms with the viewing windows, only these were being conducted in a more populated setting. She saw a Domme strutting before a trio of kneeling girls in school uniforms while the Mistress tapped her palm with a long switch.

Music with a sensual backbeat that reminded Kaela of an aroused pulse added to the ambiance. Beautiful men and women danced in cages suspended at different levels above the main floor, sometimes alone, sometimes two or three together. Along the back wall was a giant white screen, video feed showing screen close ups of different sessions happening live on the floor, interspersed with movie clips that had BDSM elements. They ranged from old black-and-white movie spankings to more current cinematic fare. The area was saturated with sexual energy, encouraging everyone to play without care or worry, adults immersing themselves in good, clean lustful pursuits. The ceiling was hung with ropes of lights and carefully placed spotlights highlighted the play areas, leaving the areas outside of them in dimly lit shadow. Provocatively dressed wait staff moved in and out of those areas, taking orders for food and drinks and offering toys and lubricants like they had on the above ground level.

Tara chuckled. "I think I could live here, Richard."

"It's remarkable," he agreed with a serious smile. "Ladies, do you think we could talk Vardalos into vacating the island and renting out the castle for our next Gathering?"

"What a delicious idea. Now, what to do first? It's like being in a great big candy store."

Tara shifted between Liam and Seanna, rubbing up against her servant like an affectionate cat as she put her hand on Seanna's shoulder, twirling one of her dark red braids. Kaela tensed as the vampire female's gaze slid back over to Garron, giving him an appraising look. As she did, she trailed her other hand down Liam's back, landing on his taut ass to take a firm hold of one buttock. Liam remained still under her touch, though Kaela had already detected his arousal, not a surprise in these surroundings. Plus, as she'd noted earlier when Garron woke her from sleep, third mark males could pretty much stay erect as long as needed, the stamina necessary to keep up with a vampire's insatiable appetites.

*So if I was your actual third mark, I'd never have to worry about ED.*

*Only if you pissed me off and I castrated you.* She wasn't in the mood to joke, but when Garron did that subtle shift again, so his hip bone was against the rise of her ass, she felt the heat of his body emanating over her.

*Don't play with fire, my lady. You'll have to be alone with me when this is all over.*

Did he not understand? Apparently her body didn't either, because the image he shot to her mind sent an erotic prickle through her vitals. The environment and her own carnal nature were only exacerbating the issue.

*Don't fight it, my lady. It's part of who you are. Study her servant the way she's studying me. She'll expect it.*

Well that wasn't a hardship. His Mistress had Liam dressed in snug jeans and nothing else. Given how compelling all servants seemed to be, he was sculpted lean muscle, no chest hair like Garron had, either because he kept it shaved or his Mistress had had it removed. Since vampires had no body hair, many seemed to prefer their servants shaved, though Kaela liked Garron's chest hair and the fine hairs on his calves and forearms.

Tara considered Garron from head to toe, covering that same

terrain. "Liam is a lovely servant, very accommodating to my needs, but he's no alpha like that one. I don't desire that in my own servant, but I admit, watching Lady Lyssa's Jacob take the Dominant role with another servant arouses me quite…intriguingly. Do you think your servant…this male…could provide us that experience? I'd like to see him take control of both Seanna and Liam."

"I think you'll be more stimulated seeing those roles reversed, my lady," Richard demurred. "I suggest tying him down and letting the two of them have their way with him. With your permission of course, Lady Kaela."

She knew that part was just a formality. Permission was automatically assumed from a lesser ranking vampire.

Tara frowned, but not because of Richard's suggestion. "I trust your judgment, my lord, but we have to remember this is a different environment. What are the rules governing your use of him, Lady Kaela?" The female overlord lowered her voice so only Kaela and Richard and the servants could hear her. "The human world can be so limiting. It's why playing in their clubs can get old so quickly. Though this one has enough variety to keep things interesting."

Richard nodded. "How far may we push him, Lady Kaela? What have you paid for?"

*An expensive resort vacation… I'm off the clock. You're mine…*

They'd given her an out. All she had to do was say no. Though paying enough money would allow them to do anything in certain dark corners of the human world, that wasn't the case here.

"With my lady's permission…" Garron stepped to her side and dropped to a knee, offering a deferential nod before tilting his head back and cocking it, giving Richard a bland look. "If it gives my lady pleasure, she can order me to do whatever she wills. I will give her whatever she needs, regardless."

Richard lifted a brow. There was so much double meaning laced in his words Kaela couldn't fault the intrigued spark in the male vampire's gaze.

"I can identify hard limits with a safe word so as to minimize disruption," Garron said. "Lady Kaela knows what the word is."

Richard glanced at Kaela. "My lady? Does he speak for your wishes?"

In so many ways she couldn't explain, though this situation didn't represent even one of them. But she had a role to play. She would encase her heart in ice and it would feel nothing. She would protect him as she protected Fran. Yet normally she could ensure her servant was given pleasure. Garron was Dominant through and through. He would get no pleasure from this.

*Don't be certain of that, my lady. This path is a twisting one, with a lot of forks. Come with me for the ride and see. There are different forms of pleasure.*

"My lady?"

She offered Richard short nod. "I agree."

"Good. He seems to have a silver tongue that belies that monstrous form."

Richard said it without any contempt, but Kaela still bristled. "Every woman has a beauty and the beast fantasy, my lord," Tara teased him. "I think he's tailor made for it. Garron, join my servants and we'll instruct you from there."

"Yes, ma'am."

He hadn't called her my lady. He wouldn't be able to get away with that at a vampire dinner, but here, where he had the latitude to do it, he took it, giving Kaela alone that honor, because when he said *my lady*, it meant something different to him, and to her.

She held onto that thought as he rose. Garron lifted her hand to his mouth, pressed his lips there. She locked her fingers over his, brought him down to her for a kiss, and not just any kiss. One full of hunger and need, and some blood-driven anger. She wasn't willing to let go of that. She expected she'd need it to get through this.

Garron's large hands gripped her hips as she bit his lip, drawing blood. She rose on her toes, licked his mouth, curling her hand around his neck. He moved his hold to her waist to keep her steady.

*You are my Master.*

*Damn right I am. Think about how I'm going to remind you of it when we're alone.*

Feeling that little internal quiver at the spark in his gaze, she gave him another nip. It would pass as the sensual response of a vampire in charge of her servant, not one who was anticipating all the ways she could serve him later. But truly, at the moment, it didn't really matter to her. She was in a fuck-all-of-them kind of mood, the usual restraint she exercised around other vampires close to snapping. This wasn't supposed to have happened.

*Hold fast, my lady. You're used to dealing with the unexpected. But this time you're not dealing with it alone.*

That thought, injected with enough force to pull her out of her irritation, was a new one. One she hadn't considered. She'd automatically locked into defense mode, into the Oh-God-something-else-I-have-to-figure-out-by-myself mindset.

*You'll have to work on that, my lady. I'll help you, even if I have to beat it into you regularly.*

She couldn't afford to lose herself in a vision of being over his lap, taking his punishment, no matter how much the resulting arousal might help her handle this situation. She'd done that for years though, hadn't she? Watching servant entertainments, imagining she was in their place, channeling the arousal to help her act the way she was expected to act.

Maybe the problem was she didn't want to have to think of it that way. She didn't want to think of him in any way other than as her Master. Or herself as anything other than his. But as usual, her ability to do that was going to be stifled. Prohibited. Shut down before she could take it as endlessly as she wanted it to go.

*Life isn't fair, my lady. We both know that. Doesn't mean we can't find our way through it.*

She felt Garron's grip on her hand, the cold metal of the choker as he slipped it off his wrist, pressed it into her hand. It was as if offering her a rosary to remind her of her faith, the covenant between them. He met her gaze one more time, a searching, penetrating look, before turning to face the challenge that lay before them both.

Seanna and Liam, directed by the thoughts of their vampires, had picked out a spot for their play. Between two nearby pillars, a spanking bench, its red leather and golden wood gleaming, was not in use. Seanna had claimed it, was already leaning against the equipment. Liam sat on it, long legs stretched out and arms crossed over his chest, the two of them looking as patient and well-synchronized as a pair of servants who'd lived together could be.

Kaela wondered if they ever had any confusion about who or what they were. Liam had shown no reaction to Tara stating her occasional preference for a servant with a more dominant side. Maybe he and Seanna accepted that they were a valued tool of their Master or Mistress, but not a vital organ, the way she would consider Garron, if he truly were her third mark servant. For his part, Garron would never accept falling short of her needs. He would surpass them and demand more of her than she could possibly imagine.

She couldn't watch this. She just couldn't. When the waiter came by, she requested a cup of wine, downed it with a quick toss. The waiter gave her a hand stamp, explaining with courteous firmness that there was a two-drink maximum for anyone actively playing.

Tara nudged her, gave her a wink and a secret smile, because vampires couldn't get drunk. "It's fun to play human again sometimes, isn't it?" she whispered, reminding Kaela she was a made vampire, like her. But not like her. No one was like her.

Seanna gestured to Garron playfully, bringing him over to the other two servants.

*Watch me, my lady. You look away, I will be very annoyed with you. Tell me if you like what they're doing, if you'd like me to do it to you.*

Richard had drawn over a table and three chairs from another area so they could more comfortably watch the scene unfold before them. Kaela took one of the chairs he gallantly pulled out for her and Tara. Since the Region Master seemed to consider what their three servants were doing prep work for the real demonstration, she was having to listen with half an ear to his casual discussion of the Council, recent policy decisions. She wished he'd shut up. In her lap, she wound the choker around her wrist, worried the clasp until it locked. She managed to pinch her flesh, but the bite of pain helped.

Despite her aversion to watching, she found herself unable to disobey Garron, her gaze glued to everything happening. Seanna ran her hands over Garron's chest, scoring him with her scarlet nails. Even if their vampires were conversing, both servants were well trained enough to know every movement was a performance. Liam and Seanna were a striking pair, drawing a crowd. But when Kaela saw other staff members drifting close, she knew those were for Garron. If Garron was as well-known as a Master as he seemed to be at Club Sin, finding out he was about to play a bottom role would be spreading like wildfire. They'd want to see how he handled that.

As Seanna continued to explore Garron's chest, tugging his chest hair in a way that made Kaela want to break every slim brown finger, Liam was adjusting the restraints on the spanking bench. Eyeing Garron's massive frame, he doubled the straps to increase their strength, causing a ripple of appreciative laughter among the staff members, as well as the audience, who were only a beat behind in catching on.

Garron's attention seemed to be entirely on Seanna, though, as if what Liam was doing was of no concern to him. When Seanna bent to get a closer look at one of the scars on his abdomen, run her lips across it, Garron's hand landed on her head, the long braids. He gave one a rough tug and her a feral grin. "Need me to draw you a map, woman? Where your mouth needs to be is about a foot south."

Seanna gave him a return smile that didn't need fangs to be dangerous. She dropped her hand, clasping his cock and balls through the slacks in a squeezing grip. A thirdmark's grip, tight enough to make him grunt. The woman he was taunting was old enough to be his grandmother. Maybe great-grandmother.

Kaela tried not to tense. *Seanna's a service sub through and through, but she can be a service top when ordered to do it.*

*Tell me something I don't know, my lady. No offense, but be quiet. I need to focus.*

She blinked at that, but she saw the way his gaze locked with Seanna's as he closed his hand on her wrist. He could have made it a wrestling match, what Kaela would have expected, pitting strength against strength, but instead he caressed the pulse in her wrist, followed it up to one of the braids brushing her forearm. Winding it around his fingers, he held it fast. While there was a light smile fixed on his face, his dark eyes never wavered.

She held that gaze for a time, but at long last, her eyes flickered. Though she didn't look away, her grip eased on his genitals.

"I expect it's going to be easier for you and Liam to have your way with me if I'm undressed," Garron said in a mild tone.

Seanna lifted a brow, but after a pause, she straightened. Putting her hands to his belt, she slid the tongue from the buckle, her long fingers taking advantage of the terrain, the prominent outline of the head of his cock near the top of the zipper. She fondled him as she lowered it, started to remove the slacks and boxers beneath, pushing them down his hips.

He'd picked up on Seanna's essential nature like a hound on a familiar scent. This was as intuitive for him as any other session, and he was sinking into his headspace, picking up every nuance.

It impressed her, helped manage her fear for him, but the down side was the ugly spurt of green through her. This was *her* Master, he was… No. He wasn't hers, was he? Just for this week. Or had been, until fucking Theodosius Vardalos had allowed Tara and Richard to come here during the same week. There was no way that was a coincidence. She just couldn't figure out his motivation.

*Just because you aren't the one handling my cock doesn't mean you aren't part of this scene, my lady. Keep your attention on me. And you* are *mine, in a way Seanna or any other sub on this whole island, in the whole world, never will be.*

That brought her startled attention back to him. His gaze met hers once more. It was a brief contact, but his look burned to her soul. He turned his attention back to Seanna.

"Don't forget the shoes," he reminded her.

Her lush lips curved. She spidered a hand on his chest, backing him up two paces and giving him a light shove that had him sitting on the spanking bench. Garron watched her lift and straddle one of his legs, putting her butt in his face with a playful taunting wiggle as she removed one dress shoe and sock. When he gave her a pinch, she tossed her braids back, shooting him a look full of erotic promise.

"You'll be at my mercy in a few minutes, big man," the black woman warned.

"I sincerely doubt that." He flicked her braids. "Little girl."

Liam chuckled at that, straightening from where he'd finished adjusting the straps. When Garron rose, he stepped out of his slacks and boxers, folding them over his arm before Seanna took them and his shoes away from him, set them aside. Tara made a pleased humming noise at the sight of Garron's glorious nudity, his semi-erect cock which left no doubt it was proportioned to the man. Kaela noticed the crowd watching had grown larger, was starting to press closer. Vardalos trained his people well, because the staff was already on it, producing velvet rope barricades with antique gold posts to cordon off the space. It allowed the three servants room to perform without interference, and the vampires' table was within that barricade, so no one would make the unfortunate mistake of blocking the view of the Master and Mistresses in charge of the scene. But even those staff members couldn't help ogling Garron. She wondered if he'd ever been completely naked like this in front of them, where they could see the powerful terrain of his body, the map of scars about which he showed no self-consciousness.

"He's lucky to be alive," Richard commented, her very thought when she'd first seen the extent of them. "A fighter and a survivor. This one bears close consideration, my lady."

Though she had her legs crossed and was leaned back in her

chair, a position of casual interest, her mind had one emphatic response. *Never.* Looking at how wondrous he was, how he was handling himself, she could never subject him to the horrors of the vampire world. He'd been through enough.

*Not your decision, my lady. And you've thought about the idea more than once since I first brought it up.*

*Didn't you say you were trying to concentrate? Should I tell you to be quiet now?*

*Only if you want to feel my belt before dawn. Trust me, I can draw blood with it, make you beg for mercy.*

She caught the glint in his gaze. Then Liam approached him from behind, set his hands to Garron's waist.

Faster than even a vampire could follow, Garron pivoted, captured the male's wrist and hand and turned them, using the other hand to twist Liam around and shove him face first onto the spanking bench. Though Liam started to struggle, he stilled almost immediately. Kaela realized Garron's hold had nothing to do with strength and everything to do with the angle. Third mark or not, if Liam resisted the hold, the wrist would break.

If it was a real fight, Kaela suspected Tara would have ordered her servant to do whatever was necessary to get free, including accept that consequence, but they were in front of human witnesses who didn't know about things like vampires and third mark healing abilities.

"Shouldn't sneak up on a guy," Garron said mildly. "There's a good lad." He gave Liam a pat on the ass and let him go, hauling him back up before shoving him back.

"As I said," Tara purred, "it's a pleasure to watch the dominant ones. Especially when they're stripped. Can you imagine the pleasure of watching the early Olympics? All those naked, muscular male bodies. A shame none of us are old enough to have seen that."

Liam shot Garron a look that seemed more annoyed with his own lack of anticipation than with her Master. His gesture toward the bench was almost polite. Though from the light in Liam's eyes, Kaela knew he was anticipating some payback when he had Garron strapped down. It was part of the usual play between servants, and Garron seemed to be falling into their rhythm easily enough. So far it might not be so different from group sessions in Club Sin. Except he didn't usually serve as a bottom, so Kaela couldn't calm the nerves jittering in her stomach.

Richard's gaze had sharpened. "His reflexes are quick. Military training?"

"Yes. I believe so."

Garron positioned himself in front of the spanking bench, arms crossed over his broad chest, feet spread shoulder width as he eyed the other two servants. "So how do you want me? Or rather, how do your Master or Mistress want this done?"

He asked pleasantly enough, though the spark in his eyes would be enough to cause anyone pause. Exchanging a glance, Liam and Seanna moved forward as one unit. After a quiet conversation where he was probably telling Garron what he was doing, Liam knelt and cuffed his spread ankles, locking the straps into the bolts in the floor. Seanna moved to the other side of the spanking bench and crooked her finger at him.

"Think you can bow to a lady, big man?"

"I bow to my lady, always," Garron responded. "But she allows me to respect the wishes of other beautiful women."

Though he was turned in profile to her, Kaela knew he gave Seanna a wink. When he bent forward, the audience behind him had an enviable view of his ass and heavy testicles. Tara took her wine and rose, wandering to that angle to take her fill. "Lady Kaela, I don't know how you're going to leave him here. I'd put him in an extra big suitcase and kidnap him off the island."

Kaela managed to give her a tight smile.

As Garron leaned over the spanking bench, Seanna drew his arms down over the edge, cuffing them to the floor. She adjusted the length in the chains so he was held at a ninety degree angle, upper abdomen flat against the bench. When Garron's mouth cruised over her hip bone, Seanna cupped Garron's skull and moved so his mouth was over her mons. Pushing his head down roughly, she propped her high heel against one of his stretched out arms so she could direct his mouth between her legs, against the tight latex that molded her sex.

"You just work on that like a good lad yourself," she crooned, though Kaela noted some breathlessness to it, since Garron knew exactly how to use his lips, with or without the interference of clothes. The thought of his mouth on her own pussy made her dampen further, even as she seethed at Seanna's fingers tracing those scar lines on his head. But her attention was snagged by Liam. He'd stripped off his clothes and had taken a trio of lubricated condoms from one of the waitstaff.

*No. Garron, I will stop this. You need only say…*

*If I want you to stop it, I will command you to do so, my lady. Can you feel what I'm thinking as I'm eating her pussy? Focus.*

The crude command snapped her back. She wanted to close her eyes, get lost in his head, but she knew that would give their connection away. So she kept her eyes trained on them, though she dove inside his head, blocking out what she was seeing in front of her. It wouldn't be the first time she'd done that.

*Except this time I want you in the here and now. Watch and listen, my lady. Take the journey with me.*

As he nibbled at Seanna's labia with his lips, he was imagining Kaela's, the way she got so slick for him and writhed against his face, making those sexy whimpers. He was going to be making her come with his mouth before dawn, and he considered this good practice. Watching Seanna get more aroused with his skill, the way the woman was starting to grind against his mouth, Kaela wanted nothing more than to be in her place. Or Garron's place, with him behind her, putting his mouth on her…

*I'll put you on your elbows and knees, my lady. Straddle your head so my cock is between your shoulder blades. I'll part your ass cheeks, put my mouth on your cunt, my tongue up your tight little rectum as you huddle beneath my body like a captured rabbit. You'll wiggle and cry for mercy, which I'll never give you. You'll scream out your climax until you're hoarse, just like this one will before I'm done with her.*

Her tissues contracted between her legs, imagining it. With her enhanced senses, she could hear every stroke of his tongue, the faint suckle as he teased Seanna to the point she was sure the woman was wishing her Master would allow her to remove her clothing, but vampires tended to enjoy drawing out their servant's sensual agony. Though it seemed Seanna and Liam were acting organically, Kaela knew their decisions were being governed by their vampires, since Richard and Tara had fallen silent, their attention focused on what lay before them.

Richard had his eyes trained on Kaela's Master like a hawk. It made Kaela uneasy.

Liam probed between Garron's ass cheeks, squirting additional lube into his rectum from a small sample tube. She registered the cool trickle of the lube through his mind, his mild distaste as Liam gripped his balls, fondled them as he worked in the lube.

It wasn't supposed to be this way. Damn it, she didn't care about the consequences. She could stop this, pass it off as a hard limit, acceptable in the human world.

*Nothing here will be unbearable to me, Kaela. But beyond that, it's not your choice to stop this, is it? I'm your Master. The only one who can call a halt to it is me.*

She pushed even farther into his mind to see if he was trying to protect her, if somewhere inside he was screaming in protest at being treated this way. All she felt was…a solid calm. Was it really more about what she could handle seeing done to him, than what he could handle himself?

*You wouldn't be the first sub who turned away from a Master because he didn't act dominant enough for her.*

No, God no. It wasn't that. She almost surged out of the chair in reaction. She had to will herself to stay where she was. *It's not that, Master. Not that at all.*

*Prove it. Shut the hell up, stop whining and watch.*

*Whining?* That snapped her spine up straight as a board. As he shot her another glance while brushing his lips over Seanna's thigh, she lifted her chin, refolded her hands on her lap. Fine. She would watch. God damn him.

His lips curved. *That's my girl.*

As Liam started to ease in, Garron's powerful thigh muscles tensed. The crowd let out a startled gasp and even Tara jumped as he threw his weight back. The decisive move impaled Liam inside him when the servant had to grab Garron's hips to prevent losing his balance.

"Don't do it half-assed, kid," Garron growled. "Put your weight into it. I don't want it to tickle. I want to feel the burn. Think you've got enough of a dick to manage that?"

Liam's jaw set. Taking an even more firm grip on Garron's hips, he complied, hard enough that his pelvis smacked against Garron's ass and he won a grunt from her Master.

"Atta boy," Garron growled, and went back to teasing Seanna's cunt with his mouth.

There was a ripple of nervous laughter from the crowd, a smattering of applause, quickly silenced by the attentive staff. Kaela closed her eyes briefly.

*Kid? He's at least three times your age, Garron.*

*He's a sub, Kaela. You're nearly two hundred, right? Christ, that burns.* He grimaced. *Being a Master has nothing to do with who looks like they're on top. It's who* is *on top that matters. That battle all happens in the head.*

Proving it, he'd ramped up his aggression with Seanna as well, nipping, sucking, getting more of his mouth involved so she was working her hips up against him in a coital rhythm. She had one hand on Garron's shoulder, nails digging in so that Kaela smelled the first fragrant whiff of blood being drawn. When some of it trickled from under her hold, Tara's nostrils flared as if she'd scented perfume and Richard leaned forward even more attentively.

Seanna reached out with her other hand and Liam leaned forward to clasp it. The secure hold on one another increased the strength of their movements. As Liam thrust forward, Seanna could lean back against his hold, tilt her hips even more up to Garron's mouth, a seesawing rhythm that had both servants moving toward climax quickly. Garron's cock was an enormous, thick staff jutting out beneath him, swaying as Liam slammed into his ass. The look of it made Kaela keenly aware of how empty her pussy was, her thighs tightening in her cross-legged position.

*If I was free…* Garron's mind voice was distracted, Liam's stimulation in his ass bringing him closer to climax, a simple physical response, cause and effect, *I'd make sure those legs stayed open. No pleasure except what I give you, my lady.*

He gave her pleasure just by being. His voice in her head was enough to make her come.

She could choose to set aside her anger at the situation, let the pleasure of feeling everything Garron was feeling flood her mind. He wasn't beaten down by this. He was immersed in one thing. Proving to her that it meant nothing. *Me coming because…someone's stimulating my dick and ass? That's biology, my lady. Nothing more… It doesn't change…who I am, what you are. Does it?*

Logically, she knew his point was valid. Her Master might be being fucked, but he was in no way subjugated, because nothing emanating from his body suggested surrender. All in the eye of the beholder. She saw Seanna claw at his shoulder, hanging on as he teased her higher and higher. She probably had a screaming desire to remove the barrier of those latex pants, so Garron could stab that clever tongue into her folds. But Richard wasn't allowing her to do that.

Garron's thighs were hard ropes of muscle, his body moving against Liam rhythmically as his inner muscles clasped Liam strong and sure, milking his hard cock. Liam had to release Seanna to press his hand into the center of Garron's back, his other fingers digging into Garron's hip.

"Mistress…" Liam gasped it out.

Tara gave an imperceptible nod a scant second before the orgasm gripped Liam. One blink later and he would have been suffering her punishment for not being able to wait. An experienced servant usually had more restraint, except Kaela knew he was a true submissive as well, not only trained but desiring to respond to a Dominant's touch, even if it was ironically coming through the pull of Garron's muscles, stroking Liam's length.

Through Garron's mind, Kaela could feel that demand upon her own body. And not just her. As her gaze swept the perimeter of the velvet rope, she could identify the submissives by who was leaning forward unconsciously, as if compelled into the wake of Garron's demands upon the other two servants. It was clear to anyone with eyes who had control of this situation.

*Even if I didn't, my lady, it wouldn't mean anything. It's a performance. That's all.*

Richard must have given Seanna permission at last, for her throat arched and the woman threw her head back, all her long braids pattering against her tight-as-a-drum ass as her own climax took her. She clutched Garron's head as she ground herself against his face. Kaela did everything she could not to yearn toward him, her body throbbing, needy. It was as if he was showing her exactly what he could do to her, holding it tantalizingly out of reach.

*One of the side benefits of this. I can torment my lady until she'll do anything to be fucked by her Master.*

"Gods above, I'd love to see him go toe-to-toe with another alpha at one of our get-togethers," Tara offered. Throughout the performance, the female vampire had moved between vantage points, enjoying the pump of Liam's ass, the writhing of Seanna's hips. At one point, she'd stepped in to caress Seanna's quivering breast in her tight corset. Then she'd trailed the edge of her wine glass down Garron's rippling back while she stroked Liam's thick blond hair, all while her servant was ramming his cock into Kaela's Master.

Now the female overlord returned to the table. Setting her wine glass on the tray of a passing waiter, she took a seat next to Kaela. "Our servants are a cake walk for him, but can you imagine him paired with someone like Jacob? Or Devlin, Lady Daniela's servant? That one has a cock like a horse. You're being cruel in such a lovely way, denying him his own orgasm. His cock is thick as Liam's arm. I bet he'd explode at the barest stroke."

She'd forgotten. She had to give him permission to come, and verbally, because they didn't know she was in his head. Eying Garron's turgid member, she wasn't sure what to do. But she was a service submissive, after all, and her Master needed to come. Liam was pulling out and Seanna was leaning over Garron, bracing herself on his shoulder as she got her breath back.

*You don't do anything, my lady. I decide when I come. If I need you to say it aloud for their benefit, I'll tell you when and what to say. Your only job is to tell me if something doesn't fit their expectations, because it's my job to protect you. Protecting you means making them believe what they want to believe.*

He lifted his eyes. Even tied down as he was, the potency of his gaze wasn't diluted, and the power of his words only increased it.

She thought of the tattoo on his back--to protect and serve. She'd been able to be an effective overlord because Lady Lyssa had told her to serve. Was he able to serve for similar reasons--because it was another manifestation of being her Master?

*Now you're getting it, my lady.*

Maybe so, but she still resisted the idea. Yes, as he said, it was a performance. One that could drain the soul, if it had to be performed over and over, in myriad, excruciating ways. As extreme as this might seem to some of those watching, it was nothing in the vampire world. Rules and structure like this didn't exist. Servants were property, who lived, died, thrived or suffered according to vampire whim.

Liam had moved to release Garron's arms. When Garron straightened, he put a steadying hand on Seanna, who was still disoriented from the force of the orgasm. After Liam released his ankles from the restraints, Garron passed her over to him. Tara's servant brought her back to Richard, pressing her into a kneeling position by him. Liam, still naked as his Mistress obviously desired him to be, took a position behind her.

Meeting Kaela's gaze, Garron went to one knee, bowing his head as if merely waiting for her next order. His words in her mind were a provocative contrast.

*When I come tonight, it will be in your cunt, my lady. I'll put you on your back and spread your legs for my pleasure.*

"Have you flogged him yet, Lady Kaela?" Richard asked. "With that broad back and handsome ass, I expect you couldn't help yourself."

Kaela pulled her attention from Garron to meet Richard's eyes. Things inside her froze anew at the look in his cool eyes. He wasn't irritated, which would be a definite warning sign, but he was intrigued by the challenge Garron presented, a human who presumed to remain in control of a situation where he wasn't supposed to have control. Vampires loved nothing better than to prove their superiority. If they outranked another vampire, they would take steps to make it clear they held the upper hand. A human who didn't perceive himself as inferior to a vampire might as well have a target on him. Vampires would dedicate extra time to changing that perspective decisively, brutally. Richard would be limited in what he could do here, but even so, her gut twinged unpleasantly at what he might do.

Richard motioned to a panel between two pillars that displayed a cornucopia of floggers, paddles and single tails. "Do you mind if I enjoy the pleasure? It seems he needs a stronger hand than our servants possess to help him get out of a Dom's mindset."

He began to rise, because of course her assent was merely a formality.

*Kaela…*

"No."

She'd spoken more forcefully than intended. Richard stopped, looking back at her, a brow raised. But she had a unique knack for recovery, didn't she? On almost the same breath, she continued, "No, I haven't whipped or flogged him yet, my lord. If you don't mind, I'd like to be the first one to do it."

"A bit possessive already." Tara smiled. "She may be thinking about that extra large suitcase after all."

Richard offered a polite bow. "In that case, gentlemanly instincts trump rank, my lady. I wouldn't deprive you of first blood. It will allow me time to negotiate a wager with Lady Tara as to whether a man's hand or a woman's will help him mind better. I'll take my turn when you're done."

Kaela managed an acknowledgment she didn't want to give before she rose, moved with purpose toward that panel of choices. She felt Garron's attention following her, even as his eyes remained on the ground. It gave her a view through his eyes of his bare feet. Like all of him, they were oversized. He probably wore a shoe size well into the teens.

Frankenstein's monster was what the porters had called him. Yet Garron wasn't the monster. Richard and Tara, beautiful as freshly formed ice on tree branches, were the true monsters. Same as those who made tigers perform in the circus, showing the crowd how they could make the powerful predators jump through hoops, do despicably cutesy things. The trainer might even think it was okay if she or he had a bond with the creatures, or if they were born in captivity, deprived of any knowledge of the life they were meant to live. The last circus she'd attended she'd wished the creatures had sprung from the ring and eviscerated every goddamned member of the audience.

*Easy, my lady. Tune into my mind.* She heard his sternness. He was concerned about her, she could feel that, and he was probably smart to worry. The way he'd aroused her, taking her along for the ride with Seanna and Liam, had helped, but the rage was still on a healthy simmer. She stopped before the panel, stared at her choices. She wasn't seeing them, though. She was trying to figure out how to go with this. All the different challenges she'd faced throughout the years, and this was one where she was groping for a direction.

*I thought I'd already taught you better than that. Where does a sub look for direction?*

*Her Master.*

*There you go. Now look at the choices and tell me what you know how to use, if any of them.*

She knew how to use all of them. Yet there were certain things that she rejected out of hand. A paddle? No. Just no. Floggers were versatile, but she found her gaze drawn to the single tails. Most subs didn't know how to use one, but most of them hadn't had to be a Dominant for as long as she had. She was very good with a six foot single tail, and the threat and strength of it, the skill and control required, would honor those same qualities in her Master.

*Well thought, my lady. Come show me.*

She grasped her choice, turned around. He stood in front of the bench, to all appearances waiting for her verbal direction Through his mind, she could tell his ass was sore, since the last time he'd experienced anal sex had been quite some time ago. She was surprised he'd experienced it at all.

*At Eden, Masters and Mistresses role play as subs occasionally to understand more about the submissive mindset, my lady. As well as to make sure we know how different punishments and sensations feel. I've had my ass taken by some quite formidable Mistresses with strap-ons that I'm pretty sure were borrowed from Lucifer's toy box.*

*How about another Master?*

Tara's suggestion about pitting him against another alpha servant came to mind. While watching Liam fuck her Master had done little for her--his attentions to Seanna were far more stimulating to Kaela---now she couldn't deny a guilty twinge imagining him fighting for the upper hand with one of the alpha servants.

Garron snorted in his head. *Women, even submissive ones, are as intrigued by two strong males going at it as men are about watching two curvy females pleasuring one another.*

*So have you ever had a Master…do that?*

*One or two, because we're expected to learn about the pleasures of same sex domination and submission as well. It's about sensation my lady, not preferences. Haven't you done the same, watching Fran submit and experiencing pleasure through her? You've learned to arouse yourself regardless of the circumstances, to make it work for you.*

At the peak of an evening of vampire socializing, when it seemed everyone around her was copulating or absorbed in some type of pleasurable power exchange, she could close down her awareness of everything but the grunts and cries of pleasure and lose herself. She'd learned how to blend. Touched bodies, demanded surrender, inflicted pain…and to make that work, she couldn't stay detached. She'd learned to channel the pleasure in ways where she did in fact experience it as well, even if it rarely went below the physical.

*The body is entirely neutral, my lady. It just likes sex. It's the mind that fucks up our compass. So do you know how to use that single tail you're holding?*

*Yes. Quite well.*

*Good. You mess up and you'll pay for it.* A mental pause. *Perhaps that wasn't the best incentive to make you do your best.*

His wry humor loosened up some of the tension inside her and reminded her again that here it was just play. He could end it if he wished by indicating it was a hard limit, because this was the human world. So he was right. Stop whining, just enjoy it in whatever way she could. That's what he was demanding, and if she couldn't be anything for him after she left the island, she would be his in all ways while she was here. That was one gift she could give him.

Closing her hand on the handle of the single tail, she let the thong and fall uncurl. His hands were loose, eyes trained on her face, everything about his body language saying she was the only one who existed for him, no matter the crowd, the watching staff members or vampires. "Move to the pillar," she said shortly. "Put your hands on it."

As he complied, he moved with that unconscious grace powerful animals had, strong and confident. It was as if he were fully dressed, not naked and just ass fucked. He knew who and what he was, and he wouldn't let anything shake that.

*You should pay yourself that same compliment, my lady. Almost two hundred years couldn't change your determination to honor who you truly are, which is why you're here on Eden with me.*

"You don't expect him to be so beautiful with all those scars, but he is," Tara remarked. "If he were mine, Kaela, I'd tie him down and feast on him for days. What an intriguing tattoo…"

Kaela tilted her head in acknowledgment while she suppressed the urge to turn around and gouge her eyes out. A very female reaction, she knew.

*An appreciated one, my lady. Like all men, I love a good cat fight. Particularly if bikinis and a vat of mud are involved.*

She was *not* going to laugh. Though the urge took her by surprise, since humor wasn't the type of emotion she was used to quelling during this kind of thing. She took a stance a few paces behind him, watched him rest both palms on either side of the wide pillar. As he did, he tilted his head so she saw him capture her in the corner of his eye. Being in his mind, it was an unusual effect, like seeing her image in a mirror looking back at her true self. Because he saw her true self. Through his vision, by wrapping his feelings about it around her, she could see it as well.

Nothing that she had to do would change that vision. She could be who Tara and Richard expected her to be and yet be what she truly was. That wasn't new. But for the first time in her life, the contrast didn't feel so isolating to her. It actually was...arousing, because Garron was still in control. He was with her, in her mind, supporting her, helping her, not making her feel so alone.

This could work. It could work.

The realization was so startling, so earthshattering, her mind shut like a trap to everything, even him. She had to blink, orient herself. Remind herself of the flip side.

Yes, it could work, if it was all about her. But it wasn't. Being a Master was so much his nature, it didn't matter what he told her, she was not going to be talked into signing him up for three hundred years of doing exactly what she'd been doing, pretending to the world. Especially in the brutal vampire world, which made her current locale look like the "you-must-be-under-48-inches-to-ride-these" kiddie area at Disneyland. She couldn't ask him to do that.

He'd realized she'd shut him out and was giving her that Master look that reminded her that was one of his non-negotiable points. *Open your fucking mind.* She didn't have to read it from his mind to read it from his face.

He must have read something from hers, however, because he straightened from the pillar, concern creasing his brow as he half turned toward her. She shook herself out of it.

*Turn all the way toward me.*

He stayed still, didn't twitch. It took her a beat to realize she hadn't said it aloud. Out of the two of them, he was the one keeping his wits about him for this hazardous game of Simon Says. That proved it. She couldn't even keep her mind straight about him in a human environment. What if she let it slip in the vampire world who was the true Master and who was the slave? They'd tear him to pieces.

*Kaela, we deal with this first.* His mind voice was even, firm, as if they had all the time in the world, as if she wasn't on the edge of losing it. *You can do whatever you need to do. I've got you.*

"Turn toward me," she said quietly. Probably too quiet for any human to hear and definitely too soft for him, but the third mark, temporary though it was, had also helped his hearing. Plus he was looking at her face. He complied and faced her, an exceptionally intimidating-looking male thanks to his size and scarring. As well as that jutting cock, still hard and unsatisfied, a different, delicious form of intimidation, because he'd made it clear he was waiting to take her, would fuck her senseless when this was over. He'd said he'd remind her who he was, but she didn't need to be reminded he was her Master. Every vibrating, yearning cell of her body, heart and soul knew.

His gaze flickered, his jaw flexing. She felt the flood of emotion from his mind, nothing in words, but nothing needed. She'd just stepped into a boat, and he was the water that surrounded it, bearing her aloft, pulling her into the center of his being so she could do this.

She tested the whip a few times, loosening up her wrist. Then she positioned herself, focused on her canvas. She flicked the whip toward him, worked her way forward until the end was snaking out to tease his chest, his lower abdomen, his upper thigh. Then she cracked it, the popper snapping inches from his flesh with that startling gunshot noise.

It was deceptive, using a whip. When pain was involved, the whip appeared to tease and caress, just whispers of noise. A crack usually meant nothing had been touched. He knew that, but it was instinct to flinch.

He didn't.

He trusted her. She stepped into the role she knew, giving out quite a few of those caresses, until his flesh showed the crisscrossing of faint red lines, and he was twitching with it. She'd worried about irritating his scars, but he let her know they weren't a problem.

*Do your worst, my lady. I'm all yours.*

His gaze never left hers, and his erection never flagged. It seemed with every strike, every flex of his muscles, the rock set of his jaw, she was getting more aroused. Her nipples were tight, her pussy wet, her body aching for his touch.

When she couldn't bear it any longer, she caught the fall, coiled the whip and set it aside. Moving in, she pressed her body against his, wanting to put herself against all those red marks she'd caused. She wanted to kiss every one of them, finish on her knees, take him in her mouth, bring him to climax. Lifting her face, she kissed him, clasping the side of his throat with one hand to delve deep. He made a growl against her mouth and she answered it, pricking him with her fangs.

*Tell me to keep my hands down, my lady.*

*I don't want to.* But she said it aloud, as he started to raise them. "Hands down."

He put them down but clenched his fists, conveying a note of impatience, a promise of retribution for ordering him around, even though he was the one who commanded the order. The dichotomy of it made her dizzy. She was happy to be punished for obeying him, for not obeying him, for the pleasure of serving his pleasure, his desire to inflict pain and drive her to screaming climax with it.

*You are a temptation like no other, my lady. Ease back, now. That's enough.*

A vampire wouldn't prolong the intimacy of a kiss, but there was something reckless and dangerous brewing inside her, a macabre ebullience that wanted to test the boundaries of her life, tell all of them to go fuck themselves and immerse herself in him.

*You'll behave, my lady. There will be time for you to act out later. When I can deal with it in full measure.*

She met his gaze with a glinting one of her own, and he almost gave her a savage grin, anticipating it. God, she needed him. Needed him forever.

But she couldn't have him. The pain of that came back like the thrust of a stake. His eyes darkened, his mouth tightened, but she stepped back, averting her gaze and facing Lord Richard, who stood with his hand out.

"You did promise me, my lady."

"I don't recall a promise, Lord Richard. I remember an assumption on your part."

Tara's attention snapped to her. Liam and Seanna did the same before quickly looking down, the typical reaction of most servants when vampires squared off. Duck and cover.

Dealing with servants touching her Master, binding him, was one thing. Difficult enough. But a vampire handling him, inflicting pain on him, was an entirely different matter. Faced with the reality, a wall came down inside her. Not just no, but hell, fucking, over-my-dead-body no. She'd seen vampires do things to servants that surpassed the tortures of the damned. But hey, it was okay, because with a little blood from the Master or Mistress, the servant would be fine, hunky dory. Maybe some pesky mental scarring, but that was on the inside, so everything outside stayed pretty. Had to keep priorities straight, after all.

Garron had been through hell physically, emotionally. Whether or not he accepted it, she was as responsible for protecting him as he was for protecting her. Thanks to her most recent disagreement with

Fran, that dear beloved woman who was the closest thing Kaela had to a real friend, she knew those two things weren't in conflict. Hadn't Fran stepped over the line of her stringent InhServ training because of her concern about her Mistress going somewhere she couldn't watch after her?

*Kaela. Give him the whip. Remember, according to club rules here, I can call a halt to it if I desire, no reflection on you.*

She knew enough about men and their testosterone surges to know how likely that would be. She would have rolled her eyes at him if she wasn't in the process of holding a staring contest with Lord Richard.

"My lady?" He had a brow raised, his eyes glittering but his expression suggesting he was giving her the chance to correct the impression she'd just given, that she was refusing him.

*Kaela, I mean it. There's* no *risk in this for me. You're endangering yourself needlessly, which will piss me off more than anything else you could possibly do. Give him the fucking whip.*

He was telling her what to do and expecting her to obey. But stepping out of the path between Richard and Garron… a mental quiver went through her. It was the same shiver of nerves she usually cast in iron in the blink before she decided whether or not the vampire in front of her needed to be taken down.

*You're a vampire overlord. You control every situation. That's what you do every day of your life. This is when you decide how much you trust me or if you've just been playing sub the past few days. Honor your Master.*

The arctic coldness of those three words shot up her spine. She glanced over her shoulder. His face had gone impassive, entirely unreadable. She felt like snarling in frustration, but an icy calm stole over her, numbing everything.

"My apologies, my lord." She channeled every façade she'd ever pasted on her face to fool a Union general or a vampire. The result was a beatific smile, laced with a good deal of unbridled lust. For the first time with respect to Garron it was a feigned reaction, because there was nothing arousing to her about this. "My servant is quite worked up, and I intend to make good use of that impressive hard on." She handed over the whip. "If you deflate it, I'll be annoyed. I'd appreciate your consideration of that."

"I haven't seen your passionate side before, my lady. Usually you're so in control." Richard's expression eased. "I'll try to resist my baser urges, but I also know you're quite capable of returning a man to full attention with no more than a smile."

Tara rolled her eyes. "Charmer," she said, nudging Kaela when she came to stand beside her. Kaela responded with a faint smile, but everything else in her was concentrated on Garron.

When he met Richard's gaze, Richard gave her Master a humorless smile. "Definitely not used to playing the submissive, are you, boy? If you lower your eyes, I might have mercy."

Garron didn't lower his gaze.

Richard gave a nasty chuckle. "Lady Kaela, if you should decide to make your arrangement with this one…permanent, I think we'll be in for some interesting social events."

The Region Master pointed to a frame positioned to the left of the spanking bench. "I want you there. Seanna, come bind his arms on either side of him. Ankles, too. Stretch him out."

As Seanna moved forward to comply, Richard went back to the panel and switched out the six-footer for two four-footer single tails. He preferred a Florentine method, Kaela recalled, and he could cut into flesh or barely brush it, flicking a fly from the air.

*Close your mind if you need to do so, my lady. I'm fine. There's nothing he can do to me that should cause you distress. It certainly won't cause me any, unless it upsets you.*

Her mind started to narrow down to a thin crack of light, but for different reasons. Things were getting far more still inside of her, everything focused on what would happen next.

The first time Richard drew blood, he would die where he stood, no matter what she had to do to accomplish it.

Garron had heard that. His gaze flicked to her, startled, but then Richard began. He hadn't warmed up like Kaela had, but maybe he was just that familiar with whip play. Or maybe he'd intended to make his first strike exceptionally memorable.

He threw hard and fast. The two whips snaked out and sliced into Garron's back, both direct strikes on his scars. Garron arched up against his bonds, all his muscles bunching into rock hard tension to absorb the pain, his mouth stretched back in a snarl. The crowd let out a startled gasp as the skin split, crimson gashes that would draw blood.

*Fucking bastard. Stand down, my lady. Stand. Down.*

Only two things saved Richard from her wrath. Her initial

moment of shock that he truly had dared something that brazen in a human environment, and the instant response of the two staff members who'd been standing inside the cordoned area to ensure people didn't lean over the velvet ropes too far. They'd shifted forward as immediately as if they'd been police trained, and perhaps Vardalos ensured that very thing, given what contingencies they might face in a BDSM club with a wide variety of guests.

Regardless, they'd cut into her path. She still might have mowed them down without impunity if one of them hadn't spoken up sharply. And if Garron hadn't repeated his explosive command in her head.

Tara reached out, caught her hand and tugged her back. "It's okay, you won't get into trouble," she whispered. "Richard knows what he's doing. It's not the first time he's played in a human club."

She could care less about being in trouble with the club, but she managed not to jerk her hand from Tara's grasp, instead extricating it with a stiff nod. She remained on her feet, though.

The staff member who had spoken up was Louis, the fire play Dom. His blue eyes sparked, his dark-stubbled jaw set. "Sir, blood play has to be sanctioned by a staff member, prior to execution."

"My bad, Lou." Garron cleared his throat. "I'm one of those who can sanction it, and I told him he could."

Louis's gaze slid over his fellow Dom, noting how Garron straightened stiffly. He didn't have to have Kaela's inside view to register the agony pin-balling through her Master. Louis's lips twisted, but Garron held his gaze in a lock, giving him a slight head shake. The Dom sighed, nodded grudgingly. "My apologies, sir," he said to Richard, though there was no apology in his hard tone. "But keep in mind we monitor this kind of play closely. Regardless of Master Garron's sanction, we will stop the session if it becomes excessive."

Tara bit back a sigh. "Human clubs," she muttered to Kaela.

Thank God for them. Kaela shifted her attention to Richard. He'd paused during the interruption, his expression neutral, almost bored. He acknowledged the warning and set his stance again.

*I won't stand here and allow him to cut you up, Garron.*

*He was just proving a point, my lady. Watch.*

Kaela remained tense, standing, but as Richard resumed, she saw Garron was correct. Richard used the blood running down Garron's back as his pallet. As he flicked the two popper ends along Garron's back, he started to spread those drops in a brush-like pattern, around Garron's original tattoo and then lower, an artistic display that impressed the crowd and had them leaning out against the velvet ropes for a better look.

In other circumstances, the artistry might have impressed her as well, but Kaela knew that flicking motion came with a repetitive sting, a pain that mounted as the whipping continued. The way Garron started jerking against the manacles was expected, though she hated it. But she also noticed something else. With his legs bound shoulder length apart, it made his genitals far more vulnerable. Yet though Richard occasionally licked those poppers against his testicles, Garron remained as hard and aroused as if Richard wasn't threatening his genitals at all.

She had to know where his headspace was, so she broke the rules and delved into his mind. Immediately she was surrounded by an array of erotic images, none of which included Richard or registered the pain of the flogger. Garron was imagining her straddling him as he made her ride him hard in their bed. Naked, her body oiled and slick as she rose and fell upon him. She was so aroused she was out of control, bending to bite him like a wild animal. Her ankles were chained to the bed, her wrists manacled behind her back. She was his prisoner…

Some pain finally penetrated, the grimace on his face becoming a snarl as Richard flicked the lash with extra enthusiasm over Garron's torso, his thighs, snapped at his balls with too much zeal. Kaela almost moved forward again, Louis tensing to her left to do the same, but in that brief second, Richard stopped. He surveyed his handiwork, stepping over to the table to pick up his wine glass, take a sip. As he circled to the front to consider Garron, her Master's gaze locked with the Region Master's once more.

Tara slid her hand into the crook of Kaela's elbow, squeezing. "Look at that hard cock, the way he's looking at Richard. You should keep him, my lady. After all these years, you know we have a sense for the humans that are meant to be a part of our world. Every time he looks at you, it's as obvious as a thunderstorm."

She raised her voice. "I think this one is a draw, my lord. I don't think it matters whether he's being whipped by a Master or Mistress. He only belongs to one person here, and I think we know who it is."

"Yeah. Himself." Richard took another sip of wine. "A true

Dom."

He tossed the whips to Louis. "I assume you have to have those cleaned," he said dismissively, and then nodded toward Liam and Seanna. "Let him loose."

Kaela took no small satisfaction at the look Louis aimed at Richard, an expression the vampire missed only because he turned away from him. Though she'd enjoyed watching the fire play, she'd kept her distance. Most vampires didn't like close proximity to flame, and Louis looked like he'd happily find a couple blow torches to teach Richard some manners.

Then Richard's focus was on Kaela, drawing her attention. "He's a stubborn one, my lady. All cock and attitude. Tara tends to be a bit more romantic about these things. The weakness of women."

"Chauvinist," Tara said without malice. A faint smile crossed Richard's face, but Kaela wasn't fooled. His eyes stayed cool.

"Stubbornness in a servant can be a challenge at best, a curse at worst. There's a high percentage of servants who have to be killed by their vampire within the first five years of their lives because they don't work out."

"Lord Brian has that serum that separates a vampire and servant now," Tara reminded him, speaking low enough only the three of them and the servants could follow the conversation. "And the memory serum that erases the servant's memory of our world."

"Which has only partially effective results, if the data coming back is any indication. Most of the Council still thinks execution is the safest course of action." Richard shook his head. "I wasn't making light of him, Lady Kaela. That one is a true Master. He won't be able to bend enough to be part of our world."

"It doesn't matter," Kaela said. Her voice was hollow in her head, even as it came out the way she intended. Casual, indifferent. "I'm enjoying him only on the island."

"Well, if you're leaving tonight, maybe we'll enjoy him for the rest of the week," Tara said with a wink.

She needed to leave. She couldn't bear to be here any longer. "You'll have to take that up with Garron, my lady. My understanding is he's engaged with other clients throughout the rest of the week."

She squared off with both vampires, gave them a courteous bow. "My apologies, but this is where we part ways. It's well past midnight and I need to prepare for my early evening departure. It's been a pleasure seeing you."

She said a few more things along those lines. Though she knew she seemed abrupt, her words a little forced, it didn't really matter, did it? If she wasn't taking him with her, he was in no danger from her erratic behavior. And she wasn't lying. She had something vital to do before dawn came, something that was boiling up in her breast and would no longer be denied.

Richard had said the obvious, yet the shock of hearing him say it aloud told her she'd almost let herself believe otherwise. Which brought back the anger that this situation had occurred at all, that what had started out as a fantasy had had to be ruined by her reality.

As Kaela moved away, she saw Tara lean forward, heard her teasing comment to Richard. "That was as close to a pissing match as I've seen between you and a human, my lord."

It was nothing less than the truth. Though Richard had been the one with the whips and the perceived power, it was clear Garron had kept the upper hand. In short, vampire or not, he'd proven who the top Dom was.

And as Richard had implied, in the vampire world, humans died for infractions far less than that.

## Chapter Eleven

Seanna and Liam were in the process of unchaining Garron. Louis had also stepped forward to ensure Garron was truly fine--and probably to mutter "what the hell were you thinking?"--so she had a few vital seconds to establish a head start. Kaela closed her mind to any question or demand Garron might toss out to reel her back. Focusing so hard on that, she almost ran into Bridget, the velvet-corseted woman who'd been at the private staff entrance into Club Sin.

"Would you please make sure Master Garron gets the care he needs?" Kaela fished out a generous tip, transferred it into the woman's hand. "He has cuts that may need treatment. A massage would be good if he'll agree to it."

Despite her obvious curiosity at Kaela's abrupt departure, the woman's eyes lighted at the possibility of getting her hands on all those lovely muscle groups. Kaela contained the urge to snatch her money back, not that she thought cash was the woman's biggest incentive. "This will cover the cost of a *professional* masseuse. And please return this to him. He…uh, he took it off his wrist so it wouldn't be damaged during the scene and I was holding it for him."

She unclasped the choker from her arm and extended it to Bridget. The way her hand shook as she did it elicited a look of concern from the woman, but as Bridget's lips parted, Kaela hastily overrode anything she was about to say. "I received a message that Theodosius Vardalos needs to meet with me," she said brusquely. "He said one of his staff members could tell me where to find him at this time of night."

Bridget's fingers closed over the silver links. It took an enormous act of will for Kaela to let go of the choker, draw her hand back, but she managed it. "Can you tell me where I'm supposed to go?"

A place like Eden operated 24/7, so Kaela had assumed its Master might observe odd hours to keep it running. It didn't seem to surprise Bridget at all that Vardalos was up at this time of night, but her brow arched.

"A meeting? As in face to face?"

Kaela wasn't in the mood. "Is there any other kind of meeting?"

Bridget gave her a searching look, but pulled out her phone, dialed someone she said was Vardalos's admin. Since she'd lied about the meeting, Kaela wasn't surprised when Bridget's brows rose at whatever the admin said, but her contingency planning was cut short when the staff submissive broke the connection and nodded. "Yes, Lady Kaela. He's expecting you."

So he was willing to meet with her. His mistake.

The woman instructed her on the Master of Eden's whereabouts and Kaela left her, moving swiftly toward the ground level. By the time she was halfway across the BDSM outdoor area, she was moving at full speed, not caring if someone was confused by something faster than the speed of a human but looking a lot like one crossing their paths. She knew such things were quickly dismissed. No one wanted to believe in fantasies. Not really. Reality was what one knew.

She could kill a vampire where he stood or reduce a submissive to quivering fear. Those things were real, but none of it was true.

*My lady, do not do this. Goddamn it.*

She realized she hadn't shut her mind to him as securely as she'd thought. She was still so hungry for his voice, to have any part of him inside her. In a matter of hours, she'd never see or hear from him again. She forced herself to shut her mind to his protests. Even now, his wrath could make her knees weak. That was her weakness to manage, as it always had been.

*We're done, Garron. Fantasy over. I'm sorry. None of this is your fault.*

Richard had accepted the situation tonight, but if Garron was at a vampire dinner? Vampires held grudges, and Richard would make it his mission to bring Garron to his knees in whatever way that indulged his whims.

Bridget had said Vardalos had a night time office in one of the castle towers. A staff member was waiting to give her access through either a small elevator or a winding staircase. She chose the staircase.

The lack of human scent along the endlessly spiraling steps said it was rare anyone came this way. That suited her purpose just fine. The courteous, slim young man who'd let her through might have thought twice about letting her come up here if he'd known she intended violence once she reached her destination.

As she reached the top, she stepped into an anteroom between the elevator and Vardalos's office. The elevator had polished wooden doors, limned with brass. The heavy oak panel doors across from it were cracked open. Disappointing, because she really wanted to wrench them off their hinges. Pushing that aside, she stepped through them.

The room reminded her of a wizard's study. The huge desk was scattered with opened old books, scrolls on the floor. Two walls were all shelves of more books, bisected by a window seat that had three tall windows. The center one, a colorful stained glass, was fully revealed by the drawn curtain. The only light in the room came from it, some type of spotlight outside or a trick of the moon.

He was sitting in the shadows of one of the flanking windows. The curtains closed over it were a relentless black. He had his profile to her, though shadows cloaked his features, much as they had Garron that first day on the dock. She could tell Vardalos was looking out a crack in the curtain, though. There was a bemused expression on his face, as if he wasn't really thinking about a vampire exsanguinating him.

"Do you think you can play games with me, Mr. Vardalos?"

The more she'd exerted herself to get here, the more enraged she'd felt, and not just because of what she'd had to watch Richard do to Garron. It was the whole intrusive situation, how she'd needed and wanted this fantasy so much she'd taken leave of her common sense to embrace it. It was Garron himself, everything she'd ever wanted in a Master.

"Not at all." He turned his head slightly. If she'd had mortal sight, she wouldn't have caught it, but she got a very brief impression of a badly scarred face, one that would make Garron's look like fresh snow. "What can I do for you, Lady Kaela?"

"You promised me discretion. The privacy to make my fantasy into a reality without danger. Two vampires suddenly having the same week on Eden? That's no coincidence. You deliberately risked my life. *His* life."

She wouldn't forgive that. Her life was irrelevant. So many emotions were choking her, she was back to wondering if it was even going to be worth living after she left Eden.

"Garron accepted the risks when he told me he wanted you--and you know I gave him all the information I had about your world, enough that he fully understood those risks." His voice stayed even, that authoritative timbre enough to send shivers up her spine. She quelled them with her anger.

"No one fully understands those kinds of risks until it's too late."

"No. I suppose that's true. We, each of us, take a great deal on faith." He tilted his head, and she realized he still had his eyes on that crack in the curtain. The opening dropped a shaft of light across his thigh, so she saw the crease of his slacks, his other hand resting on that braced leg.

"Why did you do this?" She couldn't keep the pain from surfacing. *Why did I do this?*

He turned that scarred visage to her for a full second, something she expected he didn't do often. Then the shadows reclaimed him. "I bent one promise to deliver on a more important one, my lady. What I really do here is make you see how to turn your fantasy into your reality. I've given you your fantasy, not just for Eden, but for always. You had to believe it was possible for you to have a human Master who's also your full servant. You're angry, frightened and unbalanced, which makes me think I was successful. The rest is up to you. The choice is yours."

She sincerely considered tossing him head first through the window. "Even gods aren't that arrogant."

"Believe me, they are. And then some. Here comes your reality now. He made excellent time."

Lights from three lamps came on, flooding the office with a golden light. The sound of that switch being flipped turned her toward the doorway, where Garron stood. When she glanced over her shoulder, she saw only Vardalos's back, clothed in a well-tailored black suit. He made his exit through a panel in the wall that seamlessly closed behind him.

Garron was winded, angry and dressed, all things she regretted. She pivoted away from him, facing that spot Vardalos had vacated. Staring out the multi-colored panes of glass, she didn't think she could bear looking at her Master, at what she wanted so much. The anger was receding, leaving a weariness.

"I didn't come here for some magical solution to all of this," she said slowly. "Just a break, a temporary break from always being expected to be something I'm not. That's it. It wasn't supposed to get this complicated. You weren't supposed to be…everything I hoped you'd be."

"Sorry to disappoint."

She would have laughed, except she was pretty sure any emotional response like that would crack her open entirely. "Garron, I can't do it to you. I just can't. In my world--"

"In your world, it's different. Servants have the choice to be servants and every other choice belongs to the vampire. I get it. But nothing's changed about what I told you earlier. There are worlds inside of worlds, and I'm talking about the only one that counts. The one we create between you and me."

He'd closed the distance between them. She shuddered at his nearness. She wanted to tell him not to touch her, that she couldn't bear it, but she didn't have the strength to deny him anything. Except this one thing.

"What they did to you tonight, that was nothing," she said, low. "Richard and Tara are actually quite decent, as vampires go. It can be so much worse. It's not just a matter of you not being able to handle it, Garron. I don't think I could stand by and let it happen. I would get us both killed, because I won't bear seeing my Master be treated like less than he is. Like something he's not. Once they figure it out, you would be killed in front of me. I'd be executed or put under an overlord's direct supervision, someone who could beat me into the vampire they think I need to be."

"I've actually found beating you brings out more of your true self."

She shook her head, tried to move away, but he wouldn't let her. He closed his hand over hers at her side, just held it. When he slid his other arm around her waist, trying to turn her, she resisted. He moved his large palm to her neck, curving his fingers around her nape. "Kaela, look at me. You haven't met my gaze since I came into the room."

Because it was too hard. Too hard to show him everything she wanted, because she couldn't hide it, not when it was just the two of them. But she obeyed, and that muscle in his jaw flexed as he saw it. His fingers were gentle, strong. "Just breathe with me," he murmured. "Let's just take a minute and let the universe stop spinning."

"And let you get your breath back," she observed, laying a hand on his chest, rising and falling faster than usual. His heart was still racing.

"I tend to put on some speed when someone's going to kill my boss. He is the island's major employer."

"I believe he's the island's only employer." His wry humor, his touch was helping, even though she shouldn't let it. Shouldn't let her defenses down. "I wasn't going to kill him. Probably."

Garron gave her his crooked smile. Backing up a pace or two to Vardalos's desk, he propped his hips on it and drew her with him so she was standing between his spread feet. She put her hand back on his chest, her fingers curling into the silken mat of hair because he'd only donned slacks and shoes, his shirt having been sacrificed to the used toy bin. It had looked like a nice shirt. She owed him another one.

"They'll wash and return it to me. The laundry does miracles here." He touched her face. "You like to hear stories, right? I want to tell you a story. Will you listen?"

She stared at the gleam of the dark hair curling over her knuckles. He smelled so good, that aftershave scent. He'd dressed up for her tonight. "That may be the first time you really asked me anything. Most of the time you just tell me the way it's going to be."

"Yeah. I'm having a lax moment. You freaked out on me."

She gave a half snort at the understatement of that. "Tell me a story." She wanted to get lost in it. Go to sleep in his arms, never wake up.

He touched her chin, but he didn't make her lift her face. "You know why I went into the military?"

She shook her head.

"I was a foster kid, Kaela. No family to call my own. Ran away a few times until I settled down at a reasonably decent place, which meant they kept me fed and clothed, didn't smack me around or try to do worse to me. But one of those times I ran away, I found a place to sleep in an alley, next to a garbage heap. Bad smells are part of that and you keep your ears sharp for rustlings, because that means rats. Usually you just move away when the smell's too bad or the rustling is too loud."

He paused. "Something made me look that night. I found a pair of newborn twins, still bloody from being born. Somebody had stuffed them into the garbage. Not on top, in the open, in the hopes someone would find them. They were under other trash bags, someone wanting them to die there. Ironically, though that didn't give them a lot of air, it kept them warmer."

Thinking of the infant he'd found in the explosion, her heart tightened.

"Yeah. It was another reason finding that arm affected me the way it did, not that something like that needs anything to make it worse. But when I was holding that little arm, it took me back to that night."

He looped his arms loosely around her waist, drew her closer, his knuckles resting on the rise of her buttocks. "I didn't even think. Just took off my shirt, wrapped them both up and ran. The nearest hospital was a couple miles away. I could have hailed any adult, a cab, whatever. It was a wretched part of town and I didn't trust anyone, but it wasn't that. All I could think of was getting them there. When I stumbled into the ER, peeled back my shirt and showed them to the on-duty nurse, I remember how the whole waiting area just burst into activity. Not just the nurses and doctors. It seemed even the people there for treatment, everyone from street trash to the middle class wife who'd cut herself with a knife, were suddenly invested in making sure these babies had a chance. You know, one of those rare scenarios where you wake up from your life and realize it's all for one, and one for all."

Her throat ached. "Vampires don't have a lot of those moments."

"No, I expect they don't." He released her to take her hand once more, rubbing his thumb over her knuckles as if lost in thought.

"What happened?" She made herself ask when the silence grew and added to that ache, to the point she couldn't bear what wasn't being said. All the things she wished could be.

"One of them was already dead." He shook his head. "I remember this young doctor coming to tell me. He looked tired, overworked, probably doing his residency. Yet he still had heart enough to go look for the kid who brought them in, and tell me the twin had been dead for a few hours before I found them. If he hadn't, I'd have always wondered if those twenty minutes I spent in the alley before I looked had been the tipping point for her. But he didn't leave it there. He shook my hand and told me, 'To that little girl who survived, for the rest of her life, no matter where you are, what you're doing, even if you never see one another again, you'll always be a hero.'"

He raised his gaze to her. "You know the very first thing that crossed my mind? 'Well, that kinda depends on the life she has from here forward, doesn't it, doc?' I don't know what kind of life she has. I hope it's a good one. Sometimes when I can't think of anything to pray for, I pray for that. When I woke up in the hospital after getting blown to bits, the first thing I thought was 'I hope she had a good day today.' Everything bad that happens in my life, I go back to thinking of her."

Seeing how it mattered to him so much after all these years, reminded her of the girl she'd been, standing by Jared's grave. Some things never healed.

"Garron--"

He shook his head. "I'm almost done. Let me finish. When I sat down with a recruiter on my eighteenth birthday, he told me the army could become my family. I've been lied to a lot in my life, and I knew some of that was propaganda. But he was one of the ones who believed in it, because he'd seen it work. It did for me. The point of all this is, I realized what things are meaningful, and what things you do to get by. We all put on masks, but my lady, over all these decades, you let that mask become part of your face, take over your soul. We took it back, you and me, in less than three days. You made me feel a connection that I know is real, true, and permanent. Meant to be. That has to mean something, something that translates beyond this island."

Tears spilled out of her eyes and he reached up, brushed them off with gentle fingertips. When he closed a hand on her shoulder, she knew she was rigid. As if hardening herself to receive a blow that was going to hurt almost more than she could bear. He kept on pressing, though.

"I told you I started as a bell boy here, and when they're short-handed, I still do it. When I bring bags to people's rooms, take care of what they need, I enjoy that, because though they might not get it or see it this way, they're looking to me to watch out for them and their belongings. Caring for someone as a Dom is just a different form of what you feel as a submissive, and my understanding of that is what made every minute of what we were doing with those vampires possible. I know who I am, my lady, and what matters and what doesn't. I want to be with you. That's one of the real things that matter. That's worth everything else."

If she continued to stand here, he could talk her into it. But though he was an incomparable Master, a male who'd made her feel things she hadn't felt in so long, he didn't have a hundred and seventy-five years of seeing what she'd seen.

Earlier, she'd thought if she could have ten days again with Jared, knowing she would lose him afterward, she would still take those ten days. But if she could have him back only as a vampire's servant, she knew what her answer would be. Servants were property, slaves, subject to the whim of not only their own vampire, but any vampire more powerful than her. There were just too many more powerful than her.

She couldn't do that to anyone she loved.

He'd given her access to his mind, heart and soul, so there was no way to deny it. She was falling in love with him, and he was falling in love with her. Nothing to hide, but it had to be denied.

There were sacrifices you made when you loved. While those sacrifices might break the heart, what was worse than a broken heart was the poison of regret, of a choice that couldn't be unmade or forgiven. By the time Garron understood the reality the way she did, there would be no going back. She'd have three hundred years, a servant's normal lifespan, to see that poison grow in his gaze, and root in her own heart. Or less than five, if Richard's prediction came true. Best to leave it all here, untouched by any of that.

There was no way he could understand. She had to accept that. The man who was such a hero that he rescued a baby when he was little more than a baby himself, who'd come back from a near death injury that had lost him three close friends, would never believe there was a challenge that could break him beyond bearing.

She drew her hand away from his, stepped back. Closed her mind down to him and lifted her chin. She kept her eyes flat. She imagined she was back in that drawing room with Greg, every decision calculated inside an impenetrable shell. "It was only supposed to be ten days, Garron. It wasn't supposed to even touch what was going to happen when I left here. What I wanted was a ten day fantasy. Not a gateway back to my reality. There is no gateway there. Not for us."

She took a breath. "You've opened me up to…possibilities. I'm grateful for that. Maybe I can find something like it in my world. But I won't bring you into it."

His eyes snapped with temper. "Possibilities? Like a vampire Master, one who can force you into things, overpower you?"

"No. Yes. It's for me to figure out. No more arguments. Please."

She held an even tone, her blank face.

He studied her. Though it took a visible effort, he reined back his temper. As his attention on her sharpened, she remembered his ability to read auras. She remained still, hurting for them both, but she knew the moment he read her resolve, and truly understood she couldn't be budged. While his ability to recognize that should have been a blessing, it felt like anything but.

His expression suddenly became as impassive as hers. Not cruel, not unkind, simply neutral. "If you're any indication, I don't think all vampires can be classified one way, any more than humans can," he said, low. "If what you truly desire is a vampire Master, one who won't use your submission for political gain or a power trip, it's merely a matter of time and looking."

It was impossible. Almost as impossible as her finding a human Master in a handful of days at a paradise resort who could break her heart. "I can always hope." She made herself say the words, suffered through the slight tic under his eye, a masked flinch. "Though it's not as easy as that."

"No. Nothing worth having ever is." He straightened, and she steeled herself not to take a step back. "So this is your decision."

"It is." She put out her hand, a gesture she realized was ridiculous. He stared at it, let it hang in the air long enough she was about to draw back, but he closed his fingers over it. Lifted it to his mouth, pressed his lips against it. She closed her eyes, imagining herself as tightly furled as a flower bud, not destined to open until spring. Until the sun came out again. An ironic thought for a vampire.

When she opened her eyes, she saw he was studying her face. He wasn't one to give up easily, auras or no, but he was also an exceptional Master. One who knew exactly how much or how little to push a submissive and when she'd reached her limit. When she could go no farther.

She was sure he knew she was breaking apart inside. The question was her resolve, and no matter what else she wanted or needed, that was bone deep. He wasn't going to move her on it. She just wanted to get away, was even now drawing away from him.

When he let her go, she'd rather have been stabbed through the heart with a wooden stake than lose the touch of his hand. He kept those shrewd eyes on her, and though she felt stripped naked, she managed to stay on her feet, keep her chin up. Dignified.

"If you're taking any advice, my lady," he said at last, "I'd say look for love first, then a Master. Because if you find love first, it will help pave the way to the other." There was a slight softening to his mouth, which made her yearn to touch him, but she didn't. She imagined herself rooted to the ground.

He cleared his throat. "Maybe you needed a few days here to understand that your submission truly needs to be a bigger part of your life, my lady. You need to figure that out before you reach a dangerous breaking point again. The kind that brought you here."

He was as calm and closed off as she was. Only suddenly she remembered she had access to his mind. He couldn't close it the way she could. If she could reach out for just a moment, she could figure out what was going on behind that passive countenance, touch his heart, his emotions. She had no right to do that at all, but she couldn't bear this to be her last impression of him.

Her mind was closed tight as a safe, and yet he proved just how good his intuition was, his ability to read her. An expression crossed his face that was dangerous, dark.

"Don't," he said softly, a command that was a threat.

She recoiled, physically stepped back. "I'm sorry. I will…do as you suggest. You showed me…so much. I didn't intend for any of this to hurt you," she added desperately. She wanted to say so much more, but she knew she was floundering.

"I know that, my lady. Are you still leaving at dusk tonight?"

"Yes." Though that word weighed a thousand pounds on her heart as well.

He nodded again, the same wooden gesture. "I'll make sure those arrangements are made. The phone in your suite will be reactivated so you can call the main desk if you need anything. If you change your mind about staying, you can let them know that as well. We won't be booking anyone in that suite since you paid for the full ten days. You'll have access to the club if you wish to join Richard and Tara, or if you desire to play on your own."

"I won't," she said, too quickly. But it was true. Not here, not without him. Maybe no one else, nowhere else, ever again.

He moved, brushing past her to the door. His scent, the heat of his skin, almost made her sway on her feet. She tried to keep her eyes on the wall of books so she didn't have to watch him leave, but she couldn't stop the shameful words that came to her lips. "Will I see you before I leave?"

When he said nothing, she turned. He'd stopped at the doorway and his dark eyes had fire in them. Hellfire. "No, my lady. We're done."

He said it in that same neutral tone, but she flinched anyway. His jaw eased, though only a fraction. "I have a few more days of vacation. I'll be spending it elsewhere. I think that's best for us both, don't you agree?"

She nodded, her throat too tight to speak. A sigh lifted his massive shoulders and he gave her a different look, one full of so many emotions she couldn't bear any of them.

"From here forward, I'll have two girls to pray for. I'll think of you often, my lady, and hope for your happiness."

The door closed behind him. Kaela stared at it. Was there anything as wrenching as the symbolism of a closed door, one never to be opened again? The likelihood of her ever finding a Master like him…in her world… The odds were better that she could turn back time for him to go back to that alley, find those abandoned babies earlier so he could save them both.

"Lady Kaela?" She blinked, realized she'd zoned out for about ten minutes. Now a middle-aged woman was standing at the door. Despite the late hour, she was dressed as if for a full day at the office. This was likely one of Vardalos's admins.

"Is everything all right?"

No. Of course not. What a stupid question. But she answered appropriately. "Yes, thank you."

He hadn't touched her again. Just a terse good-bye. She'd known him less than a week. It should hurt like a splinter under a fingernail, sharp but not fatal, something that once removed would ebb off quickly. Instead the splinter was the size of a railroad spike and it was lodged in her heart, making it difficult to breathe. But she didn't need to breathe. She was a vampire.

The admin hesitated. "Mr. Vardalos said he would refund your trip in full, as a courtesy."

She shook her head. "No. Tell him he can keep it. I got what I paid for, and more. I have one condition, though. Pay Master Garron. This was no vacation for him."

Brushing quickly past the bemused woman, she headed for those endless spiral of stairs. She didn't want the elevator, which would still have Garron's lingering scent. It was time to go back to her room, to pack. Once she rose at dusk, she could return to reality. The sooner the better.

Everyone knew it was best to rip off a Band-Aid quickly.

§

At dawn, she stripped and laid on the bed. She was tempted to burrow under the covers but she lay on the top, exposed and cold, staring at the ceiling. It was pressed tin that glinted from the candlelight wall sconces. She hadn't wanted the electric lights. When the dawn came, the waterfall sparkled with the sun's rays. Turning on her side, she watched.

Jared had said she was a creature of the night, one who embraced the moon more than the sun. "My witch," he'd called her, on a night when he left their bed to find her sitting on the porch steps in her night rail. She was watching the moon soar across the star-strewn sky. He'd sat down on the step above her, his legs on either side of her body, and stroked her hair. "My red-haired witch."

Was it eternal, the struggle to know what to do, how to live, how to exist in a way where there was a balance? Was there any place where the weak weren't preyed upon, and where the strong weren't always trying to beat them down from weakness into nothingness?

She was one of the strong ones, impossibly strong. She knew she was capable of going on for centuries more, serving Lady Lyssa, protecting those whose care was charged to her, or whose care she assumed. Like Garron with those twin babies. They were so alike in some ways. In many ways. Fighters, killers. Saviors, but not in the grandiose, messianic sense. More like the basic Webster's definition as one who saved something, someone, because the circumstances allowed it to happen. She supposed it amused the Powers That Be when someone was proclaimed a hero, since They knew it would take only a flick of the dial of Time to make it a second too late. Then the hero was just another face in the crowd, someone too slow to act.

What if Garron hadn't looked in the trashcan? The second baby would have died while he slept fitfully only a few feet away, his dreams plagued by what tomorrow would hold for a runaway. Or what if he'd had a few more terrible life experiences under his belt, such that when he saw the baby in the trash, he'd thought, "she's better off dead" and replaced the lid?

Was there anything worse than the death of hope?

Kaela turned away from the water, closed her eyes. She'd get some sleep, get on the plane. She'd have a few days before Fran returned. She'd do paperwork, follow up on several territory matters. Maybe read some books or visit a couple gardens in the area she'd been meaning to check out at night, when she could slip in and dwell there, a shadow among the shadows.

"Garron, I wish…"

She took a breath. She didn't have her mind closed to him, a final act of respect to her Master, but she'd also respected his demand she stay out of his head. So she spoke to him in her own mind, in the forlorn hope he might be listening.

*I want you to know there's nothing another vampire could do to you that would make me think less of you. As cliché as it sounds, I know this is about me, not you. I don't know if it's possible to love someone after only a few days, but I know I think too much of you to ever pull you into my world. I wish I could be with you once more. I know that's wrong and cruel of me. Selfish, because I know I hurt you. But I miss you so, Master. I feel like if I could be yours, just one more time, I could endure everything else. I don't want my last memory of you to be in Vardalos's office.*

From his closed expression at that last moment, she was sure he wasn't listening. This was just her way of comforting herself, rambling on like this. She even hummed a little song, trying to get herself to sleep. Would Garron like her to hum him to sleep? She had a good singing voice and had done that for Jared, wrapping her arm around his waist, resting her cheek on his back, letting the vibration of her voice take him into dreams. She hadn't had the pleasure of watching Garron sleep yet.

If he had come home with her, she would have wanted to do things for him, the way Fran did things for her. There were too many demands on her as an overlord for her to do all the things that Fran did, but she could make him breakfast, taking tiny samples of the food herself to ensure it was fit for human consumption. It had been so long since she'd cooked… One didn't tend to cook for one, and a vampire didn't cook at all. Though sometimes hot chocolate spiced with blood was good…

She was thinking nothing but nonsense. She shut her eyes tighter, hoping, wishing for oblivion.

*I didn't give you permission to sleep, my lady.*

Thank God. She shuddered. The reverberation of his voice in her consciousness brought an ache into her throat so strong it choked off word or thought. She wanted to tell him he didn't have to do this, but she would have lost that fight. She wanted him so much that when his fingers slid along the arch of her foot, she quaked all the way down to her bones. Her small cry cut through her from mind to core.

He slid onto the bed behind her, and another wave of relief went through her at the warmth of his naked body against hers, legs under her hips and fitted to the backs of her knees, chest against her shoulders and blessedly hard cock against her buttocks. He was a furnace.

"Christ, you're freezing." He wrapped his arms around her, held her as she shook.

"I--"

"No talking unless I tell you." Pushing her hair to the side, he put his lips against her throat. She didn't think anything could surpass the excruciating, bittersweet pleasure of him being here with her, granting her last wish, but then her heart broke as she felt him wrap the choker around her neck, re-securing it.

"I told you it was yours to take with you, my lady. So you can always remember who your Master is."

Her eyes closed in painful bliss as he put his mouth over it. When he slid his hand down her hip, around to her ass, she opened her legs to him.

"Good, my lady." She arched against him as he probed her cunt, stroked her rim, exploring and reacquainting himself with what was his. She felt it in his touch, heard it in his head, and wholeheartedly agreed. Yes, she was all his. It wouldn't matter if she left tomorrow. She'd never again feel a touch like this, the one that told her she'd found her Master. God bless his memory, even Jared had not awakened this level of submission, a hunger to give him absolutely everything he demanded, even if he asked for her very life.

"Good. Because I plan to be very demanding. Beyond what even you think you can give."

He pushed her onto her stomach, stretched her arms out to either side. He left the bed only to pull cuffs out from beneath the mattress, two at the head, two at the foot. He locked her in them, adjusting the ties with a sharp pull so she was stretched out to the muscle-straining point.

She turned her head, but he slid a full mask over her head, closing her into darkness. It only had a mouth opening, so her enhanced senses of hearing and smell were muffled, her sight taken away. The inside of the mask smelled like cinnamon and heat. She didn't have to be told to stay out of his head, though the temptation to try and figure out what he had planned was fierce. She didn't have long to wait, though.

She cried out at the strike across her hindquarters. The switch, she was sure. That lick of fire was unmistakable, followed by another one.

"You won't break those bonds, my lady. If you refuse or disobey a single thing I demand of you before sundown, I leave."

He spoke against the mask so she could hear him and she could tell he meant it. He wouldn't be taking any shit from her. He was showing her just how hard a Master he could be, fully unleashed.

"Now stay still. Absolutely still."

She froze in place, even though it was a struggle as he doled out the punishment, five strikes, ten…fifteen. She was shrieking, the pain incredible, and when he reached twenty-five and stopped, her ass and thighs were on fire.

"Too much noise." Her head was pulled up and a large ball gag forced into her mouth. Steel, cold and smooth, and immediately slickened by her saliva. She made an involuntary grunt as he cinched it around her head, tight. Tighter, the size of the ball pinning her tongue down.

"Those straps will leave an impression at the corners of your mouth. Until they disappear, it will remind you you're such a bad girl your Master had to gag you."

The switch came back, three more times. Her eyes almost rolled back at the pain. He replaced the switch with his mouth, and her body caught fire a wholly different way.

Licking, nipping, suckling. He adjusted the straps holding her ankles so he could slide his hand beneath her mound, lift her up enough to nuzzle her cunt, start eating her pussy as if it was the only thing he planned to do with his day. She writhed, and his mouth and touch disappeared.

"Five more strikes to teach you to stay still. I've been holding back, my lady, being overly gentle. I think you need to understand just exactly what you've taken on."

By the time he was done, he had her trained to stay motionless while he sucked, licked and tongue-fucked her pussy to near climax, even as she quivered like a tuning fork. She lost track of the number of switch marks it took. Even with her healing powers, her ass was so tender that on the last few strikes she'd had all she could do not to crack her enamel on the ball.

He rubbed his hand over her abused ass, gave it a smack. "I think you're wrong, my lady. You have very impressive self-control. I can reinforce that with lessons like this, teaching you how not to interfere if some of your vampire friends are giving me a workout."

No. She'd made her decision. This wasn't about that. She bit back a howl as the switch cut into her backside.

"Your hand curled, my lady. You're a statue until I say otherwise."

She felt the press of his knees against the inside of hers, his thighs against hers. Oh God, he didn't mean for her to stay motionless while he…yes, he did. She didn't know whether to worship him or curse him.

His cock pushed between her legs, and it felt like he was adjusting, angling himself for the best entry point, since her hips could only rise several inches off the bed. But he was determined and worked himself in, a tight, precarious glide to the root, a feeling that had her cunt spasming with orgasmic need immediately, especially when he also brought his chest against her shoulder blades, his lips to her neck.

She wanted to beg, but he'd said no speaking, no noise, inside or out. So she came to pieces, experienced a climax while motionless, which was like glass being cracked an inch at a time, until it shattered entirely. She couldn't hold back the noise, the scream, the fever-like shudder and jerking of her body.

If he'd pulled away from her as a result, she might have died of need, but he didn't this time. He kept going, still hard and enormous inside her, until she was done. Then he pulled out.

"That's round one, my lady." As she was still gasping inside her dark world, wishing she could see him, he released her bonds, but only to flip her over, rebind her and straddle her waist.

She'd said she wouldn't do it, but she couldn't help it. She had to look through his eyes. He stood over her on his knees, looking down at her from his towering height. Thank God, his gaze was on his cock as he clasped a hand around it, began to stroke. He shifted his attention from it to her breasts, quivering from the rough rhythm that was making the whole bed move. Then he focused on her mouth, stretched by the steel ball gag. Her arms, pulled out to either side of her, making her helpless to him. Her head, covered by the full head mask, obliterating her identity. It didn't matter who she was. She was His. That was all that mattered.

Despite the fact she'd just climaxed, her cunt clenched, wanting that cock inside, stretching her.

"Yeah, you're needier than any sub or slave I've ever had. Since you have to be the overlord in your world, you need to be taken over completely, hard and rough, before you can let go. Your Master has to leave no doubt in your mind who's in charge. I don't need to read your mind, my lady. You want to suck me off, be fucked by me again. Over and over until you're so sore it will make you cry when I take you, but you'll want me anyway. If you want all that, you're going to have to work your ass off for the privilege, aren't you?"

She nodded, but he caught her jaw. "And you get the fuck out of my head. Last warning. You don't get to see through my eyes. You only get what senses I allow you. Got it?"

Another quick nod, and she was in darkness again. So she had to imagine, strain to hear the rasp of his breath, feel the rhythmic movement of his thighs brushing her, his hips jerking over her as he approached climax. The blissful first spurt of come splashed on her belly, her breasts. As he released, his hand landed on the pillow next to her, that hot fluid hitting her breasts at closer range, her neck, her lips. She couldn't lick them with the ball gag stretching them, but she wanted to do so, so much.

She was moaning, a plea, a noise she couldn't stop. He collapsed next to her, and she could feel him breathing hard, but at length he propped himself up and caught the strap on the top of the head mask, using it to hold her still as he started spreading his fluid over her with the other hand. Over her breasts, teasing her nipples with it, into the cleavage. "Son of a bitch, look at that. My dick's getting hard again. I'm going to take advantage of this third mark while I've got it. Better than Viagra. Do you want me to fuck your cunt, my lady? Say, 'yes Master'. I like hearing a sub struggle to talk around a gag. Makes me harder."

"Yes…Master."

His chuckle was cruel at the muffled sound of her voice, but there was a sensual note to it too. The oddly gentle brush of his thumb over her lips told her that he had as many emotions churning though him as she did herself. Maybe more, because he couldn't make her change her mind. Though he was her Master in every way, she was withholding a vital choice. She suspected that could push Garron Rand's nature the way Vardalos had pushed her, to a line past which his control would be tested.

She trusted him with everything, though. No matter how cruelly he wanted to punish her, she would take it, treasure all of it. God above, if he wanted to stake her, she'd give him that as well and die happy.

He'd heard that, she could tell, for there was another significant pause, his hand lingering on her mouth. She made another needy noise, but he straddled her again, this time high enough on her body he could do just what he'd threatened earlier. He slid his cock in that slick valley between her breasts, cupped the curves in his hands and started moving.

"Just a slow, leisurely fuck of your gorgeous breasts. Every man's dream, especially with your mouth gagged like that, the mask keeping you focused only on what I'm doing to you, nothing else."

"Yes, Master." Another muffled attempt to speak, because she wanted to please him in whatever way she could. She could give him anything but what they both most wanted.

"Stubborn vampire bitch."

He kept working himself in between her breasts until her hips were jerking in simultaneous coital rhythm, until he reached back and gave her cunt a smart slap to still her. When he came again, she smelled his come as it bathed not only her neck but the mask itself.

"You're going to be a mess when I'm done with you. But you like that, don't you? Time to change position."

Before she could respond to what she was sure was a rhetorical question, he'd released her arms and legs and hiked her up over his shoulder, bracing his hand on her ass to carry her. She couldn't tell where they were going, but she thought they might be in the living room. Or maybe another room entirely. He'd left her suite, but she thought he'd taken a different way from the main doorway. Through the musk of his release, she smelled something else. A musty odor.

Dank. Though she couldn't see, her surroundings seemed darker.

"They haven't decided what to do with this room yet, so it's just empty space, concrete and wet stone. With a few piles of rope and some good sturdy hooks." He spread his hand over her bare ass, made her groan around the gag as he inserted two fingers in her pussy, rubbed his thumb over her rectum. "I'm the spider and you're going to be my fly, my lady. Once I have you all tied up, I plan to suck some of that lovely blood of yours, while I can still enjoy the taste of it."

He put her down on her hands and knees. She was starting to realize how far he was going to take all of this tonight. While she was a little frightened at what was clearly going to be a protracted lesson about her absolute subjugation, a far larger part of her was embracing it emphatically.

He introduced another smooth metal ball, this one into a different orifice. He pushed the slick steel into her anus, and she made a quiet noise of worry at its size, but her muscles released, letting it in. He pushed, stretching her, and the hook attached to it curved out between her buttocks, over her tailbone.

"An anal hook. One of my favorite pieces to use with problem subs." Another steel ball was placed inside her pussy, again pushed in so it stretched her. An odd vibration started in both channels, as well as a force that pulled the ball in her ass against the channel wall, and the one in her cunt upward.

"Magnetized and designed so every movement makes them vibrate inside you like pretty chimes. Now you can twitch if you desire, my lady, because the more you do that, the more crazy they'll make you. But no major movement, or I'll get the switch again."

From the pressure against it, she guessed he'd attached rope to the anal hook. He proceeded to tie her as he'd described, passing rope over and under her thighs, her waist and hips, creating a full body harness. He also worked a second harness around her breasts, cinching the ropes so tight the curves swelled inside their hold, like the fairy-dressed girl in the cell. Which of course meant he had to stop often to fondle and squeeze, remark on the stiff peaks of her nipples. When he tightened all of the ropes, all those pleasure points were stimulated.

Using more rope, he wrapped her elbows together in front of her. He wrapped rope around her thighs, calves and ankles as well, like a spider binding prey, just as he'd described. But she noticed he slipped a foam-like cushion between her elbows, wrists, ankles and knees first.

When he was done, she would have toppled, but he'd clipped lines to the harnesses and the strap on top of her head mask. Along with the one tied to the anal hook, the ropes kept her hips, shoulders and head up, her back arched.

"Vampire strength or not, the more layers of rope, the stronger the binding. No weak point for you to strain against. Want to try, my lady? Struggle, now."

The switch landed on her bare ass, and she yelped, began to writhe. He kept doing it, coming up beneath her to let the switch land on her swollen breasts, her soaked pussy, back to her ass. He was making her undulate and writhe in the bonds like a tied woman trying to dance, and those balls were vibrating, stimulating her ass and pussy.

"Master…" She wailed it through the gag. She came, just gushing as he kept striking her, making her move whatever way he wished. Like a lion tamer again, making his lioness move back and forth, spin on the head of a pin if needed. She'd thought Richard was an artist with single tails. He should have the pleasure of seeing Garron wield a switch.

She was still convulsing with aftershocks when her body left the ground. As he suspended her with rope, her thrashing succeeded in spinning her. He caught her hair, brought her to a stop and kissed her fiercely, nipping her lips, kissing her eyes, her brow through the mask, stroking her hair with such tenderness she wanted to cry. He put her head down, rubbed his cock over her masked face, pushed her nose into his testicles. He straddled her head and held her there between his thighs as he adjusted something in the ropes above her.

She was nothing but an object now, his object, no senses to identify anything, totally dependent on him. She inhaled his scent as much as she could through the mask and realized her moans had become the keening of a wounded animal, a sound she hadn't made since she was first turned and had such blood hunger she would have done anything to slake that thirst.

"My ferocious vampire. Dangerous, deadly. Mine." He caught the head strap, yanked her head back so roughly she felt the pull from neck to hips. "Who's in control of you, my lady? Not just when you're trussed up like this, but anytime? Every moment of the day, every moment you sleep or wake. Who owns you?"

*You.*

"Who?"

*Master.* She swallowed. *Sir. Please…* She couldn't think of anything now, couldn't reason or rationalize. She wasn't Lady Kaela at all…

"No? Who are you?" He sounded menacing enough to send a ripple of true fear through her.

*Yours. Your property. Your submissive. Your slave.*

"Say it out loud."

She did, the effort making shameful saliva on her lips, over the edge of the mask.

"I can do anything I want to you."

She nodded. "Yes, sir. Yes, Master."

He stood up, sending her spinning with a hard shove. He kept doing it, sometimes smacking her ass, tweaking a breast before he pushed her off again. Then he caught her, unbuckled the gag and pulled it free before putting his mouth over hers for a hard, branding kiss.

Everything a demand, seemingly violent, out of control. But it wasn't. When he pulled out the gag, he'd guided it with his fingers, held her steady, made sure it didn't knock against her teeth, chip her fangs. When he kissed her now, he unzipped the mask, took it away, cradling her scalp and holding his thumbs over her eyes, a mute command to keep them closed as the kiss drew out. His fingers dug into her hair, hard, scalp pulling.

*You're mine*, that gesture said. *All fucking mine. I cherish you. Love you. Love you enough to hate you, to be angry, but to channel all of it into this, a night that tells you who owns your very soul. And who owns mine.*

She wanted to touch him more than she wanted anything in her whole life, but he wasn't in the mood for mercy or kindness beyond that slight easing of his touch. He replaced the gag, put a regular blindfold on her and kept on going, as if he hadn't already pushed her past the breaking point.

He held her suspended for awhile, experimenting with nipple and clit clamps. Then he wrapped her up in what felt like Christmas tinsel before passing his hands over her, electrifying it with tiny licks of sparks. Having seen electric play before, she knew he had a violet wand attached to him, probably shoved in his waistband so the electricity could conduct through his hands. He took her back to a screaming orgasm, leaving her writhing and jerking in her bonds. After he stripped her of the tinsel, he used a different attachment to the wand, stroking it between her legs, up over her breasts, until she came again.

When he finally lowered her from the suspension, she was exhausted. Her pussy and ass were throbbing around those steel balls. He freed her from his "web", putting her on the cold floor to remove the balls and hook, but left her arms wrapped and legs tied tightly closed. She laid there, her heart thudding in her ears, aware of his heartbeat, his breath, the heat that pulsed from him, strong as ever. He wasn't flagging in the slightest.

As if to prove it, he lowered himself to the ground behind her. She made a soft sound for mercy as he stroked her hair, but then he slid up behind her, let her feel the thick steel bar of his cock. "You're still serving your Master, my lady. No break for you."

He pushed his cock into that tight opening and her pussy welcomed his invasion, rippling over him, her hips trying to lift and lower to accommodate his thick size. She had no energy to reach a climax, but this time his intent was to only give himself release, which perversely started to arouse her once more. As he held onto her waist and thrust into her with animal-like focus, hips slamming against her ass, she was moaning again. When he came, she felt the searing heat of it in her cunt and then on her thighs as his semen spilled out of her, wetting the ropes when he pulled out. Pulling her up to her knees by her hair and a steadying hand on her throat, he fed his cock between her lips.

"Clean me off, my lady. I want to be nice and polished for the next thing I'm going to do for you."

And she thought a vampire had stamina?

He let out that sexy, scary chuckle, telling her he'd heard that loud and clear, and was confirming it. God, she wanted in his mind. But he'd said…

"I meant it, my lady. Pull that shit and the night is over. But you keep your mind wide open to me. That's part of the same deal."

Whether he'd intended to prove it to her or not, he'd shown her he understood what drove vampires to dominate their servants in such elaborate, demanding sexual games. Garron had a Dominant's drive to see what a submissive would do for Master or Mistress, to serve them beyond their physical or emotional capacity to do so. While she'd been horrified by the few times she'd seen that forced by vampires with the wrong kind of relationship with their servant--whether or not they acknowledged such a qualification was possible—when trust and devotion were part of the Master-servant relationship, it was different. To a servant who had that, nothing would ever be too much for a Master or Mistress to ask. Fran showed such devotion, hoping for that kind of relationship, and Jacob obviously already possessed it with Lady Lyssa.

Garron was showing Kaela she was the same kind of sub.

With a vampire who understood and valued it, like what Kaela had witnessed between Lady Lyssa and Jacob, there was a savage beauty to it, an emotional well that Kaela had longed to experience for herself.

He pulled himself free of her mouth, bent and put her over his shoulder, lifting her once again. As they moved forward, she began to detect faint noises and music that became louder. He was taking her back to the club. Her stomach quaked at the thought. Then a door opened and closed, and the scents told her they were back in his private room, which helped her relax. She didn't want to be around anyone else, didn't want to share him with anyone else tonight. She smelled something sharper, something she hadn't detected the first time she'd been here. Fire. Smoke.

He unwrapped her arms and legs, massaged them briefly. It was functional care, not caressing, making it clear it wasn't aftercare. Yet he was still gentle about it. Did he know how devastating that was, to be on the painful end of a switch with him, then feel the press of his lips on those welts? Like the stroke of his hands now, their firm strength as he checked her muscles, cared for her, made sure the kind of pain she was experiencing was what he wanted her to experience. The kind that had sent her into screaming orgasm--how many times now?--even as he broke her down so completely, she knew she was his slave entirely.

She'd seen a human-sized wheel in here on their last visit, so she knew that was where he put her this time, scooping her off the mat and fixing her arms and legs to the pins so she was spread out once more. From the clasp of steel at her wrists and ankles, she realized he'd reinforced the bindings with the ones that were strong enough to hold a vampire. He inserted a new gag, a rubber phallus that filled her mouth, stopping just short of her gag reflex.

"Scream all you want this time, my lady." He put his hand against her cheek, pressing her face to the wheel. Then he bit her throat, snapping down like a pit bull and holding on.

The erotic wave was immediate. She wanted to break free, hold him, take him into her body. Despite all the climaxes he'd given her, feeding him was a whole different level of erotic give and take between them. She needed him inside her.

"Do you feel you've earned that, my lady?"

She wanted to scream yes, but the part that had surrendered to him spoke instead. *That's for my Master to decide.*

Her mind voice didn't sound like herself. It was small, quiet...waiting on his will and desires.

Something plastic pressed against her throat. He was catching the blood in a container, and then she felt him painting it on the inside of her thigh, then higher, underneath her arm, below the arm pit, against the swell of her left breast.

There was only one reason to put a vampire's blood on her unbroken skin. To anchor a mark, make it a permanent scar. Now she understood the smell of fire. A part of her responded in terror and alarm, but another part of her let out a sigh of longing and relief so deep, she wanted him to do it now, now, now, before anything could change his mind.

"I won't change my mind, my lady. You may be in charge of the decision to leave here without me. But you're not going to go on with your life as if this never happened. From now until the day you die, you'll carry my mark. Two of them."

The way a third mark servant carried the mark of her vampire until the day she died. Some said even into the afterlife. With a spurt of sadness, she realized that had been another indication that the third mark on Garron was a temporary magic, because upon a third marking, a sign of it would appear on the flesh of the servant, a cross between a birthmark or a brand. The shape of it was determined by forces beyond the control of vampire or servant, but it always had a significance. That mark hadn't appeared on Garron. Not that she'd seen or he'd mentioned.

"No, my lady. But maybe that's not so much a shortcoming of the island's magic as much as it is an indication of the magic between you and me. Maybe you're the one meant to carry the marks, not me."

The marks he put on her would say that she, Lady Kaela, would always belong to Garron, her Master, no matter what she had to be to the outside world.

He was against her from breast to knee as he nipped her sharply again. "You aren't being given a choice, my lady. This is my decision, not yours."

She shuddered under his touch. *Yes, Master.*

He stepped back. There was no preparation, no "1-2-3", or "hold your breath." She smelled the heat a second before the brand was pressed against the side of her breast. No creature could bite back a scream before the touch of fire, but even amid the anguish she felt a wave of exultation as strong as a climax, the blood burning all the way to the bone, making it permanent. She heard a rattle of what she assumed was the branding irons and a fresh one was placed against her inner thigh. She screamed against the rubber phallus as the mark burned so close to her pussy she felt the wave of heat wash over her labia. Now she understood why he'd bound her with the vampire irons--to ensure her legs stayed reasonably still. To protect her, even knowing she healed from everything.

He stepped back, leaving her the scent of her blood and burning flesh. Then he was kneeling, his mouth on the brand between her legs, nipping at the abraded flesh, making her gasp from the pain of it. A pain that became something else as he moved his mouth up higher and began eating her pussy.

*I'm starting all over again, my lady. Dusk is hours away yet.*

§

Garron guessed only the oldest vampires were capable of staying up all day, because there were points at the height of noon she blacked out, lost time. Yet Garron never stopped. He was like a man possessed. She wasn't getting on that plane with a single second of their last day together lacking his demands. As she kept surfacing, showing a hazy awareness of him, he plundered, stretched and fucked every orifice, marked her inside and out with his come. Flogged, whipped, paddled, switched and caned her. Made her suck him off three times. Made her come so many times he lost count himself. He put his mouth on those brands over and over, and she came at least once from his touch there alone, something he'd always treasure.

Along with every other thing about her.

Finally, in those last couple hours before sundown, he stood over her, breathing hard. She was a crumpled heap of silken limbs and red hair, her cuffed wrists close enough to him that her limp fingers were resting his foot, a mute plea for mercy. Or for it never to stop. The raging pain in his chest understood that completely.

He removed every restraint, including the mask and gag, and carried her back to her rooms.

She was so exhausted she had no strength at all, but when he laid her down on her bed with unspeakable tenderness, he kept his eyes on hers, showing her he'd never love a woman so much in his life again. Because he was a brute who couldn't stop himself, he slid his cock inside her one last time. Gentle, because he knew just how sore she was, but relentless, irrevocable. A tiny sigh left her lips, the tips of her fangs showing. It broke him inside when she found the strength to hold him, wrap her arms and legs around him. He felt the rough dollar-sized area of the brand on her inner thigh against him. She held on as he rocked them both like a sensual cradle, and shattered from what he heard in her mind.

*I love you, love you, love you…Master.*

Maybe it was crazy to know and feel something so intensely after such a short time, but he didn't doubt it at all. Else it wouldn't hurt like being blown up all over again.

He eased himself down on her when they both shuddered to a climax. Pulling out of the blissful heat of her cunt was almost the hardest thing he'd ever done. Since she didn't have the strength even to bite him, he found his pocket knife in the jeans he'd left on the floor and cut the vein in his throat. Pulling her on top of him, he guided her mouth to the wound. He wouldn't have her leaving the island so tired she couldn't defend herself.

It gave her strength, but she still needed the sleep. She fell asleep with her mouth on his throat, like an exhausted baby. Curling her against him, he held her, dropping kisses on her forehead, her lips, stroking her silky skin. There wasn't a human sub in the world who could have taken everything he'd done to her and still wanted more, but she had. If he hadn't had the third mark he wouldn't have been able to dish it out, but she'd brought out every desire he'd ever wanted to exercise on a sub who belonged to him unequivocally. Which only left him wanting to do more, go even deeper, explore even more with her.

But this was it. Up in Vardalos's office, he'd seen it inside her, on her face. She'd known he'd read it from that dark, unhappy energy around her. There was the hard limit line, the one a Dom knew couldn't be forced, not without dire consequences. This one was her decision, damn her to hell. And he was afraid it would. It pissed him off that the reason she was making the decision was to avoid sentencing him to the same. But he couldn't bully her on this one, much as he wanted to do it.

She could have changed her mind at any time during the past few hours. Yet she hadn't and he hadn't asked her to do that, at least not directly. It wasn't the kind of thing that could be posed as a question. So he'd done the only thing he knew how to do. Give her a night--or day, rather--to show her it was possible, to give her another way of thinking about it. Maybe it hadn't been fair, trying to drive a chink in her armor about it, but fair had nothing to do with any of this.

Truth, he knew he couldn't bully her into anything. A light smile touched his lips. Yeah, she was submissive to the core, but she was a kickass sub. From the way she'd confronted Vardalos, it was clear she'd put any man's balls in his throat if he ever pushed the wrong button, including him. She'd done it a couple times, hadn't she?

It made her willing submission such a sweet treasure.

She was also protective. The way she'd nearly neutered the guy at the pool proved that. Unfortunately, that protectiveness was part of the problem they were dealing with now. But he wouldn't change that about her, any more than anything else. It was all part of what made her so damn appealing.

The plane was scheduled to leave at eight p.m. to get her back to the mainland and safely tucked away somewhere before the following dawn. By tomorrow night or the next she'd be back home, to her life. Pushing away the desolation at that thought, he lifted her. She murmured a protest.

"Just sleep, baby. I'll get you cleaned up and ready."

Though he'd rather take a dive into acid than do a single thing that put her closer to leaving the island, he started up the shower, got it hot, and put them both in it. She stayed in that semi-somnolent state while he washed her hair, her body, exploring every crevice. Since he couldn't help himself, he lifted her against the wall, entering her once more. Not to climax, but just to feel the give of her body, her acceptance. Her arms and legs held him, her lips against his throat, his name a sigh on his lips. She'd remember him at the last as a pleasant dream, and he supposed that was the best way.

He dressed her in panties and his T-shirt, brushed a kiss on her forehead. When he laid her back in the bed, he trailed his fingers over the infinity link choker, the thigh brand, once more. Like the one on the outside of her breast, under her arm, it wasn't large and would heal in the way brands did, making it difficult for anyone to really know what it said or meant. She'd know what it was, though, because he tucked the plates in her hand.

His dog tags. She'd wear their imprint forever in those two intimate places, long after he was dead and gone.

*Give her a happy life, Lord. Give me the strength to let her go do that.*

Plenty of people lived happy lives where they had to pretend to be something they weren't. They learned that there was more than one way to be happy. He hoped to God she could do that. He hoped he could figure it out as well.

He placed the call to the front desk to have her woken in time to catch her plane. Then he left her suite, forcing himself not to look back.

## Chapter Twelve

She kept his T-shirt. She assumed he wouldn't mind. Despite it dwarfing her, she'd worn it over a short skirt, but packed a plastic laundry bag inside her carry-on so once she reached Miami she could change shirts, arrive home looking appropriate. The bag was so she wouldn't lose his scent. It would be the first thing she took out when she got home. She'd fold it under her pillow, wear it when Fran wasn't with her.

Which would be soon. She was going to send Fran back to the Council. It wasn't fair to keep doing this to her. Kaela would request a second-mark from the Council staff. Not an InhServ, but one who had no expectations beyond being her secretary and a functional blood donor.

She looked through the square plane window. Joely was firing up the engines, the craft shuddering and bobbing. In a moment, they'd be moving across the water and in the air.

According to the note from Theodosius, given to her at check out, the energies of the Bermuda Triangle would dissolve her markings on Garron once they flew out of its boundaries. She wouldn't be able to reach Garron's mind, know where he was. Hear him in her head. He would wink out of her existence.

> *While your trip may not have been everything you hoped, my lady, it is my sincere wish that you visit us again. As often as you like.*

She wished she could come back. Once a year, maybe twice a year. Be whatever she wanted to be with Garron here, and not risk him in any way. But she couldn't come back, couldn't do that to him, any more than she could do it to Fran. He would become her pre-dawn fantasy now. Her only one, flavored by the painful precious reality of what she'd had for just a short time.

*There is nothing more powerful and frightening than choice. It's the field on which courage and love are tested.*

She closed her eyes, remembering those words, as well as others. In ways large and small, he'd told her he'd be her servant. That he *was* her servant, as well as her Master.

*Please start up the plane. Get us out of here.* She was going to bend, to break. She'd made the right decision. Or had she?

After barely three days, this wasn't supposed to be such a momentous decision, but it felt like it. Almost as fateful a decision as her turning, all those years ago. She'd actually spent her first fifty years wondering what had compelled her to make that decision. Then she no longer questioned it, because it was no longer relevant. What was done was done. She'd embraced her strengths, turned them into an iron shield and made it work for her.

Just as Seth, her vampire sire, had anticipated she would.

§

She'd gone straight to Jared's grave after the war. Well, as straight a path as a penniless woman with no remaining family could take. Once she'd been released from the prison, she made it back to the farm by begging and other means. The methods hadn't mattered at that point, but getting to Jared's grave had. She wasn't sure what she'd do once she arrived there, but seeing the marker was all that had mattered to her. Everything else had shut down.

The farm had been burned to the ground, nothing left. His marker was there, though it had been kicked over. She set it back straight, cleaned the area around it, despite night closing in and the rain that started to fall. She'd stayed there, kneeling in the mud, her clothes and hair plastered against her, not really caring if she stayed that way forever. Which was probably why the hand landing on her shoulder hadn't alarmed her. She'd barely had enough interest to lift her head, blink water that wasn't all rain out of her eyes.

She'd looked up into the dark eyes of a compelling stranger. Remarkably clean shaven, given that the gray Confederate coat and trousers he wore had seen far better days. His weapons were well maintained, however, which told her his priorities. He held out a gloved hand.

"Come with me," he said. "I've been waiting for you."

Something in his touch made her obey. Maybe it was her natural compulsion to respond to a true Dominant. A compulsion she'd thought had been buried deeper than Jared's body. But she followed the male through the rain and the darkness. He didn't have a horse, and her exhaustion and near starvation claimed her by the second mile. Only her goal to get to the grave had kept her on her feet this long, so when she crumpled to the wet ground, she figured he'd leave her there.

He stripped off his coat, wrapped her in it, and carried her onward. For hours it seemed, before they'd reached a cabin in the swamps.

He'd removed her wet clothes, toweled her hair and fixed her soup. After spoon feeding her, he tucked her into bed like a child. As she stared at him with numb eyes, trying to figure out what he wanted, wondering if she cared, he pulled a chair up next to the bed.

"Before we go forward, it's important for you to understand that Jared knew who and what I was."

That got her attention. She blinked at him as he closed his hand over hers.

"Warmer, but not warm enough," he observed. "You want to die. But you're too strong to take your own life. You have no direction, no compass, but you can't be compelled to do evil." A faint smile crossed his lips. "Which shows a rather remarkable will. Jared loved you. If he has awareness of anything in the afterlife, I'm sure he still does. Our paths crossed, we fought together. When he died, he died in my arms, and gave you into my care. So you'll stay here for a time, and we'll see what we'll see."

He rose, stripped off all his clothes. "Let's get you warmer."

She assumed he wanted to be paid for his kindness with what all male strangers seemed to want from a woman traveling alone with no obvious protection, but that wasn't the case. He circled to the other side of the bed, slid into it with her. He had brown hair that reminded her of a dull copper kettle and was soft as silk when it fell over her bare shoulder. That happened when he slid both arms around her, pulling her back against him.

"Go to sleep, Kaela. Your Master has sent someone to care for you."

She was too tired at that point to ask what he meant. But that changed as the weeks passed, as she slowly started to learn why Seth went into the root cellar during daylight, why he bullied her into learning a variety of fight styles and weaponry. Though he never let her deny him the intimacy of seeing her naked, holding her or touching her when he desired, he never once made any sexual demands on her, even when her long dead libido started to stir. She despised that about herself, not wanting to respond because of the things this obvious Master triggered inside her. She only wanted to respond that way to Jared.

Then one night, Seth had come up behind her while she was cooking dinner for herself, and he'd fed from her throat. By that time, she suspected what he was, though facing the truth of it was startling, especially when it didn't repel her. He didn't hold any part of his nature back that night, and she couldn't stop herself from responding when he reacquainted her with her desires. She cried through it, but she wanted him to take her, make her surrender to her own pleasure, and he did, until the tears dried up.

But he wasn't interested in acquiring a servant. He told her about all of that, about the structure of the vampire world. Eventually, he also told her he had been given permission to turn her, but the choice was hers.

"Why would I want to live forever?" she asked. "When I could be with Jared much sooner as a mortal?"

Seth liked to play the lute and was trying different tunes on it, sitting in the doorway of the cabin. They hadn't left it in months, such that there were times she felt like they were the only humans left in the world. Or, in Seth's case, humanoid. It was like she was in a fairy tale, the girl lost in the forest. "Vampires are sexual Dominants," she persisted when he didn't respond. "You said so. That's not me."

He shrugged. "I think the chemical changes during a turning take whatever alpha qualities a person has and expands them. So that if they weren't true Dominants before, they are afterward."

"Always?"

"Always."

"So you think changing my essential nature is a good thing?"

"Maybe I just wonder if it will work that way, and how you will handle yourself if it doesn't." He shrugged again. "Vampires are known to be like cats, cruel in our curiosity. We all have different sides to us. Unexpected ones. I may be mostly one thing, but I'm not all that one thing. We have purposes to serve before our day is done."

"But I want to be done. I don't want… I want Jared."

"I know." Seth looked at her with compassion, but also an implacability that didn't let her hide from the truth. "You know it's not yet your time. There's a reason he told me about you."

"He was just a man far from home talking about his wife, missing her."

"Nevertheless."

"I may respond to you…taking charge, but I don't love you."

He laughed, eyes sparkling at her. "I know that, dear girl. This isn't about that. This is about you getting a chance to be more, to not be old and used up before you're thirty. You don't belong in this world, this human world, anymore. You've walked the line between living and dead too long, but you're not ready to join the dead yet. I can give you time to decide which one you are. See if you survive. You liked being a spy, helping others. You did it for Jared first, honoring his memory, but you found you were good at playing those politics, succeeding where others failed, protecting those who needed to be protected.

"You were raped"--his gaze flickered--"Yet you don't think of yourself as a victim. You detached, survived, moved on, figured out your next step. You don't even have nightmares about it."

"It was rape, but most of it wasn't brutal, except that prick captain with his damned cigars. Just lonely men using a woman they considered the enemy." Yes, it had been worse than that, but as Seth said, she was good at compartmentalizing. He saw it, nodded, didn't pursue it.

"The vampire world is at an odd crossroads. There's a Council of sorts, trying to deal with our on-again, off-again territory wars. Trying to figure out ways for our species to survive our own power games and blood thirst. I could see someone like you being of great use in that world, a stabilizing influence, if you survive your first fifty years. Look at it this way. If you let me turn you, and you change your mind, all you have to do is sit in a doorway like this until the sun rises. Poof, you float away on the wind as ash."

She narrowed her eyes at him. "What about my immortal soul?"

"First time I've known you to worry about that." He grinned. "You probably startled the poor thing, asleep like an old friar in the corner. If there's one thing humans *or* vampires know less than nothing about, it's their immortal souls. Some days I suspect only beasts, trees or butterflies understand its true nature. End of discussion. Your deeds are your map to the afterlife, Kaela. You can only make choices about your earthly life and hope for the best about everything that comes afterwards."

§

She'd made her decision, hadn't she? She hadn't had any clear sense of whether it was the right or wrong decision. In the end she'd gone on gut feeling.

*"Do you want me in your mind, Kaela? Unable to hide any thought from me, no need to speak aloud because I already know what you want and need, even when you can't quite tell yourself?"*

She thought of those words Garron had said to her. Was she wrong, not to give Garron the same option Seth had given her? He'd thrown her into a dangerous world, but by that time, she knew all about living in a dangerous world. He'd told her everything he could to prepare her for it and gave her the choice.

If she went that way with Garron, how would she know she hadn't rationalized, serving her own needs and ignoring his? Sacrifice was the only way to keep herself in the clear on that. But maybe that was the point Seth had been trying to make. There was no keeping clear when it came to choices that affected the soul.

Garron had told her it was his choice. Could she look at his scarred face, see the scars in his soul, and really believe she had a better grasp than he did of the consequences of choices? In the end, it was the peace made with those choices that mattered.

She looked along the jagged boardwalk, toward the castle rising high above them. A monument to things that endured everything. Battles, weather, ignorance. It had even persevered when brought God-knows-how to a whole new place, faced with a new reality, a new set of challenges.

"Garron Rand." She said his name quietly to herself. Said it in her mind. *Garron Rand. Garron.*

She'd been strong for close to two hundred years. She'd survived, but if she wanted to keep surviving, she had to make the right decision here. Vampires usually embraced their selfishness, and just like the human race itself, that self-centered attitude kept them alive, sure of their superiority to everything else. Until something knocked them down and reminded them forcefully what humility was--that they didn't know everything, and sometimes things had to be taken on faith. And what the heart wanted.

*Serve me well, Lady Kaela.* Lady's Lyssa's voice again. Three simple words. The head of the Council had left the rest to her, how best to do just that.

*Garron.*

Her heart rate speeded up, along with her pulse. She wasn't speaking his name to keep her company. She was calling him. *Garron.*

The sudden silence filled her with dread. Had it already happened, that break between their minds? Was he back at Club Sin, lining up his next submissive session? Had she meant so little, that he could dismiss her that way? *Bastard.* She imagined dismembering the faceless submissive, one lovely long limb at a time.

She was losing her mind. Of course he wasn't doing that. He'd been her Master. He was her Master. He'd left the choker on her, and she put her fingers over the heavy links of the chain she'd refused to remove. She took a breath, inhaled the scent of his T-shirt. With every movement she could feel those two brands, still tender, a dull throb she'd embraced. He hadn't given those things to anyone else.

*Master. Please forgive me. Please answer. God* damn *you, answer me.*

*Yes, my lady?*

There was amusement in his mind voice, and it brought relief, as well as a little exasperation. *Were you just waiting, seeing how desperate I would become?*

*My lady, I'm not a sadist.*

*Yes, you are.* She closed her eyes, smiling as her heart beat faster. *Please come home with me. Be my Master…and my servant.*

*You only had to ask.*

Her eyes sprang open, verifying the scent the small crack in her window had brought her. He was walking down the dock, a duffle slung over his shoulder. He was coming to her, but she couldn't wait that long.

"I need out. Let me out. He's coming. He's joining us."

Joely glanced back at her, then out at the dock. She smiled at Kaela. "Just turn the latch, my lady."

As she said it, Kaela was a blink from wrenching the door off its hinges and throwing it to the side. She was out of the plane in a flash, down the docks, not caring who might see her moving faster than a human could move. It was dark, and he was all she could see.

She flung herself in his arms, forgetting her strength, forgetting everything but him, but fortunately he'd dropped the duffle and she only knocked him back a few steps. He rocked on his heels but kept his balance, holding her tight against him, cupping the back of her skull.

"I'm here, my lady. I'll always be here."

"I won't be able to bear it if they hurt you. I won't."

"They can't hurt me past bearing if you're mine." He let her slide down to the dock, though he kept her in his arms as he gave her his steady look, the one that calmed her and made her want to beg for his mouth at the same time. "Do you understand that?"

*I want to. But if the worst happens…*

"It's the risk we take," he said, matter-of-fact. "The only question worth answering is, is the risk worth it? Is it something we can't live without?"

"I already know my answer to that."

"Yeah, you do." He gave her a cocky grin and she pushed at his chest. She didn't budge him, a testament to the bull strength of the man.

"And I guess you being here is your answer?" she demanded.

"Yeah." He touched her face. "I told you it was my choice. I was waiting you out, just out of sight and down wind, but if you'd waited one more second, I was going to be down this dock and on that plane. I was going to camp outside your door until you agreed it was my choice to make." He frowned. "Where did you say you live?"

"I didn't. California."

"Christ. Crazy liberals and overpriced coffee. The sacrifices I make."

She snorted at that. "If you camped outside my door, Fran would call the police. We'd file restraining orders."

He smiled, slid his fingers into her hair. "I'm coming with you, my lady. Everything I face in your service will be my choice. Everything you face from me behind closed doors will be your choice. Agreed?"

She nodded, and her heart hammered up in her throat again as he bent and captured her mouth with his, a hot, fully invasive kiss where he made it clear who belonged to who, his hands roaming down to grip her buttocks, knead with bruising force as she spoke her pleasure in his mouth, little unintelligible noises of need.

He kept one possessive arm around her even after he broke the kiss, bent and retrieved his duffle. As they proceeded to the plane, Joely shot him an amused look.

"Wondered when you were going to show up," she called out over the idling engines. "Figured starting her up would light a fire under you."

"Mess with me, I'll tell Roan to put you over a spanking bench next time he's here."

"Yeah, not going to happen. Too into Miranda now." Joely smirked at him and turned her attention to the controls. As she revved up the engines again, Garron tossed his bag into one of the empty seats behind her and helped Kaela in, directing her toward the back of the plane with a firm pressure against her lower back. He gave her the window seat as he slid into the seat next to her, his thigh intimately against hers. The plane rocked as he settled, making Kaela smile.

While Joely verified they'd put on their seatbelts and reminded them of basic safety instructions, Kaela thought about the heat of his thigh against hers, his arm around her shoulder, his scent in her nose, not from the T-shirt but from the actual man.

The plane started to taxi over the water, the engine noise increasing to the point conversation was no longer possible. Garron leaned against Kaela, glanced meaningfully downward.

*Why aren't your legs spread so I can play with your pussy, my lady? I intend to make you come at least three times on this trip. The first time before Joely levels the plane out.*

Her lips parted as his strong hand settled on her knees. When she spread them, she swallowed a needy cry as he put his hand under the skirt and began to stroke her with capable fingers. Every nerve surged toward that touch, as if how often he'd brought her to climax last night had become muscle memory, such that her body merely needed his command for her to climax again.

*That's my vampire.* Bending his head, he dropped a kiss on her shoulder. *Not a sound. I know you're a screamer, my lady, and we don't want to offend Joely's delicate sensibilities. Or distract her from piloting the plane.*

She'd faced a lot of challenges as a vampire and as a human, but she wasn't sure if that was one she could surmount. She didn't think any woman could stay silent when overwhelmed by an orgasm at Garron Rand's hand. But she'd be more than willing to take the punishment for failing to follow a direct order.

He pushed her over that edge in twenty seconds, his fingers playing with her clit, stroking her labia, his arm tight around her. She pressed her face into his broad shoulder as she shuddered against him.

*Beautiful, my lady.* He brought his fingers out from between her legs, touched her lips, let her smell her musky climax on them. *All for me.*

She realized she had tears on her face, her throat thick, but for once, for all the right reasons. He traced a track, put his mouth against her ear.

"You know, that fantasy you have about waking up in a Master's arms? I have my own part to add to that." He cupped the side of her face, tilting it up to him with an insistent thumb, the pressure just enough to make her eyes spark and her body still, attuning itself to whatever her Master desired.

*I spread my slave as I desire, to fuck her or use my mouth on her. Maybe both. I want to start the day, or the night as it were, with her begging. After she comes, after she's nice and wet, I take her to the bath, get her cleaned up and dressed for the day.*

"Then I take my place behind her, watching her back, serving her, keeping her sane and safe." His voice rumbled against her ear again.

Her eyes darkened as he raised his head and met her gaze, brushed a kiss over her mouth. *A Master serves, my lady. As I said before, it's just a different form of it, but we get to the same place with our sub--a complete understanding of what we each need and desire. I take the breath and you exhale it, without even thinking. We're that close.*

*If we can remember that,* he added, dark eyes burning fire into hers, *and keep working toward it, it won't matter what the world demands of us. We'll be okay together.*

"Maybe better than okay," she whispered. He answered her by pressing his response against her mouth.

"Absolutely."

###

*Elusive Hero is part of the Invitation to Eden series and a book of the Vampire Queen series. If you'd like to know more about Joey W. Hill's work or that series, visit her website or the Vampire Queen series page at:* www.storywitch.com *or* www.storywitch.com/series-vqs.

**The Vampire Queen Series**

Vampire Queen's Servant

Mark of the Vampire Queen

Vampire's Claim

Beloved Vampire

Vampire Mistress

Vampire Trinity

Vampire Instinct

Bound by the Vampire Queen

Taken by a Vampire

The Scientific Method

Nightfall

Elusive Hero